CW01021260

NOËL

CHRISTMAS AT MAGPIE COTTAGE

THE MAGPIE COTTAGE CHRONICLES
BOOK ONE

CRESSIDA BURTON

Enjoy!
Cressida Burton

Copyright © 2023 by Cressida Burton
10th anniversary second edition
Published by Magpie Cottage Books

First published in 2012 under the name Cressida Ellen Schofield.

All rights reserved.

No part of this book may be reproduced in any form or by any electronic or
mechanical means, including information storage and retrieval systems,
without written permission from the author, except for the use of brief
quotations in a book review.

This book is a work of fiction. Any similarity to persons, living or dead, is
purely coincidental.

Cover design by CJB Designs 2023.

For my mother, Alexandra, & grandmother, Sylvan…
…responsible for unforgettably magical Christmases since 1971.

CONTENTS

23RD DECEMBER

Pulling into the driveway of Magpie Cottage and catching her first sight of the house in which she had grown up never failed to give Evie Lovell a rush of warm pleasure, but never more so than on a frostbitten night in late December. There was something so evocative about the blue, red and green fairy lights that were, each year, carefully attached to follow the miniature pointed gable of the front porch, and the traditional holly wreath that hung from the eternally wonky peg on the front door. This year two topiary trees, spherical with long slender trunks, had been carefully positioned at either side of the door. Both had been draped with coloured lights similar to those that graced the porch roof. The only difference was that whereas the porch lights had been used for years and only ever had two settings — on or off — these new lights twinkled merrily. They were jolly, welcoming; hopefully portentous of a wonderfully merry Christmas filled with happy memories to be recounted throughout the coming New Year.

However...

...This was the Bingham family Christmas and it very rarely occurred without incident or squabble. In the same way that the resurrection of the fairy lights was an annual certainty, the disruption of Christmas was equally consistent. Each and every year something would happen to render the holiday less than perfect. Two years ago there had been a power cut that had lasted from half past nine on Christmas Eve until seven o'clock the following evening. Christmas lunch had consisted of bread, cheese and cooked meat instead of the traditional turkey which had sat, baleful and raw, on top of a rapidly defrosting fridge. At least the glut of candles had been suitably festive as they had all sat around and stared at each other over the Monopoly board because, as the telly was out of commission, no one could think of anything else to do. The year previous to that hadn't fared much better. That was the year one of the family cats had to be put to sleep by the vet on Boxing Day. The trail of incidents stretched back to when Evie was a child and one of her sisters had been rushed to A&E with a broken arm, having slipped on the patio flagstones after sneaking out of the house at midnight on Christmas Eve hoping to catch a glimpse of Santa. Yes, something would happen.

What that something would be was yet to be determined, but the potential was vast and varied. Becca, Evie's immediately younger sister, had just broken up with her long-term boyfriend and was both moping and moribund. Her youngest sister, Natalie, was, at best, an overbearing, overachieving, bitchy show-off who was not only prone to bouts of introspective, uncompromising narcissism but was also guaranteed to strop if she didn't remain the centre of attention. Rather like a twenty-three year old version of a toddler, Evie thought with a mirthless grimace. Finally there was Dan, the youngest of the four Bingham siblings, and who was an irrepressible wind-up merchant who far too often put his inherent love of humour ahead of the feelings of the recipient of his sarcasm and jibes. As if that wasn't enough, her father had just retired six months earlier and was now at home full time, embracing life after work with gusto, but resulting in her mother growing increasingly resentful that her domain had been breached and causing her to flap and obsess even more than usual, if that were in any way possible. Factor in the increased emotional tension of the holiday season and the likelihood of peace on Earth and goodwill to all parents and offspring was very slight indeed.

Worse still, it was Evie, who no one would expect to upset any spiced-apple carts, who had to acknowledge with considerable reluctance that she had her own potential bombshell to drop. At the moment that bombshell was currently safely concealed in a C4 Manila envelope and buried deep in her oversized handbag, but Evie couldn't help but imagine that that envelope was burning a very large, guilt-ridden hole in its side. Its contents had already been the source of a cataclysmic series of arguments between herself and her usually horizontally laid-back husband, Nick, resulting in him bolting back home to his parents' house in Newcastle just so he could put some space and time between them to enable him to think. If he'd reacted so angrily there was no way that her family wouldn't react with equal if not greater resistance. In fact, Evie reconsidered, the envelope didn't contain so much a bombshell as an unpinned grenade. Yes, it would surely be she who would cause the annual Christmas disruption.

At least they had traversed the treacherous M62 safely, Evie thought. Always a worry in wintertime, it had been a singularly unpleasant journey with the motorway like glass and an arctic wind whipping mercilessly over the Pennines. The trouble with the M62 was that you never knew when it would be shut due to unfavourable weather conditions, which weren't uncommon considering its elevation, and heavy snow had been forecast. Traffic had ground to a halt just past Halifax, causing two-year-old India, who had been fast asleep in her booster seat, two middle fingers of her left hand in her mouth, to wake with a start and promptly begin to grizzle. India was a pretty child with pale skin, ebony hair and dark knowing eyes the deep brown of black coffee, all of which she had inherited from her mother's side of the family. Unfortunately her usual doll-like beauty seemed to be permanently marred by a severe bout of the 'terrible twos' which caused her to exhibit voluble tantrums when she couldn't get her own way. Rather like her Aunt Natalie, Evie thought sourly, predicting that one of these tantrums would land within the next half hour. And if that weren't enough, India's ill-humour appeared to have transmitted to Angus, the Lovells' West Highland White Terrier, who had been peacefully snoozing in his cage in the boot but had begun to growl at the driver in the car immediately behind them, tiny pointed teeth bared, whilst peering peevishly through the increasingly misted-up rear window of the hatchback. Trapped in the driver's seat, surrounded by cars on all sides and with no chance of stopping at roadside services anytime soon, Evie had no option but to sit out the increasing racket. Not even the familiar Christmas tunes on the radio eased her discomfort. As the song said, everyone was driving home for Christmas.

Still, they had at last arrived safely in Nether Ousebury, a small, picturesque North Yorkshire village sitting under the stern, Matron-like protection of the northern edge of the Vale of Loxley, where Evie had spent her childhood years and where her parents had every intention of seeing out their retirement. The Bingham family home was comfortingly familiar with its rustic, L-shaped form and cottage-style windows. Set back off a quiet ginnel called School Lane, and away from the relative bustle of the village's main thoroughfare, Magpie Cottage had been given its name because a ceramic mural of a lone magpie in flight had been set in place directly over the front door during construction. Living walls of holly and pyracantha, peppered with seasonal red and orange berries, bordered its well-kept cottage garden, providing a wonderful feeling of seclusion from the adjoining properties.

It only seemed like two minutes since Evie had been home for Hallowe'en and the Binghams' annual bonfire night hootenanny, but no doubt she would be made to believe that an eternity had passed since her last visit. Since India had been born her parents had become increasingly greedy about the time they spent with her. God forbid that her paternal grandparents should have more access to the little girl than they did! Last year, when Evie had spent Christmas Day with Nick's parents in Newcastle, there'd been mutterings of territorial resentment from her own parents.

Freezing air encircled Evie as she climbed out of the car. She let Angus out of his crate and he leapt to the ground with a grunt of disapproval before proceeding to cock his leg on one of the new topiary trees. At that very moment the front door opened and a glorious, biblical mass of golden light spilled onto the gravel drive with her mother's familiar shape silhouetted in the centre.

'Thank goodness! You're here at last. I've been so worried,' Margaret Bingham cried, rushing out to hug her daughter. Her youthful, barely-lined face was illuminated with joy at having her eldest daughter at home once again. Dressed in a new Phase Eight dress, which had been part-camouflaged by an apron, she had obviously been to the hairdressers earlier that day as her gradually greying ebony hair was wonderfully neat and coiffured. Margaret Bingham always made a huge effort for Christmas. It was the time when she could indulge in being a mother, grandmother, wife and domestic goddess extraordinaire. There was nothing she loved better than gathering her flock around her for a few days whilst she bossed and fussed over them until they were driven to distraction. Each and every year she strove to create the perfect Christmas and relentlessly encouraged her family to join her in her enthusiasm. This year would be no different, although her family had long since cottoned on to the fact that the perfect Christmas didn't exist.

'I tried your mobile several times but you didn't answer. I was imagining all sorts of dreadful scenarios. What sort of start would that have been to the holiday?' Margaret Bingham was also a consummate worrier.

'Hello, Mum. Merry Christmas! Sorry, but you know I can't pick up when I'm driving. It was a terrible journey and I'd just got moving again.' Evie's protestations fell on deaf ears as she returned her mother's hug.

'Still you're here now. It's been too long, Evie. And how's my beautiful granddaughter?' Margaret poked her head into the car to catch a glimpse of her only grandchild. 'Oh, she looks just like you. So pretty.'

'Pretty? Pretty filthy and crabby, more like. Plus she's worked herself into a proper snit. Would you mind taking her in? I don't want her out in this cold,' Evie said. In her opinion, India looked far from pretty with her dress all creased and blathered in biscuit crumbs and melted chocolate. Nor was her dog doing her any favours. She'd just caught sight of him yet again misbehaving. 'Angus, stop that!'

'What's he doing?' Margaret casually glanced over her shoulder in time to see Angus's short white tail disappear round the back of one of the topiary tree plant pots. 'Oh, don't worry about that. Chewbacca's been cocking his leg up them for months. I tried some deterrents your father bought from his other place of residence: the garden centre. Honestly, love, I don't know why he doesn't take a sleeping bag and foldaway bed and stay there permanently. Anyway, nothing worked so, quite frankly, I've given up.' Margaret disappeared into the warm light, India wrapped possessively in her arms. 'Come on, dog.' To Evie's indignation, Angus trotted in after her, the very picture of obedience. 'I'll send your father out to help with your luggage. It'll do him good to do something useful.'

Within minutes Bernard Bingham had appeared. Dressed in grey cords, a button-down Argyle cardigan and tweed slippers, he was a little more portly than when Evie had been a child, and with considerably less hair, which was now much greyer, but none of that mattered. Despite missing the busyness of work, he looked less lined and more relaxed than he had in years. His eyes sparkled behind a pair of battered-but-favourite reading spectacles that were so old they should have been carbon dated.

'Hello, cookie,' he said, his arms stretched akimbo.

'Dad! You look marvellous. Retirement is suiting you,' said Evie as she was engulfed in a bear hug.

'Oh, it is, it is. I feel like a new man. And motherhood is still suiting you. I've just seen the adorable India with your mother. My, she's grown. It's been so long since we saw you last. You must come and visit more often.' Bernard reached into the car and pulled out a couple of travel bags. 'Thank goodness you're here safely. Your mother has been fretting because you weren't answering your phone.'

'I was driving and couldn't pick up,' Evie repeated, already exasperated.

'That's exactly what I told her, but she wouldn't listen to me. Anyway, how's my favourite daughter?'

'You mustn't *say* that,' Evie scolded, thinking of her two sisters and how hurt (in Becca's case) and angry (in Natalie's) they would be to hear their father say such a thing.

'I can, because it's true. You might not be as clever as Becca or as beautiful as Natalie but you're still the best, and my favourite nonetheless. The other two are both flawed. I can't come to terms with Becca's lack of ambition.'

'Nat has plenty of ambition. She's achieved more than any of us. You must be proud of her.'

'Ah, but Natalie has a little too much ambition which

means she doesn't care whose toes she steps on. I can be proud of her achievements but not of her behaviour as a human being. You are the balance between your two sisters. You were the firstborn and have always been my favourite. I've often said to your mother that we should have stopped at you and not bothered with the rest.'

'Well, we'll keep that as our secret then,' Evie said quickly, feeling distinctly uncomfortable. Something about her father's words was agitating her conscience, niggling at thoughts she didn't want to acknowledge at that moment. Pushing these unwanted thoughts away with a mental strength born of years of being the eldest of four, she leaned into the car and retrieved several bulging gift bags from the back seat. 'We don't want to upset anyone,' she added briskly, slamming the car door shut with her bottom.

'We certainly don't. Is that everything?'

'Uh-huh. Nick's bringing the rest of the stuff with him.' Evie couldn't quite meet her father's eyes. 'He's got all of India's presents. It would have been difficult to hide them from her if I'd brought them with me. She's getting so crafty.'

'Ah well, children are, you see. Your mother and I had a terrible time with you three girls when you were kids. Always rooting in cupboards and searching under beds for your presents,' Bernard said, lost in reminiscence. 'Mind you, your brother was a good boy. He was never a 'searcher'.' Bernard deposited the travel bags in the hall before going back for more.

'Are you two coming in or not? There's a dreadful draught from that front door,' Margaret called from the kitchen. 'The kettle's almost boiled.'

Bernard gave his favourite daughter a knowing smile.

'She's been driving me mad all week,' he said. 'She'll create the perfect Christmas if it's the last thing she does. If anything she's doubled her efforts of last year. Earlier I caught her leaping around in the lounge like Tinkerbell on acid spraying Crabtree & Evelyn's *Noël* into the air in anticipation of your arrival. The sofa cushions are drenched but at least the reek is keeping the wretched cats off the furniture.'

Evie grinned as she pressed the blipper that locked her car and, linking arms with her father, walked into the house which, as it always did at Christmas, smelled of home cooking, an excess of cinnamon and pine tree, and of chopped apple logs burning in the grate. The hallway was so full of bags they had to slalom round them to get to the kitchen, which, usually tidy and immaculately organised, was even worse chaos. The York stone floor was strewn with Sainsbury's bags-for-life, none of which had been emptied despite most of the kitchen cabinet doors being wide open. The windows were steamed up, courtesy of the pans simmering on top of the red Aga that dominated the room. From the adjacent utility room — nicknamed the 'futility room' by Margaret because she never reached the end of her chores list — came the choral whirr of the dishwasher and the washing machine. Some comedian, probably Dan, had wound a length of pink tinsel around that telltale sign of the serious cook — the garlic plait — that hung on the pantry door. Half the heads had already gone which indicated that Margaret had been indulging in a cooking frenzy. On the work surface, tucked into a corner, a small television was showing a cookery programme. A half-written recipe littered a floury work surface. Evie grinned again. Yes, it was wonderful to be home.

India was sitting at the big kitchen table happily tucking into a bowl of ice cream far too large for a child her age but Evie couldn't be bothered to chide her mother for her indulgence. Plus, if she were busy feeding India then she, Evie, might escape her mother's continual attempts to 'feed her up'. Ramesses, the family's supercilious, self-opinionated black cat, was stretched out across the back of the Aga, gently snoring, white bib and belly ceiling-wards and legs suspended as though on puppet strings so that he wouldn't catch them on one of the hot plates. Angus had settled down under the table where he had found a half-gnawed chewstick. A hamlet of dog and cat beds lay empty in the corner, the animals all much preferring one of the nice comfy beds upstairs instead.

Evie sat down next to her daughter and began to wipe smeared ice cream from her face and dress. An attempt to remove the still half-full bowl resulted in the onset of a temper tantrum. Against her better judgement Evie capitulated and left the bowl where it was.

'Will there be enough hot water for me to give her a bath?' she asked her mother as a steaming mug of tea was plonked in front of her.

'Plenty. Bernard, will you ask that degenerate son of yours if he wants a cup of tea? Whilst you're at it take Becca this, will you?' A further mug was passed to Bernard, who shuffled out of the room. Margaret watched with a warden's eye then, once she was satisfied her husband was out of earshot, she turned to Evie in conspiratorial tones. 'Thank goodness you're home, Evie, to provide a bit of sanity to the house. Only you can sort everyone out. Everybody has been bickering about the sleeping arrangements. There's so much to do and neither your brother nor your sister are being any help. Look at these shopping bags! Just abandoned where they were dumped. Mind you, it's not Becca's fault. That wet fart boyfriend of hers said he wanted to have a 'break' from the relationship in order to think things through, whatever he means by that, and she's taken it very badly—'

'Yes, I know. She rang and told me.' Evie didn't feel it necessary to add how painful it had been to hear her usually merry-natured sister sobbing down the phone, such was Becca's devastation over the split.

'—I don't know why she bothers with him but I suppose it's her decision. Mind you, I can't say I'm sorry he won't be here this year. He was such a nuisance last year. Picking at this, poking at that… Anything any of us did was wrong. Nothing was as good as his mother's. Honestly, I wanted to ask him why he didn't just go home to his bliddy mother instead of annoying us. Of course I didn't, for Becca's sake, but, oh, he was trying. Anyway, as a consequence Becca's moping around with a face like a smacked backside hoping that the phone will ring, and of course it never does, at least not for her. Daniel doesn't have any such excuse, however. He used to be such a lovely little boy but since he's gone to university he's become a monster.'

'In what way?' Evie said. She'd seen her brother a couple of times during his first semester at The University of Manchester as, living in Chester, she was now the one geographically closest to him, and had believed he had taken to undergraduate life very well.

'Well, he used to be so tidy, and temperate. Now all he can do is drink your father's beer straight from the can — apparently using a glass just makes more washing up, as if that was an activity he was ever involved in — and listen to the most horrendous music imaginable. His bedroom had to be mucked out before I could put your Grandpa in there. He never washes and his hair is far longer than any of you three girls' hair was. It looks frightful. Greasy and stuck out at all angles thanks to all that gloop he smothers on it. Furthermore, he keeps disappearing on the proviso that Chewbacca needs a walk, except he forgets to take the dog with him. Just wanders off with an empty lead and collar in his hand.'

'So what's he doing?' Evie was genuinely baffled. Daniel, as both the youngest and the only son, had a tendency to get away with stuff. It was most unlike their mother to criticise him.

'Smoking!' Margaret declared in outrage. 'He's been seen strutting through the village, puffing on a cigarette as though he's Mick Jagger. He thinks I don't know, but I do. As I said, he's been seen. And, he's got a crush on the new barmaid in The Half Moon, which means he's already spent most of the money we'd allocated for next term in the pub. Every night he rolls in pie-eyed. He could drink your Great Aunt Ada under the Christmas tree and we all know what a dreadful old soak she is. I don't know what I'm going to do with him.'

'I'll have a word—' Evie ventured, thinking she really must say hello to the rest of her family. Her mother, however, had no intention of stopping soliloquising.

'Nor do I know what Natalie is up to. I haven't heard from her in weeks. She promised she'd be here by the twenty-second so she's already late by a whole day. I've had to double her and Becca up in Becca's room. No one will be pleased about *that* but I had to make room for Great Aunt Ada somewhere and, much as I was tempted, I couldn't really put her in the garden shed. She and your Grandpa have been bickering all day, at least they have when your Grandpa is awake. Not that that stops your bliddy great aunt. It's of little consequence to her that her tirades are falling on deaf ears. She continues regardless. Worse still, Grandpa has insisted on bringing that ghastly parrot of his even though I asked him not to. It's still got bowel problems, you know. It's already done its business all over the landing carpet. I'm going to have to hire a Rug Doctor in the New Year, it's so bad. I simply despair.'

'It must be great having Dad home every day, though. I expect he lessens your workload,' Evie said, hoping to steer her mother onto a less contentious topic.

'You must be joking! He's become insufferable since he retired. He's always under my feet, leaving his newspapers and gardening magazines everywhere and monopolising every television in the house. It was better when he was out instructing. Do you know what he said to me a week ago? I'll tell you. He said: 'Margaret, I've worked to provide for this family for thirty-five years and so this Christmas I intend to have a good long rest'. I couldn't believe what I was hearing. 'What do you think I've been doing for the past thirty-five Christmases?' I asked him. 'Sitting with my feet up whilst Christmas organises itself?' He must think that Christmas cards write and post themselves and presents are wrapped in the night by a North Pole elf. He seems to believe that if he chops a few sprigs of holly off the bush and brings the tree in, he's done his bit for the year.'

'Father Christmas brings the presents, so they don't need to be wrapped,' Bernard declared, strolling back into the room and noticing his young granddaughter watching her grandma with interest. 'India knows that, don't you sweetheart? Goodness, have you eaten all that ice cream?'

'I hope she's not sick,' Evie said, lips pursed.

'Your mother called me a 'horrid little man' last week. Then she wonders why I prefer my garden's company to hers, ha ha.' Bernard gave his wife a fond kiss on her rigid white cheek. 'Look at her, desperate to burst with righteous apoplexy but actually rather charmed by me. Has she got all her grievances off her chest yet? She's been storing them up for days, awaiting your return. By the way, Dan says, yes, he would like a cup of tea and why hasn't his pig of a sister been to say hello yet?'

'Well, he'll just have to wait. What does he think I am, a waitress? What I want to know is why Nick hasn't travelled down with you,' Margaret continued, nevertheless reaching for the kettle once more. 'Term broke up more than a week ago and yet he's flitted to his folks in Newcastle, leaving you to drive all this way by yourself. What can be more important than the safety of his wife and daughter?'

'I'm perfectly capable of driving by myself, Mum. Nick's only gone home for a Christmas party, which he deserves as he's been working like a dog since the end of term, marking papers. He's staying with Carol and Malc tonight and will travel down in the morning,' Evie said blithely, looking askance at her mother. She took stock of her mother's face, which had taken on a disapproving, knowing expression. 'It's no good pulling faces, Mum. He's entitled to see his family and old friends sometimes. India and I monopolise what little free time he gets as it is. It would have been unfair of me to kick up a fuss. Anyway, you get India and me all to yourselves for one night. I thought you'd like that,' she added craftily.

'Always the diplomat,' Bernard said sagely.

'Well, I don't know why you have to dash off early on Boxing Day. We're all going to the pantomime and you don't want to miss that. It's Old Mother Hubbard this year. Perhaps I could get a couple more tickets. I'm sure Nick's parents won't mind if you stay another day.'

Before Evie could protest the phone jangled. As Margaret reached for the receiver Evie took the opportunity to escape.

'Can you watch India for a few minutes whilst I say hi to Becca and Dan?' she asked her father, who nodded happily.

'REMEMBERED US, HAVE YOU?' was Dan Bingham's sardonic greeting as Evie entered the familiar lounge of Magpie Cottage. His grinning face belied his words of beration. Even Becca, who was wallowing in the depths of dysphoria, managed to raise a wan smile when she saw her elder sister. The two of them were sitting side by side on the ancient squashy sofa that was impossible to get out of after half an hour as it moulded itself to one's bottom. Dan had his stockinged feet propped up on the occasional table. Next to them were the remains of a packet of half a dozen mince pies, of which only one was left, and a copy of the *Radio Times*, which resembled an explosion of technicolour fluorescence having been highlighted in several different coloured pens to indicate who wanted to watch what over the holiday.

'You'll never guess,' he said, his expressive, sarcastic face split by a wide grin. '*Songs of Praise* clashes with *Top of the Pops*. There'll be fisticuffs.' From beneath the bridge of Dan's legs Chewbacca, the family's fat, greedy chocolate Labrador, who had a whippy tail that could bruise any thigh and a tendency to wipe his slobbery chops on any available clean fabric, gave two cursory thumps of his tail in recognition. He was too lazy to stand up to greet Evie properly. Boo and Hiss, two new adorable silver tabby kittens that Margaret had rescued from certain death after they were abandoned in the village by a family who moved away, were batting an illicit shiny red bauble to each other behind the sofa. Realising that the fibreglass sphere could easily shatter and cause harm to tiny paws, Evie reached down to pick it up. Why was it that nobody else ever thought of these things?

In the corner of the room stood the Christmas tree that their father had dug out of the garden for yet another year. It was completely bare, which caused Evie to raise her eyebrows. All the usual other trimmings were present in the room: poinsettia, candles, tinsel, the mantelpiece littered with Christmas cards that no one had got round to hanging from the cardholder. She presumed there must be some reasonable explanation and so refrained from comment. Instead, she turned back to her brother, who was now tapping her leg with his foot. It was very irritating.

'I was trying to put off the awful moment of being reminded that I was related to you,' Evie retorted, deadpan, giving her brother a playful slap on his corduroy leg. 'What the bloody hell are you wearing? No one's seen flares as big as that since the Titanic went down. Hello Becca, how are you feeling?'

Becca's bottom lip trembled and her already reddened

eyes welled up. Dan swiftly snatched up the last mince pie and rammed it into her quivering mouth.

'Don't start that again, you silly cow,' he said, the gentle tone in his voice counteracting the harshness of his words. Despite being effectively silenced by an excess of dry pastry, Becca's owlish eyes portrayed the intense gratitude she felt towards her brother, who understood fully that any display of kindness was the quickest way to set her off. Frantic chewing allowed her the time to compose herself.

'Not great.' She gulped down the last of the pie. No wonder she was such a bloody heifer! 'Better now that you and Dan are home. Mum's been unbearable: full of opinions and advice every ten minutes and all of it either sanctimonious or redundant. Who was on the phone?' There was no need for her to mention that she hoped it was the on-off Gregory.

'No idea. Mum means well. I've barely been in the house ten minutes and I've been grilled and lectured in equal measures on a litany of topics. I've also been advised of all your shortcomings, Daniel, so you needn't sit there looking innocent,' Evie said, grinning. 'Smoking — honestly!'

Dan instantly looked sheepish.

'He's only trying to compete with Grandpa.' Becca defended her brother, nodding at the slight white-haired figure asleep in one of the easy chairs, rolling tobacco and Rizlas perched on one of the chair arms. 'Poor old bugger. That must be the first peace he's had all day. Great Aunt Ada has been bending his ear ever since she arrived. She's upstairs having a sleep, thank God. No doubt recharging the batteries for her bitch-o-meter. She's been heinous ever since she arrived, complaining about everything and generally making a nuisance of herself. She's already decimated a bottle of Dad's gin since yesterday morning. Why can't she buy her own booze? She's rich enough. She's no more than a bloody old miser. I hate her and wish she wasn't here.'

'Hush, it'll only cause problems if you're heard,' Evie said, casting a furtive glance over her shoulder. 'We have to be kind to her since Great Uncle Bruce died. She has nowhere to go and she is Grandpa's sister.'

'Besides which, we have to be nice to the auld hag to ensure that she leaves all her hundreds of thousands of bar to us instead of the local cauliflower tops' club,' Dan hissed. Both Becca and Evie ignored him deliberately.

'It's all right for you. You're dashing off up north to Newcastle on Boxing Day for your second Christmas with Nick's lovely *sane* family. We have to put up with her until New Year,' Becca said to Evie. 'Worse still, I have to share my room with Natalie. She's like Great Aunt Ada's younger clone. Evil: then and now.'

'This is why we're having the pie-fest,' Dan said, pointing to the empty packet. 'Our motives are twofold: firstly, to try and cheer up poor grieving Becca and, secondly, to help shift my bitch of a hangover. We only started them forty minutes ago. We both feel sick. There's another pack in the larder if you want one?'

Evie assessed her own increasing waistline and bottom. 'I'd better not. I don't need fattening up. I've put on so much weight I'm positively pear shaped.'

'The technical term for that is pyriform,' imparted Becca who, because she struggled with her own weight at the best of times, gave her an empathic look.

'Nonsense! There's nothing on you and there never has been,' Margaret said, bustling into the room. 'That was your sister on the phone.' Becca's shoulders visibly drooped. 'She said she's just landed at Leeds Bradford and will be with us in about an hour and a half. She said she has a surprise for us.'

'If she's at the airport then there's no way the surprise can be that she isn't coming,' Becca muttered, thinking of her sister's scheduled presence in her bedroom.

'Rebecca!' Margaret was shocked. Dan pretended he hadn't heard his mother's admonishment.

'Yule be lucky — ha ha! That was last year's surprise and we can't be that fortunate two years on the trot. I can't believe the lazy bitch has flown up from London,' he commented, reaching for the telly pages. 'She must be coining it in. Maybe she's bringing us super-fabbo Christmas presents this year, for a change.'

'Daniel, don't say such things about your sister,' his mother snapped.

'Why not? Bitch, she is, ye-e-es.' Dan's imitation of Yoda was spot on. 'She's always lording it over the rest of us. She'll be even worse this year after getting her wonderful promotion. It's Bec I feel sorry for, having to accommodate her in her room. What time is she due to descend so we can set up an unwelcoming committee?'

Evie frowned with disapproval. No one was more aware than she of how trying her youngest sister could be. Easily the most ambitious of the Bingham children, Natalie had landed a cushy job working for the BBC within five minutes of graduation and had since risen to the dizzy heights of junior television producer. It had only taken her eighteen months and, whilst her mother was giddy with pride, the rest of the family were reservedly unimpressed.

'Let's hope we get something more exciting than a DVD of her latest programme this year,' Becca said sulkily. 'It's a bit grim and gritty for me.' Natalie had been working on a critically acclaimed drama series, called *Deep Blue,* about life on a North Sea oil rig.

'You're only jealous because Natalie has a far better job than you do. I don't know how you sleep at night, Rebecca, knowing that you're wasting those wonderful brains of yours. You could have done anything but instead you choose to waste your time working in that ghastly call centre and waiting for that so-called boyfriend of yours to make his mind up about whether or not he actually likes you enough to marry you.' It was as though the words wouldn't stop pouring out of Margaret's mouth. Becca didn't respond but shot her mother a look of pure hatred and stalked from the room. Evie was sure she saw the first glisten of tears in the corner of her sister's eyes.

'Well done, Mum,' Dan said sarcastically, voicing Evie's secret thoughts. 'That was really helpful.' Dan was equally blessed and cursed with the gift of having the courage to always say exactly what he thought. Too laid back to be bitchy for no good reason, he never held back when he believed someone had to be either defended or ticked off.

'Well, she just sits there like a sack of spuds and doesn't attempt to change anything,' Margaret said, refusing to be repentant. 'Oh, I give up with all of you. I'll be in the kitchen preparing dinner should anyone care.'

Dan watched his mother depart in silence.

'That good, eh?' Evie asked. Dan rolled his eyes.

'Becca's gutted and Mum just won't take it seriously. I mean, none of us like Gregory but we have to put up with him, just as we do Nick,' Dan said, eyes flicking sideways to see if Evie bit at his little joke. She didn't, much to his disappointment, and so he returned to his theme. 'She's just floundering. I've been trying to cheer her up but I'm afraid I'm not much good at it as I can only see things from a male perspective and can't do all that listening-and-being-supportive shite. Plus I just tend to say what I think, which isn't always helpful. All I'm good for is dragging her down to the village pub and forcing booze down her throat. Do you want to come with us tonight? I'm sure the parentals will be happy to babysit. They're always moaning about not seeing enough of India as it is.'

'Gawd! You'd think I never came home, the fuss they make. I might just take you up on that offer on the proviso that I get India off to sleep in good time. I'll go and see if

Mum needs any help with dinner. She seems more frazzled than anyone else,' Evie said. Dan flicked the channels on Sky so fast that they blurred before her eyes.

'I'm glad you're home, sis. It's always calmer when you're around,' Dan said, a note of seriousness creeping into his tone. His eyes never left the television. 'You're the only one who has the patience to deal with everyone. Oh look, *Home Alone* is on.'

'Didn't you know that I secretly moonlight as a referee? I don't really illustrate children's books for a living. It's all a cover.'

'A book cover. I doubt many men would complain if you were running round the pitch in some skimpy shorts, even if you are growing a fat arse,' Dan laughed.

'Cheek,' Evie said as she wandered back into the kitchen. She found her mother furiously beating eggs in a bowl. For a moment she was mesmerised by the way her mother's entire body twisted and shook from the exertion, even when she had stopped beating.

'How long is dinner going to be? I thought I might get India's bath out of the way, if that's okay,' she said.

'We're not eating until your sister arrives from the airport, which should be about an hour and a quarter,' Margaret said. 'Paella, followed by chocolate Yule log.'

Hence the eggs, Evie thought. She was relieved that her mother had an agenda for the eggs rather than merely venting her spleen on them. Dan chose this moment to jog comedically through the kitchen, detouring on his way to the downstairs loo.

'I'm just about to make a Yule log of me own,' he said, patting his stomach as he passed by them. 'Ladies.' And off he went, leaving his mother and sister gaping after him with incredulity.

'I see what you mean,' Evie said, referring to her mother's earlier comment that her brother had metamorphosed into a monster. Margaret merely rolled her eyes. 'I've brought India's dinner with me so I'll heat that up later. She might set her head down before dinner… with any hope. That way I'll get some peace, although I have to say Dad's doing a marvellous job keeping her entertained. Where are they?'

'In the back lounge watching cartoons,' Margaret snapped. 'Nice for him to spend so much time with our only grandchild whilst I slave away in here. Honestly Evelyn, if it weren't already too late for you I'd seriously recommend not having any children at all, and certainly not more than one.'

'I'll go and retrieve my daughter and send your errant husband back to you, then,' Evie said with an uncomfortable smile. Her mother's words had hit the same particularly sensitive nerve that her father's had earlier. Still having no inclination to deal with it, she began to sidle out of the door.

'By the way, your father and I have moved our things into your old room so you and Nick can have ours. We thought it might be more convenient for you to have use of the en suite rather than battling with that horrible lot for the bathroom. I know it can be difficult when you have a little one. Dan should have put your bags in there already, providing his busy schedule of doing absolutely bugger all hasn't prevented him from doing so.' Leaving her mother to her own mutterings, Evie fled.

TEN MINUTES LATER, with India safely encased in her cot and a shallow bath running, Evie tapped on Becca's bedroom door.

'D'you want to help me with India's bath? I thought we could have a catch up,' she called through the closed door. Inside the room, red eyed and racked with misery, self-pity and guilt at being so miserable at Christmastime, Becca translated her sister's words as 'I'm not Mum, you can tell me all about Gregory whilst I listen and don't judge'. Grateful for having such a calming, understanding sister and yet at the same time wondering how her two sisters could be so different in nature, Becca replied that she'd be out in a few minutes. Even though it was likely that they'd both end up in The Half Moon later with Dan, Becca was pleased for the opportunity to speak to Evie in private. There were some things that only sisters could help with. Mopped up, she plodded into her parents' en suite.

'I swear this child was a cat in a former life. She hates getting wet,' Evie said, grinning up at Becca as she lowered India into the bath. The little girl wriggled and squirmed as she broke the surface of the water. 'I have to make these sessions as swift as possible otherwise we're subjected to the screaming abdabs.'

Becca smiled and splashed some warm water onto India's writhing body. No one in her family was aware of her desperate need to settle down and start a family of her own. It tore at her insides like a physical wound.

'She's adorable. You're so lucky. I can't wait to have kids.'

Evie considered her sister carefully.

'Has Gregory contacted you at all?' she ventured, seizing the opportunity to bring him up.

'I received a Christmas card 'from Gregory',' Becca made air quotes with her fingers, 'but there was no 'love' and no gift. All the gifts I bought for him are wrapped and lying at the bottom of my wardrobe in disgrace. I've worn the same shoes for days now just so I don't have to go down there for a different pair,' she added with a hollow laugh. 'The last time I heard from him was last week. He rang me at work to tell me he missed me and that he was finding life difficult without me.'

'That sounds promising.'

'Not really. I asked him outright if he wanted to get back together and he said no. I was furious as well as upset. I asked him what he was playing at ringing me up and he had the temerity to tell me that he was feeling down and he didn't have any one else to talk to. I was so angry I rang that spiteful battle-axe of a mother of his and dropped him in it. I disturbed her in the middle of a bridge foursome and ranted for about fifteen minutes before she got rid of me. Even she was put out by what he'd done. Probably terrified we'd make up. I bet she's thrilled about all this. She never liked me despite her earnest assurances to the contrary. She could never admit to it either because that would render me instantly vindicated. As long as she can make him believe that she likes me, and I'm the one being difficult, I don't have a leg to stand on. Bloody bitch. I know Mum can be a pain in the arse sometimes but she's positively saintly in comparison to that old bag.'

'Mum only says what she thinks is best,' Evie said as she battled to rub a splodge of baby shampoo into India's hair. 'Stop wriggling, you little minx. She means well, even if she is misguided.'

'She keeps nattering that I'm not eating enough,' Becca said. 'Those mince pies are the most I've eaten in days.' Evie had already assessed her sister and thought she looked pale and tired from the anxiety of the break up. She also agreed with their mother that she was losing far too much weight as a result of pushing her dinners round her plate instead of eating them.

'You are very drawn,' she said. 'Mum's just worried.'

'It's not that I'm not eating. It's just that all food turns to ashes in my mouth, much like the Apples of Sodom. And I wish she'd stop badgering me about my job,' Becca continued. 'I already know that answering telephones all day in a call centre isn't the most glamorous of jobs. I don't need reminding on a daily basis.'

'I think she feels frustrated that you're not maximising your potential. You are wickedly intelligent, Bec, far cleverer than me, or even Nat,' Evie said.

Becca gave a snort.

'More like she can't boast about me when she's down at the WI,' she said. 'She harangued me for hours last week about how she hadn't been able to write anything decent about me in the Round Robin letter. 'What am I going to put about you, Rebecca?' she said.' Becca's impersonation of their mother was uncannily accurate. ''That you still don't have a decent job or that you've lost your boyfriend? The glories of your academic career are very faded now. Your sisters are eclipsing you, you know.' I don't know why she has to write that awful thing. Doesn't she know that everyone laughs at them?' Evie grinned, thinking of how she and Nick always howled when they read their friends' efforts. 'It was full of guff about Dan going to university and Nat's new job and how wonderful they both are. There was even a paragraph all about you and how you're a fabulous mother and how you manage to juggle being a mother, wife and career girl with effortless competence,' Becca muttered.

'Is that what she thinks?' snorted Evie. 'Then she's seriously deluded. I'm so far behind my deadline for the book I'm illustrating I'm afraid the publishers will tell me to bugger off and bring in another artist to replace me. If it makes you feel better I've already had a grilling on why Nick is coming down tomorrow rather than tonight. I daren't tell her the real reason.' Evie looked askance at Becca, who didn't seem to hear what she'd said but continued to splash a giggling India with foamy water. Half disappointed, half relieved, Evie continued. 'No one's exempt. Anyway, it's all one-upmanship with her. Next year, just tell her a load of bollocks to keep her quiet. Dan'll concoct something for you. His ability for coming out with shite when he wants to get out of trouble is remarkable. I'm sure he can expand his skills and create an excellent alter ego for you.'

'He's been great at defending me,' Becca admitted. 'He

was such a blemish when he was at school but he's so much more fun now. Not that he's in Mum's good books either.'

'So I gather,' Evie said wryly. 'But this isn't getting you organised. What are you going to do about Gregory? Anything, or are you just going to sit tight?'

'I haven't decided,' said Becca. 'I'm so confused. I want to ring him but Dan says that's the worst thing I could do and I should just back off, but it's so hard. I miss him so much. Dan caught me texting him yesterday and rugby tackled me in the lounge before I could send it. Then he ran off with my mobile and won't tell me where he's hidden it.

'The worst thing is that I know everyone will have a better Christmas with him not here. Last year was awful. You missed it all, being up in Toon Town. Mum and Dad tried to be so welcoming, even though I knew they didn't like him. They bought him some wonderful gifts and tried to involve him in everything and he repaid them by ensuring that everyone knew that he wasn't impressed. He never said as much, it was all by insinuation. No doubt it all paled in comparison to his mother's glorious efforts. I swear he's Oedipal. Later he fell asleep — clearly from boredom — and snored even more loudly than Grandpa. He only woke up when Christmas tea was served, the greedy pig. I remember because he whipped the last piece of pork pie with egg from under Dad's nose. Dad was furious. I don't even know *why* I miss him so much. Sometimes I can't even bear to think about him without seething.'

'That's not like you, Bec. You're usually so laid back.'

'Lazy, you mean,' Becca said. She gazed down at India with a wistfulness that was almost painful to witness. At that moment Evie realised Becca wasn't simply grieving the loss of a boyfriend but the loss of a potential future, of a hoped-for lifestyle she'd prayed would evolve from mere dreams to actuality. Becca corroborated this as she continued. 'I always hoped that one day he'd wake up and realise he did actually love me. That we'd get engaged, then married and eventually have babies of our own and then, once I'd provided her with a bloody grandchild his mother might like me a little better and I'd finally be accepted into their family.' Becca's face contorted into a mask of miserable fury. 'I *hate* Christmas. It's for no one but children and lovers.'

This wasn't the moment to burden her sister with her own woes, Evie realised as she put a comforting arm around Becca's shoulders.

'It's for families, and we'll make sure you have a great Christmas this year.'

WITH EVIE and Becca safely occupied with India's bath, Dan seized his chance. The rest of the family were downstairs and therefore wouldn't disturb him either. He snuck into his own bedroom and resentfully surveyed the mess Grandpa had made. There were itchy nylon slacks and enormous greying Y-fronts as far as the eye could see and the air was fusty from the smell of pensioner and stale cigarette smoke. Worse still, there was a strong whiff of bird shit courtesy of Vera Lynn, Grandpa's slack-bottomed parrot. Despite his mother's most vehement protestations, the parrot accompanied Grandpa on all his visits to Magpie Cottage and never failed to defecate throughout the house, terrifying the cats with every squawk. This year had been no exception but because of the landing carpet incident of earlier that morning Vera Lynn had been banished to her cage in disgrace. She had been covered with her white tablecloth, which should have silenced the creature, but Vera Lynn was a crafty and garrulous bird and was aware someone had entered the room.

'Who's there?' she crawed from beneath the tablecloth. 'Who's there?' was one of her favourite stock phrases, of which she had about half a dozen. 'Here comes the vicar!'

That was another. Dan closed the door quietly behind him. No man of the cloth would ever have plotted such an outrageous deed.

'Time you and I had a little chat, Vera Lynn,' said he, a wicked expression eclipsing his attractive, wide-mouthed face as he whipped the tablecloth off the cage like a cabaret magician. 'If you're going to stay in my room we're going to have to increase your vocabulary.' Dan believed that Vera Lynn's few phrases were getting a little tired. In his opinion, it was time this old bird learnt some new tricks.

DINNER WAS DELAYED. Evie had successfully achieved her goal of having India bathed, fed and put to bed in plenty of time and had even managed to snatch a couple of precious minutes to pour herself a rare glass of wine and flick through a Christmas magazine that was lying around on the occasional table. It hadn't been her that had held up her mother's schedule. Natalie was, as per usual, late. All the Binghams sat in the lounge… waiting.

Natalie finally burst into the house, an hour later than promised, like a whirlwind, leaving in her wake open doors and abandoned stacks of matching luggage which she was confident would be dealt with by someone less important than herself. She was easily the most beautiful of the three Bingham sisters despite them all sharing the same attractive colouring and features that required little artificial embellishment. Margaret wondered if they just sat better on Natalie or if it was the fact that she had striking pale blue eyes, the colour of a clear winter's sky, which made her so stunning. All her other children were dark eyed. Margaret also wondered if it was a coincidence that the only other family member with such cold, piercing eyes was Great Aunt Ada.

If possible, Natalie looked more beautiful than ever. But then, Becca thought sourly, she had the money to buy on-trend clothes, have the latest celebrity haircut and colour, and all the other beauty treatments and paraphernalia any young London executive should have. Even Evie felt a stab of inferiority as she took in her sister's size eight figure, two-tone hairstyle and fabulously expensive clothes. Somehow Natalie made beauty look so effortless — or was it money that made it so?

Dan was still wondering what the 'surprise' was when it, or rather he, was presented to the family.

'Everyone, this is Christian!' Natalie announced. Everything she said always sounded as though it should have an exclamation mark after it, as though everything she had to say was of the utmost importance. 'He's an actor and we met during production of my show.' She pushed forward a long, thin individual who had pale brown hair cut into a shoulder length bob that was even glossier than her own, a finely kempt goatee beard and who was wearing a hideous pastel blue suit accompanied by a couple of flowing scarves in contrasting shades that made him look like a deepening swimming pool. He was extremely attractive, but in an arty, intellectual way which gave him a rather supercilious air.

'Reeeally?' Margaret asked, her sudden new-found interest in her unexpected guest eclipsing all worries and concerns about not having sufficient beds, pantomime tickets or smoked salmon tians for Christmas lunch. 'What will we see you in next? Line of Duty, or maybe a soap such as EastEnders or Coronation Street?'

Bernard cast an amazed glance at his suddenly skittish wife.

'I consider such commercial roles to be rather lightweight. I'd only consider looking at something somewhat meatier. Perhaps Chekhov or something along the lines of a Merchant Ivory production,' Christian's tone was decidedly snooty.

'Oh.' Margaret was so taken aback that she turned her attention back to Natalie.

'Tea, sweetheart? How many sugars?'

'None. She's watching what she eats,' Christian said. Evie and Becca stared in amazement at their sister's acceptance of this decree.

'I'm also watching what I eat,' Evie muttered to Becca. 'Later I'm going to watch myself eat three courses, plus bread, and wine.' Becca giggled for the first time in days.

Natalie plonked herself onto the sofa, crossing her legs in an elegant motion. All eyes turned to her, simply because that was what always happened. It was as though it was mandatory. Her eyes scoured the room, first assessing Becca from head to foot, then Evie. She commented on neither. In Natalie's opinion it was vital that she was more attractive than both her sisters, as she would never be more intelligent than Becca, or more beloved than Evie, and she had to be the best at something. Whether or not she was more attractive than Dan didn't concern her, even if he did look like a girl with that dreadful birds-nest mullet. For the most part she ignored him, this being a habit borne from childhood when Dan's birth had meant she was no longer the cherished baby of the family. By the same extent she now resented India, whom she also always ignored.

'How's work?' Margaret asked, knowing this would be the most expected question. Natalie smiled prettily.

'Fabulous,' she said, fluidly flicking her long, glossy, black and blonde hair over her shoulder. 'The last series of *Deep Blue* was well received by the viewers in addition to being critically acclaimed. We're hoping for at least one Bafta nomination. Of course, most of the credit must be attributed to yours truly.'

'What about the actors, scriptwriters and the director?' Dan asked bluntly. 'Didn't they have anything to do with the show's success or is your glorious self going to take all the plaudits?' Dan took very little nonsense from the youngest of his three sisters. Natalie had bullied him mercilessly when they'd both been children and, much like Becca, he had a remarkable memory.

'Of course they did, but they need leadership,' Natalie snapped.

'More like dictatorship,' Dan retorted, reaching for a handful of crisps from the bowl his father had brought in with him. Natalie chose to ignore him and turned her attention to the Christmas tree.

'I'm so glad you've decided to 'go green' with the tree this year, Mum,' she said. 'It's very commendable. Christian regularly campaigns to have the trees in London decorated more sympathetically. He once strapped himself to the Christmas tree in Trafalgar Square so that the authorities couldn't put the lights on.'

'You must have been plucking pine needles out of your bum for weeks after,' said Dan. He couldn't imagine this stuffed shirt doing anything as energetic as tying himself to an evergreen tree by means of protest.

'You've no idea how much energy all those fairy lights use up and what damage baubles cause to the environment, not to mention it being degrading to deface a naturally beautiful living entity,' Natalie carried on, pointedly ignoring Dan. To a man, the Binghams stared at Natalie, who had not previously shown any commitment to preserving the environment but conversely had every electrical beauty gadget known to woman and who could regularly be seen in front of a mirror polluting the air with a thick white cloud of hairspray. 'The collective electricity required to light all the sets of fairy lights in this country alone costs hundreds of millions of pounds.'

'Bullshit!' Becca breathed in Evie's ear, who struggled to suppress a giggle.

'You deface yourself with your make-up, hair dyes, manicures,' Dan said icily. 'Then again, you're hardly a naturally beautiful living entity. You need to put all that slap on your face to make yourself presentable.' Natalie's face contorted into a mask of fury.

'What do you know? You're nothing more than a troglodyte,' she retaliated.

'Will you two stop bickering!' their mother snapped. 'Dan, be nicer to your sister. It's Christmas. Good will to all men, and all that, which includes sisters. And Natalie, I haven't 'gone green' with the tree at all. I've left it bare so that my children could dress it when they finally all arrived home for the holiday. That's what everyone will be doing after lunch tomorrow. Guests are welcome to join in if they please.' Margaret directed this last comment at Christian, who looked horrified at the prospect. 'Dinner will be served in ten minutes. We'll be eating in the kitchen although it will be a tight squeeze.' She shot Natalie a look that clearly said 'no thanks to you'.

Evie, Becca and Dan reluctantly tore their attention from the box of decorations they had been casually eyeing up whilst Bernard shook his father awake.

'What? Who's there? Is it the damned Nazis?' Grandpa yelled.

'No, Dad, just dinnertime,' Bernard said with extreme patience before turning to Natalie. 'Could you please go and retrieve Great Aunt Ada? She's in your room.'

'What's she doing in there? And where the hell are we sleeping?' Natalie asked imperiously. The use of the word 'we' caused raised eyebrows all round.

'*You* are bunking up with Becca,' Margaret said.

'You're kidding! Christian and I have been living together in London,' Natalie protested angrily. This was a lie, but then the truth wasn't a close associate of Natalie's.

'As this is the first time you have bothered to tell either your father or me about this, you should consider yourself to be batting on a very sticky wicket. You will share with Becca, and Christian can doss down with Dan in the den,' Margaret said.

'Fucking hell,' Evie heard Dan mutter in her left ear. She had to stifle another giggle.

'I bet Evie and Saint Nicholas don't have to sleep apart,' Natalie continued. She was spitting like a chip pan.

'Evelyn and Nick are married.'

'So where's Gregory sleeping? Is it going to be all boys together? Lucky you, Christian. Between Dan's stench and Gregory's snoring you'll think you're back on set.'

'Gregory won't be joining us this year,' Margaret said, matter-of-factly. Natalie's eyes swivelled round to Becca, who was looking distinctly uncomfortable.

'Thank goodness for that,' Natalie said frostily. 'He ruined Christmas for everyone last year with his pissing and moaning.'

Becca turned scarlet with mortification.

'Wouldn't matter if he were here,' Dan said, grabbing Natalie by the shoulders and propelling her out of the room. 'It's someone else's turn to ruin Christmas this year.' His meaning couldn't have been clearer. 'Go and rouse Ol' Aunt Aggro. I'll make sure my new room-mate is made comfortable.'

Dinner should have been a jolly affair. To the soundtrack of carols on Classic FM, Margaret presented a splendid seafood paella accompanied by a large bowl of fat black and green olives and several different breads hot from the oven. She had also prepared traditional lamb chops, potatoes and vegetables for Grandpa and Great Aunt Ada in an attempt to prevent the phrase 'I'm not eating any of that foreign muck' from gracing the conversation. However, whereas her own family fell upon the food like savages, all having been brought up to have good, healthy appetites, Christian sat motionless, staring at his empty plate with a pained expression on his face.

'Tuck in, Christian,' Margaret advised jovially. 'My family have never understood the 'family hold back' rule. The saying 'stretch or starve' is more appropriate to this lot.' As she spoke she filled her own wine glass from one of the bottles of white Rioja Bernard had reluctantly produced from his sacred wine store.

'I can't eat this,' Christian said bluntly. Natalie opened and shut her mouth like a fish.

'Oh, do you not like seafood? Not to worry, there's plenty of chops and potatoes should you prefer that. Grandpa and Great Aunt Ada both have sparrow appetites, and I always cook far too much. It's no trouble to rustle you up a plate.' Margaret really couldn't have been more accommodating.

'No thanks,' was the uncompromising reply. 'I don't eat meat.'

'Ah, a vegetarian,' Bernard said with a sage nod of his head. 'Not a problem, dear. There are plenty of those Linda McCartney meals in the freezer that we bought for Dan's student friends. Perhaps Natalie could organise one of those for her… friend?' He couldn't bring himself to say boyfriend. The thought of this lanky fop sharing a bed with his youngest daughter was one upon which he didn't care to dwell.

'I'm not a vegetarian,' Christian said in indignation. 'I'm a macrobiotic.'

'A what-o-biotic?' asked Margaret. Dan was killing himself with laughter, his chair tilted onto its hind legs as he arched himself back in mirth.

'Macrobiotic,' said Becca in between mouthfuls. 'It's a—' She wanted to say fad diet, but felt it would be rude seeing as Christian had pretty much only just stepped over the threshold. '—Specialist diet. It's basically a vegan diet, but on 'roids. So, as well as no animal products, he can't eat or drink anything processed. It's basically green leafy vegetables, beans and brown rice and stuff.' As always, Becca amazed her family with her encyclopaedic knowledge.

'Well, I don't understand any diet that stops you eating meat but encourages you to take steroids,' Margaret said.

Becca's head sank into her hands. She daren't even look at either Evie or Dan, and she certainly wasn't going to try and explain matters to her mum.

'What can you drink?' Dan asked, intrigued.

'Freshly boiled and cooled water, not bottled, and absolutely no tap water.' Christian shot the jug of water in the middle of the table a look of disgust. 'Freshly squeezed juice, and some alcohol, but it has to be organic.'

'You can't drink tap water but booze is okay? That's the diet for me,' Dan said. 'You seem to know a lot about it, Bec. Have you dabbled?'

'Err, nope!' Becca said, taking a large bite out of a chunk of sun-dried tomato bread for emphasis. To her own amazement she was hungry for the first time in days. Must be Evie's presence, she thought. 'I like my grub too much.'

'You can tell,' Natalie interjected, looking pointedly at Becca's thighs. She herself hadn't touched the bread basket. Becca bristled but said nothing. 'Although this misery trip you're on has done wonders for your figure. I can actually see the Bingham cheekbones for once.'

'Best diet ever,' Becca said sarcastically.

'So how do you know so much about it?' Dan persisted.

'I just read it somewhere,' Becca said with a shrug of her shoulders. 'Lovely paella, Mum.'

'Lamb's a bit tough though.' To Great Aunt Ada, complaining came as easily as breathing. 'Any more plonk, Margaret?'

'Becca has a freakishly good memory; better than any elephant's,' Natalie told Christian without a trace of admiration in her voice. 'Never get into an argument with her. She'll dredge up every misdemeanour you've committed since birth.'

'Nevertheless, none of this is giving me any clues as to

what I can give you for your dinner. I suppose you don't eat turkey either, or smoked salmon?' Margaret looked positively crestfallen. Matters weren't helped by Christian giving her such a condescending look that Dan felt his temper rise. It was all right for him to criticise his mother; that was his privilege in response to her constant badgering. What was not okay was for some stranger — and they didn't come much stranger in his opinion — that Natalie had picked up somewhere along the way to come into the family home, at Christmas no less, and upset his mother.

'I think it's Natalie's problem, not yours, Mum,' he said coldly. 'After all, she has rather sprung this on us. There's nothing you could have done having been given so little notice.'

'What's the problem?' Grandpa boomed, having only just realised that something was the matter.

'Natalie's young gentleman doesn't eat meat,' Great Aunt Ada said, smiling fondly at her favourite grand-niece.

'What's wrong with him?' As ever, Grandpa didn't mince his words. 'Doesn't eat meat, indeed! In the war you ate whatever was available, and you liked it. There was none of this namby-pamby vegetarianism. You were lucky to get vegetables at all. Usual fodder was Oxo soup and stale bread. Yes!'

'For God's sake, not the bloody war again. And there's nothing wrong with being a vegetarian,' Natalie snapped.

'No there isn't, but it's still rude to drop this on Mum with absolutely no prior warning,' Dan replied disagreeably.

'I wouldn't recommend you start India on the macrobiotic diet, Evie. Research has shown that it's deficient in calcium and vitamin D and can cause rickets in the young.' Becca smirked at Natalie, who was seething in her chair. Evie, who had been shovelling paella into her mouth at a rate of knots, merely shrugged to indicate that it was never going to happen.

'The thing that I don't understand,' Dan said, now bored with baiting Natalie. 'Is why do meat-eaters have to accommodate vegetarians in their own home when the favour isn't returned? Not once have I been guesting at a vegetarian's house when, upon discovering I am not of their ilk, they've produced a nice, fat, juicy steak they'd stashed in the freezer in order to accommodate my dietary requirements.' Everyone except Natalie and Christian roared with laughter. 'It's the fact that they're not prepared to compromise both ways that bugs me.'

'Much the same can be said about smokers.' Margaret fixed her only son with a stern eye. Dan shut up. 'Natalie, what can I give the poor boy? I can't bear to see him sitting there with his empty plate, like Oliver.'

'Stop fretting. He can have a plate of veg,' Natalie grumbled. Only the look of disapproval on her father's face stopped her from further griping. 'We'll get him something suitable to eat tomorrow.'

'Can I at least find you something to drink? I've got some herbal teas,' Margaret offered.

'I'd like some more wine.' Great Aunt Ada held out her, yet again, empty glass. Everyone ignored her.

'Are they organic?' asked Christian.

'I don't know if they're organic but they are Twining's,' said Margaret, which in her own opinion gave them the seal of approval. Christian accepted a strawberry and elderflower teabag, although no one knew whether it was because it was permitted or because he was being polite, the latter of which in fairness didn't seem likely. Dan, in a moment of rare philanthropy, offered to boil the kettle. He unwrapped the teabag and swung it in front of his own face like a hypnotist.

'These teabags aren't so much fruit flavoured as fruit scented,' he said to no one in particular, sniffing the teabag before dropping it into a mug. He couldn't imagine drinking anything worse.

'What's for pudding?' Great Aunt Ada asked. 'Can you top me up?' Once again, she held out her glass. Once again, she was ignored.

'Chocolate Yule log,' said Margaret, looking daggers at Dan as though to say 'I bloody dare you'. 'And some strawberries for Christian.' Natalie shot her mother a grateful look and even Christian looked appeased.

'I don't like chocolate cake,' complained Great Aunt Ada untruthfully.

'Strawberries for you as well, then.'

Dan plonked the steaming mug of herbal tea in front of Christian, who was by now eating the remains of a dish of steamed vegetables, and began to grill him on his diet.

'So, if you can eat beans, does that include baked beans?'

'No.'

'Bummer. And you can't drink cold drinks such as fruit cordial or lemonade,' Dan mused.

'Not even bottled water.'

'But you can drink alcohol?'

'Only certain types. Absolutely no spirits or alcopops and only organic wine and beer,' Christian said.

'Oh! Well, in that case you won't want to come to The Half Moon with Evie, Becca and me. I'm pretty sure they don't serve any organic slosh,' Dan said happily. 'You should drop a card in the suggestions box, Nat. For next time.'

Natalie, who would have enjoyed a trip to the local boozer if only to get away from her mother, looked furious. There was no way she could contend with Dan's simple logic. She was still silently seething when the next exocet came from her mother.

'Natalie, what's the matter with your dinner?' Margaret had noticed that Natalie had picked out every prawn, mussel and piece of calamari out of her paella and arranged them across the top curve of her plate in a perfect semicircle.

'I don't eat living creatures any longer, Mum. I've realised the error of my ways,' Natalie said sanctimoniously.

Evie, seeing that Dan was wearing his predator's expression, changed the subject.

'I need to go into Loxley tomorrow to pick up a couple of last-minutes.' She turned to Becca. Loxley, technically a city courtesy of its historic cathedral, was the closest large town to their village. 'I thought you might like to meet up for a coffee after you finish work.'

'Great, I finish at one o'clock. God, I hate working on Christmas Eve. It should be a bank holiday,' Becca said. 'Shall I meet you under Marks's clock?' The clock suspended above the big Marks & Spencer store in Loxley's town centre had always been a traditional place for locals to meet.

'It's not like you to be so disorganised, Evelyn,' Margaret said in surprise. 'I thought you were a done-by-the-first-of-December type who hates shopping on Christmas Eve.'

'Well, I've been busy with the book,' Evie said, her eyes darting. Even Becca was staring at her sister in disbelief. As soon as their mother's back was turned she mouthed: 'Do you really need to go shopping?' at Evie.

'For a couple of things, yes. I've been a bit distracted with work this year. Plus I'm just throwing Mum off the scent. Thought you might like to get away from her for an hour or so,' Evie hissed back. Becca smiled. She loved her elder sister above all other people, and this was just one example why.

Any further interrogation from their mother was averted by the sharp ringing of the doorbell. Margaret threw the tea towel she'd been clutching down onto the kitchen side in vexation.

'That'll be more dratted carol singers,' she said. 'I wish they'd all sugar off.'

Evie felt her eyebrows lift in surprise as Margaret strode crossly out of the kitchen.

'I thought Mum encouraged carol singers,' she said. 'What's happened to make her go off them?'

It was common knowledge in the Bingham household that Margaret, who sang high soprano with the WI and who could easily hit top C sharp above middle C, enjoyed toying with unsuspecting groups of half-baked carol singers, who sang the first lines of *We Wish You a Merry Christmas* before holding out their expectant, grubby hands, by betting them that they couldn't hit a higher note than she could. Only if they could do so would they get any money. Invariably, they all left defeated and empty handed.

'Her usual trick backfired this year,' said Dan, grinning. 'Yesterday one of the kids who'd been stung by Mum last year brought along a ringer from his scout group and hustled her. Apparently this angelic-looking kid sings boy soprano with the Loxley Cathedral choir and can hit top F sharp as clear as a bell. It cost her seven quid and a bag of fun-sized Mars Bars. She was livid and more than a little bit embarrassed. Talk about being left with eggnog on your face.'

Everyone, bar Christian and Great Aunt Ada, yelled with laughter.

The remainder of dinner passed without incident. Once everyone had left the kitchen, Evie collared her parents in the utility room.

'I'm going to ask a really big favour,' she began but her mother pre-empted her request.

'We can't babysit, love. We've been invited next door for Christmas drinks,' Margaret said. 'I know you wanted to go to the pub. I'm sorry.'

'It isn't that. Please don't make Becca share her room with Natalie. She's fragile right now and she could do without the company. Natalie said she and Christian have been living together in London, and she is a big girl. There's no reason for them not to share a room. You let Nick and I share a room before we were married.'

'That's different. We knew Nick, and you two were in a serious relationship. Natalie's only twenty-three and before tonight we didn't even know Christian existed. We've no idea who this chap is. I'm sorry, Evie, it's too much to ask,' said Bernard. His indulgence with his eldest daughter had never extended to either Becca or Natalie. 'Natalie has no regard for anyone but herself and she has to learn.'

'She won't learn, Dad. The only people who will suffer from this are Dan and Becca and that's not fair. It's their Christmas too. Please don't punish them for Natalie's selfishness, especially Becca.' Evie could see her father wavering.

'I'm not sure, cookie. It's a lot to ask,' he said.

'Besides which, there's nowhere for them to go.' Margaret was shoving a tablecloth and ten linen napkins into the washing machine.

'They could sleep in the dining room. Nick can bring his parents' double airbed tomorrow. If they could make do with the sofa cushions for one night, and Dan gives them a hand to dismantle the dining table, it'd be agreeable to everyone,' Evie argued.

'Except to my Christmas lunch. Where do you suggest we eat that if we have no dining table?' said Margaret.

'We could eat in the conservatory. There's plenty of room for the table, and it's all trimmed up so it'd be nice and festive,' Evie said. 'Please?' For a few minutes the three of them looked at each other. Evie had no further case to argue so she remained silent whilst her parents thought things over.

They were disturbed by, of all people, Natalie. 'What's going on in here?'

'We were just discussing sleeping arrangements,' Margaret said, casting a sharp look at Bernard who shrugged his shoulders to indicate his surrender. 'We've decided that you don't have to sleep in Rebecca's room. If the pair of you can cope, you and Christian can slum it in the dining room but only on the condition that you move the dining table into the conservatory.'

'Thanks,' said Natalie.

'Don't thank us, thank your sister,' Bernard said. Natalie turned to Evie, her eyes as round as saucers.

'I did it for Dan and, more importantly, Becca,' Evie said. 'You could be a bit nicer to them. They are your family.' Natalie's mouth twisted as though she'd eaten something sour.

'There's just one more thing, Natalie,' Bernard said. 'I'm rather disappointed that you never even asked your mother or me if we objected to you bringing a stranger home for the holidays. What exactly do you know about this jack-a-dandy? Are you sure he's an actor?'

'Of course I'm sure. He starred in an episode of *Deep Blue*, which, surely you can remember, I produced. Why would you think he isn't what he says he is?'

'Well, you did become involved with that fellow who convinced you that he was a member of *Jools Holland's Rhythm and Blues Orchestra*,' Margaret said. 'He fed you that tall tale for months. We only caught him out because he let slip that he didn't have any plans for New Year's Eve.'

'This is different,' Natalie sulked.

'I very much hope so. Your mother has worked tirelessly to make this Christmas happen and I don't want anything spoiling it,' said Bernard. Margaret, unused to her husband wearing his disciplinary head in the house as opposed to in his instructor's car, was looking at him with admiration. She ran a hand down his arm. Evie and Natalie beat a hasty retreat. Neither needed to witness their parents getting frisky.

'Thanks for that,' Natalie muttered.

'No probs, although you can do me a favour in return,' said Evie. 'Mum and Dad can't babysit tonight and I've really got my heart set on going to The Half Moon with Dan and Becca. I thought, seeing as you two are staying in, you wouldn't mind keeping an eye on India. I doubt she'll wake up. All you have to do is listen for her on the intercom and make sure none of the cats get into the room. I don't want them sleeping in her cot in case they suffocate her. If there's any peep out of her just ring my mobile and I'll come home straight away.'

Natalie reluctantly agreed. It looked like she had no option but to resign herself to a night in front of the box.

MARGARET LIKED to think of herself as the quintessential hostess and was therefore horrified to have a guest that she couldn't provide for. As each of the Bingham children were aware, their mother had a simple motto: if it moves, feed it — if it doesn't, polish it. It was a mantra by which she lived her life and it had always set her in good stead for any housekeeping occurrence. Every housekeeping occurrence except Christian, as it turned out. Here was a guest that she had no idea how to accommodate, and it was bothering her. It was due to this that she found herself scouring the darkest corners of her extensive pantry minutes before she and Bernard were due at their neighbours. She emerged triumphant. Prize in hand, wine glasses in the other, she marched into the lounge and plonked both down on the occasional table directly in front of Natalie and Christian. Natalie stared at her mother, silently wondering what she was up to.

'Rhubarb wine!' she declared happily. She beamed at Christian. 'It's made by a chap in the village and, as far as I know, is completely organic. It's not to mine and Bernard's taste so you are more than welcome to have it.' Christian picked up the bottle and inspected it. Local produce. He nodded in approval.

'Thank you,' he said. He didn't elucidate further.

'I really don't like fruit wines, to tell you the truth. It's been languishing in the pantry for a couple of months now,' Margaret babbled on. She had expected a more enthusiastic reaction to the wine. Natalie cast a dubious eye over the bottle.

'It'll be like rocket fuel,' she said.

'Best not let Dan near it then,' said her mother briskly. She ran her eyes across the table, letting them rest on India's babycom. 'Is that switched on?'

'Ye-e-e-es. Please leave,' said Natalie impatiently. It was bad enough that she was being forced to stay in, with Grandpa and Great Aunt Ada acting as chaperones. She didn't want her mother deciding to join them at last minute. She was still angry with Dan for diddling her out of a trip to the pub. She'd find a way to pay him back for that.

With these venomous thoughts in her head she watched her mother leave the room.

EVIE, Becca and Dan had smothered themselves in coats, scarves and gloves before venturing outside. It may well be a mere five-minute walk to The Half Moon but that was no reason to be complacent. It was bloody cold outside. The gravel driveway crunched satisfactorily underfoot as they set off.

'Did you see that the forecast has predicted snow for tomorrow? Woo hoo!' Dan said as they slid out onto the icy pathway. His breath was a cloud of white.

'I did,' Becca said quietly. Normally she would have been so excited about the prospect of snow but now her face fell as she remembered a daydream she'd had about her and Gregory exchanging presents on Christmas morning in front of a roaring fire whilst the snow fell outside in romantic silence. Well, that wasn't going to happen now. Even the weather was conspiring against her. Thankfully she was distracted by her feet sliding out beneath her and had to grab hold of the wall next to her to keep herself from falling down. Evie, in turn hanging onto Becca, gave a yelp of surprise.

Evie thought Nether Ousebury had never looked so beautiful. Everything was lit by a fat, silver moon and the dark sky glittered with cold, blue stars. Most of the villagers had trimmed their houses with fairy lights; others simply left their curtains open to proudly display their illuminated Christmas trees or Scandinavian welcome lights. Adjacent to the shadow of the village church the vicarage shone like a beacon of goodness. In the window a cat sprawled across the sill, happily sleeping. On Christmas morning the bells of the church would ring out for all to hear, heralding the birth of Christ. Tonight the air smelled of woodsmoke and anticipation. Somewhere a dog gave a couple of short, sharp barks. The cat raised its head but didn't move.

As Evie, Becca and Dan walked alongside the village green they admired the twelve-foot tree that had been erected by the parish council for the first time ever. Its lights were reflected in the sheer, frozen surface of the village pond. Cars with frosted windscreens and roofs loomed out of the darkness. Ahead of them they could see the warm, golden lights of the pub enticing them to enter.

As they pushed open the door a wave of warmth and noise greeted them. Col the Landlord called out a salutation as they sat down. He had got to know Dan's face very well over the past week and a half. It took the three of them five minutes to remove all the layers of clothing they had donned just ten minutes ago. Beside Evie a mountain of outerwear grew.

'I'll get 'em in. Now, who's going to give me the money to pay for them?' said Dan, eager to get to the bar to see if the girl he had a crush on was working. Evie coughed up, rolling her eyes as she handed over a twenty.

'I want change, you chancer,' she said. She was glad to see that Col the Landlord had stacked a roaring fire in the grate. Tinsel had been draped over every possible surface and in the background the jukebox was playing the final strains of *Fairytale of New York*. The pub really couldn't have been more congenial. 'I think my feet are just about defrosted.'

As Dan made his way back to the table, glasses forming a triangle in his hands, *Santa Baby* started playing on the jukebox. Dan whistled along as he sat down, listening for a few bars as Eartha Kitt crooned her extensive wish list.

'She's a greedy bitch, isn't she? Not once does she ask for something selfless like world peace, nor offers to give a hefty donation to Dogs Trust or Cats Protection. There is absolutely no irony in this song at all,' he said. 'For some reason I'm reminded of Natalie.' Which neatly evolved into a three-way bitch-fest about Natalie's new boyfriend.

'Christian — boy, was ever that a misnomer,' Dan commented, skimming the froth off his pint of bitter with a loud slurp. 'He's a lanky streak of piss, isn't he? Seems very full of his own self-importance to me. Organic wine, my arse! I thought Mum was going to burst into tears. Oh look, the quiz is on. Fancy a crack at it? With Becca on our team we'll win no problem. First prize is a crate of Grolsch. Give us a quid to enter, Evo.'

'Give us my change and I might,' Evie said shrewdly. She and Dan exchanged money. Dan collected a quiz sheet.

'What shall we call ourselves?' said Becca.

'Bingham Over Here,' said Dan. 'That's what we can say when they ask us what we want them to do with the prize.' He hadn't underestimated Becca's brain power. She produced a list of correct answers: Florizel Street; Charlotte Dujardin; Idris Elba; The Move — *Flowers in the Rain*; Triskaidekaphobia; Vince Lombardi. Three drinks apiece and thirty questions and a tiebreaker later they had acquired twenty-four bottles of lager.

'Hurrah!' cried Dan. 'Well done, Becs. Now, let's get another round in and admit that we've all been dreading the arrival of Natalie.' Evie gave her brother a playful slap. 'I thank you, Evie, for preventing Becca and me from having to endure either of them in our sleeping quarters.' Dan raised his glass to his sister in a mock salute.

'At least she's family,' Becca said dolefully. 'Last year I made everyone endure Gregory. What do you think of him, Dan? Honestly.'

'You want my honest opinion of Gregory? He's a pecker. Gregory Pecker!' said Dan, laughing at his own bad joke. 'Oh, you wanted me to be more specific? He's a whinging mummy's boy with a superiority complex counter-unbalanced by a hefty dose of paternal overshadowment and paranoia. Plus he's overly concerned with doing what's appropriate rather than what's right. Don't look so sad, Bec. You can do so much better. Furthermore, why doesn't he shorten his name to Greg? That's much cooler.'

'What about this girl you fancy?' Evie said, keen to change the subject, despite personally agreeing with her brother. Becca had adopted an expression of utter misery since Dan's candid speech about her ex-boyfriend. 'Is she working tonight?'

Dan craned his neck so that he could see the bar. 'That's her with the blonde hair. God, she's gorgeous. She's called Rachel and she lives in Greater Ousebury.'

'How do you know that?'

'Misguidedly offered to walk her home one night. It was a bloody long walk.' Greater Ousebury was three miles away. 'At least it wasn't raining. I didn't get in until quarter past one. I tripped over the milk bottles and woke everyone up. Mum went nuts.'

'Has she got a boyfriend?'

'Don't think so. She's at Leeds studying French and German. Would that make her trilingual?'

'You wish!' Becca laughed. She had snapped out of her funk, Evie noticed with relief.

'If she hasn't got a boyfriend and she let you walk her home then I'd say you're in with a chance,' Evie said. 'Are you going to walk her home tonight?'

'In this weather?' Dan practically shrieked. 'I'd freeze my bollocks off. Tonight, she can get a taxi like she normally does.'

Evie and Becca exchanged glances. 'Ain't love grand?' said Evie drily. 'We should be getting back. I don't entirely trust Natalie to look after India.'

'Hang on a sec.' Dan shrugged into his coat. 'It's now or never. I'm going to ask her for a date.'

EVIE'S RESERVATIONS were not without foundation. She, Becca and Dan arrived back at Magpie Cottage cold but merry. Dan was staggering beneath the weight of the crate of beer, slipping and sliding everywhere. Evie and Becca were no help whatsoever as all they could do was giggle at his misfortune. However, all merriment ceased when Evie discovered that not only had the babycom been left in the kitchen by an absent-minded Natalie but she had also left the bedroom door open and Ramesses was happily sleeping in the cot with India, curled round her feet like a fur muff. Amazingly, India was fast asleep, fingers in her mouth. After she had despatched an irate, protesting Ramesses onto the landing and reassured herself that her child was unharmed, Evie stormed downstairs to find her sister similarly curled around her new boyfriend on the sofa. Christian had fallen asleep with his mouth open. The television was blaring out and both Grandpa and Great Aunt Ada were looking bootfaced. Clearly Natalie had been hogging the telly too. Evie threw the babycom at Natalie, who hollered in protest.

'I asked you to do one thing, Natalie. India could have suffocated or been scratched,' Evie fumed.

'She's all right. Rammy wouldn't hurt a fly.' Natalie gazed back with innocent eyes. She didn't move a muscle. She was still aggrieved at being demoted to the dining room floor from her own considerably more comfortable bedroom. It hadn't taken long for her to realise there'd be no telly, a makeshift bed that would no doubt be bumpier than a sack of potatoes, and a frightful draught whistling in from the hallway. Worse still, the dining room was geographically furthest from the bathroom.

'Perhaps not intentionally. Why are you so bloody unreliable? All you care about is yourself. You're *very* lucky she's not harmed,' Evie said. From where she was standing she could see into the conservatory. It was tellingly bare. 'Have you moved the table into the conservatory?'

'Yes.'

'Have you assembled it?'

'Oh, bloody hell! Do I have to do everything around here?' As Natalie sat up Christian woke with a sudden splutter.

'Welcome back,' Dan said drily. He was watching the exchange with interest, *Radio Times* in hand. Christian, perhaps wisely, excused himself. Natalie stood up and brushed down her clothes.

'Damned cat hairs,' she muttered. She paid no heed to Evie whatsoever. Becca and Dan promptly flopped down onto the sofa.

'That's the last time I do you a favour,' said Evie. 'I wangled it so you and Christian could sleep in the same room. I rang Nick's parents and asked if I could borrow their airbed so you'd be more comfortable. How do you repay me? You neglect my child and don't do the one chore asked of you. Well, you can assemble that table in the morning.'

Natalie pulled a face at Evie. It was intended to incense. It worked.

Further remonstrations were averted by the return home of the senior Binghams. They appeared to be in a very convivial mood as they joined their children in the lounge. Bernard instantly removed the *Radio Times* from Dan's grasp and lowered himself into his favourite chair. 'What's on the box?'

'Don't get comfy. There's still lots to do before bedtime,' Margaret said. Bernard looked beleaguered. 'Did you three have a nice time?' She had noticed, and decided to ignore, the taut expressions of each of her four children.

'We won the quiz,' said Dan proudly. 'And I have a date with the best looking bartender in North Yorkshire.'

'Well done,' Bernard said, looking impressed.

'It was mainly down to Becca,' Evie said. She was hoping to boost her sister's standing with her father.

'Hardly,' Becca protested. Her mother mistook modesty for idleness.

'When are you going to accept that you're wasting your brains, young lady?' Margaret asked. She turned to Evie. 'I'm trying to get her to apply for *Millionaire* but she just refuses. It's not even as though she'd have to go on by herself. They have those mother and daughter specials.' Margaret looked to the ceiling, hands clasped. 'Why won't you apply? Why?'

'I bet you'd do great on the TV, Bec,' Evie said. 'You did get a first.'

'Such superior cerebral capability.' Dan ruffled Becca's hair. 'Nat's never forgiven you for it. Especially as she only got a Desmond.'

'A 2:2 is perfectly acceptable, thank you very much. Anyway, I got a wonderful job straight after graduation which is more than either of you two did.'

'Only because you're a gobshite and can talk your way into anything.'

'Daniel, your language has been simply frightful since you came back from university,' Margaret complained.

'I agree,' Bernard chipped in from behind the *Radio Times*. The remote lay next to him like a weapon about to be fired. 'There's a good film on tomorrow night starring that fellow from *Titanic*. What's his name? Leonard Capstick?'

'No television tomorrow. We're all going to midnight mass,' Margaret said. A collective groan rent the air. 'Natalie, can't you arrange for us to be on *Millionaire*?'

'No I can't. For one thing I work for the BBC, not ITV,' Natalie snapped. She turned to face her three siblings who were all crammed onto the sofa. 'Can you please get off the sofa? Christian and I want to go to bed and we need the cushions.'

'What if we want to sit up for a little longer?' Dan said.

'Oh, you are all so selfish!'

'*We're* selfish?' Dan asked. 'How do you work that out? You're the one who wants to take the sofa cushions away.'

'I've had a very long day. I was at work at five thirty this morning and then I had to catch a flight, delayed I might add, so that I could be here, as that's what Mum wanted. I'm tired and I want to go to bed. What's so selfish about that?'

'*The Nation's Favourite Christmas TV Moments* is on in ten minutes and we all want to watch it,' Dan explained, pronouncing each syllable as if he were speaking to a small child.

'Well, I'm watching it in the kitchen. Some of us still have chores to do,' said Margaret. 'Bernard!' It was a command to come. With a sigh Bernard rose from his chair and joined his wife. He had just got comfy, too.

'There!' spat Natalie. She watched her parents leave the room. 'Not everyone is as bothered as you.'

'Come on, guys,' Becca intervened. 'We can watch it in my room. Nat can have her precious cushions.'

In the kitchen Margaret was manhandling the turkey. It was perched on a large roasting tray that she was trying to force into an already overfilled fridge.

'What am I going to do with this turkey, Bernard? It just won't fit in the fridge,' she shrilled.

'Wrap it in foil and leave it in the woodstore. It's cold enough,' Bernard said vaguely. He flicked on the television. If he was going to be denied the telly tomorrow he was going to get as many viewing hours in as possible before then. 'It won't come to any harm in there.'

EVIE, Becca and Dan congregated in Becca's room. They stretched out sideways across her bed, lying on their bellies.

'Nat's going to be unbearable all week, isn't she?' Becca asked as she flicked on the television. Morecambe and Wise in sailor suits danced and somersaulted across the screen. Dan began to chuckle.

'She'll settle,' Evie said. Her mouth opened and stretched into a great yawn. 'I think I'll have to give this programme a miss. I'm pooped.' She climbed off the bed. 'I'll see you guys in the morning.' Having said her goodnights she padded back to her own room, careful not to wake India, who was still asleep in her cot. With any luck she'd sleep through the night, Evie thought, whilst peeping out of the en suite's window as she brushed her teeth. The garden was bathed in moonlight. It really would be marvellous if it snowed! Checking her mobile she saw Nick had sent her several text messages. Traffic allowing, he'd be with her by lunchtime tomorrow. He hoped India was okay and he was looking forward to seeing them both. There was absolutely no mention of the epic row they'd had before he'd packed his overnight bag in a temper and stormed up to Newcastle earlier that morning. Equally happy to push that particularly unpleasant topic under the carpet until after the holidays, she sent Nick a carefully worded, non-committal goodnight text before turning out the light. That bullet dodged, she fell asleep within minutes.

CHRISTMAS EVE

During the night the temperature plummeted even further. Silently, with stealth, a severe frost crept across the land, turning leaf, blade and slate hoary-white. Churned earth in the fields solidified whilst winter flowers and trees were frozen into mute immobility. In the garden Bernard's beloved planters looked forlorn and frost-weary. It wasn't the snow that had been promised, but on Christmas Eve a fierce frost was the next best thing.

As a watery December sun rose pale and low in a pink sky, roads and pavements sparkled as though India had upturned a tube of silver glitter across the village.

Outside, on the brittle lawn of Magpie Cottage, a fat robin slalomed round the separated remains of the previous night's discarded bread, keen to make a choice selection before some other hungry birds came to feast on such tasty treats. It was being closely observed by Boo and Hiss, who were circumnavigating from polar opposite ends of the garden. Fat and replete on the utility room windowsill, Ramesses supervised their tactics, confident that he could do better but with absolutely no intention of proving this. As the robin took flight, a chunk of ciabatta lodged in its beak, the two young cats were deprived of their living breakfast. On the windowsill, Ramesses stopped cleaning himself and settled down for a nap. He had long since learned that chasing fresh food was pointless, especially when the two-leggeds were so keen to offer the same without condition.

In the kitchen of Magpie Cottage, Angus and Chewbacca hovered by the back door. Frost or not, business still had to be attended to, plus there were some new and unusual scents emanating from outside. As soon as an accommodating human hand opened the door the dogs shot out into the garden and began circling the patio furniture. Chewbacca, roused from his habitual lethargy by the presence of an exciting smell, found the need to cock his leg several times. Angus followed suit in order to maintain his stature. Neither the plaintive cries of the human at the back door nor the encouraging rattle of spoon against tin can could lure them back inside. Why bother with tinned meaty chunks in jelly when there were such unexpected delicacies to be had just lying in wait for them? This wasn't pre-packed; this was the real thing.

Losing patience, Margaret reluctantly put a slippered foot onto the doorstep. 'Those wretched dogs.' She had no option but to retrieve them by their collars. Singing happily because her flock were all at home and Christmas could now start properly, she stepped outside.

'I saw three ships come sailing in, on Christmas Day, on… *Oh! I Say!*'

Margaret's shriek of shock was of such pitch and length that it caused all three cats to scatter from their respective posts and Evie, upstairs and warm in bed, to wake with a start. For a few moments she lay paralysed beneath the sheets, too alarmed to function. Terrible thoughts assaulted her ability to reason and her maternal instincts turned to her child.

India!

She turned to face the cot. It was empty. Panic rose. She noticed the door slowly opening. Surely whoever entered must be a harbinger of doom?

'Happy Christmas Eve!' It was Nick, unexpected and holding two steaming mugs of coffee.

'Where's India?' The words flew out of Evie's mouth before any thought of her husband's surprising presence registered.

'Good morning and hello to you too,' Nick said sardonically. 'India is safe and sound with your father. Your mother listened on the babycom to detect her first stirrings and snuck in to collect her, as, I gather, she believes you to be exhausted and 'could do with a good lie in'. She also sent these up.' Nick raised the two mugs to chin level. 'Not even instant granules but Marks & Sparks' finest filter.' He set them down on the bedside cabinet.

Evie's small smile acknowledged her own foolishness.

'I can't believe you're here so early. I wasn't expecting you until lunchtime at least.' Nick's festive greeting had reminded Evie that it was Christmas Eve and she was suddenly keenly aware that she didn't want to spoil the holiday with their ongoing argument. 'I missed you yesterday,' she added truthfully. Unbidden, compelled by forces beyond her control, she raised herself up and snaked her arms round her husband's neck, breathing in his familiar scent, which was tainted by just the slightest hint of last night's beer and citrus shower gel. His dark hair had long since dried but not before it had slightly dampened the collar of his sweater.

'I missed you too,' Nick said, also thankful that the previous day's row seemed to have been temporarily shelved. Encouraged, he lowered himself onto the very edge of the bed. 'I woke unintentionally at the crack and figured I may as well get an early start. It was worth it too, not only because there was no traffic but also to witness your mother's face when she opened the back door.' He gave a short laugh but

Evie just looked baffled. 'Drink that coffee before it gets cold. It's freezing outside.'

'Has it snowed?' Evie asked hopefully.

'No, but it's white over with frost. My car door handles were frozen solid this morning.'

Venturing from the cocoon-like warmth of the bed, Evie padded over to the window and drew back her mother's Laura Ashley curtains. As she looked out on the back garden of her childhood home the artist in Evie eclipsed all other aspects of her nature. For one perfect nanosecond she forgot that she was also a wife, a mother, a daughter and a sister.

'It's so beautiful,' she breathed. Everything was still, the trees statuesque and the few late autumn flowers static and submissive. All the usual vibrant colours, the red of the berries and the nandina leaves, and the verdancy of the grass, had been muted by the blanket of frost. In the centre of the lawn her father's birdbath was frozen solid and a couple of disgruntled sparrows pecked belligerently at its surface. As Evie traced her fingers across the inside of the window, following the filigree pattern the ice had made on the outside, she made a mental note to defrost the birdbath. 'Where's my palette?'

'There's no time for painting.' Nick, silently sidling up behind her, unhooked the curtain from his wife's hands. It dropped back into place, shutting out the garden, and Evie the wife and mother returned, somewhat reluctantly. She felt her spirits droop. There never seemed to be time for painting these days.

'What time is it?'

'Half nine.'

'What? That's not early at all! Where is everyone?' The house was curiously quiet.

'From what I've gleaned from the barrage of information your mother chucked at me as soon as I walked through the door—' Nick said. Evie smirked into her coffee. Oh yes, that sounded like her mum. '—Becca's at work, the poor bugger. Dan's still asleep in his makeshift pit. Nat and some strange bloke are in the lounge watching unutterably boring television. Your grandfather and great aunt are both in there too, sniping at each other. Do they ever stop? They're just Nat and Dan in ancient replication.' Grandpa and Great Aunt Ada's spiky sibling relationship had never ceased to be a source of fascination for Nick. 'Your father's fled to B&Q, taking India with him, so he can buy a new hedge trimmer, and your mother is furious about your father going to B&Q to buy said new hedge trimmer.' Nick paused for breath, a naughty smile playing about his lips. 'I daren't tell you what the dogs have done.'

Evie settled back onto the bed and tucked her feet beneath the duvet where it was still warm. She would allow herself only five minutes more! It didn't matter that she was in her thirties and married with a child of her own. There was still something irregular and forbidden about sleeping in her parents' bed. Somehow, inexplicably, it was wrong.

'I must get up. There's loads to do and I promised Becca I'd meet her outside her work at one o'clock,' she said. Upon hearing this Nick's face darkened by a fraction. It was a displeasure borne of disappointment rather than irritation.

'You're going out this afternoon? But I just got here.'

'I'm sorry. It's just that Becca's really cut up about this whole Gregory business and Mum isn't helping. I thought it might cheer her up a little, plus give her a break from Mum for a while. We won't be long, I promise. Just a cup of coffee. I'll be taking India, which instantly puts a time limit on proceedings. Anyway, we can't be out long because Mum's having kittens about nothing being ready. The tree isn't even decorated yet and she'll want to oversee that. Although, how she's going to achieve that whilst at the same time prepping the turkey I'll never know. You've got to see it, it's enormous.' To Evie's bewilderment Nick smirked. 'No doubt you'll be subpoenaed to assist.' The smirk was instantly removed. 'Goodness, this coffee's good.'

For Evie, the most appreciated luxury of the day was that she had all the time in the world to pamper herself, which was something that, thanks to India, very rarely happened. Furthermore, although her parents' bed remained discomforting and alien, their bathroom was decadence itself. Knowing that her mother wouldn't object, she helped herself liberally to whatever toiletries she saw fit and emerged, almost an hour later, wonderfully clean and relaxed. She even had time to style her hair and paint her nails. It was some small consolation for not being able to paint the view from the bedroom window.

She wandered into the kitchen — a bustling one-woman cottage industry — to be greeted by yet another steaming mug of coffee and a stack of bacon and crusty white bread sandwiches.

'Eat those. You're skin and bone,' her mother commanded briskly. She was assembling a huge holly wreath with a circumference the size of a dustbin lid. 'Ketchup's on the table.'

'Skin and bone? I've put on a stone and a half since summer,' Evie said. Nevertheless she accepted the plate.

'You'd never tell. Help yourself, Nick. It'd do you good to get some decent grub in you.'

'Yes, because of course I starve him at home,' Evie said sarkily.

'Don't be cheeky, and you've got sauce on your chin.' Margaret appeared to be participating in a lucid, motherly conversation without actually thinking about it. 'There's so much to do. I've still got this wretched wreath—' A piece of holly was garrotted beyond redemption. 'Buggeration! This wretched wreath to finish and your bliddy father has disappeared to the shop to buy a hedge trimmer. A hedge trimmer, for goodness' sake! What does he need a hedge trimmer for on Christmas Eve? I swear, if I divorced him in a court of law I'd cite that bliddy garden as co-respondent. To make matters worse, Grandpa and Great Aunt Ada have been at each other's wrinkled throats all morning and, to cap it all, Natalie's young man hasn't eaten a morsel all morning. There's nothing I can offer him. I can hardly wave a plate of bacon butties and a mug of coffee in front of him, can I? I've never felt so inadequate as a hostess.'

Nick looked bemused.

'Nat's new chap is an actor and he's a macrobiotic,' Evie explained. Nick's only response was to sport an expression that visually depicted the question 'why?'.

'I haven't even begun to think about preparing tomorrow's lunch. It'll be *Nine Lessons* from Cambridge before you know it.' Evie noticed that her mother suddenly looked distressed and that caused her to remember something.

'I heard shouts and shrieks earlier. What was all that about?' she said. Next to her Nick sniggered. Distress morphed into outrage, Margaret marched over to the back door and yanked it open. Freezing air stole into the kitchen.

'The bliddy dogs have eaten the turkey,' Margaret shrilled. 'Flesh, carcass, giblets — all gone. There's not so much as a measly leg left, only a few gory remains scattered across the patio flagstones. It looks like a poultry explosion.'

A pitiful attempt at suppression failed to prevent Nick from emitting a distorted snort of laughter. Margaret rounded on her son-in-law.

'Only a man could find reason to laugh. Your father was exactly the same; no penance whatsoever.'

'Why would Dad need to be sorry?' Evie asked innocently. 'Surely he didn't tuck into the bird also?'

Nick had a sudden mental image of Bernard, Chewbacca and Angus all sitting round a table, napkins hanging from their collars and knives and forks in their hands and paws respectively. He clamped a hand over his mouth. Margaret shot him a withering look.

'Of course he didn't, you foolish girl. He let the dogs out first thing without giving the bird a second thought. They must have thought it was Christmas.'

'It *is* Christmas,' Nick howled, unable to contain himself. Evie kicked him on his shin. Pushing her chair away from the table she joined her mother at the back door.

'I don't understand,' she said.

'What's to understand? It's quite simple. They dragged it out of the woodstore and ate it,' Margaret snapped.

'I understand how they ate it. What I don't understand is how they opened the woodstore. It's padlocked.'

'Mebbe they used the tur-*key*,' said Nick, his face twitching as he tried to curtail another burst of laughter. Both Evie and Margaret turned to glare at him.

'Instead of making clever remarks, you could make yourself useful by going outside and taking a look,' Evie suggested snippily.

Nick was back within minutes.

'The door is still padlocked but the side window has been popped out. Something has walked the fence like a tightrope and clawed the glass out, then dragged the bird out onto the patio. The prints are too big for a cat. I'd put my money on Fantastic Mr Fox.'

'A fox? Oh, it was a super turkey too. I ordered it from the butcher in Greater Ousebury weeks ago. I only collected it yesterday,' Margaret mourned. 'I've already rung the butcher this morning but he isn't carrying any stock that wasn't pre-ordered. The turkey can't be replaced. There's nothing for Christmas lunch. We'll be eating beans on toast — again! — and not even that will be suitable for that micro-robotic boyfriend of Natalie's. Oh, this is going to be the worst Christmas ever. For goodness' sake!'

'For fox sake,' Nick snorted into his bacon butty, not helping.

Evie glared at him. She was seriously worried that her mother was about to burst into tears. She thought fast. If her mother weren't going to be occupied with preparing Christmas lunch she'd be unbearable all day. She had a brainwave. One that would serve the dual purposes of appeasing her mother and annoying her unrepentant husband.

'Nick'll go to Sainsbury's whilst I'm in town with Becca. I'm sure he'll be able to pick up something, even if it's a couple of frozen chickens,' she said. She ignored Nick, who was treating her to a look of death.

'Did someone mention Sainsbury's? Great! Can you pick some bits up for me too? I'd never get any of this lot in the village shop. It's only good for chocolate and newspapers.' Natalie, having appeared from nowhere, was fiddling with a sheet of foolscap. She let it flutter down onto the table in front of Nick, whose presence she didn't acknowledge. She'd never forgiven him for being good-natured, attractive and professionally successful but, even more than that, for being so devoted to her good-natured, attractive and professionally successful eldest sister. 'Thanks.' She exited the kitchen as quickly and quietly as she had entered. That way she couldn't be refused or retained.

'Merry Christmas to you too, Natalie,' Nick muttered. He studied the piece of paper. It was a long list of macrobiotic foods. Evie waited for her mother to tell Natalie off. It never came. Margaret was too busy still chuntering about the turkey — or respective lack of.

'Mary Berry says the success of Christmas lunch is all down to preparation. How can I prepare if I don't have the requisite ingredients? Delia says preparation should ideally begin at the same time as *Carols from King's*. Nick, would you really go to Sainsbury's? There's plenty of cash in the kitchen kitty. How wonderful of you to offer. Not like your father, Evie. I'm going to kill him when he gets home. It was his idea to put the turkey in the woodstore in the first place.'

'So long as you let me retrieve my child before you commit mariticide,' Evie said. She glanced at the kitchen clock. 'I hope he's home soon. I'm meeting Becca at one so we'll have to set off at least an hour before. Can you drop me near the cathedral, honey?'

'Could you also drop me in Greater Ousebury, honey?' Dan wandered into the kitchen wearing a three-day beard and an unironed Glastonbury Festival tee shirt. Yesterday's baggy cords had been replaced by the skinniest of black jeans that were hung halfway down his backside and showed at least four inches of underpants. His long hair had been pulled back into a ponytail and had been secured with a bobble he had nicked from Becca. He high-fived Nick on his way to the utility room. Evie, Nick and Margaret all heard the pantry door open followed by the clanking of beer bottles.

'What are you doing in there?' Margaret called, her eyes narrowed in suspicion.

Despite needing a hearing aid, Great Aunt Ada's finely tuned booze-radar had picked up on the rattle of glass against glass and within seconds she also appeared in the kitchen, her puckered, disagreeable face for once optimistic.

'Did I hear you opening a bottle, Margaret?'

'Oh, Aunt Ada, good news! Nick's kindly offered to go to the supermarket to see if he can buy us a replacement for tomorrow's lunch. Isn't that wonderful?'

Great Aunt Ada wasn't the only one who was less than impressed. Nick grimaced. Never before had he been so aware that there were some definite downsides to one's mother-in-law believing that the sun shone from out of your aperture.

'It's not man's work to collect the groceries whilst you go gallivanting round the shops,' Great Aunt Ada scolded Evie.

There was no good humour in her chastisement. 'It's your duty as a wife to look after your husband. All this role reversal would never have happened in my day. It just wasn't done.' Great Aunt Ada gave a great, emphatic sniff.

Dan's grinning face appeared round the utility room doorframe. He was holding his hand out to his great aunt in the shape of a telephone receiver.

'The 1950s are on the phone for you, Great Aunt Ada,' he said. His blatant cheek was not well received. Furthermore, his reappearance reminded his mother of her truncated grilling.

'What do you need to go into Greater Ousebury for?' she asked, arms folded.

'I'm meeting some of the lads from school for a catch-up. We're going to crack open a few bevvies, watch *Star Wars* and compare all our unis.'

'Don't you ever get bored of watching those wretched films? You'd better be back this afternoon to trim that tree. I want everybody present,' Margaret warned. Dan rolled his eyes.

'I'll be here, I promise,' he turned to his sister. 'I've taken a dozen beers from our winnings.'

'And you can put four of them back,' Evie said sharply. 'I'm no mathematician but even I know twenty-four divided by three does not equal twelve.'

'What's going on?' Nick asked. 'What beers? Nobody mentioned beers to me.'

'Dan, Becca and I won the pub quiz in The Half Moon last night. First prize was a crate of Grolsch which,' Evie added to Dan, 'I am not going to be diddled out of. About turn! You can have a lift but you are not having my beers.' Dan reluctantly set four green bottles onto the table.

'What do you need a dozen beers for?' shrieked Margaret. 'Don't you be coming in sloshed.' Dan began to slide out of the room, carrier in hand. 'I wish you'd wear something respectable. Those trousers make you look as though you should be reciting Shakespeare. And for cripe's sake, can't you shave? You look like a burglar's photo fit with all that fur on your face,' Margaret called after him. Fortunately for Dan the slamming of a car door distracted his mother's attention. 'That's your father,' she said. Evie shot out of the room on the pretence that she was desperate to see India but in actuality it was so she could give her father a heads up on the fact that her mother was seething about the turkey and that she believed he was to blame for the whole fiasco.

'Hello, cookie,' Bernard called as he lifted India out of his car. 'Look what we bought at the store.'

'No offence, Dad, but I'm not really interested in hedge trimmers,' Evie said, pulling a face. She took India from her father. With a sigh she noticed that her daughter's face was yet again blathered, this time with melted chocolate and biscuit crumbs. There was a long thin Ribena stain on India's new Monsoon dress, and which Evie had earmarked for Christmas Day. Her mother must have taken it that morning when she had taken India. Despite having had such a lovely lie in and peaceful morning, Evie still had to try very hard not to resent her mother for her interference.

'Not that, *this!*' Bernard proudly produced a half-sized wooden signpost that was gaudily painted with a stylised snow scene. It had a wintry pastel blue post that sported vertical bright red lettering. 'See? It's says 'Santa Stop Here'. India and I thought it would look good by the front door so that there's no chance that Father Christmas will fly past.'

'Fat chance,' Evie muttered under her breath, thinking of the mountain of presents India was due to receive the following day. 'Anyway, I need to talk to you about a couple of things. Firstly, Mum is on the warpath. We've ascertained that a fox ate the turkey last night but she blames you, as it was your idea to put it in the woodstore. Just to warn you.

Secondly, don't get comfy. Nick needs to get his car out in a couple of minutes and you're blocking him in.'

Bernard scratched his head as he surveyed the plethora of cars that were crammed into the driveway. In addition to his own recently decommissioned hatchback, which he had used for instructing, there were also Evie, Becca and Nick's cars, plus the rental that Natalie had picked up from the airport, and the ancient, rusty eyesore that Dan claimed to be 'doing up'. Margaret had never passed her test, despite her husband's many attempts to render her independently mobile, so at least she didn't have her own car to further clutter the driveway.

'It looks like a car dealership's front lot,' Bernard grumbled. Some of the cars were parked dangerously close to his beds and borders and he feared for the well-being of a couple of his best shrubs. His chipper mood was fast diminishing. He had envisaged a quiet afternoon playing with his new garden toy but he knew he could kiss that goodbye. Instead he would spend the afternoon being pig-whipped by his irate wife in atonement for the turkey debacle. If he didn't come up with a watertight excuse he would be trimming pie crusts rather than hedges until kingdom come. It really was just too much.

As Bernard stood and pondered over both his violated front garden and his ruined afternoon, Evie slipped away, taking India with her. That soiled dress would have to be changed. Perhaps she could handwash it later. There was no time now, as she would have to round up not only her child and husband but also her brother. Ten minutes later, once everyone was assembled, Bernard was still muttering about the excess of cars. 'It's just like 'Butterflies',' he complained as he reversed out into the road.

'Do stop moidering, Bernard,' Margaret said sharply. 'All you have to do is shunt a few cars round. I have to produce a Christmas dinner for ten out of thin air, including one which has to contain no real ingredients in order to placate Natalie's macro-bionic guest.' Evie, Nick and Dan hastily climbed into the car. Retreat was the only option when Margaret used that tone.

As soon as the car had pulled out of the driveway of Magpie Cottage and all dutiful waving had ceased, Dan's head popped in between the two front seats. He held a piece of paper in his hand.

'Whilst you're at Sainsbugger's could you do me a favour and pick me up a few bits?' he asked Nick.

'What bits? I'm not buying you cigs so don't even ask.' Evie whipped the paper away before Dan could retract his hand. Her eyes scanned yet another shopping list. 'Two four-packs of John Smith's! Why?'

'I've drunk most of Dad's and he's going to notice soon.' Dan wasn't repentant, simply matter of fact.

'You're incorrigible,' Evie said. Within five minutes they were approaching Greater Ousebury. 'Where do you want dropping?'

'The Green Dragon is fine.'

'I thought you were watching films at a friend's?' Evie was instantly suspicious. Nick pulled up outside the pub. The management had already switched on the gaudy Christmas lights, which were twinkling enticingly around the windows. Nick wished he were joining Dan for a couple of pints instead of being packed off for a festive bunfight in Sainsbury's.

'Yes, after having a couple in the pub. I thought I'd explained that.' Dan was all innocence. He climbed out of the car, carrier bag swinging and clinking.

'Don't be late for dinner. I'm trusting you!' Evie shouted at Dan's retreating back. With one sole hand of acknowledgement raised above his head, Dan disappeared into the pub. The door opened and shut like a trapdoor. Evie turned to Nick.

'I doubt we'll see him again before the birth of Christ.'

❋

LOXLEY CITY CENTRE WAS BEDLAM. Evie shoved India's buggy through the crowds. In Cathedral Square a group of students were busking for some last minute Christmas present money. They were singing Christmas carols a cappella and an admiring audience had gathered round to watch. Above the singers loomed a fifteen-foot Christmas tree covered in coloured lights the size of light bulbs. Groups of teenage girls dressed in miniskirts and denim jackets loitered outside New Look and McDonald's, garishly coloured tinsel woven into their ponytails and plaits. Every other person was weighed down with bulging carrier bags and harassed expressions. Evie moved on, absorbing the atmosphere. On The Parade, the town's main thoroughfare, the annual Christmas fayre was in full swing. Chart favourites from Shakin' Stevens, Sir Cliff and Slade were blasting out from vast, bulky speakers the size of fridges, whilst little kiddies zoomed round on miniature fairground rides. The entrance to Marks & Spencer was so outrageously congested that it defied description. Evie could do nothing more than stare in slack-jawed amazement, scouring the masses for her sister then waving frantically when she finally spotted her.

'This is crackers!' Evie laughed as Becca elbowed her way over. 'Remind me again why we thought this would be a good idea.'

By their feet, looking painfully thin in sharp contrast to such festive excess, a homeless person sat and begged for money. A lean, shaggy terrier with pleading eyes sat by his side. Evie, feeling sorry for them, tossed a couple of quid into his raggedy hat.

'Ta, love. 'Appy Christmas.'

'Natalie says we shouldn't encourage them,' Becca said thoughtfully.

'I don't care what Natalie says. It's Christmas,' Evie said.

They moved away, passing a mobile vendor who was selling hot chestnuts by the bagful. Their delicious earthy scent lifted into the bitterly cold air and gave it a wonderfully Christmassy feel.

'I wish I felt more festive,' Becca said as she peered into the beautifully dressed window of Boots. Not one of the luscious products displayed would change her life, no matter what the subtle marketing promised. It didn't matter how shiny her hair, how long her lashes or how enticingly feminine her scent, human beings could only be manipulated to a certain extent and Gregory was immune to all manipulation except his mother's.

'How about a festive Starbucks? Would that help?' Evie asked lightly. Her motives for meeting up with Becca weren't entirely philanthropic. She still desperately needed to confide in someone and Becca had always been her first choice. Her mother would only worry and obsess, her father wouldn't understand and Dan would just take the piss. Ironically, Natalie was most likely the one best equipped to have any empathy for her situation, but relations with her had sunk to such a low that asking her advice was unthinkable. Yes, it had to be Becca.

'It might,' Becca answered distantly. She was prepared to try anything to cheer herself up. Twenty minutes later, having battled for a free table, they were sitting opposite each other, a cream-loaded hot chocolate in front of Becca whilst Evie sipped on a skinny latte. Christmas jazz was being piped into the packed coffee house. India, already fractious, was temporarily distracted by a strawberry fruit drink and a caramel wafer.

'This latte is marvellous but I daren't even imagine how many calories it contains.' Evie leaned back in her chair and smacked her lips. 'I can't remember the last time I stuck to my diet. It's no good for India either. I must re-introduce her to the wonderful world of vegetables after the holidays. All my good intentions have gone to pot.'

'No point bothering until after you're out of Mum's reach. She seems keener than ever to feed us all up,' Becca said gloomily. 'In her opinion I'm underweight, you're underweight, Dan's positively emaciated—'

'Dan doesn't consume food, only beer.'

'Wow, it's taken you all of twenty hours to figure that out. Mum still doesn't know,' said Becca.

'She has a fair inkling,' said Evie, thinking of earlier that morning. Becca fell silent. Despite her affection for her sister she couldn't help but be envious that their parents took Evie, and only Evie, seriously. She scanned the room briefly.

'I can't believe all these people are doing their shopping on Christmas Eve. If I hadn't had to work I wouldn't have left the house at all today. I mean, even if they get everything bought they still have to wrap and tag them,' Becca said.

'Some people like the last minute rush,' said Evie with a shrug. 'Can't see the appeal myself.'

Becca stretched. It was such a relief to have finished work for the holidays. She wouldn't have to go back until the day after Boxing Day, which gave her two and a half days reprieve from a job that was hardly satisfying and fast becoming barely tolerable. This she relayed to Evie whose first response was to pull an uninterpretable face before pushing her half empty mug away from her.

'About jobs, Becs... I wondered if you'd let me have your opinion on something,' she began. India, now bored, promptly began to grizzle. 'I wondered how long it would be. This child has the attention span of a gnat,' Evie continued irritably.

'Do you want to make a move?' Becca, misinterpreting Evie's meaning, got to her feet and turned to retrieve her coat from the back of her chair. She saw something on the other side of the room that made her swear. 'Shit!' She sat back down with a thud.

'What's the matter? We don't have to leave just yet. Nick's not due to pick us up for another half hour,' Evie said, keen to stay put and chat. She seemed unaware than Becca was upset. 'I feel like a louse for sending him to the supermarket. He hates food shopping.'

'It's Gregory,' said Becca.

'Oh, I'm sorry. We haven't really had chance to have a proper chat about him.' Evie was filled with remorse but India had started to wail, and heads were beginning to swivel with annoyance.

'I mean, it's Gregory, and Evil Edna, his mother. They're here too, over by the newspaper stand,' Becca hissed. She'd daydreamed about bumping into Gregory in town but the many scenarios she'd envisaged had been nothing like the reality. She'd imagined herself looking fabulous and Gregory being stunned into making a declaration of love for her. Well, in her tatty work clothes and with no make-up on, that wasn't about to happen. She'd also imagined herself being impervious to him, brushing him aside with a nonchalant indifference that left him confused with longing for her. That wasn't going to happen either. Butterflies were killing each other with very sharp weapons in her stomach. She felt nervous and confused, not knowing whether to sneak out without being seen or directly approach him. Evie made the decision for her. The window of opportunity to talk to Becca had closed, plus she was craning to eyeball the arsehole who had upset her sister, but was doing so to the soundtrack of India's shrieking. It didn't make for a very discreet manoeuvre. All heads in the coffee house turned to look at Evie, including Gregory, who, upon recognising Becca's sister, looked distinctly uncomfortable.

'Come on, Bec. We're going to wish them a merry Christmas,' said Evie grimly. Whether they like it or not, she added silently. She had already rammed India's bobble hat onto her ever-moving head and was fighting to add mittens to the ensemble.

'Evie, I don't think this is a very good idea,' Becca protested.

'Nonsense, he's seen you now. If you don't say hello he'll think you're frightened of speaking to him.' Evie began to wheel India's buggy round the closely-set tables.

'Hello Edna. Out doing some last-minute shopping too?' she asked. 'Hello Gregory. You're well hemmed in.' He was in fact pressed as far back against the wall as he could be. He reminded Evie of a cornered rat, and that irony was not lost on her. Gregory's mother was looking daggers at Evie, who was blithely continuing, seemingly oblivious to the discomfort she was causing but actually more than aware. 'Anyway, we just wanted to wish you a happy Christmas. We're heading back home now. This little one is getting a bit fractious, as you can hear. I think someone's excited about Santa. It was nice to see you.' And with a flick of the head that clearly communicated the exact opposite, Evie wheeled away. Becca remained behind for a few moments. She and Gregory stared at each other for no more than twenty seconds before Becca muttered 'Happy Christmas' and scuttled after her sister. She was going to *kill* Evie. She had never been so mortified in all her life.

Evie was waiting for her by the door. 'Well done.'

'Well done!? I wanted to crawl into a hole and die,' Becca screeched. Her face became vulnerable. 'Has he followed me? Is he at least looking?' There was hope in her voice. Evie cast a quick look behind them. Gregory and his mother showed no signs of moving. Evie shook her head.

'Sorry, Bec,' she said. 'But, even though it's hard to believe right now, I've just done you a massive favour. He'll call you within the week. I guarantee it. You're in his thoughts now and not even his mother has control of those, despite what she might think. Come on, let's get you home.'

By sheer force of will Becca remained composed until she was seated in the back of Nick's car. Only then did she put her head in her hands and sob, overcome by the strain of the encounter. There was so much for her to think about. Every last inflection of the head and every flicker of the eyes would be desperately analysed for clues of Gregory's intentions. Thoughts would no doubt go round and round in her head until nothing made sense. This thought brought on a fresh wave of tears. India, astonished that another being could make more noise than she, stared, silenced at last. As they drew up to a red light Nick leaned into the back and gently patted Becca's knee.

'You have my sympathies, Bec. After an hour fighting the masses in Sainsbury's that's exactly what I feel like doing.' His comment was neither flippant nor disrespectful and because of that it raised a small smile. Second only to Evie, Nick was the most calming, reassuring person Becca knew. India started to wail again.

'Did you get everything?' Evie asked. She was unwrapping a rogue Wagon Wheel she'd discovered in the glove box. She rammed it into India's mouth, simply to shut her up.

'Pretty much,' Nick said. He manoeuvred the car out of the town centre. 'I fought off an angry granny in the frozen foods aisle just to get my hands on the last two measly turkeys. They're not very large but at least they're the right bird. Some of Natalie's stuff was a bit tricky but I think I covered everything. Now can I go home and relax with a beer?'

'You wish. It'll be a quick lunch and then it's tree trimming time.'

In the back seat Becca gave a loud groan.

❄

MARGARET WAS SURPRISINGLY THRILLED with the turkeys. They were nowhere near as impressive as the organic behemoth she'd originally bought but, as Nick had correctly surmised, they were the right meat and her Christmas dinner could go ahead as planned.

Preparations were already well underway. All the vegetables were peeled and chopped and resting in cold water in the pantry. The stuffing was prepared and covered with foil, ready to be reheated. Three dozen chipolata sausages had been wrapped in streaky, smoked bacon and just needed popping in the oven a half an hour before Christmas lunch was to be served. Smoked salmon starters and a rum-soaked pudding had also been prepared in advance and the cheese board just needed unwrapping.

Proceedings had come to a natural interval, which meant that after a late lunch of soup and sandwiches they could all adjourn to the lounge where the tree awaited them. Grandpa and Great Aunt Ada wouldn't participate but would observe from their respective perches in the armchair of their choice. However, as was inevitable, someone was missing.

'Where's your brother?' Margaret set a tray laden with slabs of homemade Christmas cake, mince pies and little bowls of olives (for Christian), crisps and nuts on the occasional table. Becca was already dibbing her hand into an enormous octagonal tin of Quality Street.

The knowing look that Evie and Becca shared was identical.

'I'll give him a ring,' said Becca, setting the tin aside. No answer.

'Well, we'll just have to begin without him. The little toerag! He promised he'd be back,' Margaret said. So much for her perfect Christmas. She began rummaging in a box of decorations. She pulled out several lengths of tinsel like a magician. 'Christian, I know you don't approve, and I respect that, but if you'd like to join in, you're more than welcome.'

Natalie rolled her eyes impatiently.

'I'm afraid I really wouldn't know what to do,' said Christian. Becca stared at him in disbelief. 'We've never had a tree at home,' Christian added by way of explanation. 'My parents don't approve.'

'Clever people,' Bernard commented crossly. 'Give this lot five minutes to start squabbling over what goes where and you may find that I don't approve either.'

'Come on kids, let's get stuck in,' Nick laughed. He threw a length of scarlet tinsel round Evie's neck, which complemented her dark good looks, and pretended to pull her towards him. 'Very pretty.'

'Pack it in!'

Evie yanked the tinsel away, causing Becca to raise her eyebrows. It was unlike her sister to be so touchy.

Natalie, despite receiving disapproving looks from Christian, had embarked on the mammoth task of unravelling the tree lights. Her grumbling was epic.

'Wait!' Becca cried, jumping up. Everyone started, worried something was wrong. Becca ran from the room and returned minutes later with a gaudily wrapped shoebox. She reached in and pulled out a compact disc. 'We almost forgot the music.' A weak cheer went up as the first strains of *Do They Know It's Christmas?* played. '*Now* we can begin.'

There then followed all the Bingham traditions of realising that one of the bulbs had blown followed by the annual hunt for a replacement, bickering about whether the baubles should be colour co-ordinated or traditional and the usual groans when Margaret produced her children's primary school creations and insisted on their inclusion.

'I can't believe you still put those on the tree,' Natalie moaned. 'They're so embarrassing.'

'I think they're sweet,' Margaret protested.

'Well, here's India's first ever contribution to the Bingham family tree,' Evie said. She produced a cotton wool and kitchen foil angel which India had made at nursery. Margaret and Bernard went into ecstasies over the angel, declaring they'd never seen anything so wonderful.

'She must have pride of place at the very top of the tree,' Bernard announced. 'Do you want to help me, India?' He lifted up his granddaughter and together they balanced the angel on the vertical, uppermost branch.

Natalie personally thought it was the most frightful looking thing she'd ever seen and was somewhat put out that it had jettisoned the rather expensive gold star she'd bought in Harrods and given to her parents the previous year. Part of her knew she should be gracious and say nothing. It was a small part, and was easily overruled by the rest of her.

'What about my star? That angel has a string and can go anywhere on the tree. My star can't be put anywhere else. I suppose it's not going to be used at all this year,' she griped. Margaret instantly looked torn. She loved the gold star. It was so gloriously posh. Evie was looking daggers at Natalie. 'Don't glare at me, Evie. There's more to this family than just you and India.'

'That's beside the point,' Bernard said. 'That angel is a precious gift.'

'And what was my star? Chopped liver? Mum agrees with me. Look at her. She's racked with her dilemma.'

'I do love that star, Bernard, and it's true that if we don't put it on the tree it can't be used, and that seems such a shame,' Margaret said. 'Evie, love, would you mind very much if the angel goes on another branch?'

Evie was so angry with Natalie that she couldn't respond and her silence was interpreted as acquiescence. With a sigh Bernard removed the angel from its perch and replaced it with the star whereupon India screamed blue murder.

'Are you happy now?' Evie snapped at Natalie. 'Upsetting

a two-year-old, for God's sake.' Not even a swiftly unwrapped chocolate decoration would appease the little girl. Evie rubbed her temple anxiously. The constant bickering was giving her a headache.

'I don't know what the fuss is all about,' said Great Aunt Ada, her mouth puckering like a drawstring bag. 'That child is spoilt. She needs some discipline.'

'She's only two,' Becca protested. 'What discipline could she need?'

'Her age is no reason to let her have her own way. It was the same with your late grandmother. Always sparing the rod,' Great Aunt Ada said. 'Besides, that star of Natalie's looks much better. She has such good taste.'

'Stick up for her, why don't you?' Becca muttered under her breath. She had long been aware that each one of her siblings was somebody's favourite. Dan and Grandpa had an understanding borne of them both having a megalomaniacal older sister, which led neatly onto Natalie and Great Aunt Ada being kindred evil spirits, and Evie would always be their parents' darling. It didn't matter how well they tried to conceal it. She, Becca, was the exception. She was no one's favourite. She watched with bitterness as Great Aunt Ada, agitated by the furore she herself had caused, sparked up a cigarette.

'Great Aunt Ada, could you please not smoke around India?' Evie asked.

'Why not?' Great Aunt Ada snapped, taking a long drag.

'Err, passive smoking.'

'Oh, for crying out loud, Evie. Stop beefing about everything. It's not like you at all. Honestly, you've become such a baby bore,' Natalie snapped.

'Well, you haven't *become* a selfish bitch, you've always been one,' Becca retaliated on Evie's behalf. Enraged, Natalie swung toward Becca, her eyes glazed with venom.

'Don't you start either. You haven't exactly got anything to boast about. Mum said you bumped into that useless ex of yours this morning and didn't do anything about it other than emulate a rabbit caught in the headlights, instead of telling him to sod off. I can't believe a sister of mine would let a man walk over her like that,' Natalie raged. Appalled silence greeted her outburst. It was only broken when Becca burst into tears and ran from the room.

It was at this point that Margaret also rose to her feet. She'd had enough of her warring children and felt that she would be happier in her own company preparing a casserole for that evening's dinner, thank you very much. She would wash her hands of the lot of them.

The rest of the afternoon passed without incident. Natalie and Christian huffily assembled the dining table in the conservatory whilst Evie tidied up the lunch pots. Aggrieved that he had been forsaken yet again, Nick took India and the two dogs and sulked his way round the village stopping only to belligerently throw some stale bread at, rather than for, the ducks on the pond. Becca moped in her room, becoming maudlin every time *Last Christmas* was played on the radio.

Downstairs, Grandpa and Great Aunt Ada watched some ghastly war film on television from within their own smoke cloud. The film, which unfortunately contained scenes of both tally-ho bravery and Nazism, triggered Grandpa to such a degree that Bernard thought his father was going to have a seizure and eventually had to escort him to his bedroom for a calming afternoon nap. By this time, flustered himself, Bernard finally escaped into the garden shed with his beloved hedge trimmer whilst Margaret whiled away the hours in the kitchen listening to the soothing sounds of *Nine Lessons and Carols* to calm her down. She wished her family would learn a few bliddy lessons. Tolerance and forgiveness would be a start, but hey ho!

✳

By seven o'clock Great Aunt Ada had drunk yet another half bottle of gin and Dan still hadn't appeared. The decision was made to have dinner without him.

'I do hope Daniel isn't going to roll in merry,' Margaret said, ushering everyone into the kitchen.

Evie personally thought her mother's hope was misplaced. She plonked India in her high chair.

'I can't believe he hasn't even telephoned to let your mother know that he wouldn't be in for dinner,' Bernard said to his daughters as they all sat down to eat. Margaret started to ladle spiced winter lamb casserole out of a vast tureen. Bowls containing boiled potatoes and vegetables congregated in the middle of the kitchen table. A special spicy vegetable casserole had been prepared for Natalie and Christian, and which was accepted without comment. A bowl of casserole was dished up for Dan to heat up on his return.

'Cracking soup, Margaret,' said Grandpa, tucking into his casserole with the tablespoon he had taken out of the carrots. No one bothered to correct him.

'There's apple pie for pud. Stewed apples for you, Christian. By that time it'll almost be time to get ready for church. I expect everyone to attend,' Margaret said.

'We'll be there,' Evie said, obedient as ever.

'Err… actually, I thought we'd give it a miss,' Nick said, interrupting. 'It's far too late for India and I've barely seen my wife these past two days.' His tone was jolly enough but Evie could sense that her husband was starting to reach the end of his rope with her family. Not wishing to start a fight at the dinner table, Evie made a pledge to speak to Nick as soon as dinner was over. For the time being she would acquiesce.

'It really is too late for India, and I've got a stinking headache,' she said. Both reasons were genuine enough but this didn't stop expressions of disappointment and displeasure from both her parents. Talk about not being able to please all of the people all of the time! She'd be lucky if she could please one, and she was damned sure that she wouldn't be fortunate enough for that 'one' to be herself.

Natalie wished she could come up with an excuse to get her out of the Christmas Eve service at the village church. To her surprise, Christian had decided that, as he had never attended a Communion service before, he would like to attend out of sheer curiosity. He had never experienced a Christmas like this one. Being an only child in a family of busy actors, it was rare that he and his parents spent the holiday together at all. Even on those infrequent occasions no great effort was put into the festivities, with no special meal being prepared and only the minimum of gifts being exchanged. Because of this he found the Binghams, and their enthusiasm for Christmas, fascinating. Only Natalie seemed ill at ease amidst all the joviality, leaving Christian wondering if she was torn between being work-Natalie, who was in charge, uncompromising and tough, and home-Natalie, who wasn't allowed to be any of these things and who was constantly being squashed by her family.

'The vicar's prepared a super sermon,' Margaret said encouragingly.

Oh goodee, thought Natalie sourly. She gazed at the tureen of lamb casserole longingly. Why had she invited Christian home when it meant she had to keep up this pretence at vegetarianism? She'd been pressured into agreeing to it because Christian refused to kiss her if she ate meat, claiming he could taste it on her breath and was repulsed by it. Only after she'd agreed to this did the terrible realisation dawn that she would have to forego her mother's miraculous cooking. There would be no turkey with all the trimmings for her this year. She would be enduring the tasteless nut roast that had been bought in last minute for Christian. Too proud to recant her reluctant pledge she poked at her vegetable casserole with little enthusiasm. Not only that, all the roughage she was consuming was making her fart louder than a klaxon. She kept having to slink off to one of the toilets just to blow off so as not to embarrass herself in front of Christian. Thank God she hadn't agreed to go the whole hog and turn macrobiotic! At least she could look forward to apple pie and custard followed by a few more glasses of wine.

'Who wants to help me and India put out some mince pies and sherry for Father Christmas?' Evie asked. India gave such a high-pitched shriek of excitement that Natalie flinched. Bernard fixed his youngest daughter with a stern eye, daring her to desecrate India's belief in Santa at her own peril.

'Don't forget Rudolph's carrot,' said Becca. 'He needs his vegetables so that he can fly quickly.'

India's eyes were as round as ten pence pieces.

'He can have mine — all of 'em,' Natalie muttered to no one in particular. Her plate was as full as it had been at the beginning of the meal.

'Pardon?' said Christian.

'I said, there are nine, name them,' Natalie said, amazing herself with her own quick-wittedness. 'Reindeer. No one can ever name all nine.' Everyone immediately started discussing the names of Santa's reindeer. Natalie wondered if she could sneak into the pantry and surreptitiously eat the casserole her mother had plated up for Dan. She got her chance immediately after dinner. With the rest of her family cooing over India as she was assisted in leaving a plate of mince pies and a glass of sherry by the fireplace for Santa, Natalie snuck into the kitchen, stole the bowl of casserole and clandestinely heated it up in the microwave before creeping back into the relative safety of the pantry, fork clutched in her thieving hand, to enjoy her illicit feast. After the blandness of the vegetable casserole, despite her mother's valiant efforts to jazz it up with some ferocious spices, the lamb stew tasted like ambrosia. Natalie congratulated herself on her ingenuity as she shovelled the food into her mouth with indecent haste.

There was only one tricky moment when Becca unexpectedly appeared in the kitchen looking for her bloody carrot. Natalie was at this point washing up the dirty bowl and Becca was too preoccupied by her search for root vegetables to notice the smell of cooked sheep that had pervaded the kitchen. Thanking the Lord above that Becca hadn't come in five minutes earlier and found her in the pantry, Natalie breathed a sigh of relief. Full and satisfied at last, she joined her family in the lounge. They were still enthusing over India, who at least was about to be taken upstairs to bed by Evie. Once they had gone, following an unnecessary round of snotty infant kisses in Natalie's opinion, Becca reached for the carrot and took a great bite out of it.

'What are you doing?' Bernard cried. What devilry was one of his children up to now?

'Look! Teeth marks!' Becca held up the carrot, which did now indeed look like a creature had been gnawing at it. 'Who's got the biggest feet?' She then proceeded to sprinkle a little coal dust on the hearth and convinced a very reluctant Christian to step on it. It left a size twelve footprint. Natalie observed all this in silent disapproval. In her opinion it was a wicked hypocrisy that parents saw fit to tell their children such a colossal lie in the existence of Father Christmas. Under no other circumstance was it acceptable to encourage young children to believe it was all right for a strange man to creep into their bedrooms, intent on leaving them what could only be described as bribes for obedience, whilst they were sleeping. No wonder kids grew up confused.

'All we now need is for someone to eat the pies and drink the sherry,' Becca said.

'I'll drink the sherry,' said Great Aunt Ada, to no one's surprise. Becca dutifully handed over the glass. Great Aunt Ada drained it in one long slug. 'Any chance of a refill?'

Nick was captivated. He couldn't tear his eyes away. He idly wondered if Dan's new-found love for booze was in fact genetic. It was only after a few moments had passed that he realised Great Aunt Ada was glaring at him.

'What?' she snapped.

'I really must give Evie a hand with India,' Nick muttered before making his escape. He joined Evie in the bedroom just as she was rocking India in her cot.

Evie looked up and smiled. 'She's excitable,' she whispered. Nick wrapped his arms around Evie's shoulders and gazed down at his daughter. She seemed to be drifting off at last.

'She's bound to be. Santa's on his way,' he murmured. He pressed his lips against Evie's temple. It was hot. 'Jesus, you're burning up.'

Evie grimaced.

'I've a bit of a headache. It's nothing. I've taken a couple of painkillers,' she said. India shuffled in the cot but didn't open her eyes.

'I thought you made that up to put your mother off the scent so we could have a night in,' Nick said roguishly. He placed the back of his hand against Evie's forehead and frowned. 'That's definitely a temperature.'

'It's probably a cold. There's one going round India's nursery,' Evie said dismissively, wriggling away. 'Anyway, I can't be ill. I don't have time. Everyone's at each other's throats and there's still so much to do.' She had begun to pick up India's discarded clothes. Drat, there was still the Ribena-stained dress to handwash. Nick gently took the clothes out of Evie's hands and set them aside.

'I don't understand why your family just can't get along with each other.' He had to force Evie to look at him. 'It's the same every time we come here. You spend all your time refereeing your family and helping your mother and it's India and I who get neglected.'

'They're my family and they need my help. They're in bits this year. Dan's fast turning into a lush, Becca's barely coping and Natalie—' Evie couldn't find the words to describe her current feelings towards her youngest sister.

'I know what's going on with them all. Becca's got problems, that I concede, but Dan's a big boy and can look after himself. He's just letting off steam. I did exactly the same thing when I was his age. As for Natalie, words fail me too. I don't understand her or that nobstick she's brought home. I understand your concerns but it's not your job to solve all their problems. Plus, they may be in bits but they're still solid. Everyone made the effort to come home, even Natalie, and God knows we've all heard about the 'several exclusive invitations to top celebrity parties' that she turned down.' Nick mimicked Natalie to perfection. 'That's got to count for something. They're all fine and they'll cope. All I'm saying is that India and I need you too.' He was trying hard to keep his voice down in case he woke the little girl. 'And we should take precedence.'

Evie stared at him in indignation. She slammed her hands against her hips and adopted an aggressive stance. 'Are you saying I'm a bad mother?'

Nick pulled a face of pure frustration. Why did she always twist his words so that he was the villain of the piece?

'No, all I'm saying is your family monopolise you. Even you complained earlier that your bloody mother is always interfering. There's the evidence!' Nick pointed to the stained dress.

'Oh, so it's my 'bloody mother' now, is it? I thought you liked my mother.' Evie continued her attack. 'Is that why you don't want us to go to Communion? Do you resent my family that much?' Evie turned away from Nick and began to tidy up again. She was snatching clothes off the floor and all her movements were fractious. As she grabbed at a pile of laundry she overbalanced and, with freakish power, knocked one of her mother's pictures off the wall as she tried to right herself. It fell to the floor with a guilty clatter. The frame had snapped in two and shards of glass were scattered everywhere. The print itself had creased in two. 'Shit! Shit! *Shit!*' Evie stared down at the broken picture in dismay. It would be her mother's favourite picture: a large print of Monet's *The Magpie* that Bernard had given Margaret when they had got married. She'd have to confess to that one, Evie thought as she reached for it. Her eyes continually flickered towards the cot. Surely the racket must have woken India? Somehow not. The little girl merely shuffled under her blanket, but did not wake.

Nick watched Evie helplessly, noting as she bent down how pale and drained she looked. How had he not noticed that before? Once again he stopped her mid-action and sat her down on the bed.

'No, listen, I'm sorry. You're jumping from one conclusion to another. You know I think your family's great. Insane… but great. It's just that I've barely seen you in two whole days and I want to spend some time alone with you. God knows we get precious little time since we've had India. I admit I was jealous this morning when you went into town with Becca. Didn't it occur to you that I might have liked to go for a coffee with you instead of being packed off to the supermarket? All I'm saying is that Christmas isn't all about the Binghams, it's about *our* family too, us three.' Nick watched as tears welled in his wife's eyes. 'You look knackered. Why don't you get into bed?'

'I can't. I have things to do,' Evie said, wiping her face with the back of her hand.

'Such as?'

'The kitchen's a tip and I have this dress to wash and dry for tomorrow morning. Not to mention a certain pillowcase that has to be attended to.' Evie jerked her head towards the cot, causing it to throb painfully. 'I can't believe I'm getting a cold. The timing stinks.'

'All the more reason for you to have a break tonight. You

washed up at lunchtime. Surely your sisters can deal with the dinner pots? I can wash the dress and we can organise the pillowcase later. In fact, I'm a little offended you thought I wouldn't want to help with that,' Nick said, smiling engagingly. 'What do you say? I'll hide that picture for now. We'll get it reframed once the shops reopen. In the meantime, you can order me about whilst you sit by the fire and have a glass of wine. It might help that headache of yours.' He gave a cheeky grin. 'If that fails I can think of something else to make a headache go away. I've got a very special present just for you.' Despite her earlier anger, Evie took a playful swipe at her husband.

'Filthy beast,' she laughed. She'd never been able to resist Nick when he embarked on a charm offensive and he looked so handsome and rugged with his thick, dark hair in desperate need of a haircut, having been left right up until the end of term to be dealt with. Just skimming his collar, it made him look more like the member of an acoustic rock band than a school teacher. Plus there was no benefit to staying cross with him on Christmas Eve, especially when he was assaulting her neck and shoulders so expertly with his lips.

'Let's go downstairs now. I'll get this blessed dress washed then I'll raid your father's wine store for something full-bodied, rich and fruity,' Nick breathed, reaching inside Evie's sweater with a cold hand. It made her gasp.

'Sounds like most of Dad's golf buddies,' Evie giggled. She had all but forgotten about their row and her headache and was beginning to feel giddy, like a teenager. Something about the night was magical. She couldn't say exactly what, it was just a feeling. Perhaps it was simply the enchantment of Christmas. Nick, however, wasn't to be put off.

'Hush. I'll get the fire roaring, candles lit, the tree lights twinkling, the wine flowing and we can settle down in front of a disgustingly Christmassy, sentimental, romantic film such as *It's a Wonderful Life*. Your family will be out for at least two hours.'

Downstairs, the front door slammed following a chorus of goodbyes. Nick drew Evie in for a long, slow kiss.

'We're alone,' he said. 'Let's make the most of it. What do you say?'

Evie gazed down at her daughter who was now sleeping deeply. She looked so perfect, Evie thought, and so peaceful.

'Isn't she beautiful?' Evie asked, looking up at her husband. It was a fitting moment for a cold Christmas Eve. Then Nick ruined it.

'She certainly is.' He paused, as though uncertain as to whether he should continue. 'You know I've been mentioning that I don't want India to be an only child?' Nick had by now engulfed Evie in his arms and was speaking into her hair rather than to her face. It was a deliberate move as he knew what a sensitive subject he was raising but he had been encouraged by her sudden, unexpected affection. 'I really want to start trying for another baby.'

It was a bad call.

Evie stiffened in his arms, then pulled away.

'Nick, you know how I feel about this,' she said. She turned away from him and started to fuss over a pile of India's dirty clothes.

It had been a bone of contention ever since India had been born. Nick, having been an only child, had often been a lonely boy and was keen for India to have at least one brother or sister with whom to play and share. Evie, as the eldest of four, didn't agree but instead believed that India would fare better as an only child. She loved her family dearly, even the at times horrendous Natalie, and was thankful for them, but she had paid the price. As a child she'd had to share everything four ways and had often had to make do with very little or even without in order to make the family budget stretch. She would have loved riding or tennis lessons and to learn to play the piano and read music, but money had always been tight on her father's sole salary as a driving instructor. Instead she had discovered her talent for painting in school lessons and it was only because she'd been lucky enough to have a wonderful teacher that she had gained her scholarship to art school. If India were an only child they could lavish all their time, money and affection solely on her. They would be able to afford the best education, a better lifestyle, a better start in life for her. Evie didn't want to leave India's future down to sheer luck as her own had been. Both of her parents had indicated that they felt the same just yesterday. Stop at one, they'd both implied.

Nor did Evie want to relinquish her own life to the pursuit of motherhood, as her mother had. She loved India above all other things, and cherished every moment spent with her, but was very aware of her own identity dissipating like vapour into her past. She had worked so hard to realise her childhood dream of becoming an artist, and more importantly an artist who earned her living as such, instead of it remaining nothing more than a pipedream hobby, and didn't want to relinquish it. Especially not now. Not when such an amazing, once-in-a-lifetime opportunity just seemed to have dropped into her lap.

Evie's perpetual battle between her family and her career had been the source of many a bitter argument, including their most recent one, but she couldn't believe Nick had chosen this precise moment to ambush her. She thought fast to come up with a lock tight excuse and plumped for an old and reliable favourite.

'Anyway, you're out of luck. I think my period's started early which rules out any full blown nookie.' It was a lie, but it would give her a few days' breathing space. Nick couldn't hide his disappointment. However, driven by the twin incentives of still being physically turned on by Nick's amorous advances and desperate to avoid a row on

Christmas Eve, Evie began to hitch up her sweater like a stripper, smiling suggestively. 'But I'm sure I can find some other way to wish you a happy Christmas.'

THE FILM WAS JUST COMING to its heartwarming conclusion when the front door slammed. Aware that she was dressed for bed in only a baggy tee shirt and some very skimpy shorts from her slender days that now did little to conceal her dignity, Evie sat up with a start. She expected to see her entire family returned from church, chock full to the brim with both goodwill to all beings and the vicar's wife's excellent mince pies, but only Dan stood in the hall. He was singing to himself. An inane smile was plastered across his face. Evie reluctantly extracted herself from Nick's warm embrace. Nick paused the film and gave a deep sigh. He might have known something would disturb them.

'So, you've decided to come home then?' Evie said as she approached her brother. She was almost knocked sideways by the beer fumes. 'Christ, how much have you drunk?'

'Enough to make me very jolly,' Dan said. He seemed delighted to see his sister and advanced on her with arms akimbo. 'Merry Chrishmash, Evie. Ha ha! Chrishmash Evie!'

'Mum'll 'Merry Christmas' you when she gets hold of you. She was going bananas earlier.' Evie dodged out of his way. Dan misjudged his step and crashed into the wall. Several pictures rattled, but didn't fall. Evie glared at them, unpleasantly reminded of her earlier breakage.

'The shong exshorts uzz to have ourselvsh a merry little Chrishmash and that's eshactly what I've done,' said Dan. He had begun to lean against the wall. 'Ding-a-linga-linga ding dong ding. Oh no, that's a different shong.'

'What's going on?' Nick came to assess the situation for himself.

'He's shitfaced,' Evie said. She had to lurch forward to steady Dan as he leaned a bit too far the wrong way. 'I don't know what to do with him. He can't stand straight and he keeps on singing *Sleigh Ride*.

'I'll put the kettle on,' Nick said. He grappled Dan. 'Let's get him sat down in the kitchen. He should eat something as well. He can have that plate of casserole Margaret put in the pantry.'

'I don't want anything to eat and I don't want coffee,' Dan protested as he was forced onto a kitchen chair. The kettle began to whistle. 'I want another drink. Tidings of Southern Comfort and joy-oy!' Dan sang along to the kettle.

'You've had plenty,' Nick said. He disappeared into the pantry. He emerged empty handed. 'The casserole's gone.' Nick and Evie exchanged glances.

'Natalie!' they exclaimed simultaneously. Dan instantly looked put out.

'Bitch ate my dinner?' he asked. 'But I want it.' He gestured to the empty table with both hands. Evie plonked a hot black coffee in front of his nose. Dan looked at her resentfully, and then belched.

'I want to open a preshent.'

'Well, you can't,' Evie said. She had by this time begun to see the funny side and was having trouble keeping a straight face. 'What you're going to do is sober up, smarten up and get your alcoholic little arse down to the church. If you show yourself at midnight mass you might just avoid being harangued by Mum for the rest of your holidays.' Dan groaned. He hated church. 'If you don't go and show willing you'll be lucky if Mum'll let you out of her sight until term begins,' Evie concluded.

'Your sister's right,' Nick added. Hope had been restored that perhaps their evening alone could be salvaged after all. Dan groaned again but began to drink his coffee. Despite his inebriated state he could concede that Evie had a very valid point.

Three coffees, two pints of water and three considerably protracted urinations later he was standing in his father's long black coat by the front door. He was by no means sober but at least he had stopped singing and leaning. Evie had wanted him to wear a scarf in consideration of the cold weather but Nick had wisely vetoed the idea on account of the fact that Margaret might just ring Dan's neck with it.

'If you go now you'll catch the last forty-five minutes and Mum just might be appeased. Go straight there, find Becca and try to behave yourself. No deliberate farts during prayers,' Evie said. She knew her brother's tricks of old. Nick propelled Dan out of the door and watched as he staggered down the driveway and onto the road. He slipped on an icy patch and only rectified his balance by rotating his arms like a windmill.

'Jesus!' he yelled, then cackled with laughter.

'Do you think we've done the right thing,' Nick asked Evie as they closed the door. They were both shivering from the cold and Evie's legs had come out in goosebumps from ankle to hip. 'If he acts up in front of your mother it'll be midnight mass murder. Worse still, what if he gets run over or falls into the village pond?'

'He'll be all right,' said Evie, 'so long as he turns left at the green. If he turns right he'll end up in the The Half Moon and that'll be the last we see of him. Still, it'll be hard for him to buy more booze without this!' Evie triumphantly waved Dan's black wallet in the air. 'I picked his pocket. Silly sod never even noticed.' Then Evie howled with laughter as something white on the telephone table caught her attention. It was the envelope containing the pantomime tickets for Boxing Night. In a moment of drunken self-amusement Dan had amended the writing so it now read:

Seven tickets for Old Motherfucker

Their mother was going to kill him!

DAN NEVER MADE it to prayers, at least not to the beginning of them. He dutifully reeled his way to the church, frightening some sleeping ducks into a quacking frenzy as he clumsily traversed the village green, before zig-zagging up the church's pathway, accidentally treading on a few graves in the process. He said good evening to each headstone he passed. Once his salutations were concluded he spied the heavy, double oak doors of the church, which were outlined by a halo of golden, ecclesiastical light. Delighted that he had reached his destination Dan shoved them with all the might he could muster, imagining that he was entering a western saloon in a heroic manner. Alas, the doors swung open with a monstrous clatter and Dan fell into the church only to find himself staring into the faces of a one hundred and fifty strong, rather startled congregation. All were kneeling or had bowed heads. He'd interrupted prayers. Suitably embarrassed he muttered his apologies and hurriedly closed the doors as quietly as he could. The vicar eyeballed him as he scuttled down the centre aisle, head swivelling from side to side as he scoured the rows of people for his family. Where the hell was Becca?

A hand shot out and dragged him into a pew. The hand belonged to his father.

'What the bloody hell are you playing at?' A few shocked gasps reminded Bernard where he was. He flashed an errant smile at the vicar as he shoved Dan down the pew towards his sisters. Face flaming red from mortification, Dan had to squeeze past not only his grandfather and great aunt but also an outraged mother and gloating Natalie. Eventually he flopped down in between an amused Becca and an unamused Christian, who ignored him. Becca nudged him and offered to share her running order. Dan grinned at her giving her the full effect of his breath.

'Christ, you smell like a brewery,' Becca hissed. Christian was still deliberately looking in the other direction, his chin raised as if to emphasise that he shouldn't be associated with such a plebeian. Prayers were resumed by a distinctly unimpressed reverend. A carol followed. Everyone stood up as the opening bars of *Whilst Shepherds Watched* were crucified by the antediluvian, hoary-haired spinster organist who had been in situ since Dan's Sunday school days. As the slightly off-key, too-slow music began to resonate around the church rafters something happened to Dan. It was as though the spirit of some primordial pagan god of mischief imbued itself in him. He was consumed with an urge to sing loudly and proudly for all to hear. Alas, the words that he sang were not traditional but referred to shepherds watching the telly as they did their laundry whilst the high-exalted archangels controlled the TV channels from the glorious firmament above. Becca got the giggles. Margaret was leaning forward, giving them both the evils but this didn't prompt them to stop. Eventually the carol came to its end and Dan was at last silenced. The vicar began a long rant about the values of Christmas.

'There's no better gift than friendship at Christmas—' he preached.

'What about love?' Becca hissed at Dan, her face contorted with bafflement.

'What about a *bike*?' Dan said, emphatically and far too loudly. A few disapproving 'tuts' could be heard.

Already bored, he amused himself by pinching a pen from Becca's handbag and doodling all over the foolscap carol sheet, altering the crude computer generated illustrations however he saw fit. He gave Mary massive tits and a handlebar moustache before drawing the donkey some rather dashing racing colours. He was in the middle of converting the stable where Jesus Christ was born into a Yates's Wine Lodge when Communion began. The organist launched into a jazzy version of *In Dulci Jubilo* which made the congregation fear for her health as she pounded the keys with aerobic vigour. Surely the exertion must finish her off? The occupants of the front pews made their way to the altar to receive Communion. Before long it was the turn of the Binghams and Bernard led his family up to the altar. They all genuflected with the exception of Grandpa, whose knees wouldn't bend even for God, in preparation of the receiving of the bread and wine. Great Aunt Ada was wondering how big a gulp of the Communion wine she could feasibly get away with taking. Dan noticed that Christian held his hands above the bar alongside everyone else. He remembered Christian mentioning that he'd never been to Communion before and began to protest noisily that as Christian hadn't been confirmed he wasn't entitled to receive the bread and wine.

'Shut up, Danimal, it doesn't matter,' Natalie snarled. She, like all the Bingham children, had been confirmed when she was a teenager.

'Yes it does, he should have his hands under the bar to receive a blessing.' Dan was like a dog with a bone. Christian, situated between Dan and Natalie, ignored them both and patiently waited, hands above the bar, for the vicar to reach him. Natalie was still arguing with Dan when the wine chalice reached her.

'Is there a problem?' the vicar asked kindly.

'*He* hasn't been confirmed,' said Dan, pointing at Christian before Natalie could speak. The vicar looked bemused.

'He has, Reverend. I give you my word,' Natalie said, smiling so angelically at the vicar that he couldn't possibly doubt her. She had just partaken of the bread but remained on her knees, pretending to be deep in silent prayer, so she could keep an eye on her brother. Not one twinge of remorse did she feel when Christian goofed the responses to the offerings of the bread and wine. The vicar had begun to look suspicious. Natalie grabbed Christian by the wrist and dragged him back to the pew.

Dan had watched all this with contempt. Then, as the chalice of wine approached his face, the feeling of contempt was replaced by something much more worrying. At the first whiff of wine, Dan's poor violated body decided that it wasn't going to consume one more drop of alcohol. Nausea engulfed him. His stomach lurched in protest. Dan knew he was going to puke. He looked at Becca in panic and backed away from the altar as though the vicar was the very devil.

'Need some air,' he rasped by way of explanation before striding with haste down the relatively empty perimeter aisle of the church and exiting through the main doors. The vicar was simply astonished and for a few moments proceedings were halted. Feeling her mother's eyes boring into the back of her skull, Becca had no option but to take Communion quickly before excusing herself. She hurriedly tracked Dan's exit and found him round the side of the church. He was propped against a tombstone. Frothy, black vomit, which looked like it also contained the remains of a doner kebab, was splattered against the wall of the church.

'Oh, *Dan!*'

'I feel much better now,' Dan said weakly. 'Talk about midnight massacre.' He was the same glistening white as the moon that was peeping round the church's square tower. Beads of beer-sweat had formed on his brow despite freezing temperature.

'Funny that, 'cause you look ghastly,' Becca said. She took a quick peek at the vomit, backing away at the same time. It smelled of Guinness and coffee. Her own stomach churned out of sheer reaction. 'Do you feel well enough to go back inside?' Dan looked horrified.

'I can't go back in there. What about that?' He pointed to the moistened wall, which had now started to steam. 'It has to be cleaned up.' Dan looked at his sister beseechingly. Becca shook her head.

'You're my brother and I love you, but I can't clean that up. I'll hurl too. You'll just have to go back inside and brazen it out. We'll say you felt faint and needed some air. We won't mention that you were sick.' Becca took a good look around. 'No one comes round here. With any luck it'll get washed away by some rain, or eaten by some wild animal, and no one will be any the wiser.'

'Do you want me to barf again?' Dan asked in disgust. He inspected himself. He was clean. 'At least I didn't get any on Dad's coat.'

'Come on, Communion's nearly finished,' Becca said. 'It's almost time for the Peace.' Dan followed her back inside. The brightness inside the church was blinding after the gentle glow from the moon outside.

'My breath's rank,' he said. His eyes were slitted like a cat's.

'I've got some Tictacs in my bag.'

They sat down just as the back pews were returning to their seats, and as the vicar began to recite the blessing. 'May the Peace of the Lord be with you,' he concluded.

'And also with you,' droned the congregation. Dan crunched several Tictacs noisily. His mother glared at him again. The vicar then encouraged his flock to share the Peace with each other and the congregation rose to their feet. They turned to each other and began to hug those they knew well and shake hands with those they didn't. Becca gave Dan a cursory hug. She was still keen to keep her distance in case he hurled again.

'May the Peace of the Lord be with you, Dan,' she said. You'll bloody well need it, she wanted to add.

'May the force be with you,' Dan replied, as he always did

when he shared the Peace with Becca. His mouth was burning from the excess of mints. Better he might well feel, but the alcohol still coursing through his veins wasn't about to relinquish control just yet. Hitherto, he had always been careful to limit his Jedi blessing only to his family but on this occasion he felt it appropriate to impart it on his mother's neighbours and friends, the vicar's wife, the owners of the village shop and the majority of his primary school teachers. All were left unoffended but certainly confused. Thankfully, just as one of his mother's more interfering friends (and there were plenty of those, in Dan's opinion) advanced on his parents, the vicar announced the next carol. Everyone returned to their seats and turned to carol number thirteen on the song sheet. A broad grin eclipsed Dan's face.

Plink, plink, plonk went the organ. The dutiful masses rose to their feet.

'*Good King Wenceslas looked out —*' they sang.

'—Of his bedroom win-der,' bellowed Dan. 'Silly bugger he fell out, on a red hot cin-der. Brrrrrightly shone his arse that night—'

'*Though the frost was cru-el, when a poor man came in sight —*' chorused the congregation.

'Playing with his tooo-ooo-ell,' concluded Dan theatrically. Poor Becca couldn't sing for laughing. On Dan's other side Christian looked appalled. Further down the row Margaret wanted to crawl under the pew and die. She'd heard every word of Dan's bastardisation of the carol. People were staring at her family in horror. How could he embarrass her in such a way? Had she been such a bad mother? Beside her Bernard harboured no such self-doubts. He was simply livid. What had possessed his son to turn up to midnight mass drunk anyway? At least the farce was nearly over. Upon the conclusion of the carol the vicar would say the blessing and that would be followed by one last singalong. Unfortunately the final carol was always *O Come All Ye*

Faithful and Dan and Becca, who had been egged on by her drunken brother and had been considerably cheered up by the evening's events, proceeded to sing the descant very badly and with great volume. As soon as the final chord faded away they both shot out of the pew as though the prayer cushions were on fire.

Margaret, by now breathing fire and brimstone, would have liked to have pursued them but was too tempted by the vicar's annual offer of a brief glass of mulled wine and festive snacks at the vicarage. She would deal with her children later. She always enjoyed the traditional after-mass soirée. She admired the vicar's wife above all others and often emulated her graceful manners and genteel fashions. Furthermore, she coveted the vicarage itself, which was always so tastefully decorated at this time of year, looking much like the pictures of immaculate spreads and innovative ideas in *Good Housekeeping*.

As she accepted a glass of mulled wine and a piece of wonderfully moist Christmas cake, Margaret noticed that people weren't being as chatty as they would usually be. Downhearted, she positioned herself next to the Christmas tree in the lounge and waited for someone to talk to her. Whilst she was admiring the Victoriana trim of the tree — it was all tartan ribbons and beaded gold garlands — Bernard joined her, glass in hand. He seemed tense.

'We can't stay long, love,' he said. Not even the lounge's roaring coal fire could warm his sprits. He'd heard some unsavoury gossip about his family following Dan's exhibition in the church and was keen for his wife to remain ignorant of what was being said. He monitored his family from where he stood. On the whole he was incredibly displeased with them. Becca and, even more so, Dan were a disgrace and even Evie had let him down tonight. At least she could be relied on to behave with dignity. On the bright side, Grandpa and Great Aunt Ada seemed to be mingling nicely with the other pensioners from the congregation and at least one of his children had bothered to turn up, even if it was only Natalie.

Sensing a rare opportunity to ingratiate herself with her parents Natalie had dragged a reluctant Christian to the vicarage, although she instantly regretted it as Christian turned his nose up at everything that was on offer from the nibbles to the value boxed wines from the supermarket. Even worse, her father seemed introverted and had responded to her chattering with blunt, monosyllabic replies. He hadn't even bothered to speak to Christian at all which, although it had irked Natalie, part of her could understand. Still, she considered as she nibbled on a mini mince pie, Christian wasn't being as much of a nuisance as Great Aunt Ada, who had returned to have her mulled wine refreshed for the fourth time. People had started to notice.

'I wouldn't like to foot the drinks bill in the Bingham household this year,' an unidentifiable voice was heard to say during a lull in the conversation. Margaret heard the comment and looked as though she was about to burst into tears. It was at this point that Bernard rounded up his family and ushered them out of the vicarage. As he trudged down Cherry Tree Avenue, shadowing his family like a sheepdog trying to keep a flock under control, he offered a small prayer to the cold, clear skies above. He prayed for the one thing he would like to receive that year. He prayed for patience.

BECCA MADE a cup of peppermint tea to settle her still groaning stomach from after such a good feed earlier, and trudged upstairs, gloomily aware that she would at some point pay the price for embarrassing her parents so blatantly. As she made her way along the landing Evie stuck her head out of her parents' bedroom.

'You got a minute?'

'Surely.'

'Okay. Hang on a mo.' Evie's head popped back in. A few seconds later she reappeared, a thick envelope in her hand. She closed the bedroom door very gently behind her.

'Nick still awake?' Becca asked.

'Nah. He's whacked.' Evie twitched her head towards Becca's room, indicating that she wanted to talk in private. 'I want your opinion on something. In total confidence.'

Intrigued, Becca led Evie into her room, where they both flopped down on the bed. Evie handed over the envelope. Becca digested its contents within minutes, her eyes moving up and down as she read the text. Her expression gave nothing away until she finally raised her eyes and met Evie's apprehensive gaze.

'America?'

'Boston.'

'Is this for real? You can't seriously be considering this,' Becca said.

'I didn't go looking for it. They asked me,' Evie said, petulance tainting her voice. '*They* want *me*.'

The job offer was a twelve-month secondment contract working for the Boston office of her current London-based publishing house. Specialising in children's picture books but branching out into computer generated graphics, it was a platinum opportunity to fuse her paint and paper artwork with the most exciting, cutting edge animation software. Visas, accommodation and travel for not only her but also her family would be included in the package in addition to a whacking great salary. It was the chance of a lifetime. The chance of her life. The only problem was that her life included Nick and India, and Nick most definitely did not want to live in the States for a year. He had made that quite plain. Several times over. Evie had tried pleadings, threats, sulks and rages but Nick had remained adamant. He didn't want to leave his own job, which he loved, or drag his infant daughter halfway across the world just so that she could be shoved into some day nursery whilst her previously work-from-home mother turned all executive and breezed into the office every day. One of the two upheavals would have been okay, he had reasoned, but not both. It was just too much to ask. Evie's counter-argument had been that it was the best time, whilst India was still in nursery, and they'd be back home in time for India to begin primary school. In the meantime they could let their Chester home for twelve months.

'Sounds like you've already got all our fates neatly organised,' Nick had stormed before leaving the house to the soundtrack of slamming doors and roaring car engines.

And that hadn't even been one of their worst arguments. The rows had been nothing short of pyrotechnic and had only been put on hold because it was the holiday season. Evie was dreading New Year, and the return to normality, which would inevitably coincide with the return to all the uncertainty and disagreement of what she should do with her future. She couldn't help but feel a little resentful that her husband and daughter were holding her back, stopping her from fulfilling her dreams, and that it was her duty as a wife and mother to ensure they fulfilled theirs and be nothing more than a round-the-clock servant and baby-making machine. Nick just couldn't understand that art, being creative, was something she had to do, rather than something she chose to do. It was part of who she was and when she denied that part of her, she suffered.

The most awful day of all had been just two days ago. Having racked her brains as to a possible solution to all their needs, she'd suggested that she exempt both Nick and India from any enforced upheaval and leave for Boston on her own, returning home perhaps once a month and with them holidaying with her possibly twice over the course of the year. It broke her heart to even consider leaving India for one day but, conversely, she didn't want to wake up sixteen years later and hate not only her family but also herself for being so cowardly. It was only for one year, she'd reasoned. Ironically, the term was fixed to cover someone else's maternity leave but she daren't tell Nick that, taking into account his almost fanatical desire to have a second child. He'd go into orbit. They could commence on a trial basis at first, she suggested. If it were absolutely intolerable she'd simply come back home. Surely it was worth a try? The end result had been that Nick had packed his bags and legged it up to Newcastle to his parents' home, officially to attend a reunion with his old school pals but both he and Evie knew the real reason was to give him space to think. All this she confided to an aghast Becca.

'What do you think?' Evie asked her. 'Do you understand?'

'What do I think? I think you're crackers!' Becca replied with bitter honesty. Although, she wasn't exactly sure how she felt. Evie's revelation was niggling at two individual and separate sore spots. Firstly, that Evie's marriage was not the perfect bliss bower she'd always imagined, something she admired and hoped to emulate one day, and, secondly, that Evie was complaining about being lumbered with the very things that she, Becca, craved and that had been snatched away from her so recently. Intense misery over her own failed love life and career made her bitter and resentful.

'You have it all: a gorgeous husband, a beautiful daughter, a dream house, a great career. You have every single thing that I want but don't have. Every single thing most women want and don't have. And yet here you are, happy to throw it all away just because you're going through some thirties identity crisis. Why don't you take a good look at what you've got before you start feeling so sorry for yourself? So, no, I don't understand. Not for one second.'

It wasn't the reaction Evie expected. It set her back on her haunches.

Before she could respond Natalie pushed open the bedroom door, wearing an expression of grievance.

'Is Dan still in that bathroom? He's been in there an age, half an hour at least. I dread to think what he's doing.'

'Maybe he's passed out,' Becca said, her brow furrowed. It wasn't, after all, beyond the realms of possibility. 'He was absolutely fractured in church.'

'Christ!' said Natalie.

'Use the downstairs loo,' snapped Evie, keen to get back to her discussion with Becca.

'I left my washbag in there. I can't take off my make-up or brush my teeth until I retrieve it.' She spoke as though she were talking to a child. 'Anyway, what are you two whispering about?'

'Nothing.' Evie shot Becca a warning look but Becca was so upset by her sister's revelation that she snatched the contract out of Evie's hands and handed it to Natalie, who raked her eyes over it, an expression of astonishment eclipsing her face.

'This is *amazing!*' she breathed. 'What a fantastic opportunity. You *are* going to accept, aren't you? You'd be able to shop in New York and summer in New England. And just think what it'd do for your CV. You're so lucky!'

Evie shot Natalie a grateful look. She'd had a feeling her youngest, most ambitious sister would understand her desire to pursue her own career.

'Nick and Becca don't think so. They think I'm being selfish.'

'Nick categorically won't agree to go. So she'd have to go on her own and leave her home and family for a whole year,' Becca said.

'So?' Natalie snapped back. 'There's the phone, and Facebook and Skype, and amazing things called aeroplanes that fly across the pond several times a day. She'd be in Boston not the depths of the Peruvian jungle. Sounds to me like Nick is being a bit of a chauvinistic pig. 'Stay at home and attend to my children, little wife. Leave the proper work to the men.' Sounds to me like he's holding you back.'

'It's not as simple as that though, is it?' Becca said rationally. Evie looked as though she was going to burst into tears.

'What are you lot talking about?'

All three sisters jumped at the sound of Dan's voice. He was swaying in the doorway doing up his belt. Natalie shot him a look of disgust. None of them felt the need to confide in him.

'Nothing,' all three said in unison. Dan merely rolled his eyes as he turned and teetered back downstairs.

'Sisters! Who'd 'ave 'em?'

CHRISTMAS DAY

The household was rudely awakened just five hours later. Not by an eager toddler keen to see if 'he'd been', as had been presumed, but by incoherent yelling and squawking emanating from Grandpa's bedroom. Bernard, Margaret, Becca, Dan and Nick (who had told Evie it was pointless them both getting up) congregated on the landing.

'What the bliddy hell?'

'It's Grandpa,' Becca said. Like Evie had feared two days earlier, Becca was aware that something would ruin their Christmas. She was beset with sudden worries that Grandpa was having some kind of seizure and would die in the early hours of Christmas morning. 'Do you think he's all right?'

'Only one way to find out,' Bernard said stoutly. He pushed open the door to the room and was greeted with chaos. Vera Lynn was flapping round the room, depositing a circular trail of defecation, whilst Grandpa, resplendent in vast greying Y-fronts, danced like a witchdoctor in front of Dan's prized life-size cut-out of a Stormtrooper brandishing its Imperial weapon. Grandpa was waving his hands above his head like a madman and bellowing with considerable volume.

'Damned Nazis! Infiltrating the house. It must be an assassin. Whatever next?' And on and on he ranted. Binghams and Bingham-in-laws alike stared in amazement.

'He's reliving the blitz,' Becca said. 'Shouldn't we stop him?' No one moved. Vera Lynn continued to randomly squawk her established stock phrases. 'Here comes the vicar!' she screeched. 'Rowntree's chocolates!' She also made good use of her new, recently learned favourites. 'Fucksake! Natalie's a bitch!'

'Somebody shut that bird up,' Margaret snapped. 'When did it learn to curse, for God's sake?'

'Craw! Fucksake!' Vera Lynn replied in poor imitation.

'Never mind its language. What about stopping it crapping all over my semester one assignments? Bloody bird,' said Dan. The noise was making his fragile head pound. Bernard grabbed his father by the arm and began to reason with him. It didn't take him long to calm his father down. Becca felt sorry for the elderly man, who now just looked confused and embarrassed.

'It's not the bird's fault. That eyesore that you insist on keeping in there has terrified your grandfather. It'll have to be removed. It can stay in the garage until Grandpa's gone home,' said Margaret. 'We can't risk him mistaking it for Hitler. He'll do himself an injury.'

'I'm not putting Bertie in the garage,' Dan said petulantly. Nick stared at him in amazement.

'You named your Stormtrooper?' he asked.

'And you named it *Bertie*?' Becca added. She and Nick exchanged glances of suppressed amusement. Margaret paid no attention to either of them.

'It's not staying in the house. It's covered in bird-doo,' she said.

'Margaret, can I have some help in here?' Bernard called

from inside the room. He had sat Grandpa down on the one corner of the bed that was unsoiled. 'We'll need some clean sheets. These are beyond redemption.'

'For God's sake,' uttered Margaret once more. She vanished into the airing cupboard.

'Fucksake! Craw!' was the inevitable echo.

'Where *did* she learn that?' Nick wondered. Becca instinctively knew the answer. She turned to her brother, who was bemoaning that his Bertie had been cruelly violated, and whispered in his ear.

'That's karma for you teaching that bird those awful new words. Don't think I haven't guessed it was you.' Dan, who was now attempting to wipe a large gritty black and white splodge from the Stormtrooper's helmet with a length of toilet roll, looked put out.

'Let's go back to bed. It's not even light yet,' said Bernard.

Evie called from the bedroom and Nick went back to investigate. India was standing up. She was grinning from ear to ear and was bashing her teddy on the side of the cot. She'd already spotted the pillowcase full of presents at the end of her cot and wasn't going to be cajoled back to sleep. A yawning Evie gave a small smile of apologetic desperation. Nick shrugged his shoulders and wandered back out onto the landing.

'Hope you've got some potent java in, Margaret, as it looks like we're all getting up now. India's wide awake.'

'I'd better wake Natalie and what's-his-name,' Bernard said gloomily. 'Margaret, get the kettle on, love.' He trudged downstairs. Natalie was renowned for being greedy about her beauty sleep. Waking her at such an early hour was not something he relished. After a few tentative taps an irate Natalie yanked open the dining room door.

'What?'

It was quite obvious to Bernard that his daughter was naked beneath her dressing robe. For a few seconds he was dumbstruck. Because of all the uproar he'd forgotten what he inevitably would be confronted with.

'We're all getting up,' he said, gazing at the ceiling. He couldn't bear to look at Christian who, equally naked, was lying on the airbed covered only from the waist down. Christian gave a jaunty wave. The father in Bernard wanted to shove Natalie aside, leap on Christian and beat the cocky little turd to a pulp.

'What time is it?' Natalie demanded. 'It's still dark. It feels like the middle of the night.'

'Just gone six. Grandpa had a nightmare and woke up most of the household, India included. She's wide awake.'

'So?'

'So, Evie can't get her back to sleep. Your mother's putting the kettle on,' Bernard said. He didn't have his wits about him at such an early hour, certainly not enough to competently argue with his youngest daughter, who was apoplectic with rage. All her and Evie's empathic bonding from the previous night was forgotten in an instant.

'Go tell Evie that I'm not getting up until a civilised hour. Christmas morning will just have to wait.' Natalie marched to the foot of the stairs and leaned over the banister. She could see the rest of her family looking embarrassed. 'Mum looks knackered, *I'm* knackered and poor Dan looks like he's about to throw up, he's so hungover. If they're honest, none of them want to get up yet. They're just too frightened to say so.'

Evie appeared at the top of the stairs. She looked furious but Natalie wasn't in the mood to be intimidated. Instead she pointed an accusatory finger at her eldest sister.

'*You* wanted a kid, Evie. *You* deal with the early mornings. Why should the rest of us be subjected to them? Keep the spoilt brat occupied until eight o'clock and then I'll get up.'

'You are so *selfish*!' Evie yelled, her voice hoarse. Her knuckles were white from where she had gripped the landing banister.

'I'm selfish? I'm not the one who expects two pensioners to get up before dawn just so your life is easier,' Natalie snapped. '*I'm* selfish?' At that moment she would have dearly loved to grass on Evie about the American job, and only didn't because she knew it was far too powerful a bargaining chip to squander. She bristled with anger, transferring her weight from foot to foot. Becca couldn't help but think that for someone griping about being tired Natalie had a remarkable amount of energy. 'FYI, I've been working a fourteen hour, seven day week for the past three months. Don't I deserve Christmas to be just a little bit about me, too? Or is it all about you and India?'

Unfortunately, Dan chose that moment to give an enormous, voluble yawn. He didn't even attempt to cover his mouth with his hand. It set everyone else off and within seconds a Mexican wave of wide-mouthed yawns went round the landing. Evie looked mortified. Not even she could argue with Natalie in the face of such overwhelming evidence.

'Fine, we'll keep her entertained until breakfast time,' she said, dangerously close to tears. 'You can all go back to bed.'

Becca would have liked to have supported Evie but, having worked right up to Christmas Eve, she was exhausted herself and was desperate to go back to sleep. She shrugged her shoulders by way of apology but Evie merely glared at her. Clearly she wasn't forgiven either.

'Come on, Grandpa, let's get your bed sorted out,' Margaret said, very matter of fact.

Natalie smirked cruelly at Evie before whisking back into the study, dressing robe billowing dramatically. Very rarely did she triumph over her eldest sister.

Upstairs, Evie retreated into the bedroom in a state of devastation, her mood black and feeling that nothing could possibly cheer her up.

❄

BECCA REAWAKENED some time before her alarm was due to go off. As soon as she opened her eyes she realised it was Christmas morning. It felt different from every other morning of the year. For one thing, there was none of the usual everyday noises, such as the chug of a local tractor trundling past the house or the melodic clunk-clank of the milkman as he went about his round, to break the silence. Yes, the day definitely had a feel of its own. It didn't make any difference whether it was a Sunday or a Monday, or any other day of the week. Christmas Day was Christmas Day and couldn't be pigeonholed as anything else. The radio alarm began to play a familiar Christmas song. It wasn't even fully light yet and so Becca listened to it in the darkness. It was almost the perfect Christmas moment, a little snapshot of time that would enable her to distinguish the memory of this Christmas Day from all the others. Then the landing light was clicked on, causing a gossamer-like golden edging to her bedroom door reminiscent of holy candlelight. Becca marvelled that a simple electric light bulb could offer so much comfort and warmth. She lay in bed as the household gradually came to life, listening as her family rose from their beds, each following their own individual, recognisable routines. It was Christmas Day at last.

After a fifty-five minute round of musical bathrooms everyone materialised at the breakfast table. Margaret had been the first down and had prepared a hearty full English for everyone. As her family filed in she was still monitoring a frying pan so full of fried eggs that all the whites had interlocked, causing it to look like one giant multi-yoked egg. Bacon, sausage, black pudding, grilled tomatoes, hash browns and mushrooms were all keeping warm in the bottom oven of the Aga. Hot fresh coffee, an industrial-sized pot of tea and jugs of fresh juice had all been set out on one of the kitchen work surfaces. Bread, butter, milk and ketchup huddled in the centre of the table. Ten place settings had been crammed round the table's perimeter.

The atmosphere was still tense from the earlier argument. Evie and Natalie eyeballed each other like boxers across the tureen of baked beans Margaret had placed between them. Great Aunt Ada was already grumbling that the bacon was undercooked and the tea had been left to mash for too long.

'Not everyone likes their bacon cremated, Aunt Ada,' Margaret said. 'Who wants toast?' Her tone was as brisk as her movements. Great Aunt Ada pursed her lips at such an undesirable response but helped herself to several rashers, which she would no doubt pick at and eventually leave. Nick stared at her in disgust.

'Don't know why she's so keen on things being cremated when she's likely to be next,' Dan muttered darkly. He was slumped in his chair, pounding head in his hands. The smell of fried food was making his stomach churn. To keep his mother from nagging he buttered a slice of toast and nibbled at it. Surely his hangover was the worst in history. He spotted a lone empty beer bottle on the side. It was waiting to be placed in the recycling box. 'You're a mean one, Mr Grolsch,' he said, glaring at the bottle as though his hangover was its fault.

Christian, after keeping everyone waiting for twenty minutes, was the last to show at breakfast. His long hair was slicked back from his face with what, ironically, looked like bacon fat, and he was wearing an all-in-one pumpkin-orange romper suit, belted with interlinking gold rings.

'Very Kansas state penitentiary,' Dan said with a twisted smile. As everyone began to load their plates with food those with sharp ears overheard him muttering to Becca that he wasn't sure whether he should slide out of the kitchen with his bum to the wall or ask if Christian would like to trade a bar of Imperial Leather for a packet of B&H.

Natalie said nothing but glowered at her brother. Drawn

by the intensity of her gaze Dan silently considered her. She looked just as composed and polished as she had the previous night with her perfect full face of make-up and newly washed hair falling to her shoulders. She had certainly bagged more bathroom time than anyone else had that morning. Whilst Dan studied her blonde and black hair a thought occurred to him.

'Pull your hair back, like in a ponytail,' he encouraged.

'Why?' Natalie was instantly suspicious.

'Go on, Natbag. I just think it would suit,' Dan said. Despite several misgivings Natalie reached behind her head and pulled her piebald hair into a loose ponytail. As Dan had surmised her hair split into two very definite sections; black at either side of her head with a big, broad, blonde stripe in between.

'I knew it! You look exactly like a skunk,' Dan said with a high-pitched, childish giggle. To Natalie's immense annoyance everyone else appeared to be similarly amused. She eyed her family balefully. Sometimes she hated them all.

'I have to agree with your brother,' Margaret said. 'I don't condone his choice of simile but I do think you've had nicer hairstyles. That two-tone effect makes you look like Cruella de Vil.'

Upon hearing this unflattering comparison Evie didn't even try to contain a loud snort,

'Oh, har har. Why don't you all piss off?' Natalie snapped, her language earning a look of stern disapproval from her father. She let her hair fall back round her shoulders. 'None of you would know style if it hit you with a wet kipper.' Natalie's shrill rattle was exacerbating Dan's hangover. It was no use. He would have to resort to drugs. He excused himself from the table and headed towards the utility. Moments later he returned, a small red box clasped in his shaking hand.

He dropped two co-codamol tablets into a tumbler of

water and watched dolefully as it fizzed and swelled like an ice cream float.

'Cheers,' he said sardonically before downing it with a grimace. His bad head wasn't helped by his omnipresent mobile phone bleeping loudly at irregular intervals to indicate that he had received a text message. This was in between several phone calls that caused his phone to vibrate madly on the table and made everyone jump as his Darth Vader *Imperial Death March* ring tone echoed round the kitchen.

'I still don't understand your obsession with *Star Wars*,' Natalie complained once Dan had finished his call. She pointed to Chewbacca's empty basket. (Chewbacca had taken refuge under the breakfast table in the hope of a forbidden treat materialising from a benevolent hand.) 'I wanted to call him Prince or Strider or something more befitting such a handsome beast but no, you had to name him bloody Chewbacca.' Upon hearing his name Chewbacca popped his head out from beneath the table next to Dan's place setting, his expression expectant.

'Chewie loves his name, don'choo?' Dan ruffled Chewbacca's ears affectionately. Chewbacca looked less than impressed. He had revealed his hiding place for nothing more than a quick pat when he had been hoping for some bacon rind or the end of a sausage. With a grunt of disillusionment he vanished beneath the table once more. Dan, noticing that his father was about to give his 'dogs are not to be fed at the table' speech, deftly changed the subject. 'There was a lad in my halls who was illicitly keeping some unusual pets in his room. The hall president got wind of it and he was kicked out.'

'What did he have?' Becca asked, agog. 'Sounds like it was something ghastly. I can't imagine they'd have been that bothered if it were just a hamster or fish.' She herself had kept a hamster in halls and no one had batted an eyelid.

'It was a baby python, called Hercules, and a tarantula spider named Genghis,' Dan revealed, enjoying the shrieks of horror that greeted this information.

'Ugh! I'd never have set foot in the building again,' Natalie declared. For once both Evie and Becca were in total agreement with their sister. They nodded their heads vehemently. 'He obviously knew what the beast would grow into when he called it Hercules. Honestly, *boys!*' Natalie gave Dan a look of such utter contempt that Becca giggled.

'That's rich. At least I've never seen a boy wearing a beast on his head. Steenky skunk!' Dan snapped.

At this point Margaret decided to intervene. Most people had by now finished their meal and so she began to collect the empty plates. Nick, ever gallant, rose from his feet to load crockery into the dishwasher. With raised eyebrows he noticed that Evie had barely touched her breakfast but said nothing. He chalked the uneaten food up to the fact that India had been fractious throughout the meal. She'd been allowed to open a couple of small presents to keep her occupied whilst everyone slept but this had done nothing but whet her appetite. Now, aware that there was a whole sack full of presents waiting to be opened in the lounge, India was becoming increasingly impatient. There was no way she was going to last through an hour-long church service, Nick thought. He would have very much liked to have backed out of the mandatory Bingham family tradition of Christmas morning family service but Margaret was already banging on about it.

'I expect to see a full complement of Binghams in attendance this morning. No excuses!' she said as she bent over the dishwasher. Her voice echoed eerily around the bowls and plates. 'Especially after the embarrassment of last night. Dan, it might be helpful if you could possibly sing the correct words of the carols today and perhaps sit still for more than five minutes.'

'Why do Christian and I have to attend?' Natalie whined. 'As the only one of your children who didn't either skive or show you up last night I think we should have an opt out.' She then uttered the words that turned her mother ashen. 'I don't even believe in God anyway. All that crap about Adam and Eve and the feeding of the five thousand and the dead being resurrected from the grave. It's all bullshite. Adam was nothing more than a bloody misogynist and Eve was just bored because she didn't have any decent career options.' As she spoke she flicked her eyes towards a cringing Evie. 'I can get on board with the ability to turn water into wine; I can see the benefits of that. As for the loaves and fishes, fancy turning up to such a big event without a packed lunch. How come we don't see 'miracles' like that anymore? I'll tell you why, because it's all fiction borne of some little man's imagination so that centuries of suckers could be duped into giving the church vast stacks of cash.'

'How can you say that?' Margaret gasped. 'Your father and I have brought you up to believe in the Christian faith. You've been confirmed, for goodness' sake. Never have I been more certain that you should attend church. I insist that you come. You must put your faith in the Lord.'

'I'd much rather put my faith in something I believe in, like air traffic control,' Natalie said, carefully selecting the last slice of lightly browned toast after mauling all the others. 'As I see it, it's air traffic control that keeps me safe when I'm in a plane, not God. As for Joseph and Mary having to ride all the way from Nazareth to Bethlehem on a donkey just to pay their bloody taxes… Would have saved everyone a lot of stress and aggro if they'd been able to use a postal system or, even better, just do it online. Bloody Inland Revenue, even in the first century they made things difficult for the average tax payer.'

'Bernard, talk to your daughter,' Margaret commanded. Bernard knew better than to get involved and remained silent, much to his wife's irritation. 'You will attend along with everyone else. I take it I can count on everyone to be present?' It was not so much a question as an order. There followed unanimous acquiescence but little enthusiasm. Nick was still loading the dishwasher, which enabled him to pull a disgruntled face without detection. 'Good! The service starts at ten thirty. I expect everyone to be ready for ten.'

AT FIVE MINUTES past ten Margaret descended the stairs expecting to see all her family obediently waiting for her in the hallway. Not one person was present. At ten fifteen the hall clock gave a solitary chime to herald the quarter hour. Still no one had appeared. Margaret was not amused by her family's procrastination. She had wanted to drift into church with grace and serenity — not with a crimson face and panting like Chewbacca when the neighbour's bitch was in season. Not even Bernard had materialised yet.

'Come on! It's nearly twenty past!' she shrieked up the stairs. She had begun to have visions of them all traipsing down the central aisle causing the vicar to pause mid welcoming address whilst the rest of the villagers sniggered into their song sheets.

Nick trudged down the stairs, India wriggling furiously in his arms, followed by Evie, who looked dishevelled and stressed.

'She's obsessed by the thought of her presents,' Evie explained apologetically. 'I have an awful feeling that she's going to be hell in church.'

'If we ever get there,' Margaret said waspishly. 'Where's your father?'

Evie was wise enough to realise that her mother wasn't aggrieved with her but simply venting her spleen and didn't take it personally.

'He came downstairs about ten minutes ago. I thought he was with you,' she said.

Becca was next to make an appearance, closely followed by Dan, who, despite having eaten a few slices of toast, was still as green as a Norway spruce.

'Oh for God's sake, you are not wearing that to church,' Margaret snapped, pointing at his lapel. Dan had pinned a button badge onto his coat. On it was a picture of Jesus wearing a paper hat and blowing on a party hooter. Beneath him were written the words 'Birthday Boy'. He'd received it on a Christmas card.

Becca was carrying a huge holdall rather than her usual petite handbag. Inside she had stashed her book and the latest issue of *FHM* for Dan so that they would both have something to read during the boring bits.

'Where's your father?' Margaret barked once more. Becca looked taken aback.

'Isn't he with you? He came down ages ago. He had Grandpa and Great Aunt Ada in tow. Perhaps he's outside. Have you checked?' asked Becca. As soon as her mother's back was turned she winked at Dan and patted her bag conspiratorially.

Margaret yanked open the front door to find her absent husband, father-in-law and aunt-in-law all gazing into a container of winter shrubs as though entranced. Bernard was waxing lyrical about the benefits of Miracle-Gro to the soundtrack of the merry ringing of the church's bells drifting over the frosted rooftops. It was debatable which was colder: the freezing air that flooded into the house or the frosty look to which Margaret treated her husband.

'I've been shouting you for ages. You could have bliddy well answered me instead of talking to your bloomin' plants.'

'Sorry love, I didn't hear you. You should have shouted,' Bernard replied blithely. 'Are we all ready? We'll be late if we don't get going soon.' Margaret simply gaped upon hearing this patronising delivery of an all too evident fact. 'Where's Natalie?' Bernard asked as he gave his family a cursory scan.

'*In abstentia,*' Becca said. 'Probably hoping that she'll be forgotten.' Becca had in fact overheard her sister muttering to Christian as they had exited the kitchen earlier that if they dawdled enough they would be left behind and thus be relieved of the whole ghastly chore. She had absolutely no scruples when it came to spragging on Natalie. It made being just that little bit older worthwhile. Better still, her tittle-tattling worked like a charm. Margaret immediately stormed over to the dining room door and hammered on it with a clenched fist.

'Natalie Ruth Bingham. You will come out this minute and you will join your family in church,' she bellowed.

A very sulky Natalie emerged. After shooting Becca a singularly evil look, which confirmed Becca's suspicions that she'd been listening with her ear to the door, she complained that she didn't have her coat or shoes on and suggested that everyone should head off. She and Christian would wander down after them.

'Fat chance,' Dan scoffed and practically threw his own coat at Natalie. 'You can borrow this. I don't mind being cold if it means you'll be in church with us on Christmas morning.' He then treated her to a false, simpering, saccharin smile. Natalie snatched the coat from him in sheer fury. She was still trying to zip up her two hundred pound boots as everyone strode down the drive.

'The gravel will drag the leather off my heels,' she grumbled to no one in particular.

'You should wear some decent shoes, then,' Dan said, grinning as he passed her.

'Nobhead,' Natalie hissed in reply. 'I'll get you and Becca for this.'

'Oo-ooh! I'm scared,' Dan mocked, pretending to be

intimidated. He jogged a few steps to catch up with Becca, Evie and Nick, leaving Natalie chuntering to herself.

Of course, Margaret's attempt to swiftly walk the few hundred metres to church so as not to be later than absolutely necessary was further thwarted by Grandpa complaining that his corns wouldn't enable him to walk any faster than a slow hobble, especially on such an icy surface. Plus his lumbago was giving him gyp. This led to Great Aunt Ada putting in her twopenn'orth, complaining about the fact that Grandpa was complaining. Then she started to add to the collective whinge that the ground was far too slippery underfoot and that she was worried about having a fall.

'At what age do you stop just falling over but instead have 'a fall'?' Dan asked. This set Becca off giggling and even Natalie gave a reluctant grin. Margaret despaired. Why couldn't her family be civilised? At least the church bells hadn't yet ceased which could only be a good thing, she reassured herself.

The church of St Jude's was set back from the village's main thoroughfare, Cherry Tree Avenue. A pretty, picturesque church, it was predominantly of the mediaeval gothic style with some decorated and perpendicular additions for good measure and had a stout, square tower graced by a gold-trimmed blue clock that had been bought by the Parochial Church Council to celebrate Queen Victoria's Diamond Jubilee in 1897. The clock had been recently restored to its former beauty, thanks to some rigorous and enthusiastic fundraising by both the parishioners and the WI. Usually Margaret gazed upon the clock face with a mixture of admiration and smugness, having been one of the principal fundraisers. On this day she merely glanced at it with fleeting relief as her family finally entered the church to discover that the start of the service had been delayed. The vicar was absent and the organist was playing *De Virgin Mary Had A Baby Boy* on repeat by way of entertainment. This gave

Margaret time to gather her thoughts. She took on the personality of a sergeant-major as she spotted an overlooked pew towards the front of the church. She headed towards it with purpose before old Mrs Monk, who lived round the corner and grew the most beautiful pink and blue hydrangeas in her front garden in the summer months, could swoop in and plonk down her ample bottom.

'Evie — you and Nick go right to the end. There's plenty of room for India's pushchair in the outer aisle. I'm relying on you two not to let anyone escape before the end of the service. Becca, you go next. No Dan, you are not sitting next to your sister. I don't trust you. You're sitting next to your father where he can keep an eye on you. That's right, Grandpa, you go in after Becca, then you Christian, Natalie, Aunt Ada… Move it along now. The service must be starting soon and I want to be seated. Whatever is the matter with you, Dan?' Margaret was distracted by her son, who appeared to be trying to communicate with Becca in tic-tac. What she hadn't seen was that he was mouthing 'my magazine, pass us my magazine' whilst gesticulating wildly with his arms. 'Just get in and do sit still. You're holding your father up.' Dan gave Becca a pleading look. Her only response was to shrug her shoulders. There was nothing she could do for him now. Disgruntled, Dan leaned past his father so as to speak to his mother.

'I don't see why we all have to come to church again,' he grumbled. 'Once is bad enough, but twice in two days? It's absolutely ridic. I'm not even a Christian, I follow the Jedi faith.' From his discussions with his friends the previous day he'd ascertained that church attendance was only compulsory in his God-bothering family. Most of his mates would be at that very moment ripping paper off presents and stuffing their faces with cranberry muffins and bucks fizz.

'You be quiet. You're lucky I haven't asked the vicar to lead the congregation in prayers for your deliverance,'

Margaret snapped. If she'd known at that time what had caused the vicar to be delayed she certainly would have carried out her idle threat. 'I wonder why we haven't started yet?' she mused. It was almost ten forty-five and many of the womenfolk in the congregation had started to fret about turkeys overcooking in left-on ovens.

The vicar finally appeared, robes swishing authoritatively as he strode through the church. His wife followed him almost to the altar before sliding into the pew directly in front of the one where the Binghams were seated. She immediately began whispering to her neighbour. Margaret's ears flapped like an African elephant's as she strained to hear.

'My husband is ever so cross about it. It's held us up no end this morning and he's even decided to change his sermon to reflect what's happened,' said the vicar's wife.

What *has* happened? thought Margaret, agog. Alas, the vicar's wife was silenced as the organ player dispensed with *De Virgin Mary* and the local primary school teacher began conducting the Sunday School choir as they embarked on a shrill rendition of *Little Donkey*. It split the congregation. Loving mothers gazed on adoringly whilst those with no personal interest thought they had heard more tuneful fingernails scraping down a blackboard. Glancing down the pew, Becca noticed that Natalie's face was like granite. At last it ended. The vicar stepped up to the altar and thanked a very dishevelled conductor.

'A very good morning to you on this wondrous Christmas Day,' he began. 'It's heartening to see so many of my flock on such a cold, frosty morning.' He dearly wanted to add that most of them could bloody well make the effort to turn up for the other fifty-one Sundays in the year too, but refrained. 'It's doubly pleasing to see so many of you in a time when the importance of faith and Christianity are eclipsed by commercialism and materialism, especially at this time of year. Never before have so few people committed themselves to a lifetime of belief in Christ's goodness as in this day and age. Indeed, for many of us Christmas has come to represent gift-receiving, overindulgence and intemperance rather than its true meaning. It's easy for us to forget that this holiday celebrates the birth of our Lord. Presents and parties should not be at the forefront of our festivities. We must remember what we are celebrating is Christmas — Christ's Mass — as it originates from our saviour Jesus Christ's birth in Bethlehem two thousand years ago. Without Christianity there would be no Christmas—'

'Not strictly true. The Christian faith nicked most of their traditions from the Pagan festival of Yule,' Becca muttered to herself. 'Plus, there's no way Christ was born in a barn in December. More likely he was born in March, according to astrological evidence.' Great Aunt Ada shushed her. Becca's only response was a sarcastic little smile. She was already bored. She made no attempt to be quiet as she rummaged in her bag for her book.

'—I was going to talk about the real spirit of Christmas—'

'The real spirit of Christmas is Drambuie,' Dan whispered to himself.

'—And how it brings us harmony and joy but,' a long pause from the vicar, 'due to unforeseen circumstances occurring last night I have felt the need to revise my sermon today. Instead I intend to tackle the downside of this holiday season. What downside can there possibly be? I hear you ask. Well, I can tell you—'

'Oh yes, please do,' Becca muttered from within the pages of the latest Marian Keyes.

'Great, a lecture,' said Natalie, simultaneously. Even India was emitting intermittent whinges of complaint.

'Excess. Excess is what makes us weak at Christmas. It surrounds us. We see an excess of expense in the shops, an excess of food on our festive tables, an excess of inappropriate behaviour at our Christmas parties and of course, the worst culprit of all, an excess of alcohol.'

Dan suddenly felt uncomfortable. He shuffled in his seat until his mother prodded him in the ribs.

'In this age of street violence, antisocial behaviour and vandalism there has never before been so great a need for temperance.' Even Natalie was astonished to see Great Aunt Ada sagely nodding her head in agreement, the bloody old hypocrite! 'We read in the papers of inner city youths stealing and mugging for drug money, we hear of school children stealing cars and causing death and carnage by racing through the residential areas of our towns. Are we exempt from such crimes in our peaceful little village? I think not. Even in our own delightful community—' the vicar smiled ingratiatingly at his flock. Most of them obediently beamed back. 'Even in this village we are not immune to such occurrences. It is with great sadness that I must report, on this holiest of mornings—'

'Wasn't that what he said about Easter Sunday?' Becca asked Nick in an undertone. Nick gave a vague shrug. His focus was on Evie, who was desperately trying to entertain India.

'—That last night, on Christmas Eve, an unknown perpetrator trespassed onto church property and, with no regard for respect or dignity, desecrated several graves.'

A gasp of horror echoed round the rafters.

'Yes,' the vicar nodded earnestly. 'It is truly dreadful. The tombs of our beloved departed were trampled on, leaving footprints on the turf and dislodging the flowers that had been lovingly left in Christmas remembrance. I'm certain that the villain was under the influence of alcohol as he left us an unholy gift of vomit down the side of the church wall which, as you all know, our community raised a great deal of money to have sandblasted to its former glory.'

Muted exclamations of shock and disbelief could be heard round the church.

'Rather like a Mexican rumble of outrage,' Nick whispered to Becca, who had to bite her lip to stop herself giggling. For the first time in fifteen minutes she sat her book down on her lap. Dan could feel his temperature fluctuating between hellishly hot and chillingly cold. Becca had assured him that his puke wouldn't be found and he'd believed her. This was a nightmare. It was only a matter of time before his mother twigged then he'd be for the chop. He'd be lucky to see in the New Year.

'Whoever this person was, he proved he had no consideration for this church, this village or any of its parishioners. It is the most heinous of crimes.'

At this point Becca gave an involuntary snort of derision that turned out to be more audible than she expected. As all heads turned accusingly towards the Binghams she herself turned towards Christian and gave him a look of disgust. He was an outsider; let him take the rap. Accusatory eyes swivelled to Christian, who looked horrified.

'It wasn't me,' he protested loudly and with genuine indignation. It was all Becca could do not to giggle. She dare not look at Nick, whose shoulders had begun to shake.

The vicar pointedly ignored the interruption and continued to rant. 'I urge you to seek out this person so they can be prayed for, and shamed as is their due.' He was clearly taking no prisoners but, as most of the villagers appreciated a good militant approach to wrongdoing, he managed not to offend anyone. 'On a more pleasant note, we must all offer our thanks to my good wife and her... err... wonderful mother,' the vicar's eyes twitched slightly at this glowing testimony to a mother-in-law he only tolerated because the Bible told him to. 'Between them they managed to rectify all the damaged caused.' An unenthusiastic round of applause followed. The vicar's wife simpered as she took a half-bow in her pew. The vicar then proceeded to pontificate about the evils of drink. Despite Evie's frantic attentions, India began to grizzle. Becca returned to her book whilst both Dan and Grandpa snoozed with their heads on their chests. They were woken with a start by the opening bars of the next carol.

After everyone had had a good sing there followed the Sunday School nativity, which was performed by the same motley crew that had sung earlier. It was an amateur production and consisted of homemade sets, makeshift costumes, forgotten lines, bad singing and a factually correct brown Tiny Tears doll as the baby Jesus, which had been wrapped in a vast white sheet that had *Property of Loxley Diocese* emblazoned on its side for all to see.

'Shouldn't that read *Bethlehem Hilton*?' Dan said, too loudly. Margaret stared at her feet. Why did her family have to embarrass her at every opportunity? Sniggers could be heard from the front rows. The Sunday school teacher was frantically gesturing for 'Mary' to turn the baby round, but the little girl didn't understand what was happening and began to cry out of sheer fright. Those with children of their own felt themselves welling up with sympathetic tears whilst everyone else wiped their eyes with laughter.

'Aren't they adorable?' Margaret said to Dan as the children began to sing *Away in a Manger*.

'Whatever,' replied Dan, not impressed. He thought the entire proceedings were absolute bollocks and couldn't wait to go home and open his presents. An early scan of the church had confirmed that the pretty bartender from the pub wasn't there, which meant that his presence in church was an utter and absolute waste of time. Thank God there would only be prayers and a couple more carols left.

If Dan was fed up with being in church then so was Evie. She was sick and tired of Nick commenting on how cute the 'little ones' were. Talk about sledgehammering his point home. She bloody well wished she were at home. She had a sudden, overwhelming urge to confide in her mother about the pressure Nick was heaping on her. Worse still, she felt rotten. Her head was pounding and she was developing a painful sore throat. Not only that, India had begun to play up to such a degree that Evie was seriously close to losing her rag. Heads were beginning to turn. She too was hoping that the vicar wouldn't linger over prayers when India began to scream in earnest. Evie wanted to crawl under the pew and hide. None of the usual tricks — toys and sweets — were working to calm the little girl.

'Why is she doing this to me?' Evie hissed at Nick. Nick didn't know what to say. People were beginning to stare. The final straw came when India's screaming caused the vicar to lose his place in the Lord's Prayer and the whole congregation, who had been dutifully chanting along, ground to a sticky halt and looked around blankly.

'For God's sake, Nick, take her out before I bloody kill her!' Evie shrilled, perfectly clear in the silence. She then dropped her burning head into her hands — she desperately needed some painkillers — whilst all her family stared in amazement. It was so unlike Evie to be so brittle, even in the face of India's tantrum.

In response, Nick scooped up his daughter and rammed her into her pushchair.

'So sorry,' he repeated over and over again as he wheeled her out. Once the doors had clicked shut the vicar continued with prayers. Evie, still seated, was now scarlet with mortification.

The remainder of the service passed in a blur and the next thing Evie knew she was standing outside the church waiting for her family. She couldn't even remember standing up and walking out. Nick was nowhere to be seen. Evie presumed he was wheeling the fractious India round the village. From inside she could hear a jazzed-down version of *Saviour's Day* being played. She wished someone would come and save her.

As though in answer to her prayers Becca appeared at her side.

'You okay?' she asked. Evie gave a wan smile.

'I feel like I'm swallowing razorblades and I've got a stinking headache,' she said. 'At least it's nice and cool out here.' The cold air was wonderfully cooling on her hot cheeks. Becca gaped at her.

'Cool? It's bloody freezing,' she said. She laid a hand against Evie's forehead. It was boiling. 'You're definitely coming down with something. I'm telling Mum.'

'I'm fine. There's no need to worry Mum. She'll only fuss and flap. It's just a cold. Although I think I'm seizing up,' Evie said, gingerly rolling her head to ease her stiffening neck and shoulder muscles. Around her she could hear everyone speculating on the 'vandalism' of the church. If she heard the words 'isn't it dreadful?' one more time she'd scream. It was just a bit of Christmas cheer after all, plus she had a damned good idea who the 'vandal' was. If her hunch was right, and Dan had been the culprit, then she herself was partly responsible as she'd been the one who'd sent him to midnight mass in the first place. That was something she was going to keep to herself if possible. Maybe she should have kept him at home where he couldn't get up to any mischief.

'Ey-up, here comes Ma Bingham,' Becca warned as her mother advanced on them. Like Evie, Becca also hoped that her mother wasn't going to bring up the subject. She was in luck. Her mother was preoccupied with thoughts of Christmas lunch now that her religious duties had been fulfilled.

'There's lots to do when we get home, girls,' she said heartily. 'Lunch to prepare.' Becca pulled a face. Evie said nothing. The only thing she'd be doing was letting India open her sodding presents so that she might just get some peace for the remainder of the day. She must be a terrible mother, she thought glumly, as all she really wanted to do was climb back into bed and sleep.

MARGARET GAZED AT THE SKY, which was slowly turning from sunny blue to muted white as she hurried home. 'The sky's changing colour. We might get a white Christmas yet.'

'Wouldn't it be marvellous if we got snowed in?' Becca enthused, thinking of her scheduled return to work on the twenty-seventh. 'If we get a decent amount then Loxley Road will be completely impassable.' She linked arms with Evie as they began to walk home. They could see Nick turning the pushchair into the driveway of Magpie Cottage ahead of them.

'That's not the attitude to take,' Margaret said, reading Becca's mind. Keen to avoid a lecture, Becca changed the subject.

'Evie's not well. She has a sore throat and a hot head,' she said.

'Mebbe it's tinsel-itis,' Dan said, striding past them. God, he needed a glass of water. And following that mebbe a glass of wine…?

Becca's ploy worked like a charm. Margaret began to flap round Evie and, as soon as they were all back at home, she dragged her eldest into the kitchen. Evie scowled at Becca and Natalie who, having been subpoenaed to help, were trailing unenthusiastically after their mother. She was cross with Becca for dropping her in it and with Natalie, well, just for being Natalie.

After a cursory check on the birds in the oven, Margaret began rooting in one of the kitchen cupboards. She handed Evie a tumbler half filled with soluble aspirin. Evie grimaced, but accepted the glass.

'It's no use pulling faces, young lady. You need to gargle

with that, and no spitting out.' Margaret propelled her to a chair. 'It's just like when you were all children. I could bank on one of you being poorly on Christmas Day. It's almost become a family tradition.'

Natalie was suddenly consumed by a memory of a Christmas many years ago when she'd been so sick that she'd been banished to the settee with a plaid blanket and a bucket by her side whilst the rest of her family had been enjoying Christmas lunch in the dining room. Just when she thought everyone had forgotten her, Evie had appeared with her own dinner on a tray and the two of them had sat and watched *Mary Poppins* on the television. It was one of the happiest Christmas memories Natalie had. Only Evie had bothered to remember that Natalie might be lonely in the lounge all by herself and had foregone her own family Christmas lunch to keep her baby sister company. She, Natalie, must only have been seven at the time. Evie would have been sixteen. Warmed by the memory in the midst of such a frosty atmosphere, Natalie smiled at Evie. Evie glowered back. She hadn't forgotten Natalie's tirade of earlier that morning, nor was she prepared to be forgiving. Snubbed, Natalie stormed out of the kitchen. Becca dithered for a few moments then also fled.

Traitors, Evie thought to herself sourly. At least it had given her five minutes alone with her mother. She seized the chance to speak to her.

'Have you got a minute, Mum? I really need to ask your advice about something,' she said. Margaret smiled at her vaguely.

'Will it wait, darling? I really need to get on. Don't worry yourself about it now. I'm sure you can cope with whatever it is until after Christmas.'

'Why do I always have to be the one who copes?' Evie snapped. 'Becca just goes to pieces and Natalie strops. I'm fed up with being the strong one.' Fed up with being everything to everyone else rather than being allowed to just be herself, and at the same annoyed at being dismissed so casually, Evie scraped back her chair and stomped out of the kitchen leaving her mother gaping after her.

'Well, I suppose we'd better get some presents opened,' Margaret said with mock merriment to an empty kitchen. She loaded up a tray with bottles of champagne and a large jug of Florida orange juice.

Dosed up to capacity, Evie slumped in an armchair in the lounge. From within the kitchen came the merry pop of a champagne cork. The thought of booze made her feel sick.

All the other Binghams were already waiting impatiently in the lounge. Dan and Chewbacca were sprawled out on the rug in front of the fire. Natalie, Christian and Great Aunt Ada were all squashed onto the sofa whilst Bernard and Grandpa were sitting comfortably in the two good armchairs. Behind them, the Christmas tree lights twinkled. Nick was sitting on the floor feeding India chocolate buttons to keep her quiet. Two unwrapped presents lay by his feet. Evie heaved herself out of the armchair and picked her way through the mass of presents that covered the floor and plonked herself down next to her husband. She couldn't even be bothered to complain about the fact that India's freshly laundered Monsoon dress was already streaked with melted chocolate. In the corner the television was showing a programme about Christmas choirs, with the carols subtitled and a round, holly-topped Christmas pudding bouncing along in time with the words, but no one was paying it any attention. Margaret bustled in carrying the tray laden with the bucks fizz, mince pies, Christmas cake and cranberry muffins. Becca ordered into the dining room and returned brandishing long-stemmed glasses. At the thought of more food both Dan and Evie groaned.

'Come on everybody, tuck in,' Margaret encouraged. She began to pour glasses of bucks fizz for everyone. Dan, having decided that the hair of the dog was the only way to combat his hangover, reached for a glass. Evie declined the champagne and settled for straight juice, thinking it might ease her throat.

'Easy on the orange juice, Margaret,' Great Aunt Ada commanded, eyes gleaming. She almost snatched the glass from Margaret's hand.

Once everyone had been allocated a drink there then began the usual mass exchange of gifts. Toiletries, clothes, CDs, Blu-rays, selection boxes and books were all unwrapped accompanied by oohs and ahhs of delight. Great Aunt Ada, watching everyone opening their gifts with disapproving eyes, embarked on her annual lecture about the scandalous expense of Christmas and how she'd received one tangerine and a bag of nuts in her stocking when she was a child, and that was if she were lucky.

'Not surprised, if she was as unpleasant then as she is now,' Dan muttered to Evie. 'I wouldn't give her a bag of soot. Tatty old witch.' He had in fact given his great aunt a book called *The Giant Book of Insults,* telling her as he'd handed it over that he was sure she'd find it of great use. It had not been received in good humour. Not caring one jot, Dan swapped his bucks fizz for a can of beer and began to concentrate on his own pile of gifts. Becca, having disappeared for a few minutes, returned with a selection of wrapped gifts and, to everyone's amazement, plonked them by Christian's feet.

'Some presents for you to open, Christian. We can't have you sitting there twiddling your thumbs,' she said. Natalie looked at her with narrowed eyes but said nothing. Only after Christian had opened a couple of gifts that had clearly been intended for Gregory did she decide to speak.

'I guess you've given up on a reconciliation seeing as you're giving away the presents that you so lovingly bought for Gregory,' she said. She turned to Christian, who at least had the decency to look embarrassed. 'How do you like charity, babe? I know that CD was meant for Becca's ex. It's his favourite band.'

'So?' Dan snapped. 'Jolly nice of Bec to be so generous to your boyfriend after you've been so mean to her.' Becca was mortified. How could Natalie expose her like that when her only intention had been to be kind? Was it so bad that the gifts had originally been bought for her ex? At least this way they would go to a good home instead of languishing at the bottom of her wardrobe all year, a cruel reminder of a Christmas ruined.

To divert all the attention from Becca's scarlet face, Bernard and Margaret presented Grandpa with his gift, which was a shiny silver Sky+ digibox for his little house. 'You'll never miss *Countryfile* again.' Not to be outdone, Natalie's gift to her parents was a comprehensive collection of all the shows she had worked on, on Blu-ray.

'We don't have a Blu-ray player,' Bernard said, confused.

'You do now,' Natalie said triumphantly. 'The latest model in region free, fully programmable, re-recordable DVD and Blu-ray players is being delivered here on the day after Boxing Day.'

'Cor!' said Dan, his eyes gleaming. Natalie grimaced at him.

'It's not for you.' She turned to her mother. 'It's not for Dan to hog.'

'What's a blurry player?' Grandpa asked. Everyone laughed except Great Aunt Ada whose mouth had puckered up tighter than Ramesses' bum.

'I don't see the point of all these newfangled recording gadgets,' she said. 'In my day there was a choice of three channels and if you missed something, tough.'

'Ah, but that was in the days of Methuselah,' said Dan. His mother hissed at him to be quiet whilst she distracted Great Aunt Ada with a miniature bottle of Cointreau.

'Who was Methuselah?' said Evie, her face blank.

'Noah's grandfather,' Becca said. 'Lived to the age of nine hundred and sixty-nine.'

'Bleedin' Christ! Let's hope Great A.A. doesn't do the same,' Dan said. He had begun flicking through Natalie's Blu-rays with idle interest.

'Your optimism is misplaced,' said Becca, under her breath. 'The terrible old bugger will outlive us all.'

Nick had to stare out of the window so that no one would see him savaging his lip in an attempt not to snort with laughter.

'Couldn't you have got them a few decent films to watch instead of all this tripe?' Dan asked Natalie, having thoroughly inspected the Blu-rays.

'Oh, shut up,' Natalie snapped. Why did Dan have to constantly take the piss? Dan smirked as he took in Natalie's furious expression. He considered how like Great Aunt Ada she looked when she was aggrieved. He gave Nick a crafty nudge and nodded his head towards his great aunt and his sister.

'Always two there are, ye-e-es. Always a master and an apprentice has the Sith,' he muttered. Nick snorted at Dan's accurate observation. On his other side, Evie was frantically gesturing and pointing at the bags of gifts she and Nick had brought.

Evie had agonised long and hard about her choice of gift for her parents. Eventually, in an attempt to not seem self-obsessed, she had elected India to be the giver instead. It was a small oil painting of her and India curled up on the sofa at home.

'Nick made me do a duplicate for him,' she said, blushing. 'It's taken from a photograph he took of us in summer.'

'I'm not surprised. It's beautiful,' Bernard said. 'My wonderfully talented Evelyn.' Evie felt a stab of discomfort as Becca's face fell. Dan didn't seem to care. Not surprisingly,

Natalie looked most put out at being usurped by bloody Evie, yet again. Matters were made worse by her mother reaching for her hanky.

'I've never received such a wonderful, wonderful present in all my life,' she sniffed.

'My turn next,' Natalie said, whipping a pile of elaborately wrapped gifts from under the tree. She doled them out. Evie, Becca and Nick each received reasonably decent gifts but Dan pulled out some hideous socks and pants plus a plain red tee shirt out of the paper.

'I chose it specially to match the colour of your eyes,' Natalie said with an acidic smile.

'No expense spent, eh?' Dan said sarkily. He chucked the tee shirt to one side dismissively. 'Come on, somebody give me summat decent to open.' He looked expectantly at his parents.

Great Aunt Ada opened her gift from Natalie. It was two litre bottles of best Plymouth Gin accompanied by a pair of beautiful Waterford Crystal tumblers in a midnight blue velvet lined presentation pack. Natalie's gift, thoughtful as it was and perfect for such an irredeemable old lush as Great Aunt Ada, made her father raise his eyebrows and her mother purse her lips in disapproval.

Natalie then presented Grandpa with a beautifully wrapped box that made his eyes gleam. After seeing the thoughtful, expensive present Natalie had given his sister he couldn't be blamed for believing that he too was about to receive something marvellous. It was therefore even more heartbreaking for Evie, Becca and Dan when he ripped off the wrapping to reveal a medium sized box of Trill. To add insult, one of the corners had been bashed in.

'That must be for Vera Lynn,' Evie said. Her voice was jovial but inside her heart sank. From the corner of her eye she noticed that her father had stopped unwrapping the gift that Margaret had lovingly given him and was instead watching the proceedings with intent.

'No, that's Grandpa's present,' said Natalie. 'He complained last year that we all buy each other frivolities, so this year I've bought him something useful.'

'You are a bitch beyond description,' Dan said. Like his two eldest sisters, he was upset by the look of disappointed understanding on his grandfather's face as he held the box in his hands. At the same time his mouth was working, moving quickly up and down so that his grey moustache looked like it was bouncing on his top lip. His dismay at what Natalie had done was only equalled by his apparent distress. The room was steeped with tension.

'Natalie. Kitchen. Now!' said Bernard, rising to his feet. Evie and Becca exchanged knowing glances. They knew that tone. Evidently Natalie was in for the bollocking of a lifetime.

'Here's another one for you, Grandpa.' Dan had leaped to his feet and shoved a parcel that looked like it had been wrapped by a lunatic with a Sellotape fetish into his grandfather's shaking hands. The comparison between it and Natalie's beautifully wrapped gift was ironic, to say the least. 'Believe me, it's better than this insult.' He whipped the box of Trill out of his grandfather's hands and carelessly flung it over his left shoulder as one would spilt salt. His gift was a boxset of ten Nazi-ass-whupping war books together with a huge jar of his grandpa's favourite boiled sweets. 'Something to remind you of the glory days,' he quipped. Grandpa smiled. He and Dan had always had a good connection borne of the fact that they both had a bitch of a sister to contend with.

'Well done, Daniel,' Margaret said, looking at her beloved son with such fond pride that Becca pretended to gag. Evie propelled India forward.

'Go and give Great-Grandpa his present, darling,' she said.

She pressed a large square gift into India's hands and watched her toddle dutifully over to the old man. Inside was a big, garish book containing a collection of photographs of birds of paradise. The front cover depicted a parrot that bore an uncanny resemblance to Vera Lynn. Once Becca presented him with a couple of newly digitally remastered Vera Lynn CDs and Evie and Nick had unveiled the new bird cage for the other, more foul-mouthed Vera Lynn, Grandpa looked much happier. By this time Natalie and Bernard had returned from the kitchen. Natalie looked furious and her eyes were reddened. Bernard still seemed tense. At least the mood was lifted when Nick opened his gift from Dan — a compact disc compilation of X-rated Christmas songs collectively called *A Very Blue Christmas*, which included tracks entitled *Holy Shit, It's Christmas!*, *Merry Fucking Christmas* and *Happy Holidays, You Bastard*. Everyone roared with laughter.

'We must listen to it,' Becca squealed as she read the tracklisting.

'Not whilst India is around, please,' Evie said. 'She has enough bad habits already without her learning how to swear.'

'Oh, *India*,' Natalie said under her breath. She was sick and tired of hearing about her sister's progeny. Anyone would think she was the second coming, the way they all went on. She was just an ordinary child. A noisy, smelly, messy child. Natalie topped up her glass of bucks fizz and downed it in one. Her father was still frowning at her. She was thoroughly pissed off with this Christmas. Roll on the New Year.

On the other side of the room, Evie was marvelling that Dan had managed to do all his Christmas shopping without having left the house once.

'I did all my shopping on the internet,' Dan explained as he cracked open yet another can. 'Everything was delivered to my front door. Minimum effort and fuss, maximum saving of my time, money and energy, plus everyone gets a fun gift to play with. Everyone's a winner, baby. I then used the wrapping paper that Mum bought for herself and married that with a generous self-helping of those homemade tags that she makes by cutting up last year's cards. Sorted.'

'So, that's where they all went,' Margaret said wryly. 'I thought I'd hidden them away from your thieving paws.'

'Not well enough,' Dan said happily. 'I didn't even bother with cards this year. I'm a poor student now. I can't afford stamps.'

'You're so cheap,' Natalie sneered. Dan pulled a face at his sister.

'Sez you,' he said. 'Oh look, Grandpa's asleep already. Isn't he ahead of schedule? He doesn't normally conk out until after the Queen's speech. Speaking of which, we haven't picked our colours for our customary sweep yet. I call aquamarine.'

'Pants, I wanted that,' Becca said. Instead she opted for peach. Each year the entire family nominated a colour as their prediction of the colour the Queen would be wearing for her annual address to the nation. Traditionally there was no stake but the winner was exempted from clearing up after Christmas lunch. It had always been a popular game.

'Primrose,' Nick said.

'Ha ha! You lose, sucker. She wore primrose last year,' Becca scoffed, high-fiving Dan.

'Rose for me, please,' said Evie with a tight smile. She was trying her very best to be jolly.

'I'll have lilac, please, Daniella,' Natalie chipped in. Getting out of chores was something she very firmly believed in. Christian, mistakenly believing that he would be excused from kitchen chores on the grounds that he was a guest in the house, refused to participate. He personally thought it was unutterably silly but dare not say so.

'I haven't got time for this nonsense,' Margaret said, standing up. Everyone gaped at her. She was normally such a keen participant. 'I've a Christmas lunch to cook, although if the Queen is wearing pistachio I won't be cleaning up once you gannets have eaten it all. Any help with preparation would be greatly appreciated should there be any volunteers.' No one spoke. All gazes were concentrated on the floor to prevent eye contact. The silence was only broken when Grandpa, still deep in slumber, let rip with a long, wet fart that made Great Aunt Ada look up in disgust. Dan sniggered like a schoolboy in chapel.

'Was that you? You rude little imp,' Great Aunt Ada snapped at him although she knew full well who the perpetrator had been. There was no humour in her accusation.

'No, it bloomin' well wasn't,' said Dan. He then began to warm to his theme. After all, farts were one of his favourite subjects for discussion. 'Although, there's no shame in a good fart. Some nutritionists claim that a healthy body should guff twenty-five times a day and that each time you suppress one you're poisoning your own body. In fact, each fart adds an extra ten minutes onto your life.'

'That can't be true. I've never heard of it,' Becca said. Natalie flashed her a look that plainly said 'of course, if you've never heard of it then it can't possibly be true'.

'If it is then Dan and Nick'll both live forever,' Evie commented, not without bitterness. 'Especially Nick. He's capable of offenders that are so long they'd add a full half hour at a time.' Becca, Dan and Nick all grinned. Even Margaret had to suppress a small smile even if she didn't approve of the topic of conversation.

'What about those around you, though?' Natalie complained. 'You might be adding hours onto your own life but all those toxic gases are whittling everybody else's away. We're the ones suffering because of your filthy habit.'

'What like? Passive farting?' Dan laughed.

'I've always maintained you should come with a

government warning,' Natalie hissed. As usual, her bantering contained genuine venom.

'Mebbe we should slap a sticker on your arse that says 'Farting Kills',' Becca giggled.

'Only if we slap one on Natalie's mouth that says 'Toxic Waste',' said Dan.

'What a charming topic of conversation,' Great Aunt Ada snapped. 'Margaret, you should really try to control your children better. Honestly, they're just like their grandmother was. No couth whatsoever.'

'Oh, get bent,' Dan muttered under his breath. Fortunately no one heard him.

'I think I'll nominate some help for the kitchen simply to prevent any further arguments,' Margaret said, deciding to intervene. 'Becca, Natalie, I've plenty of chores for you both. Evie, love, you stay there. You look like you're about to faint. Bernard, could you bear to give me a hand?'

'Oh, but *The Great Escape* has just begun,' Bernard protested, remote clutched in his hand. His expression was the very epitome of dismay.

'Sod you, then. Anyone would think you'd never seen the film before,' Margaret said crossly. 'Honestly Bernard, you know the story better than the scriptwriters. Come on, girls.'

Margaret wasn't in the mood for any dilly-dallying and, once in the kitchen, ordered her two middle children about like a schoolmistress. Whilst she dealt with the main course, Becca peeled cling film off nine luscious smoked salmon tians that had been chilling in the fridge. Boo and Hiss, having identified the whiff of fish, began to weave round her legs, both mewing piteously. Even Ramesses lifted his head and sniffed the air although he didn't bother moving as he was old and wise enough to realise that any leftovers would be coming his way. Natalie was dispatched to the conservatory to lay the table. As she walked through the lounge she was most put out to discover that her family weren't watching *The*

Great Escape after all but the most recent *Harry Potter* film. She could be heard clattering the cutlery onto the table in anger over the opening bars of the famous theme tune.

Dan, who was ramming illicit segments of Chocolate Orange down his throat bellowed at her to be quiet.

'Shut up, woman! We can't hear the telly with all that racket going on.' He then moved on to the Quality Street and was studying the tin. 'Ha! Get this. Hazelnut Whirl — May Contain Nuts. No shit!'

Christian, having been abandoned by Natalie, was seated next to a grumbling, half cut Great Aunt Ada on the sofa. In the first instance he was dischuffed because not only did she reek of booze but also that she hadn't ceased to chain-smoke Park Drive fags in over an hour. If she continued at this rate he'd end up kippered. It didn't help that the *Harry Potter* film brought back unpleasantly truthful memories. It reminded him that he had auditioned for the role of 'Sixth Former #5' but had been so ineptly wooden that the casting director had unceremoniously told him to bugger off. He was thankful when Margaret announced that Christmas lunch was served.

As the family filed into the conservatory Nick pulled his wife to one side.

'Are you all right? You look ghastly,' he asked. It hadn't escaped his notice that Evie appeared to have been deteriorating all morning.

'I feel so ill,' Evie confessed. 'I'm trying to soldier on but my head hurts, my neck is stiff, my throat is sore.' Her eyes filled with tears that she quickly brushed away.

'Why don't you go and have a lie down? I can manage India,' Nick said. He always hated to see Evie in pain.

'I couldn't do that to Mum. I'll get through lunch then I'll go to bed, I promise,' Evie said. Her mother was bringing through a tray of starters. She'd made such a big effort to make Christmas special for everyone and Evie couldn't bring herself to let her mother down. There had already been enough problems, what with Becca's heartbreak, Dan's drinking, Great Aunt Ada's cantankerousness and Christian's eating habits. Evie was keen not to cause her mother further concern, especially as Christmas lunch was her *pièce de résistance*. Nick wasn't convinced. It was his personal opinion that Evie needed rest. She was so pale she was positively ghostly. However, he was more than aware of how stubborn Evie could be and, even though he didn't like her decision, he knew he would have to accept it.

Another person who wasn't happy was Natalie. Only when everyone was seated and the starters were being handed out did she remember that she couldn't eat her mother's delicious salmon starter in front of Christian without blowing her vegetarian cover. Nor could she clandestinely eat it later as her mother whipped her plate away from her and proceeded to split it three ways for the cats. Instead Natalie was presented with an unappetising plate of wheat-free crackers and tofu pâté. To make matters worse Dan kept grinning at her from across the table. He was making himself unpopular by continually tapping the keys on his phone with all the skill of the most accomplished touch typist as he constantly messaged his friends and posted to his various social media networks until Margaret lost her temper.

'For God's sake, Dan, will you put that contraption down before I'm forced to confiscate it!'

The cats had a further treat as they also received the remains of Evie's barely touched salmon. Evie hadn't wanted to tell her mother that the salmon's fishy smell was making her feel nauseous. She was feeling so poorly that she didn't realise her lack of appetite had started to elicit raised eyebrows and exchanged glances.

A luscious main course followed a frantic five minutes as everyone scrabbled for the potatoes, vegetables and trimmings. Arms criss-crossed the table. Once again, Evie picked at her food whilst Natalie, fobbed off with a plate of veg and a slice of nut roast, stared obsessively at her sister's leftovers like a slavering dog. She couldn't even have gravy as it had been made with the juice from the two turkeys. Instead she had to make do with vegetarian stock granules that were no match for her mother's thick, meaty, golden gravy.

Dan, having found the hair of the dog singularly effective in shifting his hangover, rediscovered his appetite and managed to eat second helpings of everything, which made Natalie panic that there wouldn't be any leftovers for her to pinch later. Predictably, Great Aunt Ada found fault with everything but Margaret was so used to her whinging that she paid no attention.

Full plates were emptied and shipped back to the kitchen only to be replaced by dessert bowls. Margaret's homemade plum pudding triggered gasps of amazement as it was carried to the table surrounded by a halo of blue flame. It was declared sublime. Proceedings temporarily ground to a halt at three o'clock when the TV was turned on so that everyone could watch the Queen's speech. Everyone rushed into the lounge, more interested in her outfit than the speech itself. Dan won the sweep and then proceeded to grin and gloat until everyone became fed up and told him to knock it off. His mother told him that if he said 'won, I have, ye-e-e-es' once more she would retract the deal and leave him to deal with the pots solo. The cheeseboard was brought in. Stripped of his amusement Dan proceeded to mock Natalie in earnest. He was still so cross with her for so wantonly upsetting Grandpa that morning that he'd been subtly goading her for the duration of Christmas lunch by calling her names and slyly revealing some less attractive aspects of her personality to Christian. After Dan had called her Natbag one time too many, Natalie eventually cracked.

'It was Dan who taught Vera Lynn to say 'fucksake',' Natalie said as she coated a cream cracker with vegetarian pâté. (She was still hungry — the nut roast had done nothing to fill her up.) Her smile was nothing less than angelic. 'He also taught her to say 'frig me sideways' and 'fat arse'.' Her words were greeted by a stunned silence.

'I don't think that 'fucksake' is actually a word, in the strictest sense,' Becca said, hoping to diffuse the tension. Her attempt failed miserably.

'Natalie only pretends to be a vegetarian whilst she's around you,' Dan said, addressing Christian. 'One of her favourite things is a Big Mac with a side of six Chicken McNuggets.' He knew revealing that Natalie was not only a meat eater and a liar but also that she had consciously supported such a capitalist establishment as McDonald's would lose her some serious brownie points in Christian's eyes. 'And she sneakily ate my plate of casserole last night, the greedy cow. Vegetarian, my arse!' Natalie was so furious with Dan that she hurled the tofu pâté–laden cream cracker at him. It impacted with his chest with a splat and scattered crumbs all over Margaret's newly mopped floor.

'It was darling Daniel who threw up outside church on Christmas Eve,' Natalie hissed in retaliation. Their mother gave a gasp of horror.

'Natalie lied to the vicar during Communion. *To his face!*'

'Natalie, how could you?' Margaret said. She looked appalled.

'You think that's bad? Grandpa found copies of two titty mags called *Swank* and *Brave Nude World* in Dan's bedroom, so Dan told him that they were part of a college project to keep him quiet. Don't look so surprised, Mum. He's got loads of porn, including a video called *Cocks and Throbbers* that he taped over *Midsomer Murders* and watches whilst you're out playing bridge,' Natalie yelled. 'Think about that the next time you go round clearing up his used tissues.' Bernard choked on his food. Margaret looked scandalised and was heard to whisper the words 'my little boy—'

'Can we please not discuss this now?' Evie pleaded. She was ignored.

'Nat has a rabbit fur scarf that she likes to pretend is synthetic to ease her conscience,' Dan retaliated. Natalie's mouth formed a perfect but silent 'O'. Christian continued to stare at Natalie as if she were a stranger.

'I caught Dan with a doobie last summer,' Natalie yelled. 'And he has a bong in his room that he *claims* is an antique candlestick. Where do you think all Grandpa's Rizlas have been disappearing to? Dan's nothing but a common little druggie.'

'Daniel, is this true?' Bernard asked, his expression solemn. Dan didn't have the temerity to lie to his father's face so instead he refrained from comment. 'Well?'

'Natalie's a bitch. Oh wait, that's hardly a revelation,' Dan said with the utmost sarcasm.

'I really don't think this is the time—' Evie said, trying to butt in. Natalie turned to her, her face a mask of malevolence having not forgotten her bollocking of earlier and blaming the seemingly perfect Evie for everything.

'And you can pipe down. You're in no position to pass any judgements.'

'Natalie—' Becca said, warningly. She was horrifically aware of the direction in which the conversation had veered.

'No, Becca, let's tell everyone all about the precious secret Evie's been keeping. All about how she's planning to bugger off to the States for a year just so she can paint pretty pictures, leaving her husband and daughter behind to fend for themselves and how her marriage is in tatters from all the strain.'

Nick's head whipped round to look at his wife with the speed of a mutant but he didn't speak. He didn't need to. The accusatory look of betrayal on his face said it all.

'Is this true? Evie?' Margaret asked, her face ashen. Evie

stared back, not knowing what to say. Becca had no such reservations.

'You utter bitch!' Becca spat at Natalie. 'You were told that in confidence.'

'Did you all know?' Margaret said, still aghast. 'All of you but me?'

Dan raised his hand, as though he were still at school. 'I didn't,' he sing-songed, smiling smugly.

'Shut up, shut up. Just shut up!' There was a split second of silence as everyone turned to face Evie. She had pushed her chair back and had stood up. She appeared to be shaking. She then crashed to the ground in a dead faint.

Nick was by Evie's side in an instant. India was left screaming in her high chair.

'Are you all happy now? She's been sickening for days and none of you noticed. I told her she should go to bed but she wouldn't listen,' he said. He checked the back of her head for injuries. There were none. Chairs scraped across the floor as everyone craned to see. 'I'm taking her up. Margaret, call your doctor. I want her checking over.' With that Nick hoisted Evie into his arms and staggered out of the conservatory. Margaret flapped around behind him, panicked by her daughter's collapse.

Twenty minutes later Evie was asleep in bed having been force fed a copious amount of analgesics. Bernard had spoken to the on-call doctor who, to his dismay, wasn't their usual practitioner but a young locum whom he had never met before. He had assured Bernard that, in view of Evie's symptoms, he was certain that she'd just picked up a particularly nasty flu bug that was making the rounds and there was nothing to worry about. In his opinion there was no need for him to make a house visit. He recommended that the patient be kept warm and be given plenty of fluids and only if there was no improvement in the morning should he ring again. What the locum didn't bother to tell Bernard was that he wasn't keen to venture outside as it had already begun to snow heavily where he was based, nor that he personally wouldn't be on-call the following morning and therefore it wouldn't be his responsibility to make a house call. Regardless of these omissions, Bernard felt frustrated as he replaced the receiver. His own feelings were mirrored by Nick's as he relayed the information to him.

'Bloody quack,' Nick said. Not for the first time did he wish that he and his family were in their own home where he could take charge without fear of treading on other people's toes. Much as he enjoyed the Binghams' company he couldn't help but feel usurped at times such as these. Still, at least Becca and Dan had taken India off his hands. That was one less thing he had to worry about. He turned back to his wife, holding the back of his hand a few millimetres from her forehead. The heat emanating from it was remarkable. 'I don't care what excuses he gives, if she gets any worse I'll call him again.'

'I quite agree,' Bernard agreed. He cast a glance at the sleeping Evie. 'Are you coming back down now that she's out?'

'No, I want to keep an eye on her.'

'I'll leave you to it then,' Bernard said. Someone had to keep an eye on his warring family. It may as well be him.

IN A VAIN ATTEMPT TO amuse themselves everyone else settled down to a game of Trivial Pursuit. Due to India falling asleep on the sofa, everyone bickered over a dearth of comfy chairs. At the same time Margaret did her best to divide her family into teams that were agreeable to all. This was no easy task.

No one wanted poor deaf Grandpa on their team, Natalie and Christian were inseparable and everyone wanted Becca on their side. Eventually most people were appeased by the final segregation. Natalie, Christian and a now three parts cut Great Aunt Ada would go head to head against Bernard, Dan and Grandpa. Margaret and Becca made up a third, smaller team.

'It'll be good practice for when we go on *Millionaire*,' Margaret said to Becca, who responded by rolling her eyes in exasperation.

Inevitably, the game degenerated into chaos and a shaming display of impatience, badwill and personal insults. Christian argued over every ambiguous answer until Dan, voicing the secret thoughts of all, finally snapped at him to shut up. 'It's just a fun quiz, for crying out loud!'

Also, everyone became bored whenever it was Becca and Margaret's turn to play as they correctly answered question after question and rattled round the board, collecting coloured wedges. To make confusion worse, Grandpa felt the need to bellow the answers to every team's questions but his own to an increasingly frustrated chorus of '*it's not your turn!*'

As the game continued there remained an underlying feeling of sadness that poor Evie was lying upstairs feeling rotten with the flu and that Nick, being a wonderful husband, was also absent courtesy of his insistence that he stay at his wife's side.

The game finally concluded, for two reasons. Firstly, and not surprisingly despite being shy one team member, Becca and Margaret collected all six wedges before any other team had won even half as many. Secondly, Great Aunt Ada, who had continued to slug back G&Ts throughout the game, accidentally knocked her for once full glass over the playing board. Bedlam followed. Everyone grabbed the nearest thing that could be used as a blotter. Dan took particular delight in finding a use for the frightful red tee shirt that Natalie had presented him with earlier. Alas, he wasn't quite quick enough to prevent a generous helping of Gordon's dribbling onto Angus's head. The little dog had been sleeping peacefully beneath the occasional table and took his impromptu shower in very bad part. The rumpus woke India who, having had her slumbers so rudely interrupted, had no qualms about letting everyone know how aggrieved she was. Natalie was told it was her turn to entertain her for a while.

'Good practice for when you two have children of your own,' Great Aunt Ada said. It was debatable who looked more horrified: Natalie, Christian or Bernard.

Afternoon drifted into evening. Margaret fussed around, plying her family with snacks and drinks. Dan ate an entire foot-long Toblerone in one sitting. Grandpa fell asleep in his chair — again. Becca retreated into the conservatory, dolefully dibbing into a bucket of Maltesers as she watched the afternoon sky darken through the glass roof. The weatherman on the telly had predicted something called wintry mix. Becca thought this sounded like something you could buy a quarter of at the local sweetie shop. Nor was she sure it had been an accurate forecast. Above her the bright, fresh afternoon sky had slowly been dulled by a thick layer of lavender-blue clouds rolling in courtesy of a northeasterly Siberian wind. Snow clouds. Earlier she had been thrilled at the prospect of snowfall but the day had been blighted by Evie's collapse and Becca could muster no enthusiasm for anything. Most of her family appeared to be infected by the same disillusionment. Only Great Aunt Ada was unaffected. She had already made a large dent in the bottle of gin Natalie had given her and was laughing at some ancient comedy repeat on the television. Becca looked at her with loathing. She grabbed another handful of Maltesers and punted them en masse into her mouth. She wasn't hungry by any means, not after the mammoth lunch her mother had prepared, but eating sweets gave her something to do. Dan was so bored and desperate that he finished off a three quarter full bottle of Croft Original sherry, which he loathed.

Upstairs, Bernard tapped on Nick and Evie's bedroom door before poking his head round. 'Any improvement?'

Nick released his wife's hand from his own and crept over to the door. He slid out, leaving the door ajar so that he could hear any unusual movement.

'She's no better. Still sleeping,' he said. 'Between you and me, I'm not convinced it's the flu. I've been mentally debating whether it'd be a good idea to have another go at that doctor.'

'Better leaving it to the morning when Dr Murrin's back. I didn't like the attitude of that locum,' Bernard said. 'It's late now anyway. I can call him first thing. It probably seems much worse than it really is because it's Christmas.'

Nick considered this.

'You're probably right. How is everyone else? Any similar symptoms?' he asked.

'Everyone else seems fine. A little disappointed by this turn of events but that's all. It's Margaret I feel most sorry for. I left her in the kitchen, drinking brandy out of a tumbler and with her bottom lip quivering like Sue Ellen Ewing.' Bernard said with a small laugh. 'She'd planned such a perfect Christmas but what with Becca miserable, Dan drunk most of the time, Natalie relentlessly acting up and now Evie being poorly, I think she's given up the Christmas ghost of Christmas present. Four kids in total and not one of them both happy and healthy.'

'I know, it's been a bit of a washout, but there's always next year. That's the great thing about Christmas, it comes round quickly.' Nick paused. 'Would you mind sitting with Evie for a few minutes? There's something I have to do.'

Whilst Nick was absent Bernard looked down upon the face of his favourite daughter. She looked so peaceful whilst she slept which belied the extreme pain she had described whilst she had been awake. Bernard gazed upon Evie with fondness. She had been his firstborn and never would any of his other children mean as much to him as she did. He had always been in awe of Margaret who somehow managed to distribute her affection for her four children in equal parts despite their considerable shortcomings. He had never been able to do this. Just as he had always loved Margaret with a single-minded devotion, he adored his eldest daughter with the same unwavering loyalty. Now, watching Evie as she slept, he could only be thankful that she wasn't dangerously ill. The flu could be nasty but it wasn't fatal. He couldn't bear to lose his Evie. Not whilst she was so young. Despite the knowledge that Evie had merely fallen foul of a nasty bug, Bernard still found tears streaming down his face. Brusquely, impatiently, he wiped them away. Whatever was the matter with him? Crying like a bairn because his favourite child was poorly and that Christmas Day was ruined for him. The thought of his other three children brought him no joy at this present time, only guilt.

Nick returned just five minutes later. One glance at Bernard told him his father-in-law had been struggling with his emotions but, being a man, he decided to pretend he hadn't noticed. Better to remain stoic, he thought. If Bernard wanted to talk he would no doubt initiate a conversation. As it was, his silence spoke volumes. More concerning was the fact that Bernard was clearly as worried as he was. There was no other explanation for Bernard's extreme reaction to Evie's illness. Perhaps he wasn't entirely convinced of the young locum's remote diagnosis either. Still, best not to mention his own worries in case he was wrong. They could ring the practice doctor in the morning if her condition wasn't improved.

'I'd better get back downstairs,' Bernard said, not looking Nick in the eye. He rose from his post by the bed. 'Do you want a tray bringing up? Margaret has abandoned Christmas tea but I'm sure she'll be more than happy to rustle up a snack if you're peckish.'

Nick declined the offer. 'I'm fine, thanks. I don't really have any appetite. I might help myself to something later, if that's all right?'

Bernard didn't speak. He merely lightly rested his palm on Nick's shoulder as he left the room. It was a brief gesture but one which transmitted everything that didn't need to be said out loud.

Nick wiped his wife's forehead gently with a dampened flannel. The painkillers she had taken didn't seem to be having any success in lowering her temperature but at least the pain in her head seemed to have subsided somewhat. With a sigh he moved to the window and drew back the curtain slightly. Just as the forecasters had promised, the snow had begun to fall and a light, pale dusting now covered the garden. It was officially a white Christmas for the first time in decades. He opened the curtains fully so that the whole window was exposed.

A movement from the bed prompted him to return to Evie's side. She had woken and was watching him with pain-filled eyes. She struggled to sit up.

'How are you feeling? Any better?' Nick asked as he helped her to lift her upper body. Her skin was scorching. 'It's started to snow. Just like they said it would.'

'I can see.' Evie gave a weak smile that was so obviously the result of such a supremely brave effort that it made Nick want to weep. 'Maybe we can build a snowman tomorrow. India would like that.' Evie's throat was clearly still very sore indeed. Her voice had been distorted by the infection.

'Maybe. Let's see how you feel, eh?' Pessimism was usually an alien trait to Nick but on this occasion he felt his wife's predicted self-diagnosis was inaccurate. 'Are you hungry? I imagine your mother is hovering downstairs desperate to cook you something.'

Evie looked distressed and shook her head slightly. Even the smallest movement caused indescribable pain.

'I couldn't eat a thing,' she croaked. 'How's India? Has she caught this?'

'India is as right as rain. Full of beans and having the time of her life downstairs. She's been allowed to stay up late and everyone wants to play with her and feed her sweets. Honestly, she's more than fine.'

'What time are we setting off tomorrow?' Evie rasped. Her eyelids had started to droop. Nick didn't respond immediately. Whilst Bernard had been sitting with Evie he'd telephoned his mother and forewarned her that they might not make it up to Newcastle until the twenty-seventh. Although bitterly disappointed, Carol Lovell had selflessly assured her only son that whatever he decided was all right with her. She'd sent Evie her love and best wishes for a speedy recovery whilst at the same time hiding her own sadness that she would have to postpone seeing her family for perhaps another day or so. Nick hadn't disclosed this telephone conversation to Evie and so his mother's kind wishes hadn't been passed on. Instead, Nick stalled.

'We can set off whenever you feel well enough. Open agenda,' he said.

'So tired.' Evie's eyes were almost closed. 'Will you leave the curtains open so I can watch the snow?'

'Of course.' Nick settled back into the chair beside the bed. Evie was asleep again within seconds. For Nick, as he continued his vigil, there was nothing else to do but sit in patience and hope his wife's condition improved overnight.

BOXING DAY

The household was wakened early by the shrill jangle of the hallway telephone. It rang for seven or eight rings then was silenced as the receiver was picked up.

Upstairs, Nick, having been rudely awakened, wondered who the hell telephoned before eight o'clock on Boxing Day. He was also perplexed as to why he felt so cramped and sore until the realisation dawned that he'd spent the night in the big, lumpy armchair next to the bed. A glance at the bed told him that Evie was asleep, her ebony haired splayed across the pillow. The duvet had been pulled up to her nose as though she hadn't been able to get warm. He hoped she would feel better once she woke and that Christmas could return to some degree of normality. As it was, it was only a matter of time before India started demanding attention. Nick was thankful that Margaret and Bernard had taken it upon themselves to shift the little girl into their room for the night. It gave him breathing space, if nothing else.

India had, in fact, slept through the night for the first time in months and was arguably the only person other than her mother who hadn't been woken by the telephone. All the excitement of visiting Grandma and Grandad, waiting for Santa and being allowed to stay up *very* late on Christmas Day, had finally caught up with her. She remained asleep in her grandparents' bed long after Margaret had slipped from beneath the covers and snuck downstairs to make a cup of tea.

In the kitchen the dogs and cats hovered by the utility room door looking hopeful. The humans hadn't materialised as early as they usually did and the animals were keen to be fed and watered.

Margaret shivered as she felt the cold of the stone floor through her slippers. It was *freezing*. She filled the kettle and plonked it on the Aga's hot plate before turning to the animals. When she opened the back door to let the dogs out a rectangular block of compacted snow fell into the utility room. At this point the cats fled in terror. Evidently the overnight snow had been relentless. Indeed, it was still falling in fat, white flakes although the blizzards had, for the time being, ceased. The heating would definitely have to be turned up to compensate for the cold weather. Closing the kitchen door so that the steam from the kettle would heat the air a little she noticed the central heating gauge indicated that it had been turned off.

She was going to kill Bernard!

Only he could try and economise on the coldest day of the year. As both she and the kettle seethed their way to boiling point Margaret doled out the cat and dog food and set it on the floor, almost tripping over as five impatient creatures swarmed around her ankles.

Into the teapot went two bags. As she poured in the hot water Margaret considered the day's chores. Brunch was first on the agenda — perhaps she could prepare a large bowl of kedgeree — followed by an early dinner so that they could get to the pantomime in good time that evening. She was fed up with being late for everything this holiday. Everything also needed a good clean. The lounge could only be described as a state after yesterday's exchange of presents. Only the hoover could deal with the slivers of tinsel and wrapping paper that somehow always managed to weave themselves into the fabric of the carpet. Not to mention the needles off the tree; no doubt they'd still be finding those in high summer as was usually the case. Whilst she was at it she might as well hoover through the house and polish the surfaces, she thought. Anything would be better than sitting and worrying about Evie.

Yes, she decided, kedgeree, being fiddly, was a good idea.

Upstairs, Bernard wondered where the hell his morning cuppa was. India was still sleeping — and was also hogging the bed — so he couldn't leave the room. Sliding out of bed so as not to wake her, he peeped out of the door. Everything was quiet. Was that a good or bad sign? And why was it so bloody cold?

BREAKFAST WAS A SOMBRE AFFAIR. From the moment Margaret set the dish of beautifully prepared kedgeree in the middle of the table she knew she'd wasted her time.

Natalie refused to eat it because it contained fish. Christian refused to eat it because it contained, well, just about everything. Both Grandpa and Great Aunt Ada helped themselves to sparrow portions whilst at the same time proclaiming that they would have preferred a nice cup of tea and some plain toast.

Nor did the rest of the family give Margaret any joy. Bernard, Dan and Becca all pushed their food round their plates, each with a face as long as the first day back at work in January. Nick was, of course, absent but had refused a plate of breakfast by proxy. Only India was unaffected and put everyone else to shame by gobbling down two bowls of cereal with an eerie cheerfulness.

Nor had it helped that Margaret had just finished tearing a strip off Bernard for switching the heating off when it transpired that the thermostat was kaput, leaving her with no option but to backtrack rapidly.

Once the meal was over the family scattered to the four corners of the house. Everyone was subdued. Dan plonked himself in front of the telly with the remote control, every selection box he'd received and a six-pack of bitter. Natalie surprised everyone, even herself, by taking solace in menial housework and helping her mother in trying to track down an engineer who was prepared to make a house call on Boxing Day. Bernard entertained India by taking her into the snow-covered garden to build snowmen.

As she had done the previous afternoon, Becca holed herself up in the conservatory for the duration of the morning from where she could see her father and niece playing in the snow. She took with her a couple of new books and the memory of an early morning telephone call. By lunchtime she was nearly climbing the walls. She had to tell someone what had happened and the only person that would understand was Evie. She couldn't imagine any of the rest of her family being impressed by her news and so, when Nick sent a message down asking her if she could sit with Evie whilst he took a time-out, Becca realised her opportunity had come.

EVIE FELT like there was a metal vice circling her head, one with screws at each side that were gradually being tightened as though by some malevolent tormentor. Every noise was unbearably loud; every smell made her feel nauseous. Even opening her eyes in such a darkened room was unfathomably painful. She had never known such agony. In addition she was also aching to see India but her mother had strongly advised against it in case she passed on whatever ailment she had.

'There's nothing worse than a poorly toddler,' her mother had said with a sage nod of her head. There had been an essence of finality in her tone that Evie didn't have the energy to argue with. Therefore, with reluctance, she lay in her solitary bed and waited to feel better. Even Nick had felt the need to take a time-out, mentioning that Becca would drop in to keep her company whilst he was absent.

'What for? I'm not on my death bed,' Evie had complained. She didn't feel like entertaining guests, and certainly not Becca, who she still felt ambivalent about after their discussion on Christmas Eve.

A light tap on the door put paid to any hope of peace and quiet. Becca popped her head round the door.

'How are you feeling? Any better?' She advanced into the room but stopped short when she caught sight of Evie's drawn little face. 'Christ! You look dreadful.'

'Cheers for that,' Evie replied without humour. Becca wandered over to the window and pulled the curtain back a fraction. The cold, dazzling whiteness of daylight on a snowy morning punched its way into the room. Evie shied away from it like a vampire, squinting fiercely. The curtain fell back into place and the room was plunged into gloom once more. Evie wished Becca would just clear off and leave her alone.

'Can I get you anything? Mum's having a bleb because you're not eating,' Becca went on, apparently oblivious to her sister's mood.

'I'm fine.'

'Okay then. Anyway, I wanted to tell you my news,' Becca said. She plonked her bum down on the bed. She didn't notice that Evie winced as the bed jolted up and down. 'Gregory called first thing this morning. Guess what?' Becca waited patiently but Evie couldn't be bothered to answer.

Becca ploughed on regardless. 'He wants to meet with me this afternoon with a view to making up, although I'm not sure about the roads. Anyway, it was all because of that chance meeting in Starbucks. You were absolutely right. He said he couldn't get me out of his head after that.' Becca wrung her hands in ecstasy. 'Isn't it marvellous? I bet his mother is furious. I'm sure she thought she'd seen the back of me. What do you think?' Again, Becca waited for Evie to respond. Her face adopted an expression of bewilderment. 'Well? Aren't you pleased for me, Evie?'

Evie considered her sister for a few moments. Becca seemed so much happier than she'd been all week and yet Evie couldn't help but feel a vindictive, griping resentment of her upbeat mood. Although she could never have explained why, seething anger bubbled up inside her. Words poured out of her mouth before she could stop them.

'I'm not sure I am pleased, Becca. Nor am I sure that I care. I'm lying up here, immobile and in pain, and all you can babble about is that stupid boyfriend of yours. I haven't seen my daughter in almost a day and I'm feeling more ill by the hour. Tell me why I should care if mummy's boy Gregory has bothered to ring you? In my opinion you're better off without him, anyway. He's brought you, and this family, nothing but trouble and you could do so much better. Of course, that's if you could be bothered. Quite frankly, the last thing I feel like doing is playing agony aunt to your lost cause. Why don't you just sort it out yourself and stop asking me for advice. It pains me to say it, but Natalie was right. You're not twelve anymore, Becca. Learn to stand on your own two feet.'

Evie did feel some remorse when her sister ran from the room but as it didn't even come close to the physical pain she was feeling she decided not to call Becca back. Instead she closed her eyes and prayed she would fall asleep soon.

❄

NICK WAS BECOMING INCREASINGLY WORRIED. Evie's pain wasn't abating in any way and, worse still, she'd also started to intermittently vomit into a bucket he'd posted by the bed. The stench was frightful. The bucket would have to be emptied before it set him off too. Nick heard footsteps on the landing carpet. Desperate to collar someone he scooted over to the door and peered out. It was Becca, trudging across the landing towards her own room. A huge bath towel was wrapped tightly round her body and her hair was wet. She was visibly shivering which made Nick wonder if the water heater had packed in as well as the boiler. Becca's head shot up when Nick hissed at her.

'You startled me,' she said. Nick beckoned her into the bedroom. Becca paused before entering. She still hadn't forgotten Evie's hurtful words of earlier and had been quite happily avoiding any more confrontations. Due to this she had been establishing her concern for Evie from a distance. Now, cornered, she had no option but to step into the room.

Evie appeared to be asleep. Her eyes were closed and her body was static. Only the unintelligible ramblings that were leaving her mouth gave any indication that she was conscious.

'My head hurts, oh my head, my head, my head,' she intoned.

Becca, noticing the telltale signs of delirium, was horrified.

'How long has she been like this?' she asked. Her discomfort at being in such close proximity to Evie was forgotten. She moved closer to the bed. Evie's face was drenched with sweat. 'Is she too hot?'

'She says she's cold, in between mutterings of course. Her hands and feet are like blocks of ice. Here, you can feel them.' Nick indicated to Evie's hands.

Becca skimmed the back of her hand against Evie's arm. Sure enough, her skin was cold to the touch.

'Her feet are no better,' Nick said. He gently pulled back

the duvet to reveal Evie's feet. Nick had dressed them in two thick woolly socks apiece. There wasn't a matching pair between the four socks. 'First she's hot then she's cold. It doesn't help that the heating is buggered. Margaret gave me that plug-in fan heater so that I could regulate the temperature in here but it's been switched on and off more times than Blackpool illuminations in a series of power cuts. All I can think is that her inner thermostat is shot. I don't know what to do.'

Evie started muttering again. She was repeating that she was too cold. Becca frowned. This didn't look like flu to her. On a random whim she pulled the duvet back a little further to reveal Evie's legs. Her worst suspicions were confirmed. Evie's thighs and calves were covered in a dark red rash.

'Pass me that glass, would you?' she said, pointing at an empty highball glass on the bedside cabinet. It had contained soluble painkillers and now all that remained was some white powdery residue. Nick obediently handed it over. He watched, perplexed, as Becca rolled the glass over Evie's leg. It twitched convulsively in response to its coldness although Evie didn't wake.

'What are you doing?' Nick said, his forehead creased from frowning. For the life of him he couldn't understand why Becca was rolling a glass up and down Evie's legs. Had she gone quite mad? He repeated his question. Becca seemed to be having problems answering. She continued to stare at the glass. Eventually, she turned to face Nick. All the colour had drained from her face.

'I think Evie's got meningitis,' she said, her voice faint. She knew Nick's expression of uncomprehending disbelief matched her own.

'Meningitis,' Nick echoed. 'What do you mean?'

Becca pointed to the glass. 'The rash isn't fading. That's the most important test. I read it somewhere.' Nick knew better than to question either Becca's knowledge or memory.

Both were immeasurable. 'This is serious, Nick. The doctor needs calling again, if not an ambulance. If I'm right — and I hope I'm not — Evie will need taking to hospital.'

Nick shot out onto the landing, narrowly missing crashing into Margaret who was carrying a pile of towels so large that she couldn't see over the top of them. Her shriek of surprise beckoned everyone to the landing. Nick sought out Bernard's face.

'I don't care what excuses he gives this time, get that doctor round here,' said Nick. Everyone bowled downstairs, all talking at once in muted tones about what was to be done.

'What about this boiler? I'm not getting any warmer,' Great Aunt Ada said as she exited the downstairs toilet, clicking her fingers for Natalie to pour her another drink. She didn't seem to care that the foul reek she had created was pervading throughout the ground floor. 'What a lot of fuss over nothing. The girl's got flu, that's all.'

'Why don't you keep your stupid opinions and comments to yourself, you embittered old crone? Just fucking shut up for once!' Becca screamed. She had reached the end of her tether and Great Aunt Ada's glib dismissal of the potential seriousness of Evie's illness sliced through the metaphorical rope and cut her free.

'Rebecca! Apologise at once.'

'No Mum, you don't understand. It isn't flu. That rash could mean Evie has meningitis. She could die.' Silence hung in the air. Becca had said the very words that no one had wanted to utter. Not even Nick. Now Becca's impetus had roused in him some desire to act.

'Get that doctor round here, now! I don't care if he has to shunt his way through six-foot drifts. He's a country doctor; I'm sure he'll have M&S tyres. Just get him here,' he said.

'Marks & Spencer tyres?' Margaret said aloud. It seemed that nothing had sunk in.

'Mud and snow, Mum,' Dan said, his face contorted with

disbelief. He reached for his mother's old-fashioned address book and practically threw it at her. 'Ring.'

It took the doctor half an hour to travel the three miles from Greater Ousebury, although it seemed to the Binghams to take so much longer. With the exception of Nick and Becca, who both remained at Evie's bedside, the family sat in silence in the lounge and waited. Even Great Aunt Ada was compelled to refrain from voicing her usual assortment of complaints. Also absent from the gathering was Dan, who instead chose to sit on the front doorstep chain-smoking. Such was Margaret's distraction that she didn't bother to tick him off. As far as she was concerned he could smoke himself silly so long as he kept a look out for the doctor.

This he did and, just as the sky began to darken, the doctor was ushered into the house. Thankfully it was the family GP, kindly, bespectacled Dr Murrin, who'd treated all the Bingham children since infancy. He was directed upstairs immediately. Margaret, Bernard, Dan and Natalie followed him. The doctor took one look at Evie, taking into account the angry rash and flu symptoms. It was a brief examination but proved to be all he needed to make an accurate diagnosis. It was indeed meningitis.

There followed a shocked silence whilst everyone digested this fact. Dr Murrin took the opportunity to set out the next steps. He was brief and succinct.

Evie would need to be taken direct to Loxley Hospital, he advised. There was no point in waiting for an ambulance to be called out; he would take her himself. The roads were treacherous but he had every confidence that his 4x4 would be able to cope with the conditions. He would call ahead to warn them that he was bringing her in. Nick would travel with them. Anyone else could follow if they chose, or indeed if the weather allowed.

'What about the rest of us? Is it contagious? Are we in danger?' Natalie asked. Dan shot her a filthy look.

'Still thinking of yourself, Natbag?' he said. Natalie scowled back.

'Actually, I was thinking of India,' she snapped.

'That's a very pertinent point, Natalie,' Dr Murrin said, smiling down at her. 'I imagine you're all quite safe. The only people I would possibly worry about are perhaps your elderly guests and the little one. However, my advice is that everyone should take a course of antibiotics to be on the safe side. I can write the prescription before I leave and telephone to arrange for one of my staff to walk down and open the surgery in the village. Would someone be brave enough to drive into Greater Ousebury to collect the medicine?' He looked directly at Natalie, who nodded her head despite looking terrified.

'But we want to follow you into Loxley,' Bernard said. Becca and Dan both nodded their head vehemently. 'We can't afford to wait for Natalie.' He didn't look once at his youngest daughter. 'It's essential that we follow your car's tracks if we're going to get to the main road.'

'Then I can write two prescriptions,' Dr Murrin said impatiently. 'I can leave one with young Natalie here and you can bring the other with you to the hospital. It can be dispensed in the in-house pharmacy. Now, let's get this poorly lady moved with as little fuss as possible. Rebecca, could you and your mother try and make Evelyn as warm and comfortable as possible. Blankets and cardigans are ideal. A hot water bottle or two wouldn't go amiss either. When we're ready this young gentleman, who I trust is Evelyn's husband, can help me carry her down to the car. In the meantime I'm just going to make a couple of phone calls.'

'Use the landline. There's a phone in the hallway,'

Margaret said. Even in a crisis being a perfect hostess was important to her, but Dr Murrin was already speaking into his mobile. Nick followed him downstairs. Not once had it occurred to him that he not only might lose his wife but also his daughter. Now his brain was boggling with horrific thoughts and worst-case scenarios.

'Will India be all right?' Nick asked. 'How contagious is this? How much danger is she in?'

'I'm sure she'll be all right,' said Dr Murrin, carrying out two conversations at the same time. 'It's most unusual for a second case to occur. The antibiotics are merely a precaution. If you'll excuse me—' He indicated to his phone and turned away. Frustrated, Nick strode off.

Upstairs, Becca had begun to worry about her mother as well as her sister. As they battled to clothe Evie's stiff, pain-racked body with as many layers as possible, Becca realised that her mother appeared to be in shock.

'It'll kill your father,' said Margaret under her breath as she forced Evie's arm into a thick woollen cardigan.

'What do you mean?' said Becca, aghast. 'Do you think he'll get meningitis too?'

'No. I mean if anything happens to Evie,' said Margaret. Evie had begun to groan with pain. 'It's a portent of doom, I just know it. I just wish she'd mentioned sooner about the picture so I could have done something.'

Becca was bemused. 'What are you talking about? What picture?'

Margaret stared at Becca as though she were quite mad.

'*The Magpie,* of course. My picture's gone from the wall. They must have tried to hide it until after the holidays but I can see it behind the chair. The frame is in pieces and the print has a big crease in it. It's a sign. I'm sure of it.'

'Broken mirrors bring supposed bad luck, not ordinary pictures,' Becca said. She felt as though she were speaking to a small child.

'I know that. It's just that I've had that print for as long as we've owned this house,' Margaret said. She was becoming more and more agitated by the minute. 'It was a wedding gift from your father by way of appeasement. I never wanted to buy this house but he had his heart set on it. He adored it from the moment he set foot inside. I was never happy about that dratted Magpie baked into the bricks over the front door. One for sorrow—' Margaret paused, aware that she was rambling. She glared at Becca. 'That picture was my last defence against the bad luck. It was the outside magpie's partner, the one that defied the rhyme and made it two for joy. Deep down I've always known that wretched bird would bring disaster to this household. Can't you see? This is an omen. Oh, why didn't she tell me about it?'

Becca was appalled. She stared at her mother in stunned horror. There had never been any mention of her mother not wanting to buy the house. Nor had she ever had any inkling that her mother was so superstitious or that she'd been so afraid of the magpie after which the cottage had been named. She, along with her three siblings, had always believed the picture to be so sacred to her mother because it had been a wedding gift from her father. She felt it was up to her to reason with her mother.

'Mum, you can't blame this on the magpie. It's only a painting, same as the one above the front door is just glazed ceramic. It doesn't mean anything that the picture got broken. It's a coincidence.'

Margaret shook her head. She seemed to be resigned.

'Evie broke the picture and look what's happened to her,' she said. 'No good can come of this.'

'Don't say that! Lots of people recover from meningitis all the time,' Becca protested. 'Evie's going to be one of those. Anyway, she'll have already been carrying the virus before she arrived here, long before the picture was broken. It's got nothing to do with it.'

Her mother looked at her with pity, as though she was foolish and naïve.

'I need to get some hot water bottles for your sister,' said Margaret. 'Can you organise some blankets? There's plenty in the airing cupboard.' With that she exited the room leaving Becca rooted to the spot, gazing at the space where her mother had stood.

Nick carried Evie down to the hallway. Becca followed, making sure that none of Evie's extremities were banged on the banister as they descended. Dr Murrin had pulled his vehicle up flush to the front door so the blast of freezing air that Evie would unavoidably be subjected to was as limited as possible.

Natalie was standing in the hallway. She had already donned her coat and was nervously twizzling her car keys round her fingers. She was waiting by the house telephone for the doctor's receptionist to call and advise that the surgery pharmacy was open. She didn't want to embark on the horrifying journey into Greater Ousebury, especially not alone. She hated anything but perfect driving conditions and was cursing herself for being coerced into volunteering. Margaret, Bernard and Dan emerged from the coat cupboard with their coats across their arms. They were going to follow in Bernard's car. No one seemed to care that Natalie had been ostracised. At least, no one except herself.

'Will India be okay with the olds and Christian whilst I collect the antibiotics?' Natalie asked Nick as he passed her, desperate to have some form of communication with someone. 'I'll be as quick as I can.' If Nick hadn't been so preoccupied with his wife's health he would certainly have protested at this proposal. Instead, he gave a brief nod of his head. As he carried Evie over the threshold and began placing her in the back of Dr Murrin's off-roader the house phone shrilled.

Everyone jumped.

'That'll be my cue to leave,' said Natalie. She yanked up the receiver. After a few moments she passed it to Becca, her face blank. 'It's for you.'

Wordlessly, Becca took the receiver. Through the open door she could see Nick climbing into the back of the car. He slammed the door shut. Her parents and Dan were already sitting in her father's Corsa. The engine was running.

'Hello?' she said into the phone. A familiar, whinging voice began to grill her. *Why was she still at home? She was over half an hour late. Did she really think this was acceptable under the circumstances?* The voice went on and on.

Becca felt as though she had been frozen in place. Natalie was staring at her as if mesmerised, ashen beneath her make-up. Becca couldn't remember the last time she'd seen her little sister look so vulnerable and young. Through the open door she watched Dan wind down the window. She could see his mouth moving as though he was shouting. It looked like he was saying 'come on — hurry'. It was starting to snow again. Thick, fat flakes had begun to fall. Within seconds it had started to blizzard. Still the voice moaned in her ear. *Did she even want to try and make it work? Why had the telephone been engaged for so long? Why hadn't she rung to say she would be late? She'd better have a good reason.*

The doctor's car slid out of the driveway. Bernard revved the Corsa's engine. If Becca were going to accompany her family to the hospital she would have to leave now. She watched as Dan leant over his mother's shoulder from the back seat and tooted the car's horn. There was no time left. This was it. It was a straight choice between her boyfriend and her sister.

'I'm sorry, Gregory. I'm not coming. I've got something more important to do.' With that she dropped the receiver back into the cradle and ran out of the house, skidding dangerously on the treacherous front step. She didn't think twice about what she had just done.

Natalie, jaw hanging in disbelief at what she had just witnessed, watched as Becca hurled herself into the car. More than anything she wished she were going with them.

'Promise you'll ring me!' she called after them, a lonely figure framed by the open door. As Bernard's car disappeared out of the driveway a solitary tear zigzagged down Natalie's cheek. She closed the front door. For the second time in five minutes she jumped as the telephone rang.

THE JOURNEY into Loxley was terrifying. Nick sat in the back of Dr Murrin's 4x4 desperately trying to protect Evie from the rough bouncing and sliding of the car. It was all he could do to prevent her from falling off the seat into the footwell. If she'd been in agony whilst she'd been lying stable in bed then this uncontrollable movement must be nothing less than excruciating. He wanted to ask Dr Murrin to slow down but daren't, not only because the doctor was consumed with intense concentration but also because he appreciated the necessity for haste. Evie's life could literally be hanging in the balance.

Snow was hitting the windscreen. It spiralled in from the road ahead making him feel dizzy whenever he looked at it. The horizon was obscured by the moving storm. Only brief, static silhouettes could be seen of the hedgerows and trees by the roadside. The sky and earth merged into one white-grey blur, indefinable and remote. The deepening twilight only added to the bleakness. It would soon be completely dark.

The car engine whined from the effort of finding some traction on the icy road, which was no more than single track in some parts. Several thick layers of snow had compacted on the ice, making driving conditions even worse. The 4x4 was sliding from side to side like a lifeboat in a hurricane. Sporadic drifts formed chicanes. It was small wonder they hadn't nosedived into a roadside ditch. Nick gazed out of the window with vicious resentment. Damned snow. The collective will of the nation had invoked a white Christmas. All of them had wanted it but none of them were as affected by it as he. If the roads had been clear they would have been at the hospital by now. As it was they weren't even halfway there. Precious time was slipping away. Evie herself had wished for snow. What a frivolous, futile waste of a wish! Now snow was her enemy. Nick knew that if Evie died he would hate snow forever. He craned his head so he could look out of the back window. Through the blizzard he could just make out Bernard at the wheel. If the doctor was struggling with his vehicle then Bernard was even more so with the Corsa. Margaret looked positively sea sick in the passenger seat. They were fools to have followed but he couldn't blame them nonetheless. He merely hoped they would be safe or at least have the sense to take the longer, safer route on the trunk roads. There was so much potential for tragedy. Nick was rendered helpless as the 4x4 surged ahead leaving the little hatchback behind. Again, he wanted to say something to the doctor, ask him to slow down or stop, but he knew he couldn't. His priority must lie with Evie. Nevertheless, he couldn't quell a sinking feeling in his heart as the Corsa was consumed by the blizzard. Within seconds they had fallen so far behind that they were no longer visible and Nick knew Bernard had turned off towards the main road.

After that Nick ceased to worry about his in-laws because, beneath him, the 4x4 skidded askance without warning and slammed into a five-foot drift. Caked, impacted snow covered the windscreen, obliterating what little visibility there had been. The vehicle pitched downwards in response to the contact. The rear wheels lifted off the ground, continuing to spin madly. Everything lurched forward, including Nick. He scrabbled to keep a solid hold on his wife but she slipped through his grasp and hit the back of the driver's seat with a wallop. From somewhere within the depths of her torment, Evie screamed.

IN THE DRIVEWAY of Magpie Cottage, Natalie climbed out of her hire car and slammed the door shut. In her hand she held a parcel that contained antibiotics for herself, Christian, Grandpa, Great Aunt Ada and India. She let herself into the house, stamping her snow-caked boots on the doormat.

'I'm back! Any messages?' she called. No one answered. Natalie knew that if her mother were here she would have by now been ushered into the kitchen, where it was still warm thanks to the Aga, and a hot mug of something delicious would have been pressed into her hands. Alas, her mother wasn't here, and nor were any of her family. Surely they must be at the hospital by now? The answering machine yielded no messages and her mobile, which she'd carried like a priceless jewel in her pocket as she'd travelled, remained stubbornly mute. Natalie began to worry. Her own journey into the next village and back had been terrifying beyond description. Having only been able to drive inside the troughs that other vehicles had gouged into the snow, it had taken the best part of an hour and a half and she had never reached a speed of more than ten miles per hour. By her own crude calculations, her family should have at least reached the main road during this time and she hoped it would be clear enough for traffic to traverse. Perhaps the telephone had rung and one of the olds had answered it. Hope renewed, Natalie entered the lounge.

Both Grandpa and Great Aunt Ada were sleeping in their chairs. As usual the television was blaring at full volume. They wouldn't have heard the phone even if it had rung. Christian was nowhere to be seen. Natalie leant down and flicked the TV off. The relief she felt upon encountering the silence was much the same as when one stopped banging one's head against a hard surface. Not long after a different noise caught her attention. From upstairs came the muffled cry of a distraught child. India!

Natalie raced up the stairs two at a time. She burst into her parents' bedroom to find India trapped in her cot. The little girl was standing up, gripping the side. Her face was puce from screaming, her eyes puffy and her skin all blotchy and sore. She immediately quietened as soon as she saw Natalie.

'An-natlee,' India said between breathy sobs. 'Wan' Mummy, An-natlee. Wan' Mummy.' Natalie was appalled.

'Where the fuck is Christian?' she muttered under her breath as she picked up her niece. India was sodden, and not just from crying. 'I'm sorry, India, I'm so sorry,' said Natalie as she hugged the child. 'How long have you been left like this?' Evie was going to kill her if she found out. Ha! Everyone was going to kill her, not just Evie. 'Let's get you sorted out, sweetheart. Let's get you out of these wet clothes.'

Neither necessity nor inclination had moved Natalie to ever spend a great deal of time with India. Now, having been forced to care for her, Natalie felt curiously comforted by India's presence. She was the nearest she had to her family right now. With great care she changed India's clothes, dried her tears and sought out her favourite and most comforting stuffed toy. The next step was to provide refreshment and so, with India perched on her hip, Natalie wandered down to the kitchen. She could contain India in her high chair whilst she prepared some food.

Nothing, however, could have prepared Natalie for what she found in the kitchen. Christian was slumped in one of the dining chairs, his booted feet were on the table and a stack of ham sandwiches had been placed next to them. These he was sharing with a slavering Chewbacca and Angus. Upon spotting Natalie in the doorway he whisked the remainder of the sandwiches onto the floor. The dogs demolished them within seconds.

'That was good ham you've just wasted,' Natalie said coldly. She couldn't think of anything else to say. She plonked India into her high chair then grabbed each dog by its collar and manhandled it out of the back door. This was no mean feat as both canines were intent on licking the York stone flags to the size of a pebble where the illicit treats had fallen and were not keen on being ejected. As she slammed the back door on the dogs the magnitude of what she had just witnessed hit her. Then she hit Christian soundly round the head with one of her mother's copies of *Good Housekeeping* that had been left lying around.

'You bastard!' she yelled. 'You unutterable, self-centred, lying bastard! My sister is critically ill but instead of behaving like a human being for once you look after only yourself. I came back to find India traumatised in her crib. Did you put her in there?' Natalie didn't wait for Christian to answer. Christian merely stared at her in disbelief. 'And where do I find you? You, Christian, devout macrobiotic and self-proclaimed protector of the helpless and oppressed. I find you in the kitchen eating ham sandwiches. Ham!' Thwack went the magazine again. 'Fucking ham! — You are not to repeat this, India. Do you understand me? — You bloody hypocrite! I've sacrificed my mother's divine cooking all Christmas just to impress you and for what? I wish I'd never brought you home. How could you leave a little girl crying in her bed? She's almost screamed her lungs dry.'

'I don't see what you're getting so het up about,' said Christian blithely. 'You told me that you can't stand the brat.'

'She's my family. It's my prerogative to complain about her. You don't share that luxury.'

'Phooey! You're the hypocrite here, not me,' Christian jeered.

Natalie put her head in one hand and turned away. 'Just

get out of my sight. Go to the pub or something. After eating the flesh of a pig I'm sure a couple of beers won't do you any harm.'

'Don't worry, I'm going,' Christian said. 'Anything to get away from your crazy family.' He gave a nasty grin. 'By the way, one of the cats has been sick all over the conservatory floor. You might want to clean it up. Enjoy.' As he exited the room Natalie hurled the magazine after him.

'Cockhead!' she shrieked. A thought struck her. 'Has anyone left me a message?'

Christian popped his head back round the doorframe. 'Course not. No one cares about you. That's why you were the only one left behind.' Then he was gone. Moments later the front door slammed.

Natalie sat down at the table in despair. Next to her India gurgled. She'd been amused by all the shouting and slapstick abuse with the magazine. Natalie looked at her ruefully.

'Glad you find it funny. Still, at least you've cheered up. Now, what can I give you to eat that will shut you up long enough for me to clean up whatever ghastly mess awaits me?'

With India happily stuffing her face with all manner of unmentionable junk in the kitchen, Natalie armed herself with a bowl of hot soapy water and ventured into the conservatory. Just as she set to work on the first splodge, Great Aunt Ada woke up.

'Oh, it's you,' she called from the lounge. Her tone was decidedly disagreeable. 'What took you so long? And what's for dinner? It must be time for a drink.'

With supreme effort, Natalie bit her tongue. For the first time in her life she found herself on all fours, wearing rubber gloves, cleaning up cat sick and marvelling at how her mother managed to juggle so many tasks and remain cheerful. Never before had Natalie missed her mother so much.

❉

Two and a half hours after leaving Nether Ousebury the rest of the Binghams entered Loxley Hospital's A&E department. Bernard strode ahead of his family, his gaze fixed intently on the enquiries desk. Behind him Margaret struggled with her mobile phone. Inexplicably, she felt the need to telephone Natalie to tell them they were all right. Dan remained outside; he hadn't had a cigarette for the duration of the journey. He'd join them in a while. Becca hovered near to her father's elbow.

'Evelyn Lovell,' said Bernard. 'Dr Murrin brought her in with suspected meningitis. I'm her father.'

The duty nurse flicked through her papers without rushing. Becca couldn't believe she could be so calm amidst all the anxiety.

'Evelyn has been sent to the Intensive Care Unit,' the nurse said. She smiled up at Bernard. As she did she caught sight of Margaret who was still furiously pressing every button on her mobile. 'I'm afraid you'll have to switch that off.' The nurse pointed to a nearby sign. It was of a mobile phone within a red circle with a broad red band across it. Seeing that her mother was just about to argue, Becca intervened.

'Which is the quickest way to Intensive Care, please?' she asked. The nurse provided directions. 'I'll wait for Dan. You go ahead.'

Bernard and Margaret found Nick waiting outside a single room. He was sitting on a low plastic chair. He looked cold, wet and exhausted. Relief dominated his face as he saw them approaching. They had made it safely through the snow after all.

'I've been sitting with her until about five minutes ago,' Nick said. 'The doctor's in with her now.'

'Dr Murrin?' asked Margaret. She was staring at Nick's

sodden trousers.

Nick shook his head. 'No, he went back to the village. He wanted to stay but he's still on call. He's been marvellous. You can tell he's a country practitioner. We hit a drift on the way in. I thought we were stuck but he had a shovel in the boot. He cared for Evie whilst I dug the bonnet out of the snow.' He indicated to his clothes. 'Hence why I'm drenched. Dr Murrin left a prescription. I haven't been to the pharmacy yet. I didn't want to leave Evie.'

'That's no worry,' said Margaret. 'One of the kids can go down and get it. What do we know so far?'

Nick shrugged. 'Not much. As soon as we arrived they carted Evie off for an MRI scan and some other tests. A lumbar puncture, or something. Sounds horrible. She's been unconscious since we arrived. She banged her head when the car hit the snow. She's got a few cuts and bruises and a mild concussion but, frankly, that's the least of our worries. I'm just waiting for an update from the chap who's in with her.'

Becca and Dan hurried along the corridor just as the doctor exited the room. Upon seeing him Nick stood up.

'How is she?' he asked. The doctor looked at him gravely, also taking in the four anxious faces of the Binghams.

'I'm Dr Asbury, the house doctor on the ICU tonight,' he said by way of brief introduction. 'Evelyn has meningococcal septicaemia. This means she's been carrying bacteria that's caused her meninges, in other words the lining of her brain and spinal cord, to become inflamed, and this has also manifested itself as blood poisoning. We've prescribed an intense course of antibiotics to counter-attack the infection and these are being administered by intravenous drip. All we can do after that is keep Evelyn calm and reassured in a quiet dark place and wait and see if she responds to the treatment.'

'Can I see her?' said Margaret, clutching onto Bernard's arm for support. 'I'm her mother.'

'Of course,' said the doctor. 'Just don't be alarmed by how

she looks. It's quite normal in this situation. Plus, the injuries she sustained in the shunt are minimal. They look much worse than they actually are.'

Margaret and Bernard followed Nick into the room. The light had been dimmed which made the machinery and devices surrounding the bed seem more space age than they actually were. A nurse was studying a chart at the end of the bed. She gave a gentle, unobtrusive smile as the family entered. Margaret gave a small cry when she saw Evie's inert body on the bed. Evie was as white as the hospital sheets on which she lay. Her dark hair had been scraped away from her face and a stark, white dressing had been applied to a cut on her forehead. A speck of blood could be seen emerging through the fabric.

'It looks worse than it is,' Nick said. He had reacted the same way as Margaret just had when he had first seen Evie all wired up. Now he knew what each machine did he was less overawed by them. 'Those are Evie's drips. One is plying her with medicine, the other with nutrients. The third machine is the heart monitor. There's also an oxygen monitor. I'm told that these are a precaution only.'

Margaret looked as though she was about to faint. She reached for her hanky.

'Considering the late diagnosis of her illness she's doing remarkably well,' the doctor said. He patted Margaret's hand gently. 'I'll leave you alone. The nurses will be happy to assist. If you need anything all you need do is ask.' As the doctor left the room Nick was certain he heard Bernard muttering about suing the locum.

'You can't blame the locum,' Margaret said. She hovered her hand over the bandage on Evie's head.

'Can and will,' said Bernard, his voice rising. 'Firstly, Evie would have had those antibiotics coursing through her veins a whole day sooner. Secondly, the weather wasn't half as bad yesterday, which means the roads wouldn't have been as treacherous. These additional injuries should never have occurred. I hold the locum entirely responsible and I shall tell Dr Murrin as much as soon as all this is over and we're all back at home.' Margaret didn't respond. She was picturing the broken Monet print in her head.

'We really need to give Evie as much peace and quiet as possible,' said the nurse, trying to get her point across tactfully. 'You all look frozen stiff. Why don't you all get a cup of coffee and then come back?'

Bernard looked mutinous at this suggestion but Margaret dragged him out of the room. Becca and Dan were waiting in the corridor, both looking anxious. They were immediately despatched to the pharmacy and the coffee shop. They returned half an hour later to find their parents settled into the waiting lounge but still bickering over the locum.

'Might as well get comfy,' Dan said, plonking a large paper bag on the central table. 'Something tells me we're going to be here for some time. You'll never believe how much all this lot rushed us. Let's just say there's precious little change out of fifty quid.'

Nick had been summoned back into Evie's room, reappearing just as Dan and Becca were doling out bottles of water, antibiotics and hot drinks. He was accompanied by Dr Asbury and both were looking a little more optimistic. Evie's vital signs had improved once the antibiotics had taken hold, the house doctor told them. As a result Evie had regained consciousness.

'It's a good sign,' said the doctor. 'However, Evelyn is still a critically ill young lady. I can't say for certain that she's out of the woods yet.'

'When can you?' Dan snapped. Dr Asbury looked pained.

'The next twenty-four hours are crucial. Evelyn's body now needs to accept the antibiotics and work with them to fight the infection. As I said, the early prognosis is hopeful but meningitis is an unpredictable illness. It may fight back and, if it does, it will do so with a vengeance. As I said, all we can do is sit and wait.'

Dan was fed up with sitting and waiting. It was all he had done since Evie had collapsed on Christmas Day. What a shame the hospital didn't have a bar. He could do with a stiff drink. How ironic that it had everything else to get a frustrated visitor through the night or day: a chapel, a coffee shop, a sweet shop, a designated smoking area. Hell, it even had a hairdresser. Why not a bar?

'I'm going for a smoke,' he announced. There was no longer any need for pretence or secrecy.

'Evelyn has started to ask a great deal of questions since she woke,' Dr Asbury said to Margaret and Bernard. 'Her husband and I wondered if you thought she might benefit from being told the truth.'

THE CONFIRMATION that she had meningitis panicked Evie. Nick, Margaret and Bernard had all been present when the news was broken. No one knew whether they had done the right thing or not. An instantaneous reaction had been that Evie's heart monitor began beeping like a hyperactive alarm clock. As the nurse worked around her Evie constantly plucked at Nick's sleeve.

'I want to talk to Becca,' she rasped. Nick could barely hear her.

'You can talk to Becca later,' Margaret said. 'There's plenty of time.'

Still the urgent hand tweaked at Nick's sweater. 'Nick, get Becca for me. I want to talk to her alone. Please.'

Such was the desperation in her tone that Nick decided he had no option but to fetch Becca to Evie's bedside. He left Evie in her parents' company as he went to search for Becca. He found her alone in the waiting room. She was sitting on a plastic chair, her feet propped up on a table laden with out-of-date magazines. She looked up as Nick walked in, her face held an expression somewhere between expectancy and horror. The extreme best and worst scenarios flooded through her thoughts.

'Evie wants to speak to you,' Nick said.

Becca thought he looked absolutely shattered.

'Is she better?' she asked, full of hope.

'She's freaking out. We told her. She's frightened,' Nick said. His efforts to remain matter of fact were monumental.

Becca turned pale.

'Why does she want to speak to me?' she asked. Nick didn't respond. He had a fair idea why but wasn't prepared to voice his thoughts. Not just yet, anyway.

'You're her sister,' he replied vaguely. 'Of course she wants to see you.'

As Becca walked the few yards to Evie's room she felt her legs jellify beneath her. Up until this point she had been denied access to her sister. She couldn't imagine why Evie would want to speak to her specifically, as opposed to Nick, or their mother or father. She pushed open the door to Evie's room. Evie was lying in bed, her arms by her side. Each arm had at least two tubes attached to it. Her face was wan, with heavy grey bags shadowing each eye. She looked absolutely exhausted but she still managed a weak smile.

'Hi,' she said quietly. 'Glad you're here. Mum, Dad, I want to talk to Becca alone.' With a low huff Bernard left the room. Margaret followed, looking worried.

The ever-present nurse also exited after bestowing a brief promise that she would return in a few minutes.

'And not too much talking,' she added. 'You must rest.'

Becca sat on the chair her mother had recently vacated and reached for Evie's pale left hand, being careful not to dislodge any of the intravenous drips.

'How are you feeling?' she asked. She couldn't meet her sister's eyes. She was shocked by how cold Evie's hand was.

'Never felt worse,' Evie quipped. 'Pretty rotten but the drugs help. I feel worse now they've told me that it's meningitis. Nick said you figured it out this afternoon.'

Becca looked at the floor. 'I saw the rash when I came in to see you. I read about it somewhere.' Both she and Evie were aware of the sharp words that Evie had said that morning. There followed an embarrassing silence that was broken by Evie.

'I'm sorry about what I said this morning.'

'It doesn't matter,' Becca said quickly. 'It probably needed to be said anyway. Besides, I understand that you were in a lot of pain. It'd be enough to make anyone ratty. Not that I'm in any position to hold grudges. I've been so unsupportive of all your worries and choices, not considering your point of view. I'm sorry too.'

'That's the apologies out of the way,' Evie said. Her voice had become so faint that Becca struggled to hear her. 'I want to talk to you about something.' She paused for a few minutes as she wrestled with the words that were forming into sentences in her thoughts. 'I need to ask you a big favour, Bec.'

'Anything,' Becca said. 'Just say the word.'

'I want you to look after India and Nick if I don't get through this—'

'Don't say that! You're going to get better,' Becca interrupted. 'The doctors are working hard and people recover from meningitis all the time.'

'They also don't. I've heard the nurses muttering that I should have been medicated sooner. I know I might die,' Evie said. Her voice faded away so quickly at the end of each sentence that Becca had to strain to hear her.

'You have to rest, Evie,' said Becca. 'I can barely hear you. You must stop talking now. It must be painful for you.'

'This might be my only chance to say this,' Evie ploughed on, ignoring her sister's protests. 'There's no one else to ask, Becca. Nick'll have enough to deal with. Mum and Dad wouldn't be able to cope and I can hardly ask Natalie or Dan. You're her aunt and her Godmother. Besides, you always were my favourite. You know that, right?'

Becca looked her sister in her eyes for the first time since entering the room.

'I often wish it had stayed just the two of us. Do you remember the Christmases when we were kids, before Natalie and Dan were born? We used to share a room because you were scared of the dark and didn't like to be alone at night. We'd wake to find our presents in a pillowcase at the end of the bed, and back then we were still duped into thinking that Father Christmas had brought them during the night. Grandma Bingham was still alive then and she used to buy us a new red and green outfit especially for Christmas Day because she knew Mum liked to dress us up in those colours. She was so kind and jolly. We were also spared Great Aunt Ada in those days because she used to go and visit Great Uncle Bruce's family in Scotland.

'In the afternoon we used to play with our new toys until the family film came on then we'd all sit down together to watch it. Do you remember? After our tea we'd all watch *Morecambe and Wise*. It was just the six of us. If we'd been really good Mum would let us play Christmas songs on the record player. We'd play Slade and Wizzard and Chris de Burgh on the 45s and you'd always cry when *A Spaceman Came Travelling* ended because you loved it so much. We'd have to put the stylus straight back to the beginning. You loved singing along to the *la-la-las* and would stand in the middle of the room swinging your hips, entertaining us. You were so adorable.'

Becca didn't have such clear memories as Evie of their early years, as she was three years younger, but after listening to Evie's fond reverie, she had a sudden flood of long forgotten images of two beautiful dark haired girls dressed in festive colours. In some memories they were playing out in the snow, test driving their new toys. In others they were sitting beneath an artificial 1980s Christmas tree that had been trimmed with paper lanterns and tinsel. They'd never fought as children. At least, not until Natalie had come along six years later. Christmas had been so much simpler when they were children. These days the holidays were filled with stresses and arguments, and Becca was left bewildered as to what had happened during the interim years. What had gone wrong? Had they simply grown up? Somewhere in the depths of her thoughts the little image of her and Evie laughing on Christmas morning fought its way to the forefront reminding her of what had once been. She felt her eyes well with impromptu tears.

'Don't you dare cry, Rebecca Bingham,' Evie rasped. Becca looked at her, willing her to provide an explanation. 'If you cry then this is all real, and I mustn't believe that.' Her words caused Becca to curtail the tears but just as she lassoed her own emotions Evie's began to seep out. Saltwater began to streak Evie's pale face, causing it to look transparent. She could barely get her words out, so intense was her grief. 'They won't let me see India, Bec. I might never see her again and I can't bear it. I can't hold my baby or tell her that I love her so, so much. That's why I need you to promise to look after her. I need you to make sure she has the kind of Christmases we had. You're the only one I can trust with this. You're the only one who fully understands. Not even Nick can do this for me. Promise me, Becca. I won't rest until you do. Say you'll promise me this.' Evie's voice was becoming weaker and weaker from the exertion of speaking.

Becca noticed that the device monitoring Evie's heart rate had become erratic and her eyes flitted to and from it with panic. She must have exhausted herself by talking.

'I promise,' Becca said. She knew she had to call the nurse, and quickly. 'I promise I'll look after her and Nick.' She tried to move away from the bed but Evie gripped her hand with a freakish strength.

'Don't leave me,' Evie said. 'Not until I've fallen asleep.' Her lids lowered over her pained eyes but still Becca struggled to free her own hand. Eventually Becca prised herself away, leaned over and pressed the emergency call button. The heart monitor was still going berserk. Within minutes a nurse appeared. She took one glance at the monitor and shot Becca an exasperated look.

'What's brought this on?' she barked.

'We were just talking—' Becca stammered. The nurse rolled her eyes and began to fiddle with the machine, talking in soothing tones to Evie as she worked. Becca stared, silent. After a short while the nurse remembered she was there.

'I think you'd better go now,' she said. Becca stepped out into the corridor. A doctor was hurrying towards her. Whatever had she done to her sister? Her mother and Nick were hovering outside Evie's room and even they were looking at her accusatively.

'What did you say?' Margaret snapped. 'Have you upset her?'

'No. We were just talking,' Becca repeated. She wondered if she looked as guilty as she felt.

'What about?' asked Margaret.

'Just sister stuff,' Becca replied vaguely. 'She's just got a little emotional, that's all. The nurse is with her now.' She had no intention of ever divulging their conversation with any of her family. It would only hurt, offend or distress. 'I'm going to get a drink from the vending machine.' With that she slowly walked away, dwelling on what she and Evie had spoken about. She needed to be alone for a while to digest the conversation and to come to terms with her own reaction to Evie's words. Evie's request and her own subsequent pledge had been harrowing enough without the added angst of dealing with the happiness of her childhood memories. Worse still was the knowledge that somewhere amongst the deep horror of accepting why Evie had asked for her, to her utter shame, Becca felt a tiny glimmer of something like joyful vindication, something that almost resembled exhilaration. Whilst she acknowledged this feeling was unbidden and inappropriate she couldn't help but embrace it and take from it what happiness she could. At a time when she had believed herself to be superfluous within her family she had learnt that she had always been Evie's favourite. She, Becca, had been someone's favourite and because of that sole fact she realised she wasn't such a disappointment to herself after all.

Twenty miles away, Natalie was thoroughly sick and tired of her charges. From the moment Great Aunt Ada had woken she had done nothing but bitch about Natalie's mother and sisters. Nor had she been impressed when Natalie had banged microwaved ready meals onto the dinner table for them all. Only Grandpa hadn't complained but happily tucked into his food, causing Natalie to reconsider her longstanding opinion that he was senile, dull and eccentric. Christian's reaction to a steaming plate of Bird's Eye's finest beef stew and dumplings had been well worth it, however. Just as he was about to protest Natalie pre-empted him.

'If you can eat pig, you can eat cow,' she said. 'If you don't want it... tough! There's nothing else and I personally couldn't care less if you starved. If you leave it, it'll go to the dogs and you'll go hungry.'

After that she had given each of them their allocation of antibiotics with instructions of how many to take and how often. Then, because she was uncertain of how India would react to mandatory medicine, she crushed two tablets in a freezer bag with a rolling pin, hammering away with satisfactory spleen, and sprinkled them over a generous scoop of chocolate ice cream. Such devious behaviour worked like a charm.

Later still, she took India up to her parents' bedroom and put a kiddie programme on the television for her to watch whilst she changed the bedding that Evie and Nick had used. Natalie thought it best if she slept in that room rather than in the dining room with Christian. Firstly, because she had absolutely no desire to get within sniffing distance of the deceitful pig-eater and, secondly, India's crib was in there and she was certain that maintaining some semblance of continuity could only be a good thing. It didn't hurt either that she could draw a degree of comfort from being in her parents' room.

A further added bonus was that she could hide away from everyone else. They could all kill each other downstairs for all she cared. The only problem was that, because she'd fed India the sugar-loaded equivalent of rocket fuel all afternoon and evening, the toddler was almost hyperactive by bedtime and in no mood for sleep. Just as the tantrums were becoming unbearable Natalie was struck by divine inspiration. Hating herself, and in the certainty that she was doing a wicked, wicked thing, Natalie dosed India up with a spoonful of child-friendly antihistamine syrup she found in the medicine cabinet. Within half an hour the child was zonked.

As Natalie lay in the darkness with only the television to provide company and light, she remembered that no one had bothered to phone her to let her know how Evie was or to ask about India. Perhaps they thought she didn't care. She considered how wrong they were if this were the case. She was lonely and sick with worry. What if they hadn't even made it to the hospital? What if they were stranded en route, vulnerable and exposed? The last time she'd checked the snow was thicker than ever and still falling.

It wasn't even as though she could go looking. She was trapped in the house, with three encumbrances who she certainly wouldn't entrust to Christian's care. She was helpless, useless and more than a little bit out of her depth.

Whilst she mulled over this the other inhabitants made their way to bed. As she realised that the house had fallen silent it occurred to Natalie that the dogs probably hadn't been put out or the cats fed. She might as well check all the lights and locks too. Silently she padded through the house, turning keys and flicking switches. It was only when she spotted seven forgotten pantomime tickets for that very night on the telephone table by the front door that she finally gave way to tears.

27TH DECEMBER

Nick had never known such a long night.

For all of the previous day possibilities and probabilities had tormented him until he felt he could bear no more. He was already racked with guilt that he'd tried to apply some pressure on Evie on Christmas Eve on the subjects of job offers and babies whilst she had clearly been feeling so ill. Then Becca had gone and traumatised Evie to the extent that she suffered a seizure and things had got even worse. It was only as the hospital came to life the following morning that his thoughts drifted back to what Evie and Becca had discussed. He was confident Becca would never have intentionally distressed Evie, which left him wondering who had upset whom. Lord knows it had taken Margaret an inordinately long time to calm Becca down.

Becca was equally consumed with guilt at having worsened Evie's condition. Not even the house doctor's reassurances that seizures were a common occurrence in a patient with meningitis lessened her feelings of culpability. Becca felt as though she were to blame, and convinced herself that everyone else felt the same.

All hell had broken loose when Becca stepped out of Evie's room. Several nurses had raced to her aid and stabilised her, refusing Nick entry to the room. Evie then proceeded to drift in and out of consciousness for several hours, causing both his own hopes and fears and those of the Binghams to see-saw dramatically. Then, just as the middle of the night turned to very early morning, Evie's heart rate dropped and she slipped into a coma.

Yet another consultant gathered everyone together to impart this news.

Evie's condition was critical, he told them. If she didn't start responding to the antibiotics her chances of survival would lessen. The coma was not a good sign. It meant she was deteriorating rather than recovering.

'Will Evie die?' Becca had said. No one else seemed to be able to form any words. They had all looked stunned; as though they'd never considered Evie's life was in danger despite everything they'd been told.

'It's a possibility that can't be ruled out,' said the doctor. 'It's certainly something that you may need to prepare yourselves for. In saying that, the human body is a remarkable machine and its capability for self-regeneration and healing is amazing. It may be that Evelyn's body is just taking a time-out in order to recover. You mustn't give up on her yet. There are some things that may help that I can recommend. The next few hours are vital.'

That had been almost five hours ago, Nick reflected, and nothing had prompted Evie to wake. The doctor had taken him to one side and recommended he talk to her, advising that she may still be able to hear him from within her coma and quite often this helped to bring the patient round. Willing to try anything and everything, Nick had dredged up every topic of conversation he could think of. He recalled memories of holidays and happy days they'd had with India, and recited poems and lyrics of favourite songs, but all to no avail. Evie remained still and pale. All the while he held her hand. He had come to regard it as her anchor, the means by which he kept her with him. On one, rational level he knew he was being ridiculous but still he dare not let go in case she drifted away, never to return. He hadn't even left Evie's side in order to ring and check on India. In his own mind it was vital he remain with her; he was too frightened of what might happen in his absence to do anything else.

Both Bernard and Margaret regularly joined Nick at Evie's bedside throughout the hellishly long hours of the cold, bleak dawn, sometimes singularly, sometimes together. Neither could offer comfort or hope, only company.

Margaret seemed to be coping better with the trauma than Bernard, but it was Bernard with whom Nick felt he could speak openly. He seized the opportunity to offload some of his worries and grievances to his father-in-law whilst Margaret had slipped away to the hospital chapel for five minutes' prayer. The two men sat opposite each other, one at each side of Evie's bed.

'They've said the longer it takes for her to respond fully to the antibiotics the less chance there'll be. I don't know what I'll do if—' Nick didn't feel the need to finish the sentence. He changed the subject. 'She was so looking forward to Christmas this year. Each year I see her becoming more and more obsessed with family and togetherness. Even this year she was more concerned with everyone else's woes rather than her own well-being. She wouldn't take it easy no matter how much I badgered her.'

'Just like her mother,' Bernard said, a wry little laugh accompanying his words. He looked at Evie. In sleep she was so like Margaret had been at that age. Life may have removed the vibrant colour from Margaret's hair, turning it grey, but it had once been dark like her daughters'.

'Just like her mother,' Nick agreed. The two men exchanged knowing glances, each acknowledging what it was like to love a Bingham woman. It was a brief moment of light relief and passed far too quickly.

Something else was bothering Bernard too. *There'll be other Christmases…* Nick had said just the previous morning. Bernard couldn't help but brood on these words. Nick had been so sure there would be other Christmases but what if he had been wrong? What if this had been their last Christmas as a family? What if there were no more chances? Look at how they had squandered the time they had been given. Little did he know but Nick was harbouring the exact same thoughts and regrets.

'We've been disagreeing a lot recently,' Nick confessed, ending a long silence. 'We would have had another row on Christmas Eve whilst everyone was out at church if Evie hadn't averted it. You see, I want more children, and Evie doesn't. She's quite adamant it would be best for India if she remains an only child. I don't agree. I was an only child, and I was lonely. I just can't see how we're going to reach a compromise on this. I suppose Evie will get her own way. After all, when it comes to what happens to her own body she's in the driving seat. I still think she's wrong though.' Suddenly Nick didn't want to mention the Boston job. He cast a glance at Bernard, wondering how this news had been received. Bernard was grey beneath the usual ruddiness of his cheeks. Nick's revelation had floored him. He looked simply devastated.

'I'm sorry,' Nick said. 'I didn't mean to burden you with this. I just had to tell someone. It's been driving me crazy. Plus I feel terrible that I was heaping pressure on her whilst she was battling this… this… disease.'

'I'm glad you told me,' Bernard said. He was silent for a few minutes. 'I think I've done you a disservice. I know why

Evie is so keen to only have one child. It's because I've, in a roundabout way, encouraged that.' Nick noticed that Bernard looked mortified. 'I've never made any secret of the fact that Evie has always been my favourite child. She's always been so perfect. She never gave us a moment's trouble. She never answered back, never complained, always worked hard in school, had a couple of nice boyfriends and then she met you, settled down, married, provided us with a grandchild. What more could a parent ask for? She's so unlike the other three who are so wilful and combative. I've often told Evie that I wished we'd stopped at her and not bothered with the others and how much better her life would have been if she'd been the only one. What a thing for a father to think, never mind to say out loud. Of course I love all my children, and wouldn't be without any of them, but I don't understand them half the time.' He was silent for a few minutes, his face hardening as he thought of the grief and worry he and Margaret had endured over Christmas courtesy of his youngest three children. 'You're quite right, you know. Kids need brothers and sisters. They need to learn how to play and share. If I've influenced Evie in any way in this decision of hers I am so very, very sorry. When she's better I shall tell her how wrong I've been. Of course India should have a little brother or sister. Of course she should.' Then he beamed. 'I'm glad you chose to confide in me. It means I can right this wrong and make Evie see sense. You never know, sometime soon we might well be celebrating a new life.'

Nick noticed that Bernard was smiling to himself, happy in his own thoughts. He couldn't share his father-in-law's optimism and instantly regretted spilling his secret. Bernard clearly viewed it as more lives to celebrate; Nick saw it as more losses to mourn.

❄

NATALIE WOKE early with Ramesses wrapped uncomfortably round her neck and Boo and Hiss sprawled across her feet. The effect was both suffocating and claustrophobic. That alone would have made waking a relief but, in addition, Natalie had suffered an unpleasant night, filled with worrying, macabre dreams and disturbed sleep. There was still no word from the hospital.

At least India was still fast asleep in her crib. The antihistamine medicine appeared to have worked like a charm. Setting the babycom to loud, Natalie dressed in the nearest clothes that were to hand, scraped her hair back into a ponytail and ventured downstairs. The house was still freezing. Christian showed no sign of emerging from the dining room. Grandpa and Great Aunt Ada had both been up for hours and were now snoozing, mouths agape, in the lounge. It was the most peaceful they'd been since their arrival. Because they were both deaf, the telly was blaring out at an obscene volume. Natalie picked up the remote and switched it off. Neither of them responded. No one had bothered to turn on the tree lights.

Natalie wandered round the house in a daze. It seemed so empty and quiet now that all the bickering had stopped. Perversely, she now wished she were arguing with Dan and her sisters. Anything would be better than this hollow waiting. Outside it was still snowing but not nearly as ferociously as it had been. Natalie fed the dogs and, having rounded up the three cats too, chucked them all out into the cold. Ramesses immediately mewed to come back in but Boo and Hiss shot off into the garden, tails bushy like Davy Crockett hats. A blackbird pecked hopefully at the solid ground. Plants and trees bowed and buckled beneath the weight of their snowy burden, looking defeated and disillusioned. Just like everything else, Natalie thought miserably as she shivered on the kitchen doorstep.

Chewbacca and Angus, both having taken umbrage at the cold, pawed and hovered until they were let back in. Still bored, Natalie tidied up the kitchen, loading the dishwasher and wiping down the sides. For some reason the menial tasks enabled her to collect her thoughts.

Feeling slightly more optimistic, Natalie considered the options. Her family must have been so busy with Evie that they had forgotten to ring her, she told herself. She ignored the taunting little voice telling her that if anyone had bothered to ring it would have been to enquire about India and not her. Natalie managed to convince herself the lack of communication wasn't due to the fact that her family were stuck in the snow and had never reached the hospital at all but that they had simply forgotten about her. Still, there was no harm in making sure and after a tense five minutes whilst she scoured the internet for the right number, she telephoned the hospital helpline. It was engaged. She left it for another ten minutes. Still engaged. After a third unsuccessful attempt she gave up.

A sickening and overwhelming sense of foreboding engulfed her. This was a nightmare. She was trapped in the village with no means of finding out what was happening to her sister and the rest of her family. Even the telephone had forsaken her. Sooner or later India was going to wake and she didn't think she could cope with another full day of demands and tantrums. Then, just when it seemed there was no escape, Natalie's eyes fell on her mother's address book. Perhaps there was one more option...

Natalie snatched up the receiver once more and began to dial. If she were lucky, she'd be freed within two hours. Thankfully, someone answered within a couple of rings.

Eighty five miles due north, Carol Lovell had been practically sitting on the telephone all night, waiting for a call from her son. However, the last person she had expected to be calling was Evie's youngest sister, the one Nick had the least pleasant things to say about, begging them to drive down to Magpie Cottage as soon as they possibly could so she could be relieved of her babysitting duties and go to the hospital to see what was happening for herself. Carol Lovell's first reaction, as Nick's mother, was to say that of course she and her husband would travel down to Loxley but that they would first visit the hospital to offer moral support to their son before driving on to the cottage. Not wishing to be left literally holding the baby — again — Natalie panicked upon hearing these words.

'No, you can't. Please come straight here,' she shrilled. 'I've been here for almost twenty-four hours on my own. Evie's my sister and I have to see her. No one's told me anything.' Sensing that Natalie was close to hysteria, Carol Lovell reluctantly acquiesced. They would use their best endeavours to be at Magpie Cottage within two hours. Satisfied, Natalie set the receiver back in its cradle. There was plenty to be done before they arrived. Her mother would murder her if she allowed guests into a house that wasn't immaculate, especially Nick's parents, with whom Margaret had an amicable but competitive relationship.

A cry from upstairs made Natalie groan out loud. India was awake and would need to be bathed, fed, watered and entertained. Chores would have to wait. However, Natalie was not a successful businesswoman for nothing and soon decided that delegation was the answer. Once she had overseen the tasks that she daren't entrust to anyone else, namely clothes and breakfast, she left the toddler in the lounge with her ancient relatives. They could cope with her for an hour or so. God knows they'd done bugger all else since their arrival before Christmas. Predictably, Christian hadn't emerged from the dining room other than to use the bathroom.

Natalie pondered on how she'd ever been attracted to him

as she transferred an excess of empty beer cans and wine bottles from where they'd been dumped on the kitchen work surface into the relevant recycling boxes in the utility room. How could she have once been so smitten with him when he was so clearly repugnant to all? More importantly, how was she going to get rid of him? A further conundrum occurred to her when she noticed that the glass recycling box contained no less than five empty gin bottles of varying brands. Had Great Aunt Ada really drunk that much booze in just about as many days? Natalie was horrified. Her thoughts reluctantly turned to Grandpa and, worse still, shitty Vera Lynn. How could she leave the Lovells stranded with them all whilst she cleared off to the hospital? They had the sort of antisocial foibles that only family could either tolerate or understand. It would be grossly unfair of her to expect Nick's parents to cope with them as well as with India. There was only one thing for it: Christian, Grandpa and Great Aunt Ada would have to be taken home.

Glancing out of the utility window onto the patio, Natalie was distracted by Boo and Hiss, who were engaged in what looked to be a feline tug-o-war. She set down the last of the beer cans and yanked the back door open, painfully ripping a French manicured acrylic tip off one of her nails in the process. As she stepped out of the back door, onto snow that crunched underfoot, for a closer inspection, she realised that the 'rope' was red and squishy. It was either a mouse or a bird. Natalie's stomach flip-flopped unpleasantly.

'You beasts!' she shouted. She searched her immediate vicinity for a throwable object. The only thing within grabbing distance was a hollow plastic ball her mother used to put laundry detergent in the washing machine. The ball landed nowhere near the kittens but they shot off anyway. 'That's right, clear off. Scabby animals,' Natalie called after them. Now that the victim had been relinquished all that remained was to retrieve what was left of it. Natalie seized an empty box from the dustbin that two days ago had contained a thoughtful gift. It was about the size of a brick and would more than suffice as a makeshift coffin. Shuddering, she scooped up all that was left of what had once been a sparrow whilst two naughty silver tabby faces watched her crossly from within the sparse, severely pruned frame of her father's prized buddleia.

'Villainous, stinking creatures,' Natalie said to them as their heads disappeared back into the woody stalks of the plant. She fastened up the box and placed it out of paw's reach on a hanging basket bracket. It should be safe there until she had time to deal with it properly. At least the low temperature would ensure the poor mite's carcass wouldn't deteriorate further.

Glancing at her watch Natalie noted that over an hour had passed since she'd rung the Lovells. With any luck they should be over halfway there by now. Natalie was confident all the trunk roads would now be clear. Plus, remote though the village was, she was further encouraged by the first signs of a thaw. Stretches of cold, pale blue sky could be seen peeping through the last vestiges of the snow clouds and every so often a low, watery orange sun would appear. It wasn't hot enough to give off any heat but it did cast chequered patches of sunlight on the garden, which, as they hit the snow, were blindingly bright. From behind her Natalie could hear the telltale drip-drip-drip of ice reverting to water. For once, melting snow was a good thing.

With a sigh she realised there was still so much to do before the Lovells arrived. A shrill cry from inside the house reminded Natalie that she'd left India in the dubious care of Grandpa and Great Aunt Ada. She hurried through the kitchen and into the lounge and was relieved to discover that all she had heard was the sound of India having a tantrum. It appeared she hadn't taken kindly to Grandpa not allowing her to have one of the cigarettes he had rolled up. Natalie put her head in her hands.

Still, she thought, here was her chance to tell them what they wouldn't want to hear.

'Pack your bags,' she said. 'I'm taking you all home today.'

Great Aunt Ada looked at her as though she were an insect.

'Don't be ridiculous, you silly girl,' she said. 'We're not due to go home until the New Year. What a selfish suggestion. I suppose it makes things easier for you.'

'It makes things easier for everyone,' said Natalie. 'I'm very sorry that you feel so aggrieved but it's not open for negotiation. Nick's parents are travelling down from Newcastle to look after India whilst I drive to the hospital to be with Evie. In view of their kindness, it's only fair they have the run of the house.'

Great Aunt Ada sniffed. 'I'm not going anywhere,' she said, looking triumphant. 'You can't make me.'

Natalie eyed Great Aunt Ada with something akin to hatred. Never before had she been on the receiving end of her aunt's unpleasant nature and she didn't much appreciate it. It had become apparent that, when deprived of her usual choice of victims, Great Aunt Ada had no compunction in turning on her alleged favourite.

'We're leaving in an hour or so,' said Natalie, refraining from voicing her thoughts. Instead she chose to ignore Great Aunt Ada. 'I suggest you get started. I'll be happy to help with your cases once I've told Christian the glad tidings.' With that she stalked off in the direction of the dining room where no doubt she would receive just as difficult a reception.

By the time Nick's parents arrived at Magpie Cottage Natalie was practically climbing the walls. As naturally bossy as any kindergarten matron she had badgered the olds and

Christian until they were all seated in the lounge, waiting with their coats on. Their packed bags were stacked in the hallway, ready to be thrown into the car. None of them had yielded quietly. She had no sooner ushered the Lovells into the kitchen, being the warmest room in the house, than she was driving the three others out of the front door towards her car. She would just as cheerfully have driven the three of them over a cliff. Returning to the kitchen she found the Lovells standing in the middle of the room looking disorientated.

'Thanks so much for coming at such short notice,' said Natalie, putting the kettle on the Aga hot plate in automatic emulation of her mother. 'India's having an enforced timeout upstairs, having had a conniption fit because Grandpa wouldn't share his cigs with her. Here's the babycom. She's really distressed at being separated from Evie but can be pacified with junk food.

'Unfortunately the boiler's bust so there's no heating and no hot water. I've been relying on lots of jumpers and endless hot drinks. If you get really stuck you can always call on the Baxters next door. They're very friendly and helpful but be warned, if you linger they'll want to show you every photo of every family member they've ever known, dead or alive.

'There's enough cat and dog food to last until next Christmas. I've left a list of instructions on how much, and when, on the pantry door. Don't give the cats any milk. It makes them sick. They're fine with water.

'The fridge and freezer are both bursting with food. Please help yourselves. Cooking isn't a problem as the Aga is oil burning and hasn't been affected by the boiler conking out.

'I think that's covered just about everything. I'll get someone to call once I get to the hospital. I've got to go now. I have to drop everybody off at their homes before I go to the hospital. I just hope I'm not too late.' With that she dropped a house key on the side and, forgetting the kettle boiling merrily on the Aga, ran from the room and out of the front door. The Lovells were left gaping after her.

THE CAR JOURNEY WAS HELL, but not for the same reasons that the other Binghams had suffered the previous day. Gritters and snowploughs had been out in force overnight and even the single-track road between the village and the main road was now passable without fear of death.

It was the company in the car that made the journey uncomfortable. The knowledge of them being returned to their lonely homes prematurely had not been received in good spirit by anyone. Christian complained that he would have to fork out to transfer his plane ticket to another day. Grandpa was the only one who didn't moan but Vera Lynn more than made up for his silence. The bird wouldn't be pacified by the tablecloth and squawked long and loud, profanities spouting from her beak in between craws. In the secrecy of her own thoughts Natalie imagined grabbing the bloody bird's cage and flinging it out of the window. She would have no compunction in gleefully watching it bounce down the centre of the deserted road, red and gold plumage blurring into one as the wretched creature was churned over and over within its cage-prison like raffle tickets in a tombola.

Great Aunt Ada was the most aggrieved and thus the most vocal. Enraged that she would be kissing goodbye to an endless supply of Bombay Sapphire and at least three unwilling serfs she proceeded to give Natalie a ferocious strip-tearing. Natalie, in return, finally learnt to appreciate that she didn't like being on the receiving end when the jackboot was on the other foot and it was with an element of grim satisfaction that she deposited Great Aunt Ada on her doorstep, luggage unceremoniously dumped at her swollen court-shoed feet, before screeching off. Grandpa was the next to be offloaded and, although Natalie was too proud to offer an apology for her mean gift, she walked him to his door and gave him a peck on the cheek together with a promise to visit him in the New Year. She was almost moved to tears when she saw the look of surprised happiness on his face. Finally, she practically kicked Christian out of the car outside the airport terminal without as much as a goodbye kiss. It didn't hurt her that, despite his earlier grumblings, he seemed to be relieved to be away from her and Magpie Cottage and she knew she wouldn't be calling him when she finally returned to London.

Natalie did not appreciate the drive back from the airport. The afternoon sky was already beginning to turn to twilight and a muted pink sky foretold of yet more snow to come. Further towards the horizon a band of low lying mist was touching the tips of the leafless trees, shrouding the darkening green and white fields, and was a sure sign that nightfall was imminent, but the beauty of the midwinter's day was lost on Natalie. The temperature had plummeted once more. The thaw had clearly been temporary. Just as she hit the main trunk road back to Loxley, it began to snow heavily. She didn't feel comfortable manhandling the four-litre hire car she'd selected at the airport rental stand three days before with the sole intention of showing off her earnings to her family. Its fat, low profile tyres skidded across the already greasy road and which the fresh onslaught of snow had made treacherous. Furthermore, now she had dropped off her three passengers the car seemed bigger than ever and, because of the difference in weight, the torque had altered. Thankfully the roads were all but deserted so at least she wasn't dazzled by flickering snowflakes being reflected in other cars' headlights. The fields at either side of the road were white over but Natalie had neither the time nor the inclination to admire the snowy landscape which, because of a hint of fog, now had no distinction between the sky and the horizon. They had merged. It was almost a white out.

All in all, she was not so much pleased but relieved to reach Loxley Hospital unaware that she was about to receive a greeting even frostier than the weather. Ignoring the parking charge notice in the car park — she would pay any fine she might be given — she hurried through the bright, sliding doors of the entrance.

Natalie found her family waiting in a plain little lounge at the end of the Intensive Care Unit. The first thing she noticed wasn't her family but the tinsel round the nurses' station, which seemed inappropriately jolly, almost anachronistic, amongst such tension and misery. Both her parents and siblings were present but tiny clues led Natalie to believe there hadn't been a great deal of movement. Dan reeked of cigarette smoke. Becca had drunk so many cans of Coke that she had built a shiny red pyramid in between the piles of out-of-date magazines on the low table in front of her. Neither of them acknowledged her. Upon noticing her youngest daughter, Margaret rose and hugged Natalie in greeting.

'How did you get here? Where are India and the others?' Margaret asked.

'I telephoned the Lovells and they drove down. They're looking after India. They send their love to everyone. I took Grandpa and Great Aunt Ada home. Christian's gone, too. With any luck he should be somewhere above the Midlands by now,' Natalie said. Everyone just stared at her. 'How's Evie? Can I see her?'

Her father's greeting was acerbic. In fact, it wasn't even a greeting. 'Of course you can't see her, you stupid girl,' Bernard snapped. Natalie could tell he was angry but she had no idea that, after deliberating over his conversation with Nick, his anger was in fact directed straight back at himself. 'Whatever prompted you to call the Lovells? Now they'll be worrying unnecessarily. What a fuss! Evie will be home in a couple of days and then you'll look foolish.'

Natalie paled visibly. Margaret felt the need to intervene.

'Bernard, if Evie doesn't come out of the coma soon she might not come home at all. You may have to accept that,' she said gently. Bernard stormed across to the other side of the room and, one arm propping up his body, stared moodily out of the window.

Natalie turned to Becca who, she hoped, would be less likely than Dan to replicate their father's hostility.

'How is she? Is Nick with her now?' she asked

Dan piped up before Becca could answer.

'What do you care?' he snarled.

'How can you say that? Of course I care. She's my sister too!' Natalie cried, shocked.

'Funny way of showing it. You've been an A1 bitch to Evie since you came home. Rubbishing her presents, pissing and moaning about India and generally being disagreeable. Now you come rushing in, in this... this travesty of a mercy dash and expect us to be impressed. Shame you couldn't show Evie some respect whilst she was alive.'

'Dan! Evie's not dead yet,' Becca admonished, appalled by Dan's words.

Natalie stared firstly at Dan, then at Becca.

'Listen to yourselves. For God's sake, Becca, you're talking as though Evie's about to die and you—' Natalie turned to face an ashen Dan. 'You talk as though she's already dead.' All the while she was aware of her father glowering at her from across the waiting room. This just added to Dan and Becca's obvious disapproval of her presence. It was perfectly clear to Natalie that she wasn't welcome. She decided to retreat with grace. Her frozen hands and parched throat gave her the perfect reason to excuse herself.

'I'm going to get a coffee from the cafeteria. Would anyone like anything bringing up?' she asked. No one responded.

Natalie looked at her mother with hope. 'You look like you could use a break, Mum. Why don't you join me?' For a nanosecond she thought her mother was going to agree but then Margaret slowly shook her head.

'I would, darling, but,' she paused as if carefully considering her next words. 'Evie's been in a coma since last night. If she should wake whilst I was gone—'

Despite translating her mother's words as 'if Evie should die whilst I'm gone', Natalie's shoulders visibly drooped. She'd had an awful day ferrying vexed relatives and newly ex-boyfriends to and fro whilst all the time being separated from her critically ill sister and worried family and, although she didn't want to feel sorry for herself, she really couldn't help it. She wasn't prepared to let Becca or Dan, and certainly not her father, see this, however.

'I understand,' she said quietly. 'Shall I bring you up a fresh coffee? That one must be stone cold.'

'That's very thoughtful of you, Natalie dear,' Margaret said. As she spoke she reached out and touched Natalie briefly on the arm. It was the slightest graze of her mother's fingers but it moved Natalie in a way she couldn't have predicted. Tears welled up in her eyes but rather than let anyone see them she stalked off towards the lifts.

The walk to the ground floor seemed endless. Natalie's boot heels clicked rhythmically on the cold, grey, tiled floor. The cafeteria was as deserted as the roads had been. Once her order had been placed Natalie chose a solitary table on the outer perimeter of the café next to the floor-to-ceiling frosted glass partition. A waitress brought over her drinks. Natalie warmed her hands on a mug of coffee, the cost of which did not reflect its taste. Once her hands were near scalding point she pushed the mug to one side, slopping its contents over the table and earning herself a black look from the waitress. Natalie didn't care. She pressed her burning forehead against the cool glass partition. On the other side, curiously distorted, she could see the main entrance doors sliding open and shut as little groups of visitors entered. They carried stacks of wrapped presents, flowers and balloons sporting pretty snow scenes and jolly Santas. Clearly these people were visiting folks who were not dangerously ill. Folks who knew they were only in the hospital temporarily, perhaps suffering from broken limbs or even having babies. Not like Evie, who might not come home at all.

Walking the other way was a group of nurses who, having just finished a shift, were laughing and chattering as they headed out into the cold night air towards the local pub for a post-Christmas drink. They seemed to be totally unaffected by what they were leaving behind but then, Natalie mused, she wouldn't want to dwell on her experience in the hospital once she got the chance to leave.

A young house doctor entered the café and shot Natalie an admiring glance as he passed by, but Natalie's eyes didn't even flicker. For the first time in her life it was evident to her that beauty was no substitute for favour. With a heavy sigh she picked up the coffee she had bought for her mother and made her way back upstairs.

INSIDE THE LITTLE room Nick was still talking to Evie.

'We'll come back to Magpie Cottage when you're better. Perhaps in the summer when there'll be roses framing the front porch, not fairy lights, and the garden will be filled with lupins and hollyhocks and your mother will be plying us with barbecued food and pitchers of Pimm's, except you might not be drinking because hopefully you'll have changed your mind about more babies and be pregnant. India will have turned three and your father will finally get his wish to put a swing back in the garden. All this will seem so long ago. You might be tired and have headaches but we can get round that. First you have to wake up, and then we can concentrate on getting you better. Please wake up, Evie. Please. Your family needs you. India needs you. *I* need you. I need you most of all.' Nick rested his head on the bed beside Evie's motionless hand. Only when the room became eerily quiet did he notice that the life support had stopped beeping. Seeping cold panic enveloped him. This couldn't be happening. It must be a mistake. He pounded the emergency button with his fist. Why wasn't anyone coming to help? He turned back to his wife. She wasn't breathing.

'Oh God, Evie, no. Don't do this. Wake up. Please, come back to me. Evie, please,' he said, shaking her hand frantically. 'Wake up, wake up, wake up—'

A crash team raced in and repeatedly tried to revive her, but Evie remained still. From his banishment to the corner of the room Nick could do nothing but was forced to watch in hopeful yet appalled silence as strangers pounded and pummelled his wife's fragile body. The language was deplorable. How could it be that neither the doctors' efforts nor his own had made one iota of difference? He had done everything he could to keep her with him. He'd done everything the doctors had asked him to do. He had talked to her, he had held her hand, he had willed her to live with every fibre of his body. He felt he had been misled. She was slipping away from him anyway. Surely there was no hope.

Then there was a faint beep. Then another. And another. The beeps continued, erratic at first before becoming more regular. Nick felt his lungs contract and expand as his body took it upon itself to inhale deeply. He hadn't even been aware he'd been holding his breath. There was a palpable reduction in tension in the room as the nurses exchanged knowing glances of relief. It had been a close call. Too bloody close. They began to talk amongst themselves about how difficult the revival had been until one of them remembered Nick was still in the room, pressed into the cold, stark corner.

Almost instantaneously Nick found himself being ushered out of the room by a nurse. It was imperative the doctor had some time alone with Evie in order to assess her condition so as to stabilise her as quickly as possible, she told him. Distressed at having been separated from Evie even for five minutes, Nick was reluctantly agreeable if not happy. He felt excluded, almost superfluous, as though Evie's well-being was not his concern. Despite the nurse's kindly suggestion that he grab a hot drink and have a seat in the corridor, Nick continued to pace the floor, making sure that he didn't catch the attention of any of the Binghams, who were seated round the corner. Although he felt mean-minded about it he prayed that none of them would suddenly turn the corner and see him outside Evie's little room for fear of the barrage of questions he would be faced with. After what seemed like an age, but was in actuality only ten minutes or so, the doctor emerged from the room and indicated to Nick that he would like to speak to him in private about Evie. Nick turned cold until he realised that the doctor was talking about Evie in the present tense, not the past. The doctor drew Nick into a quiet, empty side room and introduced himself. His name didn't register with Nick, as he had spoken to so many doctors and nurses and even the cleaner at one point, although he hadn't realised this at the time. All the faces had become a blur, merging into one authoritative figure.

'I don't see any benefit in being anything less than candid with you,' said the doctor. 'Medically, Evelyn is alive. My team managed to revive her and, of course, this is marvellous, but the prognosis is not good. The current position is that there is at best a ten per cent chance of full recovery, greater still if she would wake. In those circumstances things would be very different, much more positive and with a far greater likelihood of a complete and swift recovery.'

'Wait, wait a minute,' Nick said, interrupting. 'What do you mean *medically* she's alive? And a ten per cent chance of recovery seems very low. Far too low. What exactly are you not telling me? You say you are being candid with me but it all still seems cryptic and confusing.'

The doctor gave a small sigh as he organised his thoughts.

'The cardiac failure has caused Evelyn to become drained of what little resources her body had left. Add this to the meningitis plus the seizure she had yesterday and the result is that, to all intents and purposes, she's running on vapours. I wish I had better news for you but it's very likely that Evelyn will pass away today. In the absence of her waking, the very best we can hope for is that she remains alive, but unconscious. You already know that the longer she remains in the coma the more unlikely it becomes that she will ever come out of it. Furthermore, if she ever should wake there is a very strong possibility that she will have suffered some behavioural changes and, or, cognitive disabilities.'

'You mean brain damage?' Nick wasn't prepared to mince his words. The doctor pulled a face, as though uncomfortable with the phrase Nick had used.

'At its bluntest, yes,' he said.

'So what you're saying is that either she wakes up, or there's no hope,' said Nick. It wasn't a question, but a statement.

'I'm so sorry, but it's my belief that it is only a matter of time, and very much borrowed time at that.' He had assessed Evie's condition and personally was amazed that his team had been able to revive her at all. 'I don't think she'll wake up, leastways not in time for her not to be affected.' He watched Nick carefully, observing as he interpreted what he had been told.

'Can I stay with her?' Nick asked. 'I don't want her to be alone.'

'Of course.' The doctor was impressed by Nick's equanimity, admiring his composure and ability to always put his wife's needs before his, despite his anguish. As both men rose from their seats the doctor laid a hand on Nick's shoulder. 'Do you want me to tell her family what I've told you?'

Nick considered this for a few seconds, still numbed from the shock of what he had heard.

'No,' he said. He spoke slowly, as though trying to find the right words through the grief that was clouding his thoughts. 'I'll tell them, but could you please ask her parents to join me in Evie's room? Just her parents. I can't tell them all at the same time.'

NATALIE RETURNED from the cafeteria with a polystyrene cup of rancid coffee. Only Becca and Dan were waiting in the visitors' lounge. The thought of being left alone with her hostile brother and sister caused Natalie to panic.

'Where's Mum?' she said, her eyes darting from side to side. 'I've brought her a fresh drink.' See? I am a good daughter, she wanted to add. Becca raised her head and took a good long look at Natalie. Something was different about her sister but she couldn't place her finger on what exactly. She stared at Natalie in fascination, taking in the fearful eyes and shaking hands that still clutched the disposable beaker. Some of the scalding coffee had slopped through the plastic lid onto Natalie's fingers but she didn't seem to care. Becca's attention was caught by an unusual sight, then, when she realised that she had been fixating on — of all things — a broken finger nail, the penny dropped. How could she not have seen it earlier? It was so apparent. Natalie looked frightful with her pale, un-painted face, matted hair and tatty, mismatched clothes that any self-respecting tramp would have scoffed at. Becca hadn't seen her sister without her hair and make-up done since they were kids. Furthermore, without her trademark glamour Natalie looked uncannily like

Evie. It was something in the tilt of her head and in the way she had pulled her hair from her face. Even her troubled expression was the same. A brief chill passed over Becca. She had never seen Natalie look like this before. As she continued to stare Becca wondered if Natalie had experienced something akin to an epiphany whilst they'd all been absent.

'Mum and Dad have been summoned by the doctor. I can't imagine it's good news,' she said, not unkindly. She herself was as blanched as the snow-covered rooftops outside. 'Mum might need something stronger than that coffee if it's as bad as I imagine.'

Natalie sat down abruptly. Dan was sitting in the corner, refusing to speak to either of them. He turned his head to the wall each time Natalie looked at him. He was fed up. All he wanted to do was get home, drink himself into oblivion whilst watching his favourite Christmas film, *Die Hard*, and forget all about this relentless horror.

'Yippee Ki Ay, motherfucker,' he muttered under his breath.

Back across the waiting room Natalie felt more isolated than ever. Between Dan giving her the evils and Becca studying her like a book, she began to wish she had stayed at home.

'I wish they'd tell us what's going on,' she whispered to herself.

Natalie's wish was soon granted. Margaret, red eyed and trembling from an instinctive outburst of maternal grief, had managed to compose herself before she rejoined her other three children in the waiting room and told them it was all but certain that Evie wouldn't make it through another night. She then had to watch her three children disintegrate before her eyes upon hearing the news, each reacting in exactly the same way but also remaining stubbornly alienated. Margaret couldn't help but think it was sad that they didn't turn to each other for comfort. Instead they retracted into themselves and refused to acknowledge each other. Dan leaped to his feet and flung his arms round his mother's neck but the two girls remained seated, each encapsulated within their own grief, not even able to reach out to their own mother for solace.

What did I do wrong? Margaret thought, her insides twisting painfully from this added distress. Why do my children hate each other? Instead she gave a bald little speech about how their father and Nick were still with Evie, each trying to come to terms with what they had been told, but that if they so wished they could have a few minutes with Evie before… She couldn't finish her sentence as the threat of fresh tears loomed.

Margaret had said her own goodbye to Evie whilst she felt she could, just in case. Once she had released the initial reaction of shock and despair she'd sat quietly beside her daughter's motionless body, considering the inevitable. It was amazing, Margaret thought, that even though her skin was so white it was almost blue, Evie looked remarkably beautiful. Margaret couldn't believe her daughter wasn't going to open her eyes and smile at her. It just didn't seem possible.

'Sweet dreams, child,' Margaret had said, gently brushing some of Evie's dark hair away from her face. As she ran a few long strands through her fingers, Margaret briefly thought how unbearable it was that it might never have the chance to turn grey from old age. Evie might never see her daughter grow into a woman nor have grandchildren of her own. She, along with everyone else in the family, would lose so much.

Margaret had always thought it was a truly terrible thing for any parent to have to lose a child but she had never imagined it would happen to her. Not only that but she'd had to watch her husband of over thirty-five years fling himself onto the thin strip of bed next to where Evie lay, clutching at her hand, devastated by grief. She'd always been aware of Bernard's great love for Evie and had acknowledged it as a rare and powerful bond but, as she'd watched him sob and wail, she wondered how he could ever recover from such a loss.

All this passed through her thoughts as she stood and watched her three remaining children, realising that each one was presenting a new and unique worry of their own. Dan was twitching like a drug addict and would no doubt pile into the booze and smokes as soon as he was released from her supervision. Becca had sunk deep into introspective thought and would later stew over her guilt until she drove herself to self-deprecating madness unless she was intercepted. Natalie was the most worrying of all. She sat away from her siblings, diminutive and dressed from head to foot in uncharacteristic funereal black, wringing her hands and looking like a disaster victim. Normally so composed and untouchable, she had veered so far away from her usual self that Margaret wondered if she would know how to reach her. She knew she wouldn't be able to rely on her husband for support. If he ever stopped thinking about his beloved Evie it would only be to turn on his youngest daughter for whom he had little patience or affection under the best of circumstances. It would only be a matter of time before he found some way of blaming her, and whereas Margaret would once have said that Natalie could handle even the most terrible barbs from her father now she wasn't so certain. It didn't help that Natalie had managed to infuriate her father more than ever before over the past five days. Perhaps they should be kept apart for a while, she pondered.

Almost as though Margaret's thoughts had summoned him, Bernard staggered out into the corridor a few moments later, ranting and babbling. His face was green with nausea and his legs barely had the strength to support his body. He swayed like a seasick deckhand. He was upon them all before

Margaret could intervene, leaving her with no other option but to witness his outburst in silence. He was incoherent with grief.

'How can this have happened? On Christmas Eve she was drinking wine and cracking jokes. No one should go that quickly. For God's sake, why Evie? Of all people, why take her? Why not—?' His eyes flickered to Natalie who was trying to disappear into the oversized cardigan she was wearing. She read his thoughts in an instant. She paled and her eyes filled with the bitter tears of understanding.

'Bernard, you don't know what you're saying.' Margaret desperately tried to mitigate the damage. She had known this would happen. She just hadn't known it would happen so soon.

'No Mum, let him speak,' Natalie said. She stood up. Her voice was even, albeit a little shaky. 'Let him have the guts to say what no one else — not even Dan, for once — dare say. Let him say that he wishes that it were me lying there dying rather than Evie. Let him say it because it's true. You're all thinking it... and so am I.' Natalie paused. 'I've always known Evie was the favourite. It's our family's worst kept secret. You all wish you could trade me for her.'

Becca, still sitting under the window, watched the scene unfold with clinical detachment. Her big brain had been working much faster than everyone else's, ruminating over tiny little observations no one else had noticed. It was as if the final piece of the jigsaw had been slotted into the puzzle that was the entire Bingham family. For the first time in years Becca knew who Natalie was and understood her. Natalie was Becca, and Becca was Natalie: they were both in Evie's shadow. It was just that they had reacted in very different ways. For the first time Becca could see that Natalie's bloody-minded behaviour, her relentless unpleasantness and her cloying, ruthless ambition were all reactions to their parents' ill-concealed preference for their elder sister. By the same token she, Becca, had reacted by having no desire to ever challenge Evie's crown. She had been lazy. Inaction had been her own protest.

'I don't,' she said, her voice catching. The entire family turned to face her. They watched her as she rose from her seat and crossed the room to stand beside Natalie. 'I don't wish it was you lying there instead of Evie. I wish she wasn't there at all because it's unbearable, but it wouldn't be any different if it were you. It would be just as painful. You're my sister and you're equally as irreplaceable. For all the right reasons.' Becca brushed a stray strand of hair away from Natalie's cheek. Tears were streaming down Natalie's face. Becca turned to her parents and took a long, deep breath. 'You've punished us for not being Evie for as long as I can remember. You can't continue to blame us for not being her, not now, not after all this.' She persisted in talking about her sister in the present tense. She wouldn't accept that Evie had gone, not until it was absolute and irrefutable. Not until she was convinced all hope had been extinguished.

'Becca,' Dan said. He looked appalled.

'No Dan, don't interrupt me. You don't understand how it is. You're a boy and that very fact has exempted you from this entire conversation. Mum and Dad have always accepted you for who you are because you can't be compared to Evie. It wasn't the same for Nat and me. I can't even blame Mum and Dad for that. Evie's perfect. She's everything a good daughter should be as well as being a wonderful mother and the best of sisters. We all rely on her to make our lives easier and no matter how bad things get, she can always do exactly that. She's always there for all of us and I don't know how we could possibly manage without her, but I do know that we'd have to find a way. We wouldn't have a choice. More than that, we would have to help Nick and India. They love Evie for what she is, not what she can do for them. They're the ones who need the most help right now, not us. We already have each other — whether we like it or not.'

As soon as she finished speaking Becca felt the room spin. If it hadn't been for Natalie holding her up she would have crashed to the ground. Instead she was helped into a seat by her sister and mother. As she gasped for breath she felt a cold hand creep into her own. It was Natalie's. Becca looked at her sister and was amazed to see that she was staring at her with an expression that looked something like reverence. Becca gave her a small smile. The icy hand gripped hers. Natalie had at last found an ally, and a friend.

Becca expected her father to bawl her out for her outspokenness but instead he pushed past her and staggered away. Margaret had noticed his green pallor and the beads of sweat on his forehead from earlier. His reaction to the doctor's news had been more physical than anybody else's. It was just another piece that she would have to pick up.

Natalie, still clinging onto Becca's hand, was becoming increasingly troubled by one thing in particular. It was certainly true she hadn't always treated Evie, or indeed any of her siblings, with a great deal of respect. However, she'd always been incredibly fond of the family's animals and had always taken it upon herself to ensure that any poor departed pet received a fitting interment. It was due to Natalie that there was a little corner at the far end of Bernard's beloved orchard that had become a pet cemetery. It was here that dozens of animals, everything from goldfish, rabbits, guinea pigs, rats and hamsters to dogs and cats, had been laid to rest, often wrapped in a favourite blanket or lovingly placed into a shoebox coffin with a cherished toy. Eternally soft-hearted when it came to animals, Natalie had even been known on occasion to collect up any deceased creature she encountered, be it an infant bird that had fallen from a nest in a tree or some unfortunate roadkill she'd found in the gutter, and bury them in her little animal graveyard. As a child she had always maintained that it gave them some dignity, allowed them to rest in peace, and she had fashioned childish little headstones made from glued together lollipop sticks with names written on with felt pen. If a family pet had died she had always rounded up her brother and sisters and insisted they join her in a solemn little service under the apple and pear trees. Sometimes even Bernard and Margaret had been summoned to attend, mostly when a larger pet had died. It had been her intention to add the poor, eviscerated sparrow from earlier that morning to her sombre graveyard once she returned to Magpie Cottage. That was why she had boxed it up carefully and tried to protect it from further desecration.

The only downside to Natalie's kind-heartedness had been that she would inevitably lay awake in bed imagining that the beloved creature was cold during its first night outside on its own. More often than not she had experienced nightmares containing terrifying, ghoulish images of lonely animals that were crying to be let back inside. Margaret had always consoled her youngest daughter by telling her that the animal had just joined its other furry friends and it would be happy enough because it was in good company.

Now, trying to absorb the knowledge that Evie might die, Natalie battled to come to terms with what would happen to her sister's body. A lone sob escaped her. With a sigh, Margaret sat beside her. On Natalie's other side Becca put an arm round her shoulders.

'If Evie dies where will she go?' Natalie wailed. 'What will they do with her? Where will they put her?'

'Oh, for God's sake!' Dan snapped. His bottom lip was quivering and his eyes had filled with water. Only with supreme effort had he not broken down. He himself had been tormented by the thought of them all eventually heading home, leaving poor Evie behind. Instead, he directed all of his grief into his dislike of Natalie. He was desperate for a drink. 'Just shut up, Natalie. No one cares what you think.'

'Don't tell your sister to shut up, Daniel,' Margaret said. 'Natalie has every right to express her feelings just as you and Becca do.'

'I care what you think, honey,' Becca said to Natalie. 'In answer to your question, I think they would take her down to the mortuary and from there she'd go to a Chapel of Rest until it was time for the funeral. She wouldn't be alone in either place.'

'But she wouldn't be with us,' Natalie said. Another thought occurred to her. She raised her head. Her face was pinched, her forehead creased with worry lines. 'Would they cut her up?' Becca and Margaret simply stared at each other. It was the most horrific of contemplations.

'Absolutely not,' Becca said, crossing her fingers behind her back. For once her encyclopaedic knowledge failed her. She had no clue what would happen but wasn't prepared to share that thought with Natalie. No point in distressing her further. 'There would be no mystery.' This explanation seemed to appease Natalie, who leaned in to Becca and rested her head on her shoulder. 'Anyway, it's all hypothetical. Evie won't give up without a fight. She might make a miraculous recovery yet.' What was one more lie, Becca thought. Natalie's smile was reminiscent of a child's; she was prepared to believe anything. Becca drew comfort from her sister's presence. Surprisingly, Natalie's unexpected neediness made her feel better, almost as if she were exercising some control over the situation. It gave her some much-needed grounding, something to concentrate on. It felt natural to look after Natalie, like it was her job to take care of everyone, just as Evie did. God, if the worst happened she would be the eldest.

Margaret observed the exchange between Becca and Natalie with interest. Peculiarly, Natalie was acting more like Becca always had, brooding and reflective, and in turn Becca appeared to have taken on some of Evie's more matriarchal characteristics. It was fine by her if Becca wanted to take care of Natalie, she thought. It gave her a little bit of breathing space and allowed her to focus on Dan who, by his own regular analogy, had gone over to the Dark Side and was lashing out at whoever was nearby. He was acting more like Natalie usually did, bitter and resentful. If only he would let her near him she could perhaps help him deal with his emotions. As it was he was sitting in the corner, absentmindedly shredding a *Woman's Weekly* into tickertape and scowling at anyone who addressed him. His hands moved systematically, rip and tear… rip and tear. Margaret watched as though mesmerised. The sound of rendered paper was almost hypnotic. It made her relax into her seat and allowed unbidden thoughts to enter her head.

Margaret had long ceased to worry about the pantomime tickets she had pre-booked although the thought of them did invade her thoughts briefly as she considered how desperately she had wanted her daughter to stay at home for longer than had been agreed. She recalled how she had all but begged Evie not to travel up to Newcastle on Boxing Day but instead stay for a few more days. Ironically, she'd got her wish and Evie hadn't travelled up north — but at what cost? There was no way she could have known that this Christmas would possibly be the last few days she would ever spend with her daughter. Tiredness overwhelmed her. She had a sudden and desperate desire to crawl into her own bed back at Magpie Cottage, fall asleep and be relieved, if only temporarily, of the horrors of the past day. As it was, she was still required to referee her other children. Over by the plastic seats, Dan was still venting his spleen.

'If by some miracle Evie lives you'll be marmalised for that little lecture,' he said nastily to Becca, who paled. It was the first time Dan had turned his vengefulness on her. She didn't respond but gazed at him in defiance.

The sound of footsteps on the linoleum made everyone look up. It was Bernard, returned from the bathroom. He had lost his green tinge but still looked as though he would like to tear anyone who dared to look at him limb from limb. Feeling Natalie shrink next to her, Becca thought that the phrase 'like father, like son' had never been more pertinent.

'We should start to think about going home,' Bernard said. It was evident he had all but given up. In his mind Evie was already dead. 'No point hanging about indefinitely if these quacks can't do anything useful—' He went on to blame everyone from the locum to the poor staff nurse who scurried past just as he was at the pinnacle of his tirade.

'Bernard, calm yourself, for goodness' sake,' Margaret said. 'You'll have a heart attack if you carry on like this. Plus, you're upsetting the children.'

'He's not upsetting me,' Dan snarled. 'What's wrong with a bit of finger pointing?' As he spoke he looked directly at Natalie.

'There's no point in doling out blame,' Margaret said. In her mind she saw the magpie picture. Becca, who was becoming increasingly concerned about how weary her mother looked, knew what she was thinking. She considered that perhaps her mother had the right idea. She blamed the picture. It was sure as hell a lot healthier than blaming another human being, which was what everyone else seemed to be doing.

'We can organise transport once we know something definite,' Becca said, keen to remain calm and practical. 'We've got two cars so there's plenty of space.'

'Well, I'm not getting in a car with *her*,' Dan said, jerking his head towards Natalie. 'I'd rather walk home.'

'Fine, you can go in the Corsa with Mum and Dad,' Becca said. 'I'll take Natalie back in that tank she's rented.' Even as she spoke she dreaded driving Natalie's vast hire car. She'd never driven anything larger than a hatchback since passing her test. The thought of driving a four litre, two hundred and fifty horsepower luxo-barge all the way back home on icy roads was not one that she relished.

'What about Nick?' Natalie asked in a quiet voice. Everyone instantly looked guilty. They had quite forgotten about Nick. Natalie hadn't even seen him since her arrival. He had remained stoically by Evie's bedside, save for the brief chat he'd had with the doctor.

'I'll see if there's any news,' Margaret said. 'You lot try not to kill each other in the meantime.' As she left Dan pulled a face behind her back.

'Ignore Dan,' Becca told Natalie, taking her to one side so their brother wouldn't hear. 'He's just letting off steam by being a git. He'll come round in a few days.'

NICK HAD RETURNED to Evie's side. His head was full of what ifs and if onlys. What if he'd realised sooner how serious Evie's illness was? If only the locum doctor had been bothered to venture out on Christmas Day instead of funking out. What if the county hadn't experienced the most severe snowfall on Boxing Day since the 1930s? If only they hadn't crashed into that drift. Would any of it have made any difference?

He spared a few thoughts for Evie's family. The Binghams would all be shell-shocked. The loss of Evie would shake every last one of them to their core. She was his wife and the mother of his child but she was also a daughter and a sister. She was connected to everyone; she was the central hub, the centre of the compass. All roads led to and from her. He couldn't even begin to contemplate the impact it would have on India. That would have to be dealt with later.

All this he considered as he waited. Half an hour of precious time had already passed. How long did Evie have left? Minutes, hours, perhaps a day? It wasn't even as though she were conscious and he could tell her how loved she was or reassure her that her daughter would be cherished and protected. It was so quiet. Too quiet. Desperate to make a noise, any noise, he twiddled the dial on the bedside radio until he found a station playing soft, gentle carols. The doctor had said music might help, but it hadn't. All it had succeeded in doing was heightening everyone's responses, provoking tears when they had hitherto been composed. In the end they had switched off the wretched thing as it had proved too emotive. Now Nick found it a welcome distraction from the unforgiving silence.

'Sleep in heavenly peace,' sang a lone chorister with angelic purity. He seemed to speak for Nick even if his words were cruelly symbolic. Overwhelmed, Nick stood, turned his back on the tiny figure in the bed and gazed out of the window. In the distance he could see rows of terraced houses. People had started to turn on their Christmas lights. He could see illuminated trees in the windows and the silhouettes of people as they moved around within their homes. No doubt they were all settling in for a cosy night of festive pastimes with their families and friends, eking Christmas out for as long as they could before clock and calendar crept ruthlessly towards the inevitable cold harshness of January and the reluctant return to work. They were oblivious to his pain but for the first time he didn't resent them for their good fortune. Make the most of what you've got, he thought silently, be thankful that you're not enduring this. The snow had once again begun to fall, silently and with theatrical grace. The chorister continued to sing. Under any other circumstance it would be a perfect Christmas moment.

Turning back from the window he started. His entire world gave a violent, unfamiliar shift. It couldn't be true. He must be hallucinating from the fatigue and emotion. The doctors had said it would defy all medical probability, that it could never happen, that they should brace themselves for the very worst. They were all wrong.

Evie was looking at him. Her eyes, dull from pain and exhaustion, were open.

She gave a ghost of a smile, the edges of her mouth barely upturned, so great was the effort.

'Hey,' she said, so faintly that it was barely a whisper.

Evie had woken up.

28TH DECEMBER

Becca woke early, having not slept well. Her dreams had been tormented by visions of death and loss. Despite her exhaustion following her night's sleep on a hard, hospital chair she was relieved to be awake. Grabbing the television remote she clicked on a random channel. Anything to provide some noise that would drown out the unpleasant thoughts violating her subconscious. However, not even the mindless babble of the TV could mask the shrill ringing of the telephone in the hallway. Becca glanced at her alarm clock. It wasn't even eight o'clock yet. Her heart plummeted, certain that it could only herald bad news. She pressed the mute button and listened as someone padded downstairs and picked up the receiver. Although she strained her ears she couldn't identify who was speaking or what they were saying. Realising that if it were bad news she would find out soon enough, Becca flopped back onto her pillows and considered the events of the past three days, which had been nothing short of horrific.

Becca still found it hard to acknowledge how close she had come to losing her sister. It seemed only by the merest chance, some glorious intervention, that Evie had woken up.

Even the doctors had been astonished. They had hidden their surprise of her recovery far less well than they had the possibility of her death. She herself would never forget the sight of the doctor walking towards them, more slowly than in real time, or so it seemed. Everyone had expected the very worst so, when he uttered the marvellous news that Evie had woken up, no one seemed to know how to process it. Only after the passing of several seconds did anyone react. From then on it was pandemonium with everyone hugging each other, even Dan and Natalie although they parted like the Red Sea once they realised. Everyone was in tears from the sheer relief.

Nick was with Evie, the doctor told them. She was perfectly stable and appeared to have shaken off the infection with remarkable swiftness. The initial prognosis was excellent and, in view of this, her parents could pop in to see her for the briefest of visits. He had barely finished speaking before Bernard was striding down the corridor towards Evie's room. He didn't bother waiting for his wife.

'Can anyone else see her?' Becca had asked. Best not, the doctor had replied. Despite her progress Evie was exhausted, emotional and very weak. Why didn't everyone else go home for a hot meal and a good night's sleep? They would be able to see their sister the next day.

Margaret thought this was a marvellous idea. She bade her three younger children stay put whilst she went to see Evie for a few minutes. She would then organise for them to go home. She and Bernard would stay overnight, along with Nick. There was no point in everyone having a further night of discomfort.

She returned smiling. Evie was sitting up and had even managed a few sips of water, she told Becca, Dan and Natalie.

'Did she say anything?' Becca had asked. Not much, her mother had replied with a frown. Evie had shown a little interest in India but hadn't commented on much else. She'd seemed in reasonable spirits though, but was easily upset which was only understandable under the circumstances. With that they'd had to be content.

After that Becca had been instructed to drive Natalie and Dan home in the hire car on the grounds that she was the one that Margaret trusted most to get them home in one piece.

'Just keep Dan and Natalie away from each other for as long as you can,' Margaret had told Becca, having pulled her to one side. 'If they get too unbearable you have my full blessing to bang their heads together. I'll ring you later tonight to give you an update. I'm sure everything will be all right now. The doctors are confident that we're well over the worst.'

'They were also pretty confident that Evie wasn't going to wake up,' Becca muttered. 'I just hope they're not proved wrong a second time.' Too much had happened since Christmas Day for her to be carried along by everyone else's joy and optimism. Her nature dictated that she would have to wait and see.

'I'm sure they won't be,' Margaret had said. She gave Becca a brief bear hug. 'Do be careful on those dreadful roads and message me as soon as you're home safe. And don't forget to give the Lovells a ring once you get outside the hospital. They should at least be forewarned of the impending invasion. Oh dear, I wonder if the man has been to fix the boiler yet?'

'If he hasn't I'll deal with it,' said Becca. 'Everything will be fine. Go and stay with Evie. I'll take care of Tom and Jerry over there. Don't worry about a thing.'

'You're a good girl, Rebecca,' Margaret said. She'd come to appreciate her second born over the past three days, admiring her calm, unflustered approach to her warring siblings and her instinctive care of Natalie, who continued to give her cause for worry with her pinched little face and new-found meekness. 'Thank God you knew what that awful rash meant.

I wouldn't be surprised if we have you and your brains to thank for Evie's recovery. I'm very proud of you, and so is your father.'

'I know,' Becca said, although nothing would make her believe that her father thought anything of the sort. She doubted whether he had given her, Dan or Natalie a moment's thought since Christmas Day. Still, she appreciated the sentiment.

After that she'd had the unenviable task of driving Natalie's hire car back to Magpie Cottage in the snow. At least there had been no en route incidents within the vehicle as Natalie had flaked out on the back seat as soon as they passed the city boundary. Keen not to antagonise Dan, who was still in an explosive mood, Becca hadn't even commented when he sparked up in the car. Instead she wound the window down slightly using the electronic buttons on her side. Better to freeze than to choke on Dan's ciggie smoke.

Thankfully the gritters had been out in force and they were home within the hour. Having been instructed of their impending arrival, Carol Lovell, tall and elegant with her stylishly cut blonde bob and wearing jeans and a cashmere cardigan, greeted them with warmth and a pot of fresh coffee. India was happily watching the telly with Malc in the lounge. A casserole from the freezer was keeping warm in the Aga. The boiler still wasn't fixed but Carol had called upon the neighbours and they would be more than happy to let the three Binghams have a shower.

Natalie, having been deprived of meat for days, fell upon the casserole like a starved tiger, mopping up her mother's delicious, homemade, thick gravy with enormous chunks of bread. Dan ate nothing but sat on the back step, huddled into his overcoat, swigging lager straight from the can and chain-smoking. Chewbacca sat next to him, his eyes slitted from the smoke.

The first thing Becca had done was to go and see India.

The lounge was at least warm due to the well-stacked fire that Malc had built. An older and fatter version of Nick with greying black hair and a beer belly that was a legacy from too many pints and pies whilst supporting the Magpies at St James's Park, Malc was big and hairy, like a slightly scary teddy bear. The lights on the tree had been switched on and the whole atmosphere was calm and welcoming. India was sitting on the sofa, next to her Grandad Malc, eating raisins out of a small cardboard box. She looked like she didn't have a care in the world. She certainly wasn't aware of what had transpired over the past three days. And thank goodness for that, thought Becca as she followed Carol into the lounge.

'I hope you don't think that the Christmas tree being lit is disrespectful. We thought it best to keep everything as normal as possible for India,' Carol said.

Becca couldn't reply. The inescapable normality of her family home overwhelmed her. Unable to stop herself she burst into uncontrollable sobs. The roaring fire, the twinkling tree lights and the glow from the candles all reminded her of what this Christmas should have been, but wasn't, whilst at the same time offering her comfort and reassurance.

'Oh, you poor child,' exclaimed Carol. She led Becca to a chair and sat her down. She fished in her cardigan pocket for a tissue. On the sofa India cast a moderately interested glance at her Aunt Becca before deciding that *Wallace and Gromit* was much more entertaining.

'I'm okay,' gulped Becca eventually. 'It's just been really shitty. Oh God, I'm sorry, I know I shouldn't swear but shitty just sums it up.' She tried to get out of the chair. 'Where's my phone? I promised Mum I'd message once we were home. She'll be worried sick. And I have to ring the boiler chappie. Where are Natalie and Dan? They can't be left together for any length of time otherwise they'll murderlise each other.' There was so much to do. What was that saying her mother always used when she was ridiculously busy? She could hear her in her head. 'I'm meeting myself coming back.' It had always made her laugh, but not today.

Carol forced her back into the chair. 'You stay put. I'll need to message Nick again and I'm sure he'll pass the message on. The engineer has been sorted, he's due first thing in the morning, and Natalie and Dan can sort themselves out. Other than some name calling and hair pulling they can't do each other much harm. Why don't you go and get a shower, have something to eat and try to get some rest? That way you'll be refreshed for when you go back to see Evie.' What she didn't tell Becca was that her employers at the call centre had rung several times that day asking why she hadn't been at work or bothered to call in. She didn't feel that there was any point in upsetting the poor girl further.

Carol was so unruffled and practical that Becca found herself calming down. No wonder Nick was so adept at dealing with her deranged family. Patience was obviously a genetic trait. Taking Carol's good advice, Becca retired to bed, taking a bowl of casserole with her. She decided to pass on the shower, not wanting to see the sympathetic looks of their neighbours. Nor did she want to answer their questions or accept their well-intended platitudes. If the engineer was coming in the morning she could get clean then. At that precise moment all that she craved was sleep.

BECCA CONSIDERED ALL this as she listened for whoever had answered the phone to hang up. When she heard the telltale ping of a concluded call she stiffened and went cold. There was a period of silence followed by footsteps coming up the stairs. Becca jumped as someone tapped on the door. Natalie poked her head round.

'Are you awake? Mum rang,' she said. Becca motioned for her to come in. 'It's good news. Evie's much better. She's eaten some breakfast and is perfectly lucid. Apparently she's been asking when she can come home.'

'That's *great* news,' said Becca. 'Did the phone wake you up? It's not like you to see the early hours unless absolutely necessary.'

Natalie pulled a face. 'Firstly, I couldn't sleep for the thoughts whirling round my head, driving me nuts. Secondly, I think I'm still on London time.' She gave a small smile. 'It's a world away from this sleepy village.'

'I bet it is,' Becca said, not envying her sister her frenetic London life. 'Anyone else up?'

'Carol's in the kitchen — God, that sounds like one of those ghastly flyers we get from the vicar's wife each Christmas — making coffee. She seems like such a nice lady. Malc's nice too. They drove all the way down just so that I could go to the hospital,' Natalie said. There was only the slightest hint of her former sarcastic self; her tone was mainly compliant and deferential. 'Do you want me to bring you some coffee up?'

Five minutes later Natalie returned with two steaming mugs. She handed one to Becca then paused slightly, as though unsure of what to do next. Perhaps she should return to her own room. It wasn't as though she and Becca had been on the best of terms this Christmas. Becca intercepted this thought.

'Plonk yourself down,' she said lightly. '*Friends* is on in five minutes.'

Relieved at not being kicked out, which was what she had half expected, Natalie made herself comfy on the bed beside Becca. In easy silence they drank their drinks and watched the television, but not even the high caffeine content of the coffee could keep them awake. By the time the closing credits ran they were both asleep, Natalie's head resting on her sister's shoulder. It was the first peace either of them had had in days.

❄

FIFTEEN MILES away Margaret Bingham paced the floor in the corridor outside Evie's room. The doctor was in with Evie doing some tests and assessments. Nick and Bernard had taken the opportunity of their banishment from the room to grab a quick breakfast from the hospital cafeteria. For Nick, the bacon butty was the first food he had eaten in seventy-two hours. It was only after he had consumed three sandwiches that he realised how hungry he was. Even Bernard managed a couple of slices of toast and a cup of tea. Margaret had elected to remain on the ward in case the doctor needed to ask any questions. In any event, he would give his verdict as soon as he had finished examining Evie and Margaret wasn't prepared to wait for longer than was necessary.

Evie had asked the doctor if she could return home but the doctor hadn't been keen to permit this. She was still very ill, he told her, and would need expert care. Evie had then called upon the most powerful tool she had to enable her to win her argument — her mother. Of course Evie would have round the clock care, Margaret had assured the sceptical doctor in her desperation to have her daughter back under her jurisdiction. Then Bernard had added his twopenn'orth, saying that Evie needed to be surrounded by her family in order to make the best recovery. Listening to this from her hospital bed, Evie thought nothing of the sort. Her foremost motive was that she wanted to be with India but she was damned if she was going to allow Nick to bring her precious child to her, in the hospital, where disease and illness was rife. Nick's was the only voice of dissent. As he raised his worries about the detriment that could be caused by discharging Evie too soon every eye turned to stare at him with an accusation of treachery. Even Evie looked at Nick with a blank gaze, which told him plainly that she was displeased with him and that he would pay later for his betrayal. Never before had his wife looked at him quite like that and Nick was left with an unfamiliar but distinctly uncomfortable feeling of unease.

Gradually the Binghams had worn Nick and the doctor down, firstly by arguing the case that there was no care in the hospital that Evie wouldn't get from her husband and parents at home, especially now that the drips and devices that had been keeping her alive had been taken away, needed no longer. When that failed Evie resorted to threats. She would discharge herself immediately. The doctor had capitulated but only on the condition that he make a thorough examination of Evie to ascertain that she wouldn't do herself or her recovery any harm if she were released. He also stressed that a proper schedule of care would have to be followed and she would have to agree to regular visits from the district nurse. Those were his terms and they were non-negotiable. He then told Nick and the Binghams that if they didn't agree with him on these points he would consider them to be neglectful of what was best for Evie rather than themselves, no matter what she or they might think. Looking huffy, Evie accepted the proposition.

Now all they could do was wait. Margaret was still pacing by the time Nick and Bernard returned from the cafeteria. Having eaten, Nick had lost some of his pallor. Even Bernard looked a little more cheerful, albeit still apprehensive.

'No word yet,' Margaret told them, noting their expectant faces. At that very moment the door of Evie's room opened. The doctor beckoned them all inside. They found Evie sitting up, a beaming smile on her face. Margaret instantly felt hopeful. At the same time, Nick's heart sank. He was beginning to feel like a mere pawn in the Bingham family.

'Whilst it's highly unorthodox, and certainly isn't my ideal recommendation, I will permit Evie to be taken home,' the doctor said. Margaret opened her mouth to speak but the doctor held up a hand. 'However, it's essential that she is kept quiet, clean and receives round the clock supervision. There must be absolutely no excitement, plenty of rest and good, wholesome food, and not too much time spent with the little girl. Evie still needs to recover, whether she believes that to be the case or not — and she clearly doesn't. I've explained to her the extreme trauma that her body has endured together with the risks of doing too much too soon. It's vital that you all, too, appreciate this. I can provide you with plenty of information and leaflets about the after-effects of the illness, and you must all pledge to return to the hospital if there is any disintegration in Evie's health. My last stipulation is that she spends one more night in the hospital for observation, just to be on the safe side. Other than that, you can take her home with you tomorrow.'

'That's wonderful news. Thank you, doctor,' Margaret said. 'Of course, the entire family will do whatever they can to make Evie's recovery as smooth as possible'

No one noticed that behind her back she crossed both sets of fingers as she made this statement. Just for luck.

DAN WAS PISSED OFF. He had endured three days from hell only to come back to his home to find some unfamiliar woman masquerading as his mother. Having only met Carol and Malc Lovell at family events, such as Nick and Evie's wedding and India's christening, it felt to him as though there was a couple of strangers in his house. As a result he felt that his freedom had been curtailed. Now he felt that every time he lit up, or had a little drink, or watched something he wanted on his own telly, he was being policed. Worse still, Becca, his erstwhile partner in crime, was now best buddies with Natalie, his nemesis. He didn't like that one bit.

He considered all this as he embarked on a melancholy

walk round the village. Chewbacca, not having been walked for days and desperate for a good run, was straining at the lead and earned a few sharp words for his trouble. Angus the Westie was pottering along beside him.

Balls to it, thought Dan as he passed The Half Moon, what's the harm in a lunchtime pint or two? His mind made up, he headed for home in order to drop the dogs off, and pick up his wallet. Forget that, his wallet was empty. His mother wasn't home. He would raid the housekeeping kitty instead.

Alas, his plans were destined to be foiled. Dan returned home to find his mother and father in the hallway. They still had their coats on which told him that their return had been within the past few minutes. The Lovells, Becca and Natalie were all present too. Everyone looked thrilled. Becca was the first to notice Dan loitering in the doorway.

'Dan! Guess what?' she said. Dan couldn't be bothered to guess. 'Evie's coming home tomorrow. The doctors have okayed it. Isn't it fantastic?' Before Dan had the chance to reply his mother cut in.

'It's all hands to the deck,' she began. 'This house has to be spotless by tomorrow afternoon. I want every bed changed, every skirting board washed down and every window cleaned. The bathrooms need scouring and the kitchen needs an overhaul. I'm not risking Evie catching another infection. She's still vulnerable. There'll be jobs for everyone, starting from right this second.'

Dan's groan was drowned out by Carol's pledge of assistance. That put the kibosh on any illicit midday trip to the boozer.

'What time will Evie be home?' Becca asked, taking her parents' coats off them and hanging them in the narrow cupboard that her mother liked to refer to as 'the cloakroom'. 'It'll be fabulous to see her.'

'Provided nothing has changed we can collect her

231TH DECEMBER | 231

tomorrow afternoon. Nick's going to stay overnight. He'll ring tomorrow morning once the all clear has been given,' Margaret said. 'Your father and I are going to go a little earlier so we can have a chat with the doctor about her care and to book her first visit from the nurse. We've come home so that Evie can get as much rest as possible, plus there's so much to do round here. Oh, Natalie dear, your father and I wondered if you'd mind letting us use that large car you've hired. We thought it might be the most comfortable, travel wise.'

'Absolutely,' Natalie said, looking directly at her father in the hope he would give some sign that he approved of her co-operation. He didn't. Instead he turned to Becca.

'How did you get on driving that thing, Rebecca?' he asked. 'Not too much car for you to handle? I thought you'd struggle with it. No car for a girl like you.'

'It was okay,' Becca said, immediately feeling inadequate and more than a little bit insulted. Worse still, she got the distinct feeling that her father had only spoken to her so that he didn't have to acknowledge Natalie. She'd hoped they'd all got past the resentful bickering stage. She suddenly recalled with a large degree of unease her bitter speech about her parents' favouritism and knew she would pay for that at some point in the not so distant future.

All things considered she was relieved when the doorbell rang. Looking surprised, Margaret opened the door to find a diminutive bald man in denim dungarees and a donkey jacket. He was carrying an obviously heavy bag.

'Yeh called for an engineer, love,' he said, peering into the hallway. He looked taken aback to see so many people just standing there.

'Yes, two days ago,' was Margaret's sharp reply. 'You'd better come in seeing as you've turned up at last. I have a very ill daughter for whom central heating and hot water is a necessity, not a luxury.'

'Sorry, love. This was the earliest I could manage. I

thought I'd explained that on the phone,' he said, not realising he hadn't spoken to Margaret but to Carol. The engineer turned to Natalie. 'I can see you don't look well, love. I hope you get better soon.' Natalie didn't know whether to be astonished, offended, outraged or worried and the expression on her face reflected this. Becca had to turn away to hide her desperate need to giggle.

'This way, please,' said Margaret stiffly. The engineer followed her into the utility. 'I suppose you'll want a cup of tea before you get started.'

It was the most ungracious offer of a cuppa the engineer had received in a long while.

'If you don't mind, love. I'm gaspin'. Blimey, it's chilly in here, eh?' he said. The look Margaret gave him was of sheer exasperation.

I've a right one here, he thought as he opened his bag and selected the appropriate tools. Once she had plonked his mug of tea in front of him, Margaret then proceeded to bark instructions to her family in the manner of a dictator. The engineer was thankful he'd been left in the relative solitude of the utility room, even if it did reek of alcohol dregs courtesy of the three recycling boxes chock full of empties. Jesus, he thought, as he peered into the boxes.

Ten minutes later Becca was stripping and remaking every bed in the house, Natalie was on polish-and-hoover duty and Dan, to his utter disgust, had been dispatched to the bathroom with a jay cloth and several tins of Mr Muscle.

'This is the worst Christmas ever,' he grumbled as the three of them stomped upstairs. 'One third spent humouring Mum and her freaky perfect Christmas crap, one third spent in a hospital waiting room and one third cleaning the bogs.'

'I'm surprised you can remember anything at all, you bloody lush,' Natalie snapped. Her snide comment was the first indication she hadn't quite yet descended into complete catatonia. 'More like one third in a drunken stupor, one third drying out and one third complaining about it.'

'Piss off,' was Dan's sophisticated response.

'Go on, Mrs Mop,' Becca said to Dan as she shoved him into the bathroom. 'Get cleaning. You do ball-all housework the rest of the year. 'Bout time you learned how to do it.'

'Bitch!' Dan retorted, slamming the bathroom door in her face.

Downstairs, Bernard rounded up Chewbacca and Angus intending to melt away from the threat of chores on the pretext of walking the dogs. Delighted at an unexpected second walk, Chewbacca emitted a wonderfully Baskervillian howl of such bass and volume that the poor unsuspecting engineer leapt to his feet in panic, banging his head on a low shelf.

'Ow, yeh *bass*-tard!' he yelled. He put a cautious finger to his forehead. When he drew it away he saw that it was smeared with red. He stuck his head round the doorframe hoping that Margaret was still in the kitchen. 'Have you got a plass-ter, love?' he asked.

Alas, Carol had brought India into the kitchen for her lunch believing it to be the safest place for her amidst such activity, and it was at this very moment that the little girl looked up from her plate and saw the bald, bloody head peering into the kitchen. Terrified, she proceeded to scream blue murder. Carol and Margaret were only able to calm her down with a bowl of ice cream once the engineer had been patched up and returned to the utility. It was then that India decided to echo the earlier pained expletive of the engineer.

'Yeh *bass*-tard,' she sing-songed, over and over again. As soon as she cottoned on to the fact that her grandmothers didn't want her to say this she chanted it all the more. At this juncture Bernard reappeared in the kitchen.

'I've forgotten the poopie bags,' he said, heading for the

utility. To express her pleasure at seeing her grandfather, India greeted him with relish.

'Grandad, yeh *bass*-tard!' she shouted, giving her spoon an emphatic bang on the table. Bernard looked scandalised.

'I don't believe this,' said Margaret, wringing a tea towel in distress. 'Not only is my grandchild swearing, she's swearing in broad Yorkshire. What a way to welcome her mother home tomorrow. This isn't what I wanted at all.'

Gradually the situation calmed down. Carol relocated India from the kitchen to the lounge and encouraged her to read her favourite book in an attempt to distract her from her new-found use of profanities. Bernard left with the dogs and Margaret started to scrub the kitchen floor and work surfaces until they were spotless. There was a minor hiccup when the engineer, having temporarily fixed the boiler, stomped across Margaret's newly mopped floor in his steel toecaps, leaving dirty great footprints in his wake. Determined to remain dignified, Margaret desisted from beration.

'It'll do for a while, love, but yeh boiler'll need replacing soon,' the engineer said. 'It's yeh thermostat, yeh see.'

'What's wrong with it?' Margaret asked.

'It's buggered,' said the engineer, as though speaking to a child. 'Yeh'll need to get an engineer to replace it.' And it won't be me, he added to himself as he was shown the way out. In his opinion they were a family of nutters. He'd rather chew his own leg off than come back here. Someone else could deal with them next time.

I⊤ was not Becca's destiny to have a stress free day. She should have known not to be so naïve as to think that just because Evie's life was out of danger, her own would suddenly click into place. Her day had comprised of one aggravation after another. The first had been that Dan had obviously taken offence to her improved relationship with Natalie. He had made his feelings perfectly clear that morning at breakfast by glowering at her from across the table. Next had been her work calling, demanding to know why she hadn't advised them of her absences for the past two days. Despite her explanation, which she thought any decent human being would accept on the grounds of compassion, and her apologies and assurances that she had genuinely forgotten to call in all the upheaval, she was still told that she could expect to receive a written warning upon her return to the call centre. Incensed by such a reaction, Becca promptly tendered her immediate resignation by way of the words 'you can shove your job up your arses, you unfeeling cretins'. After that she doubted she could rely on them for a decent reference. If that hadn't been bad enough Dan had overheard the entire conversation and, in an uncharacteristic fit of spite, spragged to their mother, who proceeded to stalk Becca round the house as she remade the beds with fresh linen, lecturing her as she did so. Did she appreciate what she had done? What was she going to do for money? Did she realise how much easier it was to get a new job whilst you had one? Why didn't she swallow her pride and beg for her job back? Eventually Becca lost her rag.

'You wanted me to do something with my brains,' she bellowed. 'Well, this is my chance. Why can't you just trust me?' With that she stormed into her room and slammed the door behind her. She stood in her room seething until she was summoned to a family meeting downstairs. She entered the lounge to find everyone already seated, even the Lovells.

Christ, it's an intervention, she thought.

It wasn't. Margaret wanted to establish where everyone would be sleeping now that Evie was coming home. Evie and Nick would continue to have use of her and Bernard's bedroom and en suite. She and Bernard would make do with Evie's old room and Carol and Malc could have Natalie's room. They would take it in turns to have India in with them. Natalie could bunk in with Becca. Dan was the only one not affected, much to his relief, although he was heard muttering that his room still stank of old man farts and bird shite. Everyone ignored him.

Margaret then went on to make a suggestion that, in celebration of Evie's return from the jaws of death, everyone went to The Half Moon for their dinner that night. It would be her and Bernard's treat. Upon hearing this declaration of expense Bernard's head shot up but he didn't dare say anything. Everyone was agreeable to this, especially the three Bingham children who quickly realised that eating out meant no washing up and, better still, free booze.

Trouble started when Carol declared that she and Malc intended to go to the hospital that afternoon. This caused Margaret's hackles to rise.

'I'm not sure that's advisable, Carol,' she said, rather rigidly. 'The doctor was most adamant that Evie should have no visitors to enable her to have a good rest before tomorrow. Perhaps we should respect his wishes. Sorry to be so inflexible but I have to consider what's best for my daughter.'

'I'm not going to see your daughter, I'm going to see *my* son,' Carol said, also bristling. It was the first sign of discord between the two women. 'I've barely spoken to Nick since Evie's admittance. I think he'd appreciate our support.'

Margaret looked suitably squashed. 'Well, Evie doesn't want India going to the hospital so you can't take her,' she added waspishly.

'I had no intention of doing so,' Carol said.

Natalie exchanged glances with Becca, who gave an almost imperceptible shake of her head. Clearly everyone was still on edge. Even so, Becca thought that her mother had been unnecessarily abrupt. She decided to intervene before the spat could develop further.

'Should we say a seven o'clock departure for the pub

then?' she said brightly. 'That'll give Carol and Malc a good few hours with Nick and it'll leave plenty of time for us to get organised for the grand homecoming tomorrow.'

'Sounds good to me, pet,' Malc said. He was beginning to appreciate why Evie had always spoken so warmly of Becca whenever she and Nick had visited. In his opinion she had the same ability to diffuse tricky situations as her older sister. She had managed to remind everyone of the reason for the celebration without being contentious whilst at the same time avoiding a potentially unpleasant argument. Yes, Malc Lovell took his hat off to Becca. On the other hand, Evie had never been effusive about Natalie, and Malc couldn't understand that. There was no doubt that she was spoilt and temperamental but she had also displayed a great deal of common sense and kindness over the past few days. Nor had it escaped Malc's notice that Bernard had not once directly addressed his youngest daughter since his return earlier that day. If that was the norm it was little wonder that she was prone to throwing wobblers, he thought. Personally he admired her feisty nature and her acidic wit but most of all the fact that she took no crap. She'd have made a great Geordie, he thought.

NICK HAD DOZED off over a newspaper some other patient's relative had left in the corridor when the nurse popped her head into Evie's room.

'Mr Lovell,' she hissed, so as to not wake Evie who was asleep, curled up peacefully in her bed. The nurse had to repeat herself several times before Nick came round. When she saw his eyes were open she beckoned him outside. Nick, stiff and sore from several nights' sleep in an uncomfortable chair, was moderately spooked upon first waking to see a floating head peering round the door. With a yawn he tried and failed to refold the broadsheet paper before heading over to the door, stretching as he did so. A quick glance at the bed confirmed that Evie hadn't been disturbed. She was still sleeping soundly, her retroussé nose peeping over the top of the bed covers.

After becoming accustomed to the dimmed light in Evie's room it took his eyes a while to adjust to the harsh strip lighting in the corridor. Through watery eyes, he watched a couple head purposely towards him. It was several seconds before he realised who they were. Once he did, emotion welled up inside him.

With no spoken word he wrapped his arms round his mother, comforted by her familiarity. Never before had Nick been so pleased to see her. Carol held him for a long time, loath to let him go. His father was next to engulf him in a bear hug.

'All right, son?'

'How? How are you here?' Nick asked, overwhelmed by their presence. 'I thought you were in Newcastle.'

'We've been at Magpie Cottage since yesterday afternoon,' Carol told her son, still holding his hand tightly. 'Natalie telephoned us and invited us down. We've been looking after India, who is fine and not upset or anything. I've brought you a change of clothes and your father's overnight bag.'

Natalie? thought Nick briefly. That didn't sound right. He watched his mother as she whipped items of clothing out of a carrier bag.

'Didn't anyone tell you?' Malc asked. Privately he was appalled by his son's appearance but he kept this opinion to himself. It was obvious that Nick was wearing three-day-old clothes and that he had barely eaten. He looked exhausted, unshaved, unkempt and both his clothes and his breath stank. There was a regiment of Binghams and yet it seemed that not one of them had bothered to ask Nick if he needed anything. It wouldn't have killed them to bring him a clean shirt and a pair of pants. Or buy him a toothbrush from the hospital shop.

'I've hardly seen anyone. I've been with Evie for most of the time,' Nick said. At that moment the pressure of having to keep it together for everyone else's sake finally got to him. Now his parents were here he could pass at least some of his burden on to them. His face crumpled. 'I'm so glad you're here. I can't describe it. It's been horrendous.' He sank back into a chair, his head in his hands. 'I thought I'd lost her. I was so certain… so was everyone else… and then she just woke up.' It was at that point that he looked up at his parents. They both saw the utter torment in his expression. 'I should be ecstatic and I am, absolutely overjoyed, but I still don't feel happy. I don't know what to do. Mum, Dad… she's changed.'

Carol sat down quickly. 'What do you mean?' she asked, kindly. Nick shook his head as he tried to organise his thoughts.

'She's different,' he said. 'She's not my Evie, who was warm and loving. She's cold and abrupt and—' Nick paused. 'Mean.'

'In what way?' Carol asked. 'I don't understand. She's still Evie. Her personality can't have changed overnight.'

'It can. It's a common after-effect,' Nick said. 'Temper tantrums, moodswings, aggression. At lunchtime she threw a cup at the window in a rage when she heard that her parents had gone home. Thankfully it was only a plastic cup and it just bounced off the glass but there was lemon barley everywhere. Apparently it's nothing to worry about and it'll wear off in time, but I don't know. There's no light in her eyes. They've gone dark, like there's no one in there.'

Carol and Malc exchanged worried looks. It was clear to them that Nick was starting to suffer from his food and sleep deprivation. He was obviously depressed too.

'Have you eaten today?' Carol asked. 'Have you had any sleep at all?'

'Patches. I've had a couple of sarnies but not much else.'

'Right, in that case you can go with your father and get a square meal down you. I'll stay here and keep an eye on Evie,' Carol said. She plonked the clothes and washbag into his hands. 'You can have a wash and tidy up too.'

'What if she wakes up whilst I'm gone?'

'She'll understand. I can't imagine she'd begrudge you half an hour after the vigil you've kept these past days.'

'Don't bank on it,' Nick muttered. 'You've not had the pleasure of her since she woke up.'

'In that case you'll need your wits about you to dodge whatever she chucks at you,' said Carol. 'You're having some hot food and a wash. Don't argue with your mam. I know best.'

Nick mustered a small smile. 'So India's really all right? She's the only thing Evie can bring herself to talk about.' He omitted that Evie hadn't spoken to him about anything else, not even to ask how he was. It seemed that India was her sole interest, and even that was sporadic.

'She's fine,' Carol said. 'Everyone's doting on her.' She paused. 'Everyone's been very welcoming. Margaret and Bernard are taking us to the local pub for a meal tonight in celebration of Evie's recovery. They're insistent.'

'That's the Binghams,' said Nick. 'They're lovely, but they do tend to take over. In some ways they've been so supportive but I couldn't help but be relieved once they'd gone. Of course, they didn't go until they ganged up with Evie and overruled not only me but the doctors too.'

'What do you mean?' Malc asked sharply. He'd always got on with the Binghams, believing them to be normal, everyday folk. Now his opinion was constantly mutating as he learned more about them and experienced more of their insular habits.

'The doctors don't approve of Evie being released tomorrow. Apparently it's very unorthodox and not advised.

Evie's adamant though. Once she realised that she couldn't harm India she nattered, sulked and threatened until she got her own way. Of course, her mother pledged to provide round the clock care for as long as it takes. God knows how long that'll be. I have nightmares about having to return to work and leaving Evie at Magpie Cottage. I just want to take her and India back home with me.'

'Have you talked to Evie about this?' Carol asked. Nick gave her a condescending look.

'Seriously. Five minutes with Evie and you'll realise how redundant reasonable conversation is. She's obsessed with getting out of here. She can think about nothing else.'

'She's a mother, Nick,' Carol said. 'She's been separated from her child by force for days. Worse still, she knew how ill she was. She must have been worried sick not only for herself but for India too. It's only natural. I'd have been exactly the same. No mother wants to leave such a small child without her care. It's a devastating thought. If I were Evie I'd never want to let India out of my sight again. Don't be too hard on her.'

'Mebbe, but if I didn't know better I'd swear she was viewing India as just another reason for her to get her own way.' Nick didn't have the energy to argue with his mother but at the back of his mind a tiny voice was petulantly asking 'what about me?'. He knew he should try to silence it but in truth he had neither the energy nor the inclination. He felt that he had bled himself dry in his efforts to look after Evie and that no one cared. Of course he was jubilant that Evie had survived, that went without saying, but he couldn't help but feel some resentment that no one had shown any concern for him and the impact the ordeal had had on him. The Binghams had descended like a plague of locusts and had fought and squabbled through their time in the hospital whilst wearing masks of concern. He had no doubt that their worries about Evie had been genuine but, as usual, they behaved like a pack of adolescents as they went about it. It had been evident to Nick that not one of them gave a shit about him. Even Evie didn't seem too bothered by his presence. She was more concerned about herself, which he understood whilst at the same time wishing that she had a smidgeon of time for him. He daren't voice his feelings for fear of appearing childish and ungrateful. Instead he let them churn, bitter and rancid, in his stomach until he felt sick. At times he didn't know who he hated more, his wife, her family, or himself.

'I'm sure she's just desperate to see her daughter. Look, you're tired, hungry and overwrought and you're not going to be any use to Evie until you sort yourself out.'

'Why don't you come back with us tonight? You can get a good night's sleep and have a nice dinner and a couple of pints,' Malc suggested. 'It might do you good. Refresh you for tomorrow.'

'I can't,' Nick said. 'She's being released tomorrow.' It was as though Evie had been incarcerated in jail. 'I might as well see it through to the bitter end.'

'You're going to change your clothes and have something to eat, though. I insist,' said Carol. Nick knew it was futile to argue with her and silently accepted the proffered washbag. 'I'll send someone to find you if you're needed, which you won't be. You can afford to take twenty minutes. Malc, go with him and make sure he eats something decent. I'll wait here. Now, pass me that magazine, will you?'

With no option but to agree, Nick followed his father down the corridor.

BECCA HAD SPENT the best part of the afternoon doing her mother's bidding. Aggrieved by the Lovells' obstinacy and ultimately their departure to the hospital despite her advice to the contrary, Margaret had been intolerable and had beleaguered poor Becca until she almost snapped. In the absence of Evie, Becca was promoted to chief sounding board. It was a position she neither coveted nor enjoyed and as she scrubbed, polished and disinfected, whilst at the same time being subject to her mother's unending thoughts and opinions, she was forced to question her former desire to be her parents' favourite. Margaret complained about the Lovells going to the hospital; she complained about them being in her house. It seemed to Becca that they were damned if they didn't and damned if they did, and that her mother would only be happy once they had packed their bags and travelled back up the A19 to Newcastle where, in Margaret's opinion, they belonged.

Later, as everyone was walking to The Half Moon, Becca considered how her mother had changed as soon as the Lovells had returned from the hospital, reverting to the epitome of an affable hostess. Feeling shameful and disloyal, Becca found herself questioning her mother's sincerity.

The short walk to the pub didn't do anything to raise Becca's spirits despite the picturesque, festive weather and the jolly Christmas lights in the village. Instead Becca was reminded of Evie's first night at home when they'd gone to the pub for the quiz. That night now seemed an age ago. Back then she had still had a job, a healthy sister and a brother who was also her friend. Tonight the party that made its way through the silent, snow-dusted village was fractured and sombre. The Lovells had been suspiciously reticent since their return from the hospital, so much so that Becca doubted their keenness to join her family for a meal. Being naturally astute, Becca was certain something had been discussed between parents and son and was in no doubt that that 'something' appertained to her family.

Nor was her own family offering any more joy. Her mother was already piqued at having her wishes disregarded but now she appeared to have taken umbrage to their aloofness. Natalie was clinging to Becca's side like ivy, which caused Dan to ignore the pair of them. Once her greatest ally, he was so disgusted by Becca's new allegiance to Natalie that he refused to even meet her gaze. Wise in the ways of her brother, Becca knew that he was stewing and could be relied upon to air his thoughts sooner rather than later, probably during the meal which would, of course, be the most inopportune of times. He had never been any good at bottling things up and Becca dreaded the moment when his vexation would finally be spilled. The only member of the party who Becca couldn't fathom was her father. She knew he had been very badly affected by Evie's ordeal but now he had retreated into himself. Earlier that day, when she had asked him if he was all right, he had looked at her as though she were a stranger. Worse still, he couldn't bring himself to even look at Natalie, let alone speak to her, which had the consequence of taking a further chunk out of Natalie's fast diminishing confidence. Having suffered many times as a result of Natalie's malevolence, Becca found her younger sister's transformation to meek fragility the most worrying. In many ways Becca wished for the return of Natalie's venomous streak. Cold and hard she may have been but she'd also been more than capable of fighting her own battles. Now Becca suspected that the character assassination Natalie had received from her father and brother, in addition to those awful hours she had spent at Magpie Cottage incarcerated with Christian, India, Grandpa and Great Aunt Ada, had done irreparable damage. There was probably worse still to come. Shortly after her return to Magpie Cottage, Carol, respecting Nick's wishes, had taken Becca and Natalie to one side, feeling more comfortable with them than with Margaret, and confided that Evie was acting out of character and was less tolerant than she had previously been. Upon hearing this Natalie had paled, no doubt remembering how vile she had been to her sister and her niece in the run up to Christmas

Day. Repercussions were inevitable. Little wonder Becca was worried.

Once inside the warmth of the pub they were ushered to their table by Col the Landlord. As the village was, in general, friendly and compact, he, together with most of his clientele, was familiar with all the Binghams, especially Dan, and had been asked by many of his regulars to get an update on the plight of Evie. However, what he wasn't prepared for was the twisted version of musical chairs that followed. Dan refused to sit next to Natalie or Becca and promptly disappeared to chat up the lovely Rachel behind the bar as soon as he had bagged an end seat next to his father and opposite Malc. Natalie was insistent on being seated next to Becca, who in turn was ordered to sit adjacent to her mother so that she could continue to bend her ear. Furthermore, Becca thought it prudent to keep her sister away from her father as that was another walking time bomb that had yet to explode. As she was generally feeling disillusioned with her daughter-in-law's parents, Carol was keen to keep as much distance between herself and Margaret as possible. This in turn was tricky as India wanted to sit in between both her grandmothers. Malc couldn't give a monkey's where he sat so long as someone brought him a pint.

Eventually everybody was sorted out with drinks and menus and once everyone had ordered their food Margaret set out her plans for the following day. She and Bernard would go to hospital to collect Evie and Nick first thing, she declared. This immediately raised Carol's hackles as she'd planned on returning to the hospital in an attempt to give Nick what she felt was some much needed back up. Each mother was desperate to do what was best for her own child.

'I don't see the benefit of a battalion of people converging on my daughter,' Margaret said. 'The doctors say she's very distressed from the ordeal of nearly dying.'

'I completely understand, but my son is also very

distressed from his ordeal of watching his wife almost die,' said Carol, rather waspishly. Not that any of you gave him a second thought, she wanted to add, but didn't. 'I need to do what's best for him and he's said that he wants me there.'

A brief squabble followed until the two women agreed that both sets of parents would go, but in separate cars. This neatly led to the problem of who would stay behind to babysit India. Margaret had an instinctive but well-founded reluctance to leave her three other offspring unchaperoned in the house under such volatile circumstances. With this in mind she instructed, rather than asked, Becca to take charge of both her niece and her siblings. Dan immediately looked aggrieved.

'I don't need a nanny,' he said, his lip curling. 'Anyway, shouldn't Becca be out looking for a job?' Becca treated him to a look of death.

'That can wait one more day,' Margaret said sharply. All the same, she cast Becca a look of asperity, which assured her that she hadn't heard the last of it. 'I don't trust you lot not to murder each other in my absence. Besides which, Becca won't have any problem finding work with those brains of hers. Perhaps she can find something rather more fitting to her intelligence.' Becca rolled her eyes. Ignoring this, Margaret continued. 'I think tomorrow we should have a homecoming dinner for Evie. I'm sure she'd like that. I'll prepare all her favourite dishes. It'll be marvellous. The Christmas lunch we never got to have.'

'Do you think she'll be up to that?' Becca asked, filled with doubt.

'Of course, I'm her mother. I'm sure Evie will feel much better after a decent, home cooked meal. I'll do a joint of beef, with Yorkshires and roasts. We'll have Caesar salad to start and crème brûlée for dessert.'

'You can count me out,' said Dan. 'I'm taking the lovely Rachel into Loxley for dinner and drinks.'

'You'll have to cancel,' said Margaret.

'No,' replied Dan. 'It's been organised since last week. I'm not cancelling so don't ask me again.'

'That's a very selfish attitude, Daniel. How could you plan it for tomorrow night? This is very important.'

'Well, when I made the arrangement I wasn't aware that it would clash with the welcome home dinner for my sister who had been snatched from the jaws of death. It wasn't in my diary at the time. Perhaps if I'd had a bit of a heads up I might not have been so selfish—'

'That's enough, Daniel,' said Bernard.

'Oh, let him go,' said Becca. 'He'll never stop whinging otherwise.'

'I agree. He'll only hog the wine if he's there anyway,' Natalie said. A couple of glasses of Pinot Grigio had dispelled some of her new-found self-doubt, resulting in a mini-reversion to her former self. 'Talk about Man on de Sauce.' She had intended it as a joke but no one laughed. Everyone couldn't help but notice that Dan was downing two pints of lager to everyone else's one drink. Instead there followed an embarrassed silence, which Dan finally ended.

'Thanks, but I don't need any help from you,' he snapped. He turned to his mother. 'For the last time, I'm not changing my plans. There's been precious little to be joyous about thus far this Christmas. This is one thing that's just for me.'

'You selfish little sod. You should be thinking of your sister, not yourself. You all should,' said Bernard. 'Nothing's more important than Evie.'

Ain't that the truth, thought all his other children with differing degrees of bitterness.

Dan acknowledged silently that he'd done nothing but think of his sister for days and that he was desperate to turn his thoughts to something else, something less traumatic, before it drove him to madness. Rachel, with her blonde hair, long shapely legs and splendid knockers, fit the bill perfectly.

'Don't even think about asking your father or sisters for a lift. You're on your own this time,' Margaret said, knowing that she couldn't force Dan to stay against his will. Of course, that didn't mean she couldn't make his life extremely tiresome in the meantime.

'Fine, I'll get the bus,' Dan said. He acknowledged that now was perhaps not the best time to ask his parents for a sub in order to pay for his romantic night out. Instead he turned to Natalie.

'I don't have enough coin for smokes. Nats, you're loaded. Buy us twenty Marlboro Lights from the vending machine, will yeh? I'll let you consider it a peace offering.'

Natalie shot him a look of utter incredulity. 'Get fucked!'

'Natalie!' thundered Bernard.

Thankfully, everyone was distracted by the arrival of the starters but, alas, it served only to provide a temporary spell of peace. As the first course was cleared away, Margaret recalled the ear-bashing she had received that afternoon courtesy of Great Aunt Ada, who had telephoned her niece-in-law and proceeded to tell her exactly what she thought of Natalie and the crude manner in which she had been shunted home.

Dan, already halfway through his fifth pint, was only too keen to egg his mother on. The irony hadn't escaped him, he told Natalie, that even Great Aunt Ada, her erstwhile lone fan, could finally appreciate her awful personality. Becca did her best to defend her sister by replying that Great Aunt Ada was a bitter old soak who changed her mind more times than a talent show judge. Amidst all this Natalie was trying to state her case.

'I wasn't rude to her. I simply told everyone that it was for the best if they went home early in view of what had happened. Grandpa didn't take offence. On the contrary he understood perfectly and was just worried about Evie. And as for Christian, as far as I could gather he was actually relieved to be going back to London,' she said.

'Country life not to his liking?' Dan sneered. Natalie ignored him.

'I did everything I could to help her but she was disagreeable and obstructive. She wouldn't help with India and she complained about every meal I put in front of her. Nothing pleased her.' Even as she spoke Natalie identified recognisable aspects of her own character in her accusations. It left her feeling distinctly uncomfortable. She was even more ashamed of herself when she realised no one had bothered to ring Grandpa to let him know that Evie was getting better. She made a mental note to call him the following morning.

'Now you know how I feel every time she visits,' Margaret said drily. 'Sorry, Bernard, I know she's your aunt but she's insufferable. How your Grandpa survived growing up in the same household as the old trout I'll never know.'

'I have a fair idea,' said Dan, giving Natalie a pointed look. It was at this point that Rachel sashayed over to the table with a pint of Stella that she had clandestinely pulled for Dan whilst Col the Landlord had been down in the cellar changing a barrel. Becca, having already met Rachel on quiz night, smiled and said hello to the girl who, if all went according to Dan's master plan, would be her future sister-in-law. Natalie, however, felt her jaw drop when she saw just how pretty and sexy Rachel was. She stared as Rachel gave Dan a shy smile before returning to the bar.

'How did *he*,' she pointed at Dan, 'get her to agree to go out with him?'

'Don't be unkind, Natalie,' said Margaret. 'Your brother is very attractive.'

'Yeah, to another Aye-Aye perhaps. Don't get me wrong, I can see why Dan would fancy her. She's a walking swimsuit model crossed with a free beer machine. I just don't understand how the attraction is reciprocated. I thought the references to 'the lovely Rachel' were tongue in cheek.'

'Ohhh, one can hope,' groaned Dan. He took a long draught of his complimentary beer and smacked his lips.

'So you haven't snogged her yet, then?' Natalie said.

'None of your business, nosy.' Dan said. He turned to Bernard. 'There you are, Dad. You've now met the next Mrs Bingham.'

Bernard grunted a monosyllabic reply. He'd barely spoken to anyone all evening and even then he'd only addressed his wife and son on matters concerning Evie. He hadn't spoken to Natalie at all since his return to Magpie Cottage that afternoon. Her behaviour since she had come home for Christmas was still fresh in his memory and he wasn't in a forgiving mood. Nor did he feel any better inclined towards Becca, who he was also loath to forgive for her all too accurate recounting of both his and Margaret's distribution of affection. He even spoke to Dan as if he were a friend or acquaintance rather than a son. It was as if he now believed himself to only have one child. Evie.

None of this escaped either Carol or Malc's notice. Feeling immensely sorry for Natalie, Malc started to grill her.

'Are you courting then?' he asked her. 'I'm sure you must be, a pretty girl like you.' His question brought an image of the ghastly Christian to the forefront of everyone's memories. Natalie cringed. Once again, Becca waded in to come to her sister's rescue.

'Nat and I both had boyfriends but we got rid as they weren't good enough,' she said. This was technically true on both counts despite it being euphemistically put. Neither break up had been as straightforward as Becca's words implied. It was also a statement designed to pre-empt any tricky questions about her own derisory love life.

'Oh dear. Well, if that's the case I'm sure it's for the best,' Carol said.

'Not if Christian starts bad-mouthing me all round the Corporation,' said Natalie gloomily. Then she visibly cheered up. 'Not that anyone takes any notice of him anyway.'

'What do you do, Natalie?' Malc asked. Natalie had to give him snaps for making an effort.

'I'm a producer for the BBC in London,' Natalie said. Dan rolled his eyes.

'Here we go,' he muttered. 'The Natalie Show.' No one paid any attention to him.

'Oh!' said Carol, suddenly looking excited. She and Malc turned to each other and started communicating via lifted eyebrows, nods and hand gestures in such a way that only a long term couple can. Natalie sighed inwardly, preparing for the questions that invariably followed a disclosure of her job. Can you get me tickets for a live recording? Do you get to meet a lot of celebrities? Can you get me a signed photograph of John Barrowman? Natalie prepared her stock answers. Live recordings? Yes, but only for obscure new shows that are a bit naff. Don't bother asking for tickets for Graham Norton or Strictly 'cause they were snapped up within seconds and not even staff could get hold of them. Celebrities? Of course, I see them all the time in passing but they really aren't as thrilling as everyone would think. (She never bothered to add that the first time she met Colin Firth in the Star Bar she had nearly wet herself from the excitement.) As for signed photos, I've never met the man but I can give you the standard BBC website addresses for his shows.

'This is going to sound a bit cheeky but—' Here it comes, thought Natalie. 'Our nephew, Nick's cousin, Reggie has just started work in the City and is keen to make new friends. Would you mind if he gave you a ring?' Carol said.

'Huh?' Natalie said, taken aback. She hadn't seen that one coming.

'Don't worry, pet,' Malc said, mistaking Natalie's surprise for apprehension. 'He's a canny lad. We wouldn't lumber you with someone Plug-ugly. Plus he's one of the Toon Army, so you can't go wrong there. You never know, the two of you might hit it off.' Natalie dutifully handed over her business card but knew that the 'canny' Reggie wouldn't be calling her. She didn't dare ask what the Toon Army was.

Malc and Carol continued to chat to Natalie. In an attempt to build bridges with her brother, Becca asked Dan what his plans were for his hot date the following night. Dan, in turn, defrosted sufficiently to tell her. Pudding was served, and cleared away. By this time Dan had drunk seven pints and was starting to slur his words. His eyes were glistening like a cat's. Becca yawned. She cast a brief glance at her watch. God, it was almost eleven. She hoped they could go home soon. Sensing that their ETD was approaching, Dan sloped off to say goodbye to Rachel who, having rung for time, was permitted a ten minute break. Dan disappeared out of the side door of the bar. They were still outside when the group trooped out into the cold night. They jumped apart at the sound of familiar voices.

'Howay, Casanova, man!' shouted Malc, who was also buoyed up by several pints of bitter. 'Leave the pu-ar lass alone for five minutes. Yeh'll see her tomorrer.'

Furious, Dan said a brief goodbye to Rachel before following his family home. Things had been going well up until the point when his cretinous family had appeared. Rachel had been sharing her Smirnoff Ice with him and, thus encouraged, he had been just about to lean in for a snog when Malc had rudely interrupted them. Bloody impostors! When were they going to clear off home? He walked home in a huff, deliberately lagging several hundred yards behind everyone else to have a sly smoke.

Ahead of Dan, the group passed the village green. As they did so Becca noticed one of the smaller houses had acquired a for sale sign. It was a middle property in a terrace of alms cottages and had a rather overgrown garden, a rickety, paint-chipped gate and ivy trailing up the front elevation. Despite its tatty appearance it was an attractive house. Feigning idle curiosity, she asked her mother, who was a walking oracle when it came to residents of the village, who was moving out. Margaret replied that it was being sold by one of the ladies from the WI who was moving to Bath to live with her son and daughter-in-law. It only had one bedroom, her mother told her, but had had a new kitchen and bathroom fitted recently. It had plenty of storage but needed a bit of modernisation. Becca wondered if her mother would have been so keen to big up the house if she'd been aware of the basis of her daughter's interest in it. She took a mental picture of the estate agent's name so that she could make some enquiries.

No one spoke for the remainder of the walk. Each individual was preoccupied by his or her own thoughts. Margaret was contemplating menus for the following night's meal. Bernard was thinking about Evie. Dan was daydreaming about the lovely Rachel. Becca was speculating on the possibility of house ownership. Natalie was obsessing in equal measures about her unpopularity and her impending return to London. The Lovells were worrying about Nick. India, fast asleep in her buggy, was the only one without a care. It surprised no one that, as soon as they arrived back at Magpie Cottage, each faction wordlessly retired to their respective bedrooms. It was as though they had run out of things to say to each other.

29TH DECEMBER

Everyone rose early, either by design or by force. Becca had been happy to get up as, unused to sharing her bed, she had been kept awake all night by Natalie, who had a nasty habit of kicking, punching and muttering in her sleep. Dan hadn't been so keen to leave his bed. Hungover again, he spent the first half hour of his day in the kitchen forcing down Alka Seltzer, gulping and retching like a vampire that had been forced to drink holy water. Margaret and Bernard left Becca, Natalie and Dan with strict instructions, and also a few threats, with regard to care of both the house and India before they set off for the hospital in Natalie's hire car. Carol and Malc followed in their own vehicle and made good use of the journey into Loxley to have a serious discussion about life at Magpie Cottage and how it was affecting their son and grandchild. At least the weather wasn't as vicious as it had been. Snowstorms and blizzards had turned to dreary sleet. Gradually the fields were reverting to green and brown.

Both parties arrived at the hospital to find Evie sitting in a wheelchair, wearing loose day clothes and a bootfaced expression. Neither set of parents were aware that Evie had stubbornly refused to get in the wheelchair, being mistakenly confident she could walk unaided to the hospital exit, and only the doctor threatening to rip her discharge papers in half had convinced her to change her mind. Even so, she had got her revenge by seizing the blanket Nick had attempted to wrap round her legs and, screwing it into a ball, flung it to the floor with a strength and energy that caused even the assisting nurses to raise their eyebrows. They had witnessed many tantrums and moodswings by post-meningitis patients but none had been so entertaining or carried out with such dramatic flair as Evie's. Despite this, they wouldn't be sad to see her wheeled out of their sight as she had turned into a particularly difficult and demanding patient. Let her be someone else's responsibility from now on.

Nick, standing by her side with her overnight bag in his hand, was therefore astonished to see Evie greet her parents with a beaming smile. Suddenly she had metamorphosed into her old self, which left Nick feeling ambivalent about his wife's behaviour. On the one hand, he was desperate for this phase of extreme behaviour to cease, as the doctor had assured it would, and for his sweet, kind wife to re-emerge. On the other, he was keen for Evie to demonstrate the cruel ill temper she had subjected him to since she had woken up. Now, watching Evie smiling and hugging her parents, he didn't know whether to be relieved or disappointed that she had inexplicably sweetened up.

The doctor sidled up.

'All set?' he asked cheerfully. Evie nodded her head happily.

'I can't wait to see my baby,' she said. 'Is she all right?'

'She's more than fine,' said Carol, giving Evie a quick hug. 'She's at home with her aunts and uncle.' Carol was taken aback to see Evie in such good spirits, taking into account what Nick had told her the previous day about her short temper.

'Not Natalie, I hope,' Evie said, her eyes narrowed dangerously.

'Natalie's been especially good with her,' Malc said, keen to defend his new favourite Bingham.

'I doubt that,' Evie snapped. All pretence at niceties was wiped away in an instant. 'I expect you've been taken in by her pretty face. She's a vindictive little bitch and I can't believe you've left India with her. I wouldn't trust her not to pack India off to the workhouse in exchange for a new Gucci handbag. Take me home, *right now!*'

'Anything you say, cookie,' Bernard said. Either the cruel things Evie had said about her sister didn't register or he simply didn't care. 'I'll wheel you.' He didn't notice the looks of disbelief on everyone else's face, so deep was his joy at having his Evie returned to him. With continued ambivalence, Nick still didn't know whether to be relieved or disappointed with Evie's reversion to form.

Margaret also appeared to be in denial. As the group began to move away the doctor pulled Margaret back.

'A quick word about Evelyn,' he said. 'I think it's best she isn't left unsupervised with the little girl.'

'Why ever not? Is there a health risk?' Margaret was full of concern.

'No, it's not that. Evelyn can be a little… err… temperamental at the moment and has a tendency to lash out when provoked. It's quite common but, in view of this—'

'Oh doctor!' Margaret truncated him with a short laugh that managed to be both dismissive and patronising. 'If you're suggesting that Evie would ever harm India, you're very much mistaken. Evie is a marvellous mother. I don't think she's ever so much as tapped the back of India's hand in anger. I know her better than anyone and, believe me, there's no way she would do such a thing.'

'Her husband has reason to disagree, and so do I,' insisted the doctor. 'I'm only advising, from a medical point of view, on what's best for Evelyn.' Unknowingly, he had raised his voice slightly and Evie, having a mother's trained hearing, heard her name mentioned.

'What's that?' Evie called from down the corridor. 'They're whispering about me. Dad, take me back.' Unable to refuse Evie anything, Bernard dutifully wheeled her back. 'What are you saying about me? I want to know!' She was as petulant as a child who had been told she couldn't have a bar of chocolate.

'The doctor was just telling me that you might be a little bit crabby after your ordeal and maybe we shouldn't leave you alone with India,' Margaret said, still laughing. 'Of course, I told him it was nonsense.'

'As if I'd harm my own child,' Evie growled at the doctor, reacting to his opinion exactly as he would have predicted. She looked livid.

'I was also going to advise you not to relay our discussion to Evelyn,' he said to Margaret in slightly exasperated tones. 'It isn't in her best interests to become aggravated.'

As if to prove his point, Evie could now be seen clenching and unclenching her fists. Margaret brushed this aside as mere nervousness but Nick and Carol shared meaningful glances. Carol could sense her son was desperate to talk to her, and she had a fair idea what about.

Earlier that day Nick had had a brief chat in private with the doctor who had signed Evie's discharge papers.

'I just want it noted that I do not advocate taking Evie back to her parents' house,' Nick said as he sank into a chair in the doctor's office. 'I don't agree that it's the best thing for her. I believe she would be safer and better cared for here in the hospital. Her mother will drive her mad with all her fussing and smothering and her siblings can't be trusted not to instigate open warfare on each other, neither of which will be conducive to keeping her quiet and calm. She'll be dragged into whatever triviality they're scrapping about.' The doctor had listened with sympathy, and silent agreement, but advised that he felt he had been left with no option but to acquiesce with Evelyn's wishes.

'You and me both,' Nick had then muttered. He felt he had been irrevocably overruled. Not even he, Evie's husband and the person whom she should love and trust above all others, could make her see reason. Their discussion had resulted in a bitter argument that had culminated in Evie telling Nick, rather icily, to leave her room. She wasn't prepared to believe that he wasn't having a go at her family. Nor, she told him, was he welcome to sleep in the chair by her bed that night. Equally furious and devastated, Nick had sat outside on a cold, hard chair glaring at the tinsel draped round the nurses' station. Some bloody Christmas this had turned out to be!

To pass the hours he struggled to understand Evie's personality change until, just as the nurses were changing shifts in the early hours, she displayed an amazing volte-face and had called him into the room demanding to know, with weepy outrage, why he had abandoned her. Relieved that the fight was over Nick sank into the familiar bedside armchair and tried not to dwell on his confusion and his guilt, the latter which he felt, with a considerable degree of resentment, had been manufactured by Evie to ease her own conscience. Not once did Evie apologise but, as ever, Nick said nothing and forgave her, chalking it up as yet another after-effect of the trauma she had suffered. At least the doctor had promised to have a quiet word with Evie's mother before they took her home in an attempt to vindicate Nick's reservations. Now Nick had just watched that attempt fail miserably.

'Let's just get you home,' he said. 'This isn't helping anyone.' As he turned to follow Bernard and his wife, the doctor laid a hand on his shoulder to express his sympathy and support.

'Good luck, Nick,' said the doctor. 'Remember we're here if you feel you need advice and don't forget those support group leaflets I gave you earlier.' Nick nodded his gratitude before moving on. There was nothing more the doctor could do or say.

Outside the air was bitterly cold and Evie shrank into her cardigan, suddenly mourning the warm blanket she had so flippantly discarded a few minutes earlier. Nor did it help that neither her parents nor the Lovells could agree on who was to travel with whom. Carol and Malc presumed that Nick would want to travel with Evie but she, in turn, would need an entire back seat to herself. Adding to the complications was the fact that neither Bernard nor Margaret was prepared to stand down. Eventually, in a half-hearted attempt to keep the peace and also to prevent Evie from freezing on the spot, Nick suggested Evie travel with her parents and he would travel with his. Despite everyone's surprise at this, and also Evie's lack of reluctance to this idea, it did seem to be the most sensible and feasible solution. And so, once Evie had been made comfortable, Nick jogged over to the car park and his parents' car. As his father drove away he sank into the back seat, clearly relieved to be away from his wife. When his mother quizzed him on it, Nick replied that he felt he needed a time-out from Evie, and that her unpredictability was beginning to wear his last nerve to a frazzle. Taking note of his pale face and tired eyes, reddened by lack of sleep and worry, Carol could do nothing but condone his decision.

THEY WERE BACK at Magpie Cottage within three quarters of an hour.

Becca, desperate to see her sister, had been watching from an upstairs window and had been the first to greet the Lovells. As soon as she'd seen their familiar car pulling into the drive she'd raced downstairs and yanked opened the front door. Chewbacca and Angus slipped past her legs and began circling the car. They ignored her commands to get back inside.

'Hi!' she called. 'I can't believe you're here already.' Her excitement was tempered when she realised Evie wasn't with them. With an expression of confusion she gestured towards Nick. 'Where's Evie?'

'It was better for Evie to travel with your folks,' Nick said diplomatically. He bent down to pat the dogs in an attempt to stop their frenzied welcome.

'I see,' said Becca. Her tone indicated to the Lovells that she did indeed see. It was no surprise to Becca that her parents had begun to monopolise Evie already. 'Well, let's get you inside. Natalie's waiting with India.'

Natalie, not so keen to see Evie, had opted for India-sitting and was waiting in the kitchen. India was in her high chair and the kettle was whistling on the Aga. Nick entered the kitchen and was greeted with an ear-piercing shriek of joy from India. Lifting her out of her high chair, Nick buried his face in her dress to hide the fact that a few tears had escaped from his eyes. With uncharacteristic sensitivity Natalie turned away from them and instead concentrated on the teapot in an attempt to give Nick some privacy. No one else knew where to look.

'Pooh, stinky,' India said, wriggling in an attempt to get away from her father. Her face, wrinkled in disgust, was so comical that everyone laughed, causing the tension in the kitchen to dissipate. Dan wandered into the kitchen and gave Nick a brief salute in greeting. Nick nodded back.

'I suppose I will be a bit ripe,' Nick said. 'I wonder if I have time for a quick shower before Evie gets here.'

'They can't have been too far behind us,' Carol said. 'I expect Bernard is taking it steady so as not to joggle Evie about. They'll probably be here in five or ten minutes.'

'Then I'll risk it,' Nick said. 'Who wants this bundle of

trouble?' He automatically turned to Becca. He didn't notice Natalie's face fall.

'I'll take her,' Carol said, taking India from Nick's arms before anyone could argue. Mother, son and granddaughter exited the kitchen and went upstairs, talking quietly amongst themselves. Dan slid out of the kitchen as silently and calmly as he had entered. He was followed by Becca, who also went upstairs to resume her watching post by the window. Still in the kitchen, Natalie raised a full pot of tea to an empty room and with a false, bright smile asked 'anyone for a cuppa?' before banging the teapot onto the table and flopping into a chair in despondency. She might as well be invisible.

UPSTAIRS, once Nick was safely in Margaret and Bernard's en suite bathroom, Carol pulled the dress India was wearing over her head.

'Let's get you out of that dowdy thing, pet. It's got a stain on it.' It hadn't. 'You want to look all pretty for when Mummy gets home, don't you?' India had been dressed in a long forest-green dress with a white trim that was one of Margaret's favourites. Dressing India in this particular outfit had been one of the instructions Margaret had left Natalie and Becca, alongside turning on the heated blanket and nicking flowers from vases around the house for the bedroom, seeing as fresh ones couldn't be bought. Carol was just straightening the hemline on the new red patterned dress and matching bolero jacket she had bought India as a Christmas present when Becca called from the landing.

'They're here!'

Nick emerged from the en suite with a bare chest. He had decided against a shower but had had a brief wash and brushed his teeth and hair. Flinging his filthy shirt and sweater onto the bed, he pulled fresh clothes over his head.

Despite his efforts he still looked drained and pale. Scooping India into his arms he headed downstairs.

As Bernard pulled into the driveway everyone lined up outside to welcome Evie, much to her amusement. Rather like Ye Olden Tymes, when the Lord of the Manor returned home and was greeted by his staff, she remarked as Nick opened the car door. Her eyes scoured the group for India. Nick, intending to help his wife out of the car, had passed India to Becca who, because she also wanted to help, promptly passed India to Natalie. Now, upon seeing her daughter in the arms of her youngest sister, Evie's eyes narrowed to slits. As she alighted from the car Margaret clapped eyes on India, who was now dressed in an unfamiliar outfit, and her eyes also narrowed. For ten or so seconds mother and daughter looked curiously alike. Margaret dragged Becca to one side.

'I thought I told you to dress her in the green velvet,' she hissed.

'I did,' Becca hissed back. 'She was wearing it when she went upstairs five minutes ago. Carol must have changed her.'

'For goodness' sake! Did you arrange the flowers?'

'Yes.'

'And switch on the heated blanket?'

'*Yes.*'

'I'll just go and check,' Margaret said, disappearing inside. Becca couldn't help but feel frustrated. This wasn't how she'd imagined Evie's homecoming at all. Evie had practically snatched India out of Natalie's arms as soon as she was in reach and was now cuddling and kissing her daughter. India was laughing and giggling and was clearly delighted to see her mother after so many days' absence. Becca hadn't got anywhere near her sister yet.

'Let's get you inside,' Nick said. The heavy grey sky was threatening to sleet and he was more than aware that Evie was still in the back seat of the car. No one else seemed to care. Surely she would be better off inside where it was warm and dry.

'In a minute!' Evie snapped. Nick recoiled. Becca, not having witnessed Evie's turbulent moods, looked shocked. Within a split second Evie's expression had changed from seraphic to demonic and back again. She had never seen her sister look so vicious, and especially never towards Nick, who now just looked mortified. She decided to play a safer card.

'India doesn't have a coat on. Why don't we all go inside?' she said, stepping forward. Upon seeing Becca Evie's eyes lit up.

'Becca!' she cried, holding out her arms for a hug. She was suddenly her old self again. 'You must help me settle in. Here, take this creature so Dad can help me get inside.' She passed India to Becca. The little girl immediately began to whinge, so displeased was she that she had been separated from her mother after such a short time.

Upstairs, Margaret was not happy to discover that her plans to ensure an immaculate, welcoming bedroom had been scuppered by Nick flinging his reeking shirt and sweater on the bed. Furthermore, whilst Carol had been changing India's clothes, India had amused herself by strewing her dirty clothes, which Evie had been keeping in a carrier bag under a chair, around the room. Worst of all Angus, having found a stale tripe stick in the garden, had joined the adjournment to the bedroom, eaten the stick and was now wiping his face on the counterpane. The entire room stank of cow stomach. All in all, the impression Margaret had wanted was somewhat marred.

Tutting, she scooped up all the soiled clothes into the carrier bag, intending to take it downstairs and wash it as soon as possible. However, her disapproval turned to indignation when she found the outfit she'd selected for India balled up behind the chair. All thoughts of laundry forgotten she shook out the dress. As soon as she could she would change the outfit back to her own choice.

Back downstairs Bernard was monopolising Evie to the extent that no one could get near her. Evie, in turn, only had eyes for India and was finding her father's attentions suffocating. Poor Nick was desperately trying to convince everyone that Evie needed to be in bed resting but was being universally ignored. At this point Evie had managed to progress no further than the hallway and was seated on a wooden chair. Nick wanted to put his head in his hands in despair.

Worse was to come. Natalie had tried her very best to keep out of Evie's way but, like a cruel game of pass the parcel, every time India was separated from Evie she ended up in Natalie's arms. Fortune had counteracted this by ensuring Evie didn't notice but, as Natalie found herself in custody of the little girl for the third time, fortune retracted her patronage. Carol chose that very moment to move a fraction to her left, exposing Natalie and placing her in Evie's direct line of vision. Feeling Evie's eyes boring into her, Natalie attempted a weak smile. It was the catalyst Nick had been dreading. Evie flipped. She started screaming at Natalie, calling her every name she could think off and ripping her personality to shreds. India, not used to seeing her usually placid mother behave in such a way, began to cry from fright. This Evie also blamed on Natalie. She commanded her father to retrieve India from Natalie but, shocked and distressed, India clung onto Natalie, with whom she had spent more time with than anyone else over the past few days. This only served to madden Evie further.

'I don't want you within fifty feet of my child,' Evie screeched. Natalie was visibly shaking and was doing all she could to prise India's tiny fingers off her and from out of her hair. 'Let go of her!'

'I'm trying,' Natalie protested, panicked. 'She won't let

go.' Eventually Bernard lifted India away from Natalie, treating his youngest daughter to a look of pure hatred as he did so.

'What on Earth is going on?' Margaret cried, descending the stairs. She snatched the weeping India out of Bernard's arms and carted the distressed child back upstairs. Here was her chance! She reappeared five minutes later. India, duly calmed down, was dressed in the green velvet again.

'Wasn't India wearing red five minutes ago?' Nick asked, perplexed.

'Who wants tea?' Margaret cried in an attempt to distract Carol, whose head had whipped round to stare at India. She ushered everyone into the kitchen. Feeling thwarted, Nick told Margaret that he really thought Evie should be resting. She brushed him aside. 'A quick cup of tea won't harm.' Bernard helped Evie sit at the kitchen table. He didn't seem to notice how pale she had turned or how she winced as she sat on the cold wooden chair.

Margaret was so nervous that she forgot to prepare a fresh pot of tea and proceeded to serve up cups of lukewarm, over-brewed tea. Upon taking their first sips everyone spat and gulped in disgust. Everyone except Evie who, upon taking her first mouthful of bitter, tepid tea, gave a shriek of rage and flung the cup and saucer at the open kitchen door. With remarkable accuracy the cup arced through the air straight into the utility room. It shattered upon impact with the back door. Ramesses, asleep in a basket of freshly laundered clothes, leapt onto the floor in fright, deeply cutting his pad on a shard of china before shooting out of the cat flap and into the garden. He left behind him half a dozen perfect red paw prints on the utility room tiles. Natalie flew after him, worried the piece of cup would become embedded and cause serious injury.

Nick, feeling vindicated, had had enough.

'This is ridiculous! I'm taking my wife upstairs to bed

right now. The hospital said no stress and look at what's happening. Do you all want her to have a complete relapse?' Nick indicated to Bernard and Margaret. 'You two, help me get her into bed.'

'I don't want to go to bed,' Evie snapped.

'Tough!' was Nick's reply. Carol and Malc took India into the lounge whilst Becca reached for the dustpan and brush.

Evie started sobbing as soon as she was placed on the bed. Nick, furious with himself for allowing her to be subjected to so much stress, did his best to comfort her but she remained inconsolable. She didn't want to be left alone, Evie wailed. Nick explained that he would stay with her for as long as she was awake and even then he would take India's baby monitor with him wherever he went so that he would hear her if she needed anything. This seemed to appease her slightly. Nick asked her if there was anything she wanted. Perhaps a glass of water, Evie replied. Margaret suggested she stay with Evie whilst Nick went for the water. Nick agreed and, babycom in his back pocket, he went to get the drink.

Once Evie was comfortably in bed Margaret started to tell her all about her plans for her welcome home dinner, explaining how she was preparing all her favourite dishes. Walking up stairs, with a glass of chilled water in one hand and the babycom in the other, Nick, couldn't believe what he was hearing.

'We'll wake you around seven thirty so you can come down and join us,' Nick heard Margaret say. 'I'm going to convince your father to let us have a bottle or two of champers from his store. It is a celebration after all. Everyone's very excited about it.'

Nick poked his head round the door.

'Margaret, a word please,' he said. He beckoned for her to join him on the landing. 'She'll be okay for two minutes.' He shook the babycom at his mother-in-law. With some reluctance she joined him.

'What the hell do you think you're playing at?' Nick hissed at Margaret, whose eyes widened in surprise at how angry he was. 'Evie can't sit at the table and put away three courses like the rest of us. She isn't well. She's recovering from a critical illness and that means bed rest, peace and quiet, and more bed rest. She shouldn't even be here. This house is like a bloody zoo. She should be at the hospital with professionals looking after her.'

'No one cares more for Evie than I do. I'm her mother!'

'And I'm her husband! Although everyone seems to have forgotten that,' Nick said. 'I'm pulling rank on this one. She's staying in bed until I decide she's well enough to get up.'

'But I've made all her favourite dishes.'

'So? If she wants something to eat she can have it in bed on a tray, although I suspect she'd be just as happy with a simple pasta dish, and it'd probably be better for her. Have you forgotten that three days ago we thought she was going to die? She's barely eaten in days and all you want to do is feed her until she pops. The only thing I care about is getting her back to normal as quickly as possible. Don't you think her body has suffered enough? She needs good, plain food not rich, fancy dishes. Furthermore, she needs protecting from skirmishes like that one in the kitchen. Having all those people around her was bound to distress her. She needs quiet.'

'I've never been spoken to in such a way—' Margaret said, looking offended.

'I doubt that very much. I've heard your own children say far worse to you. Now if you don't mind I'm going to sit with my wife until she falls asleep. And another thing, I don't want anyone coming up and disturbing her.' With that Nick disappeared into the bedroom and closed the door behind him with a firm click.

❄

ONCE EVIE HAD GONE to bed there was a distinct feeling of anticlimax. Margaret closeted herself in the kitchen. Regardless of what Nick had said she was still hell-bent on preparing a magnificent feast in celebration of Evie's recovery, irrespective of whether or not Evie would be present. Besides which, she had already defrosted the joint she had intended to cook.

In an attempt to get away from being assigned any kitchen chores, Becca and Natalie wandered upstairs to Becca's room.

'It's weird, isn't it? Evie's like a completely different person,' Becca said. 'Do you think she'll ever change back?'

'Yeah. Evie's tough enough. I bet you any money that next year we'll be eating our Christmas dinner and laughing about all this, including Evie. After all, they say what doesn't kill you makes you funnier,' said Natalie. Becca reflected that in Evie's case what hadn't killed her had just made her grumpier. She recalled some of the awful things Evie had said to Natalie earlier that morning.

'You mustn't take to heart what she said to you. Nick told me that she's been absolutely vile to him, so you haven't been singled out,' Becca said. She peered out of her bedroom window. The sleet had stopped but the skies were still grey and dark with nimbostratus clouds that made Becca doubt that they'd seen the last of the wintry weather. It was still damned cold.

'Let's go shopping this afternoon,' Natalie said, changing the subject and once again showing a glimpse of her former self. 'My treat. We can get new clothes, new haircuts, our nails done.'

Becca was silent for a few moments, mentally debating whether or not to let Natalie in on her secret plans. Eventually she decided it could do no harm. 'I'd like to go shopping, but not for clothes.'

'What for then? Not more books, surely? It's already like a branch of Waterstones in your room.'

'No, not books,' Becca said. Another pause. 'I want to buy a house.'

'*A house?*' shrieked Natalie, forgetting to be quiet. She clamped her hands over her mouth. 'A house?' she hissed. 'Please don't bite my head off but you have no job and therefore no income with which to pay a mortgage.'

'I'll get a job, and I have enough for a deposit from the money Grandma Gates left me.'

'You still have that? Oh my God, I spent mine within days of it hitting my bank account. How do you think I paid for all those Manolo Blahniks?'

'What did I have to spend it on? My sexy clapped-out Fiesta that's sitting on the driveway, like the jewel in the Bingham family fleet? Anyway, it's probably too late to go into town.'

'Why don't we search online? Come on, it'll be fun,' Natalie said. She looked the happiest she had all day. As Becca felt she couldn't refuse she found herself sitting in the den booting up her parents' computer. Natalie was tapping keys with a speed and accuracy that surprised Becca.

'I never knew you could type,' she said. Natalie shrugged.

'I had to do a lot of crappy jobs in order to get the one I've got now. Despite what Dan might think, I'm bloomin' good at what I do,' she said. She never stopped typing once. 'So, what sort of property are you looking for? A house, a flat,' she turned to Becca and flashed a wicked smile at her. 'A narrow boat?'

'Har har. Actually there's a cottage on The Green I'd like to have a look at,' Becca said.

'Our Green? In this village?' Natalie asked. 'Isn't that a bit close to Mum and Dad? You'd never be rid of 'em.' Now it was Becca's turn to shrug. 'Whatever shakes your cocktail maker,' Natalie added, continuing to tap. 'Is this your bad boy?' A photograph of the cottage on The Green appeared on the screen. 'There's a virtual tour. Let's take a look.' For a few minutes they studied the property, clicking on each room and watching as a camera scrolled round a full 360 degrees.

'It needs some renovation,' Becca said, looking in dismay at the woodchip on the living room walls. It was stained yellow from years of cigarette smoke. It clearly hadn't been redecorated in decades.

'That's good. Keeps the price down,' Natalie said. 'Kitchen and bathroom aren't bad. Just need a lick of paint and a good clean. Nice sized rooms too.'

'Even if they are just as tatty as the lounge,' Becca said. 'It probably needs a full rewire and damp proof too.'

'Merely bargaining points to enable you to knock down the price. Let's have a look at the garden.' Natalie clicked a few times. The garden was as unkempt and neglected as the house but despite this Becca could imagine it in high summer, gloriously transformed into a cottage garden with a multitude of lupins, hollyhocks and aquilegia, and perhaps some home-grown vegetables. In her mind's eye she saw a sleek ginger cat sunning itself on the flagstones. Maybe even a little dog…

'Earth to Becca.' Natalie was clicking her fingers in front of Becca's face. 'I've requested the particulars. They'll be here in a couple of days.' If she was expecting Becca to be pleased with her she was mistaken. Becca merely gaped at her.

'Thanks for that,' she said sarkily. 'How am I going to explain that dropping onto the door mat?'

'I didn't think of that,' Natalie said, looking sheepish. 'You'll have to come clean.' Becca gave her a withering look.

Any further discussion was cut short by the sound of a commotion in the hallway. Peering out of the den, Becca and Natalie learned that Evie had woken and was demanding attention, a drink, something to eat and more attention. Nick had done his best to accommodate her needs but hadn't done so quickly enough and had been screamed at for his trouble. The commotion they'd heard was Evie's response to her mother's attempt to reason with her. It was to be only the first of a series of incidents as Evie continued to piss people off for the rest of the afternoon, shouting and yelling from the bedroom. No one was exempt. Margaret and Carol were next in line for a telling off. Carol had changed India back into the red outfit just before she took the little girl in to see her mother, not realising that Evie had already learned of the constant costume changes from her own mother. Summoning them both she shrieked at them for a full five minutes before bursting into tears.

'I don't give a shit what she's wearing. Just leave us alone,' Evie said in between sobs. An hour later a stony faced Nick stomped downstairs. His hands were full of broken glass. Evie, having been given the wrong type of fruit squash, had immediately flown into a vicious temper and hurled her glass at the wardrobe.

'Jee-suz, she likes her projectiles, doesn't she?' Becca asked no one in particular. 'God knows how she never made the rounders team at school.' She, Dan and Natalie had decided to suspend hostilities in order to watch a film on the television. Petty griping was still permitted however.

'She's like Dark Phoenix,' Dan grumbled.

'Is that another one of your stupid *Star Wars* references?' Natalie asked. Dan looked at her with condescension.

'No. Dark Phoenix is from *X-Men*, dumbass.'

'Oh, a stupid comic book reference then. That makes it so much more acceptable.'

And so it went on. By the end of the afternoon only Bernard didn't wish that Evie were still in the safe confines of the hospital where properly trained medical staff could deal with her moodswings.

UNBEKNOWNST TO BECCA AND, more pertinently, Natalie, Dan, in desperation, had crept into Becca's room and pinched forty quid from Natalie's purse whilst they were in the den. With a twenty and two tenners safely concealed in his back pocket, he then called into the kitchen to ask his mother for the bus timetable in the hope that she would take pity on him and tell his father to give him a lift.

'Jesus,' he said as he saw how much food his mother had prepared. The table could almost be heard groaning under a mass of laden dishes. 'I don't know why Bob Geldof bothered with Band Aid. He should have just rung you up and saved himself a whole load of bother. There's enough grub to feed the world in this kitchen.' This didn't help his cause. His mother, already miffed with him and in no mood to suffer fools, didn't appreciate the observation and told him in no uncertain terms to clear off. She didn't even wish him luck for his date. Denied, Dan had no option but to stand shivering at the bus stop.

Next in line to cop for it was Becca. She slid into the kitchen with the intention of telling her mother about the house particulars but received such a sermon about her lack of employment that she fled before she got the chance.

'Perhaps you should have studied medicine. Perhaps it's your calling to save lives,' Margaret called after her, but Becca was long gone.

After that it was time for dinner. Nick took his and Evie's food up on a tray. Everyone else squashed into the kitchen.

'Why aren't we eating in the dining room?' Bernard asked as he sat down.

'The table is still in the conservatory,' Margaret replied, plonking a carafe of wine on the table. Natalie, realising it had been she who'd banjaxed the sleeping arrangements by springing Christian on her family and therefore was responsible for the table being in the conservatory, took evasive action.

'Let's have a toast to Evie,' she said. It worked. Even her father was distracted from moaning at her.

To Margaret's credit the food was sublime. It was just a shame no one had any appetite for it. Wound up and on edge due to Evie's constant rages, everyone barely ate but instead pushed their food round their plates, which was curiously reminiscent of Natalie's actions on her first night home. Margaret tried not to take personal offence as she cleared away one untouched plate after another.

UPSTAIRS NICK WAS TRYING to convince Evie to eat something. Sensing that she was being deliberately stubborn he removed the tray from her, preventing any more pieces of crockery from ending their existence wrapped in newspaper in the dustbin. He idly wondered if Margaret had any plastic kitchenware.

'This has got to stop,' he said, taking Evie's hands in his. She refused to look at him. 'Do you want to make yourself ill again? Do you want to go back to the hospital?'

'No,' was the sulky reply.

'Then let me help you,' Nick pleaded. 'I don't know what you want. I don't know what'll make you feel better. Everyone else has an opinion on what's best. Your parents want you to stay here until you've fully recovered, even after India and I have gone back home. My parents want to take India to Newcastle so I can concentrate all my energies on getting you better.'

'I don't want to be separated from India,' Evie said, still staring at the bedspread. Nick sighed, trying not to take it personally that she didn't seem to mind the prospect of being separated from him.

'I want to take you and India home with me. I love you and I love our daughter and I just want to take care of my family. What I don't know is what you want. What do *you* want, Evie?'

'I don't know what I want. Yes I do. I want to be left in peace by the whole lot of you,' Evie said savagely.

'That's a very vague answer, babe. It doesn't help me much.'

'Oh, do what you want!' Evie snapped. Nick considered this for a moment.

'Okay. We will do what I want. I'll be the decision maker. As soon as you're well enough to travel you, me and India are going home.'

'Can Becca come and stay?' Evie asked, her fingers twitching the bedcovers. Nick also considered this. He had heard snippets of conversations and had gleaned that Becca had resigned from her job, sort of. Also, if he had to have any of the Binghams under his roof he would always pick Becca over anyone else. She was kind and thoughtful and was the only Bingham who truly had Evie's best interests at heart. He couldn't see the harm but decided to promise nothing.

'I'll ask her. Okay?'

'Okay.' Evie still wouldn't meet his gaze but it was the calmest and most sensible conversation they'd had since her discharge from hospital. Nick decided to delve deeper.

'Why have you been so mean to me? I've stayed by your side throughout everything. I don't understand why you continue to punish me. I don't know what I've done wrong. At least have the decency to tell me what you're angry about.'

'I can't.'

'Why not?'

'Because I don't know.'

'You've hurt me. Badly.' Nick knew he was taking a risk by mentioning her behaviour but he felt it was the right time. On this occasion he was prepared to trust his instincts. He was right.

'I know, and I'm sorry. I love you so much.' Tears began to stream down Evie's face. To hide them she pulled the bedspread up to her face and hid her eyes behind it. She couldn't even begin to explain to Nick how confused she was, or how frightened she'd been. Then there was the bewilderment of her emotions, over which she suddenly had no control whatsoever. She didn't know how to tell him that, despite her love for him and her knowledge that he'd done everything he could, and then some more, to keep her with him, she still felt let down by him. It sounded ridiculous, even to herself, but she felt he should have known sooner how dangerously ill she was, and therefore he should have done more to protect her and India. Despite knowing that he couldn't have done a single thing more, she still felt he could have done more to keep her alive. It was a cruel, nonsensical paradox. Then there was the accompanying guilt that came with such thoughts. How could she explain it to Nick when she didn't even understand it herself? It was easiest to push him away. That way she didn't have to deal with it.

'I asked Becca to take care of India if I died,' Evie confessed. Little did she know it but in that one sentence she successfully conveyed to Nick what she was feeling.

'I know. I figured,' Nick said, also referring to more than the simplicity of his words. He cradled Evie in his arms and kissed the top of her head. 'It doesn't matter. None of it matters but you getting better. I'd do anything for you, you know that.'

'I know that,' Evie repeated, like a child. 'I'm sorry.' She was crying again.

'Shhh, it doesn't matter.' Nick continued to rock her as she wept. He found the tears easier to cope with than the tantrums. Moreover, he felt that for the first time since she had woken up he had at last reconnected with his wife. He was hopeful the worst was now over.

'So, do you want to eat your dinner? Your mother made all your favourite foods?' He asked. Evie nodded. Nick brought the tray back to the bed. 'I'll eat with you. Just have as much or as little as you want.' Sitting side by side on the bed they ate their meals. Evie didn't eat everything but at least she seemed like her old self. She even smiled a couple of times.

'Tomorrow we're going to pack up the car and go back home. I'll tell your mother tonight.'

'I'd like that,' Evie said. Nick cleared away the trays. He then lay down on the bed beside Evie, his arm curled protectively round her. Her head nestled into the nape of his neck. She was asleep within minutes. Nick extracted himself without waking her and headed downstairs, babycom once again in his back pocket. He would be able to tell Evie's parents that she was at last recovering but he suspected it would be a small consolation for him taking her away from them the following day.

REELING from the ecstasy of having Frenched Rachel all the way home on the back seat of the night bus, Dan let himself into the house. Everything was curiously silent. The hallway was deserted and even more unusual, the kitchen door was closed. The telltale murmur of the television told him someone was in the lounge. Having been on his best behaviour he had only had half of a shared bottle of red and a couple of beers in town but now he decided he fancied a nightcap. Feeling the need for something a little harder than a lager, and taking advantage of being unsupervised, he raided his parents' drinks cabinet in the den. Trying hard not to rattle them, he inspected the many bottles. Gin he vetoed immediately as he found its flavour too highly perfumed.

'Might as well drink a bottle of Chanel No. 5,' he muttered to himself. He spied another bottle and pulled it out. What the hell was this yellow stuff? He turned the bottle over and checked the label. Advocaat. Wasn't that the hideous egg stuff that his mother mixed with lemonade to make a frothy concoction that looked, but alas did not taste, like an ice cream soda float? What was it she called it? Oh yes, a snowball. He hastily replaced the bottle. 'No thanks.' Finally he unearthed a half full bottle of Bacardi right at the back. It was a bit dusty, and was clearly a leftover from his parents' coral anniversary party a year or so ago, but it'd do. He slid it underneath his coat and exited the den, only to come face to face with an obviously furious Natalie.

'So, you're home, are you?' Clearly she knew he had pinched the money.

If Natalie could've been waiting with a rolling pin she would have. Having discovered she was light to the tune of forty sheets she proceeded to lay into Dan with a ferocity that startled even him. Within seconds they were having a *Ding! Dong! Merrily on High* in the hallway. The din drew Becca out of the lounge. She was concerned their squabbling would provoke Evie and that upstairs in the bedroom there would be gravy dinners flying through the air in all directions.

'Did you have a nice time on your lovey-dovey date? Did you have a nice bottle of wine? Was the food good? Did 'the lovely Rachel' put out as a result of your wonderful generosity?' Natalie asked.

'What's it to you?'

'What's it to me? I'll tell you what it is to me. I have a vested interest in your love life on account of the fact that I sponsored it with the forty pounds you stole from my purse this afternoon. I own you, you little shit.'

'I didn't take your stupid money.' Denial was worth a try.

'Don't lie to me. Who else would take it?'

Becca moved slightly which caught Dan's eye. He hadn't realised she was there. He looked cornered. The squabble then degenerated into a venomous fight that was much more damaging than the one Natalie and Dan had had during Christmas lunch. That had been childish one-upmanship, consisting of ridiculous attempts by each one to get the other into bother with their mother. This was cruel and personal.

'What if I did take it? It's tainted money anyway, earned by an evil slave queen at the BBC. God, I'd hate to work for you. I bet you make everyone's life hell on Earth,' Dan said. As he spoke he gesticulated with his arms. Suddenly unsupported beneath his coat, the illicit bottle of Bacardi dropped onto the carpet with a guilty thud. All three stared at it.

'At least I'm not a piss artist,' Natalie said.

'Get real and stop being overdramatic, if at all possible you bloody pathetic drama queen.'

'Overdramatic?' Natalie's expression was the epitome of righteous incredulity. 'It's not just my opinion, baby brother. Everyone is sick and tired of you getting pissed and nicking stuff. I want my forty quid back, you thieving magpie. How dare you root around in my personal stuff? You'd hit the bastard roof if I went in your room without your permission.'

'Don't stand there and lecture me about people being sick and tired of me, you frigging hypocrite. No one appreciated your little stunt of turning up on the doorstep with that poncy get Christian. You didn't even have the decency to ask Mum if it was all right to invite him. You didn't care that an extra person buggered up her plans or his weird eating habits would make her feel useless and stupid. You've been mean to Becca, you've been mean to Evie and don't even get me started on what you did to Grandpa. That was absolutely unpardonable. You. Don't. Care — about anyone but yourself and that's why no one can stand you. You're a vile human being. You're a bitch! Happy fucking Christmas, Natalie,' Dan yelled.

Becca, forced against her will to adopt the role of peacekeeper, was told on more than one occasion to butt out. Nevertheless it didn't stop her from trying.

'That's enough, Dan,' she said. Thoroughly incensed, his rage fuelled by alcohol, Dan rounded on her.

'You're defending her? After everything she said about your weight? Your job? Gregory? I can't believe you've just forgiven her.'

'Who said I'd forgiven her?' Becca said.

'You haven't forgiven me?' Natalie cried, aghast.

'Oh, give over. You've done and said some absolutely rancid things this Christmas. You can't expect all that to just evaporate without fallout. We're cool now. Just let it go and stop sulking.'

'I don't sulk,' said Natalie, sulkily.

'Pfffh!' said Dan and Becca simultaneously.

From behind the closed kitchen door Margaret could hear the rumblings of an argument. At first she tried to block it out by clattering crockery into the dishwasher but after a while it began to wear her down. What had they found to fight about now? In the corner the radio was playing jolly tunes. She switched it off with a sharp, angry motion, wishing Christmas had never happened. She hadn't told anyone about her feelings, how she was thoroughly fed up of her warring children and all the baggage they'd brought home with them, and by that she didn't mean bin bags full of dirty laundry. That she could cope with quite easily, thank you very much. It was all the other stuff — the resentments, the insecurities, the selfishness and introspection — that wore her down. Like a bloody oracle she was expected to know when to offer comfort, support or advice on demand, only to be told on other occasions to bugger off and mind her own business. And what thanks did she get? None whatsoever. She'd tried to feed and take care of everyone but not once had anyone shown her any respect or appreciation. Worse still, at a time when the family should have pulled together and supported each other all her children were savaging each other, and her husband was living in his own little dream world. And as for Evie…

Margaret just couldn't fathom what had happened there. Never could she have imagined what a nightmare her daughter's homecoming would be. What the hell had gone wrong? They were all good people. She had been a good mother. All she'd ever wanted was for the family to have a nice Christmas together, in harmony. Obviously it had been far too much to ask for. It was the same every year, although no Christmas had been as bad as this one. What was it that little blond boy said in that *Home Alone* film? 'Another Christmas in the trenches…' Other families appeared to have perfectly decent, agreeable Christmases. Why did it continue to elude theirs? Did it really exist for other people or did they also conceal their own hostilities and insecurities behind a mask of festive joy.

To top it all, Nick had materialised in the kitchen just half an hour ago and told her he was taking Evie and India back home the following day. There was to be no discussion, he'd said. Evie was in agreement with him. As a couple their minds were made up. Margaret had had no option but to relinquish control of her daughter's care. Never before had she felt so absolutely defeated.

In the lounge everyone was waiting for coffee and After Eights. The thought of more expectation finally made her crack. Flopping down on to a chair she put her head in her hands and wept. She allowed herself the luxury of release for a minute or so before pulling herself together. This really wouldn't do. Tears wiped away with a clean handkerchief, she began to prepare the coffee. As she stripped the green box of after dinner mints of its cellophane she made a premature New Year's resolution. From now on she would exercise tough love with her family rather than trying to be their friend. Little did she know, she was just about to be given the opportunity to test her new resolve.

❄

WHILST MARGARET WAS in the kitchen composing herself the argument in the hallway was fast reaching gargantuan proportions. Becca was desperately trying to keep the peace whilst at the same time taking care not to favour any particular side.

'Why don't you do us all a favour and drop dead,' Dan snarled at Natalie. He couldn't have possibly chosen a worse turn of phrase. Becca could only stand and watch as the colour drained from Natalie's face. She wasn't even aware that a small gasp of disbelief and horror had escaped from her own mouth.

'Dan, that's an awful thing to say, especially after what we've all been through this week. Apologise at once and stop being such a shite,' she said. Dan was only prevented from transferring his fury to her by the arrival in the hallway of his mother. Her eyes were drawn immediately to the Bacardi, which was lying on its side, its neck pointing at Dan like a judgemental version of spin the bottle.

'What the bliddy hell is all this racket about?' she asked. 'Your sister is upstairs trying to *rest* or had you all forgotten that she nearly died this Christmas?' The tension was too much for Natalie. She burst into tears, which prompted Dan to roll his eyes in exasperation. For Becca, this was the last straw. Dan was being insupportable. She put her arm round her younger sister.

'No, but perhaps Daniel ought to be reminded again. He's just told Nat to drop dead. I can't imagine a worse thing to say under the circumstances,' she said. 'He's acting like a five-year-old and he bloody well needs sorting out.' Dan's head snapped round, his jaw hanging loose in astonishment. Never before had Becca ratted him out to their mother, who looked furious. She pointed an accusatory finger at all three of them, her face contorted into a mask of menace.

'I'm pig sick of this. What on earth were you fighting about this time?' she demanded. The question concerned Dan and Natalie but she looked directly at Becca as she spoke. It was as if she knew only she could provide a sensible and truthful answer. Uncomfortable as this made Becca she felt that honesty was her only option. She deliberately ignored Dan's expression of pleading and horror as she began to speak.

'Dan stole forty quid out of Natalie's purse so he could go on his date. When Natalie confronted him about it he lashed out.'

'Is this true?' Margaret turned to Natalie and Dan. Natalie could only give a mute nod. Knowing he'd been busted Dan opted for what he hoped was a mitigated confession.

'I would've paid her back—' His mother cut him off before he could finish his sentence.

'Right! You and I are going to have a little chat, my boy.' With that Margaret grabbed her son's arm and frogmarched him into the kitchen. The door was closed behind them with ominous firmness.

Inside Dan lowered himself onto a dining chair with some apprehension, keenly aware he was in for the arse-kicking of a lifetime. He decided to emulate the national England football squad and play defensively.

'I don't know why I'm being targeted here. Natalie has wound everyone up this holiday,' he began. As an opener, it didn't go down too well.

'I'm perfectly aware of Natalie's shortcomings, thank you kindly, and whatever action I decide to take will be mine and Natalie's business,' Margaret said. 'I'm more concerned with your behaviour at this precise moment which, quite frankly, has been no better than hers.' Dan made a scoffing sound but his mother barked at him to be quiet. 'Incessant drinking, smoking, stealing your father's beer—' Dan suddenly looked shifty, and guilty. 'So, you didn't think I knew about that, eh?

Your father isn't an idiot, Daniel. He does precious little to help me at Christmas but one of the few things I can coerce him to do is get the booze in. Did you not think that he'd notice when his cans mysteriously disappeared from the pantry or, even more magically, changed into a different brand? Natalie may have done and said some frightful things since she arrived home but you shouldn't delude yourself that you're in a position to judge her. Your behaviour has been deplorable. You disappeared all day on Christmas Eve without giving me a second thought, you turned up at church punch drunk, you were sick in the church grounds and not only have you stolen money from your sister but also from my housekeeping jar. O-ho yes, I know about that too. You've disappointed me and you've embarrassed me — then you have the gall to sit there and accuse Natalie of being selfish. This is going to stop, right now. Your first job is to put that bottle of rum back where it belongs. Then, tomorrow, I want you to apologise to Natalie and, more pertinently, I want you to mean it.'

'What if I won't?' Dan's mask of bravado had slipped but was still intact. Even he had been horrified by the list of offences that his mother had reeled off. Had he really done all those things?

'Then you'll suffer the consequences. As the youngest you have got away with much more than your sisters did, especially Evie and Becca, and you've certainly benefited financially from your father and I being better off as we have got older and settled our liabilities. If you don't start acting like a civilised member of this family you'll be treated accordingly. If you don't shape up I'll cut your university allowance and you'll either have to get a term time job or get a student loan like all your sisters did. I'm no longer prepared to sponsor this downward spiral of drunkenness and debauchery. If you don't pull your socks up — and your stupid baggy trousers at the same time because I am sick and tired of seeing your underpants — you can find a way to finance yourself. You've got two choices, what's it going to be?'

Dan stared at his mother, his jaw slack. Never before had his mother given him such a telling off. Talk about shock and awe.

'Well?' Margaret pressed. Dan had no option but to capitulate.

'All right,' he said with what his mother perceived as a disappointing lack of grace. 'I'll apologise for what I said but I still don't think it's fair that Natalie gets off scot-free.'

'What makes you think she has?' was Margaret's cryptic response.

It was only after Dan had given it some thought that he finally understood what his mother had meant.

BECCA COULDN'T SLEEP. Natalie had conked out within minutes and was sleeping with her mouth wide open. She was so out of it that Becca wasn't even worried she might wake her by playing music or turning on a light.

Becca had exhausted her usual methods for dropping off. She'd sprayed her room and bedlinen with an overpriced blend of soothing and sedentary scents. She'd read for quarter of an hour. She'd left her radio playing gentle choral carols in the dark. Nothing had worked. There were too many thoughts and arguments racing round her mind. She was worried about Evie. She was worried about Natalie. She was worried about Dan, but was also bloody annoyed with him at the same time. She was also replaying a conversation she'd had with Nick that afternoon. He'd collared her as she was walking across the landing and asked her if she had five minutes. They'd sat on the topmost step of the staircase.

'Evie's asleep,' Nick had said. 'She finally seems more

herself.' He paused. 'I'm taking her back home tomorrow. I haven't told your mother yet.'

Becca shrugged. She knew how cloying and intrusive her mother's affections could be. If Nick felt that Magpie Cottage wasn't the best place for Evie to be, who was she to disagree?

'It's what Evie wants too,' Nick continued. 'In fact, she was keen on the idea of you coming to stay for a week or two.'

'Oh!' Becca had said, taken aback.

'I thought it was a good idea too, especially in view of you not having any work commitments at the moment.'

'Word travels fast,' Becca said drily. How the hell did Nick know about her job? She'd barely spoken two sentences to him since Evie had come home. Anyway, she did have work commitments. She was committed to finding work on account of the fact that she had no income. She muttered something to this effect.

'Well, I have a proposition for you in that area also,' Nick said. 'There's no way Evie can deal with her own work commitments whilst she is recovering and I won't have time to take them on because I'll be caring for both her and India. I need someone to look after Evie's portfolio whilst she's incapacitated. So I thought of you. There wouldn't be much to do, a few phone calls and emails and perhaps some trips to the copy shop and the Post Office, and whilst the pay would be a pittance it would be enough to tide you over for a few weeks. Would you be interested?'

Becca thought for a moment. An image of the cottage on The Green loomed in her memory. Her priority had to be finding a decently paid job. Nick seemed to read her mind.

'You wouldn't have to come over until the New Year, perhaps the third or fourth. I'm not back at school until the sixth due to the way the bank holiday has fallen.'

Becca considered this. It would be nice to spend some time with Evie without the added distraction of their family. Plus,

a few days concentrated searching for a new job must yield
fruit. Surely she would have found something by the fourth
of January, even if it were just temp work? There was
something else to consider too. Something Evie had confided
in her on the day she had arrived. It couldn't be ignored, even
if it did mean betraying Evie's trust.

'What about the Boston offer? Would I need to deal with
that too?' Becca finally asked. Nick gave a deep sigh.

'Yeah, it still needs dealing with but... she surely can't still
be seriously considering it? Not after all this.' Nick held out
his hands in a gesture of hopelessness. 'Everything's
changed.'

They sat in silence for a few minutes, each lost within their
own thought processes. It was Nick who spoke first.

'So, what do you reckon? Can you do it?'

'Okay,' Becca said finally. 'But I need a couple of days to
get myself sorted out with a job first. I reckon I can be with
you by the fourth, the third at the earliest depending on how
successful the job search is.'

'Fantastic!' Nick said. 'Evie will be so pleased. I just have
one more favour to ask you... Would you mind very much if
we left a few things behind for you to bring with you? It
would make it much simpler if we could travel lightly
tomorrow.'

'I guess not. What sort of things?' Becca imagined Nick
meant the several full bags of Christmas presents, perhaps
some of India's larger toys and whatever clothes that
wouldn't be needed.

'Yes, those things,' Nick confirmed. He paused. 'And
Angus.'

'Angus!' Becca cried, wondering how she was going to fit
so much inanimate stuff plus a living creature into her tiny
Fiesta. 'Oh, go on then.'

Nick had seemed so pleased but Becca couldn't help but
think she might have been a bit premature in taking on so

many responsibilities. It certainly put her under pressure to find another job. Therefore Nick's request was yet another deliberation that kept her awake well past midnight.

At half past one she decided she needed a glass of water and, as she refused to drink water from an upstairs tap, this meant a trip to the kitchen. As she padded downstairs she noticed the kitchen light was still on and, to her surprise, she found her mother sitting at the big scrubbed table writing thank you letters. Margaret looked up and smiled as Becca entered the room.

'Hello, love. Problems sleeping too?' Becca nodded mutely. She'd expected her mother to still be angry about the earlier row in which, even though she hadn't been an active participant, she'd certainly had a hand. 'It has been rather a pig of a week, hasn't it? Sit down. I'll make you a mug of hot chocolate.'

Obediently, Becca sat down whilst her mother started to heat a pan of milk. To Becca, she seemed more serene than she had in days although she couldn't help but notice, as her mother passed beneath the kitchen spots, that she'd acquired several worry lines over the holiday. Becca also saw that her mother had written a stack of letters, which made her wonder how long she'd been sitting there. The kitchen radio was playing the same programme as the one she had been listening to upstairs.

'Your father went out like a light the moment the ten o'clock news credits rolled,' Margaret said as she spooned drinking chocolate into the milk. She then reached for the ground cinnamon and a handful of mini marshmallows. She might be taking a firmer stance with her children but she couldn't bring herself not to take the same care in feeding them. It just wasn't in her nature. 'I'm afraid I didn't enjoy the same luxury. Between Evie and her erratic behaviour and Dan and Natalie's collective foibles and grievances I'm at my wit's end. Sleep was absolutely out of the question.' The mug of hot chocolate was handed over. 'Drink that whilst it's hot. Of course, your father can see only Evie and therefore nothing else concerns him. He has no idea of what's going on with the rest of you. Oh, sorry! I shouldn't say such things to you.'

Becca gave a wry smile. 'S'okay. We all know how it is.'

'Nevertheless, your father and I will be having a little chat about it. It's really not fair.'

Becca said nothing but swilled her milk round her mug, redistributing the congealed powder collecting at the bottom. For a few minutes mother and daughter sat in comfortable silence. On the radio a soprano trilled like a canary, sounding equally exquisite and ridiculous. Eventually Becca spoke.

'I'm sorry I lost my job. I'll find something else this week, even if it's just temping. I don't expect you and Dad to bankroll me,' she said, her voice quiet. Margaret gave a short laugh.

'Oh, sweetheart, you're the least of my worries,' she said. 'I've every confidence you'll find something much more suitable than that wretched call centre. I can't say I'm sorry you've left there. I wouldn't be surprised if this turned out to be the best thing that could have happened. Better things must be round the corner for you.'

'There's something else too,' Becca said. 'I contacted the estate agents and requested the particulars for that house that's for sale on The Green. I'm thinking of arranging a viewing.'

'But that's wonderful!' Margaret exclaimed. 'I can't imagine anything better than you living in your own cottage in the village. You'd have your independence but still be close enough to pop round for a cup of tea.'

Becca hadn't been quite sure how her mother would react to this news but she certainly hadn't expected her to respond so enthusiastically.

'I thought you might be cross,' she said.

'Cross? What's to be cross about? I'm just thankful that

one of my children is looking forward and making plans. Of course I'm not cross. Just imagine, we could have barbecues at your house in the summer and come round for dinner in the wintertime.' Margaret's expression suddenly turned impish. 'Perhaps you could even have Dan stay with you during his holidays. He could gas you with those awful cigarettes and pinch your money instead of mine.'

Becca grimaced. 'Not sure about that,' she said. 'I might have to ensure I get a one bedroomed house with no accommodation for guests. Anyway, we'll see. All jokes aside, it might not be in my price range or it might be unsuitable.'

'Well, whatever you decide, I'm sure your father and I can help you out in some way,' Margaret said. 'How do you think you are set financially?'

'Not too bad. I still have my inheritance from Grandma Gates, which is a more than an adequate deposit. I need to find a job with a decent salary first.'

'You will. I know it,' Margaret said. There was a couple of minutes' silence, which left Becca with the strong feeling that her mother wanted to say something. She was right. 'Nick told me he's taking Evie back home tomorrow.'

'I know he is,' Becca admitted. 'He asked me if I would go and stay for a week or so, so I can help look after Evie and India.'

'That's good to know. Obviously I don't want them to leave but I understand why he's made this decision. I feel that I haven't handled Evie's illness very well since she came home. I wonder if I just wanted her to be better than she actually was and then convinced myself I was right. Nick was adamant that she should stay in the hospital for a little while longer but we all overruled him. I was insistent I could care for her at home. Now I have to admit he was right. I owe him an apology, and Evie too for letting her down. If she doesn't make a full recovery I'll never forgive myself,' Margaret said.

'I suppose not everything can be made better with a cup of tea and a bowl of chicken soup.'

Becca sensed that it had taken her mother a great deal to admit this.

'I wouldn't be too hard on yourself,' she said. 'It's been new territory for all of us. Everyone's been affected. Anyway, Nick said Evie was so much better this evening. He thinks the worst is over.'

'I hope so. Are you going to go and stay with them?'

'I said I'd be happy to but I need to sort out a couple of things first. Apparently it was Evie's idea. She specifically asked for me.'

There followed another short silence during which time Margaret stared out of one of the kitchen windows. Only a couple of lights were still on in the village.

'I can't help but wonder what sort of Christmas other folks have had,' Margaret said at last. 'Have theirs been all mince pies and mulled wine or have they had their troubles too?'

'I doubt that anyone's Christmas is perfect,' Becca said. 'After all, even before Evie got sick we were all in-fighting and obsessing with our own problems. Plus we had Grandpa and Great Aunt Ada to deal with, not to mention Christian and Vera Lynn.'

Margaret gave a small smile of acknowledgement before becoming serious again.

'But the world out there, they're not concerned with what's happened to us, are they? Despite all the good wishes and sermons about togetherness and opening up your heart to your neighbour no one has been affected by this but us.'

Becca lifted her head and looked out of the window too. An upstairs light went out in the house opposite. She looked thoughtful for a few moments.

'I don't believe that they wouldn't care. I think it's just that they're all busy dealing with their own imperfect Christmases. I'm sure there are plenty of people who would consider us to have got off lightly. After all, we're all still here and Christmas can continue to be a happy time for us. I think we did okay, eventually.'

'So wise, as usual,' Margaret said. She indicated to Becca's empty mug. 'Do you want another?'

Becca shook her head. 'Nah, I think I'll try to get some sleep now.' She stood up, leaned over her mother's shoulders and gave her a brief hug. Margaret gave Becca a long look as she headed for the door.

'Becca,' she called. Becca turned round, framed in the doorway. 'You know, I know I've given you rather a lot of grief over the last few weeks. I just wanted to tell you that I've been very impressed with how you've dealt with Evie's illness. If it hadn't been for you none of us would have known about the meningitis. You've tried so hard to keep Natalie and Dan from ripping each other's throats out and I think you've been very generous in your care of Natalie, especially in view of some of the awful things she's said.' Margaret suddenly looked sheepish. 'Plus you've had the courage to draw to your father's and my attention that perhaps we haven't always been fair with you four. It needed to be said and I want you to know we're not cross with you. I confess that I have been guilty of mistaking your stoicism for sloth in the past and that was wrong. This week you've acted with great maturity and grace and I want you to know that I'm very proud of you. Everyone else has gone to pieces this week. But you? It only seems to have made you stronger.'

Becca gave her mother a brief, sardonic smile. 'It was about time something did,' she said.

30TH DECEMBER

By morning Evie's rages had evolved into weepiness. It was a development everyone found much easier to cope with and lessened the tension in the house slightly. Not that it made the atmosphere at Magpie Cottage any happier, for today was the day everyone was returning home.

Carol and Malc were the first to leave. They set off just after breakfast, having thanked Margaret for her hospitality. Carol had hugged Nick long and hard whilst Malc loaded up the boot with their luggage. She promised to ring him every day to chart his and Evie's progress.

'If you need anything, anything at all, you just give me a call,' she said. 'Say goodbye to Evie for me and wish her a speedy recovery.' Evie was sleeping soundly. No one wanted to disturb her. Nick, India and Becca waved them off.

Upstairs, Natalie was moving her belongings back into her own bedroom, only to have to pack them into her suitcase ready for her own journey back to London. She had woken with a feeling of gloom and for a few minutes seriously considered staying at Magpie Cottage for a few more days. Then she remembered her father and Dan's hostility and decided that, although she would prefer to stay with her mother and Becca, perhaps London was the best place for her. Furthermore, unbeknownst to Becca and Nick, she had overheard their conversation of the previous night and knew Becca would be travelling to Chester in the near future and so wouldn't be around anyway. The knowledge that Becca was so readily willing to drop everything in order to go and stay with Evie plunged her further into despondency. She'd always been aware that Evie and Becca, having been born only a couple of years apart, shared a bond that neither she nor Dan were privy to, but had felt that hers and Becca's relationship had taken great steps over the past few days. Now, in the knowledge that Becca was zooming off to help Evie, she felt excluded and insecure. What would Becca do if she asked her to come and visit her in London? Would she drop everything as readily for her younger sister as she had for her elder? Evidently Evie and Becca were still active participants in their little club for two.

Natalie had still been undecided at breakfast and, although Dan had offered her a stilted and obviously scripted and rehearsed apology for his outburst of the night before, she still felt she didn't belong. The final straw came when she noticed a signed for but unopened package in the hallway. It had been shoved under the telephone table, clearly disregarded and unimportant. The cruel symbolism of this was all too apparent to Natalie as only she knew it was the Blu-ray player she'd arranged to have delivered to her parents. It was the deciding factor. She resumed her packing. She would go home to London that day as per the original plan.

Margaret, miserable as a direct result of everyone's departure, was consoling herself in the kitchen. She might not be physically able to care for Natalie and Evie with them living so far away but she could send them on their way with some decent food. For Natalie she'd chosen some snacks for her journey, even though she was certain that she wouldn't eat them, and for Evie she had prepared several easily reheatable dishes that could be taken back home and stored in the freezer. All that remained to be done was the labelling. They would then be ready to be stacked in the cool bag. She'd been cooking since dawn. At least Nick was pleased with them, she thought as she closed yet another Tupperware container.

'You're a wonder,' he had said. 'I won't need to cook at all. Thank you, Margaret.'

Neither of them met fully the other's gaze. Each was acutely aware that their argument of the previous night could not be allowed to stagnate and would have to be addressed at some point in the near future. Just not today. For now Nick was happy to postpone his apology to Margaret until such time when Evie needed less constant attention. He was relieved Margaret too was keen to pretend, at least on a temporary basis, that their unpleasant row hadn't taken place. It was as though a silent consensus had been reached for the sake of everyone else despite the faint coolness that still lingered.

Amidst this, Natalie wandered into the kitchen to say goodbye to her mother. Margaret, thankful for the distraction, gave Natalie her full attention and forced the bag of snacks on to her. 'And make sure you eat them.' Natalie pulled a face. 'I'm taking this cup of tea in to your father. Stay here until I get back.'

As soon as Margaret had left the room Natalie turned away from Nick, pretending to rummage through the bag of food her mother had handed her. It wasn't an act of rudeness. She was just sure Nick wouldn't want to speak to her. She was wrong.

'Natalie,' he said. Natalie turned slowly. What sort of strip-tearing was she in for this time? 'I know we dumped

India on you when we all dashed to the hospital on Boxing Day.'

Here it comes, thought Natalie. What had he found out? The swearing? The antihistamine? The overall crappiness of her care?

'I just wanted to say thanks. India has been talking non-stop about the fun she had with her Aunt Natalie and I just wanted to tell you that I think you did a really good job.'

At that moment Margaret bustled back into the kitchen.

'India's asking where her storybook is and Bernard can't find it. Nick, would you mind?' Nick disappeared book-wards, leaving Natalie staring after him with her mouth agape. She hadn't seen *that* one coming.

NATALIE WAS NEXT TO LEAVE. Becca helped her put her luggage in the car.

'Will you come and visit me in London?' Natalie said, in a rush. 'We could go to the West End and see a show or maybe a film in Leicester Square. I can take you shopping in Covent Garden and I'll even compromise my excellent taste and accompany you to TGI Friday's for cocktails and a burger.' Natalie had always mocked Becca for liking the American chain and Becca appreciated the intention behind her offer.

'I like Friday's,' Becca said with a smile.

'Someone has to.' Natalie grinned back.

'There's something I want you to have.' Becca handed Natalie a battered looking item. Natalie accepted it with something akin to reverence. She felt water well up in her eyes. Becca had handed her Bun-Bun, her favourite childhood toy. Becca had never gone anywhere without the pink, pointy-eared rabbit, not family holidays nor sleepovers at friends' houses. On more than one occasion Bernard had had to turn the family car round because Bun-Bun had been left behind. Once they had almost missed a flight because they'd had to turn back for home just as they reached the outskirts of Manchester because Becca wouldn't stop sobbing. Once as bright and pink as a stick of Edinburgh rock, Bun-Bun's fur had faded to a muted grey. He had long since lost one of his eyes and also the eye patch that their mother had lovingly crafted so that Becca wouldn't be upset by his new disability. His pointy ears were no longer proudly upright but fell over his battered face. Most of his seams had been darned and then redarned to prevent his gizzards from coming out. Of course, none of the embroidery threads matched which gave him the appearance of being Frankenstein's monster's stuffed toy. Even so, Bun-Bun was still Becca's most prized possession, and now she was giving him to Natalie.

'I can't take him,' Natalie said. 'You love him.'

'Have him on loan then. He'll keep you company until I come and visit,' Becca said. Natalie glanced at her watch.

'I have to go. I'll miss my flight,' she said, her voice cracking. She really, really didn't want to go. Becca gave her an enormous hug.

'Ring me as soon as you get there. Promise?'

'I promise.'

Natalie climbed into the hire car. She realised, with considerable relief, that it was facing the right way, which meant she wouldn't have to reverse it. In her rear view mirror she could see Becca waving from the doorstep. Disregarding the usual rules of mirror, signal, manoeuvre she continued to watch her sister as she pulled away. Becca stepped onto the gravel in her stockinged feet and Natalie saw her wince as the stones dug into her soles. Nevertheless, she followed the car out onto the road and continued to wave until Natalie had turned the corner, out of sight. For Natalie this was the final straw. She cried for the duration of the journey to the airport. If only there were windscreen wipers for the eyes, she thought sadly.

The spotty, nerdy youth at the car hire desk noticed her swollen, red eyes but refrained from comment. He knew what a ball-acher Christmas was for the lonely and the miserable. What other reason could there possibly be for his voluntary attendance at work in between Christmas and New Year? If he had somewhere better to go, wouldn't he be there? With a small, empathic smile of camaraderie he handed Natalie her receipt. He chose not to wish her Happy New Year. His instinct had correctly informed him that it wasn't what she wanted to hear and yet, as he watched her walk away, he was comforted slightly, but not maliciously, by the thought that someone who had a gold card and who was so very, very hot could still be so unhappy.

For Natalie the flight passed in a blur. The seat that had originally been intended for Christian had been reallocated to a lanky businessman no older than herself who, knees spread about two feet apart, tapped on a bulky laptop for the duration of the flight whilst at the same time ogling Natalie's slender, knee-booted legs. She realised she must have dozed off not long after the complimentary drinks had been served because suddenly the captain was informing the passengers of their imminent descent. As if in a daze she managed to retrieve her luggage and made her way through London City arrivals.

After a long journey in a taxi cab, driven by a driver who valiantly tried to chat to her but eventually gave up, she arrived back at her flat. It was still a tip from the party she'd held the night before she'd gone home. At the time it had seemed like a good idea to leave the mess. Still, Natalie thought as she dropped her suitcase in the middle of her lounge, at least she now had something to do that evening.

Remembering her promise to phone Becca she headed for her telephone. The red light of her answering machine was flashing. She hoped to dear God that it wasn't Christian, full of theatrical venom. However, when she pressed the play button the room was filled with a deep, pleasant voice that was unfamiliar to her. It had more than a hint of Geordie.

'Hi Natalie, err... this is Reggie... Reggie Lovell, Nick's cousin. I hope you don't mind me ringing you. Me Auntie Carol suggested I give you a call. I'm new to the city and would appreciate a guided tour. Errm, also, I... err... wondered if you would like to come to a New Year's Eve party tomorrow night — well, when else would it be? Honestly, sometimes I am so stupid!' Natalie couldn't help but smile at the light self-deprecation in his voice. 'Anyway, if you're interested give me a bell back and... err... we'll sort summat out. Errm... okay, bye then.' There was a pause. 'Ah, I 'spose I'd better leave me number.' Once he had left his mobile number Reggie finally hung up. Feeling curiously uplifted, Natalie looked at the digits she'd jotted down and gave her first genuinely happy smile since Evie had come home. Perhaps the outlook wasn't so bleak after all.

Becca set the receiver back in its cradle. Natalie was home safe. Plus, she seemed a little more cheerful than she'd been when she'd left that morning. Becca found herself looking forward to heading up to London for a visit. Still, that would have to wait a while. There was plenty that had to be dealt with before fun weekends in London could be arranged.

Outside on the driveway Nick and Evie were just about to set off. Evie had been her old self as Becca helped Nick get her in the car. She'd given Becca a hug and a kiss on the cheek.

'I'll miss you,' she'd said.

'It's only for a couple of days,' Becca replied. 'I'll let you know whether it'll be the third or the fourth.'

'I hope it's the third,' Evie said, smiling. 'I can't wait to show you everything about managing my portfolio. You'll do such a good job. Mind you, I'm very behind on a lot of things. There's quite a lot to catch up on.'

'Does that include Boston?' Becca asked quietly, eyebrows raised.

'Oh that,' Evie said dismissively. 'I think it's safe to say that my answer to their very generous offer will be a definite 'no'. It has to be. All things considered.' But behind her back Evie had her fingers crossed.

Angus, aware he was being left behind, was inside, sulking underneath the telephone table. Every now and then he let out a small whine of protest. It was at that point that the telephone had rung. Becca headed back outside to relay the news that Natalie had had a good journey. At the mention of her youngest sister, Evie's face had clouded over, but not from anger or annoyance. Earlier that day Evie had woken from her long sleep to discover Natalie had already left for the airport. Evie had promptly burst into tears, saying she was ashamed of being so mean to her sister and she'd wanted to say goodbye, and that she was sorry for all the awful things she had yelled at her.

'I think that's everything,' Nick said, closing the boot with a flourish. He felt more optimistic than he had in days. Moreover, he was looking forward to seeing his own home. 'Are we ready to go?' His eyes flitted from side to side in mischief, aware that India hadn't been strapped into her seat yet.

'What about me, Daddy?' the little girl cried. She'd been casting concerned looks at the forsaken Angus and was fearful that she too was to be left behind. 'What about me?'

Sensing an imminent shrieking fit, Becca scooped India up and handed her to Nick.

'Ignore your daddy. He's just being naughty,' she said, treating Nick to a look of chastisement. 'He's just trying to frighten you.' India giggled. 'If you're ready to go, I'll call Mum and Dad.'

Her parents were in the lounge watching the television and eating their lunch on trays, as they customarily did on an ordinary day. They joined Becca at the front door to wave the party off.

'Drive carefully!' Margaret called as the car pulled away. 'And do call me as soon as you get home. Two rings will do, just to put my mind at rest.'

Evie was openly crying as she waved goodbye from the back seat of Nick's car. Despite not knowing if this was because Evie was truly sad at leaving Magpie Cottage or if it was just another bout of symptomatic tears, Becca felt her throat constrict. Beside her their mother was dabbing at her eyes with a tissue. They continued to wave until the car was out of sight. Inside, Angus accepted defeat and mooched into the kitchen on a quest for food.

Even after Nick and Evie had driven away and her parents had retreated back inside to their lunch, Becca stood alone in the open doorway, looking out on to the driveway. The snow had all but thawed. A petulant drizzle and cloudy skies would herald the New Year. There was peace at last. Natalie had gone back to London, although Becca was in no doubt that she'd be seeing her younger sister very soon. Dan was upstairs in his room. Admittedly he was listening to some God-awful music but at least there wasn't any telltale blue smoke stealing under the closed bedroom door. The Lovells had gone back to Newcastle and now Nick, Evie and India were on their way home too.

Turning, her eye was caught by the copy of the long-forgotten *Radio Times* on the telephone stand. It was still open on Christmas Eve, and showed *Nine Lessons from King's* highlighted in fluorescent yellow. How ironic, Becca thought. Perhaps not so many as nine in total, but there had been lessons aplenty for her family to learn: self-esteem, humility, temperance and tolerance, to name but a few. What they all intended to do with what they had learned as they went forward into a new year remained to be seen.

And a brand new year was only a day away! Becca didn't have any plans. Dan would no doubt go into town with his mates and get lashed, but Becca didn't envy him. She'd be quite happy staying in with a bottle of wine. She'd spend New Year's Eve surfing the internet for a new job. It would be a whole new start for her. She closed the front door quietly with a small smile.

From behind her father emitted a cry of anguish that distracted her from her thoughts.

'Awww, no!' Alarmed, she spun round. Whatever had happened now? 'Margaret, help, quick! One of the bloody cats has eaten my lunch and sicked it back up in my slipper!'

Becca laughed out loud. Everything was back to normal at Magpie Cottage.

THE END

Becca Bingham's Cranberry, White Chocolate & Cinnamon Christmas Morning Muffins

These breakfast muffins are a Bingham family favourite and are enjoyed whilst we open our gifts on Christmas morning. They go very nicely with a chilled glass of bucks fizz (or ten, in Dan's case). Enjoy! Love Becca x

Preparation:

Spend 15 minutes scouring mother's thousands of cookery books for recipe like an maniac before remembering that recipe is on a scrap of paper wedged between two books. Of course it is.

Stare at pantry shelves in despair as you realise you're missing a couple of essential ingredients.

Appease any lurking dogs with Bonios before ushering them into the safety of the utility room. This is for the safety of the ingredients you've already put on the work surface, not the safety of the dogs. Razz car to nearest supermarket with hastily scribbled shopping list in paw. Park like a fool.

Stare in horror at how busy supermarket is, then wander round aimlessly for a few minutes with shopping list in one hand, basket in another, handbag in ano… hang on?

Get distracted by a stand of paperback books. Drag self away. Get distracted again by some nail varnishes in really weird but strangely appealing colours. Drag self away again. Get distracted for a third time by a celebrity magazine featuring a picture of future husband Chris 'Captain America' Evans. Stand and lust after him for a few minutes before getting a grip.

Circumnavigate entire supermarket at least three times in quest to find necessary missing ingredients. Have minor panic attack when you see the ground cinnamon shelf empty but then breathe with relief when you spot one last jar someone has craftily hidden behind the turmeric. Phew! On way to ridiculously busy checkout, sling two packets of Reese's Cups into the basket. They're not required for the recipe, you just like them.

Ingredients:

- 225g (8oz) self-raising flour
- 2 x 5ml spoon (2tsp) baking powder
- 2 x 5ml spoon (2tsp) cinnamon
- 125g (4oz) butter or baking spread
- 50g (2oz) caster sugar
- 1 x 200g jar cranberry sauce
- 1 egg (free range, or else!)
- 2 x 15ml spoon (2tbsp) milk
- 100g (3oz) bar white chocolate

- Icing sugar & ground cinnamon (mixed) for dusting.

Method:

- Once home, trip over dogs as you try to get into the utility room at the same time as they are trying to get out.
- Try and fail to remember to preheat oven to 190 C / 375 F / Gas mark 5.
- Put on some suitably festive music. Dance around kitchen like an absolute eejit for a few minutes. Be very grateful that you're not overlooked by neighbours as dancing is shameful.
- Sieve the flour, baking powder and cinnamon into a bowel. No, not a bowel. A *bowl!* End up with most of it on work surface. Mutter darkly to self.
- Rub in the butter to resemble fine breadcrumbs. Stir in sugar.
- Mix cranberry sauce, egg and milk in a jug until well blended. Do *not* splash this on white top you have (foolishly) chosen to wear. Stir into flour mixture.
- Put bar of white chocolate, still in its wrapper, on back door step and bray with a rolling pin until it is in rough pieces. (Chocolate, that is, not rolling pin. Although, if you are particularly heavy-handed…)
- Eat 25g of white chocolate. Don't worry about this: recipe requires only 75g and takes gluttony of baker into account.
- Add chocolate and mix well.
- Spoon into 12 festively designed muffin cases already neatly placed in suitable baking tray. You will inevitably drop at least one splodge of mixture onto the tray, which will then bake into the very

fabric of the metal and refuse to be removed by dishwasher, powerwasher, sandblaster… and still be there in five Christmases' time.

- Chat to dogs and cats as the muffins bake for 15-20 minutes until firm to the touch and golden brown (texture like sun?) Think about doing washing up. Don't actually get round to this.
- Put hot muffins on wire rack to cool. Realise they really are very hot. Blow on burnt fingers.
- Do NOT leave muffins unattended during cooling, otherwise either dogs will pinch them or cats will lick them. True story.
- Dust with icing sugar and cinnamon. End up with most of this on work surface. Sneeze as cinnamon goes up nose.
- Eat one muffin to check for quality. Consider this a control muffin. Eye up a second one, but resist on grounds that you don't want to be a fat knacker. (Too late.)
- Once cool, stack remaining muffins in cake tin, ready and waiting to be enjoyed on Christmas morning. They won't see Boxing Day…

Dan's Boozy Cointreau Chocolate Cream Truffles

If Becca's going to do a recipe for this book malarky so am I. Oh yeah! I can cook. That shouldn't shock you, considering my mother's proclivity for home economics. She's had me slaving away in the kitchen since primary school under the slim guise of a 'fun activity'. Don't be deceived! Just because I don't, doesn't mean I can't.

So, do you get frustrated when your mother hides all the best Christmas booze during advent, meaning you can't have a decent sesh whilst watching some festive telly? Never fear,

Dan is here to hook you up with my deliciously boozy chocolate balls of heaven.

Ingredients:

- 225g/8oz dark chocolate. The darker the better, so at least 60%. No use using Dairy Milk as the buggers'll just fall apart.
- 300ml/half pint double cream. I suppose if you have to have half a pint of something other than ale, it may as well be double cream. You can swap-in a plant-based alternative if you're dairy-free or vegan, or if you're subject to an annoying, last-minute and unexpected guest, courtesy of your bitch sister… but I digress. What else? Oh yes…
- 45ml/3tbsp lovely, lovely liqueur of your choice. Cointreau is my tipple of choice, but you could use Drambuie, dark rum, Bailey's or some sort of Amaretto. Or make a batch of each and really treat yo'self. Also, this tablespoon nonsense. You could get a miniature bottle if you like. Yeah, yeah, yeah, they're cute and all that. But, if you get a full-sized bottle, you can have a wee drinkie whilst you're baking.
- Cocoa powder. Some. How vague is that? I ask yer.
- Coating: extra cocoa powder, finely chopped nuts (which is what I'll have when my darling Mumsie realises I've included this…), grated milk or white chocolate. And, if you really want to give your fam a jolt this Christmas, source yourself some of that popping candy. Hehe…

Method:

- Break the chocolate into small but equal pieces and put this in a large bowl with the cream. This will act as your bain-marie. Not, as I called it up until about age eleven, an Anne-Marie. She's a singer.

- Place the bain-marie over a pan of shallow, simmering water until the chocolate has melted. A word of warning, not so shallow that the water boils dry and ruins your mother's best Aga pan. That won't make you popular. I learned that the hard way.

- Once all the chocolate has melted - GENTLY! - and been stirred into the cream to form a lovely shiny, chocolately ooze, leave to cool. You can hurry this up by standing the bowl in a large bowl of cold water, or, you can leave it to cool in its own good time whilst you pop your feet up and enjoy half an hour with a wee tot of your favourite tipple and the double issue Radio Times. Now, where has Becca put the highlighter pens? Do you know that she allocates each of us a separate colour pen and then analyses all our telly choices like some sort of new-age personality test? Bloody weirdo!

- As soon as the mixture has started to set, stir in your liqueur then whisk that bitch with an electric whisk until it's light and thick. Chill out by leaving it to chill in the fridge until it's solid enough to handle. Another top tip: don't make room for the mixture by taking something else out of the fridge. I once took out some very expensive crab meat, forgot to put it back, and it went off. I was doghoused for days.

- Once it's chilled, sieve some cocoa onto a small plate. Take a spoonful of the chilled mixture and roll it in the powder. Quickly shape it into a ball using your hands. Then, either re-roll it in the cocoa powder to give it a nice, even finish, or roll it in another small plate containing one of the other toppings.

- This mixture should make about 30 truffles. You can scoff 'em yourself or pop them in those tiny petit four cases to make them look all purdy and give them to someone as a giftie.

I think I'll make some for the lovely Rachel from The Half Moon. Oh yeah! She'll soon learn that I have layers...

Peace out! Dan-Dan, The Baking Man!

The Ousebury Oracle
DECEMBER. ISSUE 13.

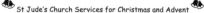

VICARAGE NEWS!

Hello Flock! Christmas is almost upon us, and I do hope you're all prepared. Every villager would be very welcome at St Jude's this December for one of our wonderful church services.

St Jude's Church Services for Christmas and Advent

Our Christingle will be held on the last Sunday of Advent. This service is suitable for your little ones, so please do bring them along. Flame-free candles will be provided, but please do return them at the end of the service as the PPC can't afford to keep forking out for them.

Christmas Eve Midnight Mass, 11:00pm prompt. The service will be followed by mince pies and mulled wine in The Vicarage. All welcome!

Christmas Morning Holy Communion. 10:30am
"Holy See" You There! God bless, Reverend Cliff

Parochial Parish Council, November Meeting. Item 1: It has been noted that several readers have left well-thumbed copies of Fifty Shades of Grey for swap in the telephone box book exchange on The Green. As this is a family-friendly facility, please refrain from leaving such unsuitable material. **Item 2:** All bin and recycling collections will occur one day later than usual due to the festive bank holidays. Could all villagers please take note and not play "bin roulette" with your neighbours, as we're told it is not appreciated. Full minutes available online at www.jobsworthsdoing.com.

VILLAGE LIGHTS SWITCH ON!

Join us for our annual village gathering on Sunday, plus very special visitor, from 3pm. Rev. Cliff will bless the tree, followed by carol singing, and then the big switch on. Mulled wine, hot chocolate and festive sweet treats to keep you warm will kindly be provided by The Half Moon. Be there!

Are moles the bane of your life? If yes, you need

HOLEY MOLEY!

Big Dougie will be round like a shot to take a pot shot at your problem. E-mole Big Dougie at holeymoley@gmole.gone

Nether Ousebury WI. We enjoyed an origami demonstration held by Mrs I Fold at our November meeting. The best Christmas chutney competition was won by Mrs Firth.

CHRISTMAS ANAGRAM!
OLE UGLY (ANSWER NEXT ISSUE)

THE HALF MOON
GOOD GRUB, WARM WELCOME, REAL ALE!
BOOK YOUR TABLE FOR CHRISTMAS & NEW YEAR NOW.
DOGS & FERRETS WELCOME!

Be in the know with your friendly, local Ousebury Oracle! For free ads, lonely hearts and situations vacant.

MERRY CHRISTMAS AND A VERY HAPPY NEW YEAR!

STILL JUST 50p WITH ALL PROCEEDS GOING TO THE CHURCH ROOF REPAIR FUND.

ALSO BY CRESSIDA BURTON

THE MAGPIE COTTAGE CHRONICLES

Noël: Christmas at Magpie Cottage
(10th anniversary edition)

Lindian Summer: Summer at Magpie Cottage
(10th anniversary edition)

THE IZZY BROWN STORIES

Incapability Brown
(10th anniversary edition)

Mistletoe & Whine
(10th anniversary edition)

FOR YOUNGER READERS

THE RAVENSBAY SCHOOL STORIES
(Featuring Taryn from The Izzy Brown Stories)

First Term at Ravensbay
Hunter Trials at Ravensbay
Bitter Rivals at Ravensbay
White Horses at Ravensbay
Snowed In at Ravensbay
Pony Girl Problems at Ravensbay

STAND ALONE STORIES

WELCOME TO THE BURTONVERSE!
CRESSIDA BURTON'S READERS' GROUP!

Keep up to date with all the news from The Burtonverse by joining
my readers' group! You'll get one newsletter a month (if you're
lucky, trust me, you won't be bombarded!) containing sneak peeks,
cover and title reveals, competitions and giveaways, author
recommendations and probably cat spam. Plus, you'll be gifted a
100% free Ravensbay School Stories ebook short story called *Paige's
Summer Pony Trek Page*, which you can download direct to your
ereader. All you need do is subscribe via the link on my website.

www.cressidaburton.co.uk

I'll see you there!

Cressidax

ABOUT THE AUTHOR

Cressida Burton knew she wanted to be a writer when she was seven years old, and never gave up on that dream. She is now — finally — a full-time author.

She writes both dark humour about family life, friendships and relationships for grown-ups — dramedy, if you like — and inspiring junior fiction for pony-mad kids age eight and above. Although, most of her grown-up fiction also contains a lot of horse and animal content, which can never be a bad thing.

She started riding ponies at age six, learning on a very opinionated scruffy bay Shetland called Olaf. She still loves horses dearly despite being told as a child that ponies were 'just a phase'. She believes she has hit the deck at least 150 times in her riding career. In her most spectacular fall she demolished a triple bar in a showjumping jump-off. She knows it was her own fault as she should've had more leg on!

Whilst all her books are set in a fictional world that's been nicknamed The Burtonverse, Cressida lives in the North Yorkshire Moors National Park with her husband — the redoubtable and very shy Mr B — and their big, floofy, orange cat, Bilbo Baggins.

www.cressidaburton.co.uk

Printed in Great Britain
by Amazon

41140375R00178